Richard Monaco published four Arthurian /Fantasy novels. Two were best-sellers and Pulitzer Prize finalists. PARSIVAL OR A KNIGHT'S TALE; THE GRAIL WAR; THE FINAL QUEST and BLOOD AND DREAMS were originally published by Macmillan, Simon & Schuster and Putnam/Berkley. PARSIVAL OR A KNIGHT'S TALE is currently available on ereads. Monaco published twelve other books between 1970 and 2000 many of which were translated into German, Italian and other languages.

All the Parsival books are self-contained and don't need to be read in any order. LOST YEARS: THE QUEST FOR AVALON involves the tangled and forbidden love relationships of Parsival, his son, wife, Gawain and others amidst the dark magical power-plots of Morgana the witch in a terroristic, plague-struck Post-Apocalyptic world swirling with mad politics and violent religious cults.

Monaco attended Columbia University where he studied English and Musical Composition. He wrote screenplays for major studios, published poetry, had plays produced, hosted a radio talk show, co-created book series, discovered and developed authors for a NYC literary agency and taught and lectured at various universities.

LOST YEARS: THE QUEST FOR AVALON

A Novel by

Richard Monaco

COVER ART
Ava Warbrick

To

Darsi Monaco
&
Jodi Armstrong Monaco
For Their Unwavering Help and Support

With Special Thanks to
Professor Leverett Butts for his Editorial Input, Assistance and
Friendship

PROLOGUE

In the Hills of Northern Wales

Predawn. The only hint of morning was where the ragged, fang-like hills subtly seemed to form like dark clouds from the general night, traced by the melting gray evanescence of first light.

On the rough, weedy, stony North Britain soil, the ashes of a campfire were a dull purple, shapeless warmth in the chill mist. Here and there, in bundles of shadow, maybe a dozen men slept, snored, shifted, sighed and groaned.

Two were awake, sitting across the blurred coals from one another. There was enough glow to outline a knight with chainmail hauberk, topped by a monk's hood and the other, a smaller man wearing the shadowy vestments of a priest, long-faced, restless, thin, intense.

They spoke softly, at first. The knight had a husky, almost expressionless tone as if he were either terribly tired or a convalescent barely holding his own.

"He'll come out to see me," he was just telling the other. "Why, we are joined together like a monster twins sharing a common body."

The small man kept weaving left and right and nervously plucking at his garments. His voice was high-pitched and often shrill, even in a whisper.

"So say you, so say you Gawain," he responded. "But what if he doth not? Do we besiege his castle with our miserable troop?"

Gawain leaned back, resting his head on the padded saddle he was using for a pillow. The summer air was rich and soft. The dew-mist was just becoming visible as the light imperceptibly intensified.

"You don't understand," Gawain replied in his weary voice, "we are not here to fight Parsival. If we fought you would probably all die and I would escape with my life."

With his right hand he touched the right side of his face through the hood: there was really no left side. A sword stroke had peeled him to the teeth. It had somehow healed. Horribly. His left hand was carved wood that could hold a shield (rarely used by him) or a sword if he wished.

"You fear him," the other shrilled.

"No. But you should. Harken, he will come out because we are brothers and he owes me."

"Have you the same mother?"

Gawain didn't exactly answer.

"False priest," he said coldly, "our mother is war and our father death. Are we not brothers?" Paused. "I ask my brother to heal me."

The "priest" was weaving forward and back, now; like a child who needed to go to the bathroom. His hands cut the grayish air.

"I?" he went shriller. "I?" I am the only *true* priest." He spoke now as if addressing a crowd. "I am the hope of the serf, peasant and all the broken and beaten men! I must have the Grail concealed by this demon Parsival! It belongs to the people. It belongs to the oppressed, the helpless, the hurt! I will forge its metal into a sword to cut down all nobles and kings, priests and bishops, aye, even to the vile spider who weaves his webs from Rome!" He stood up as if jerked to his feet by an invisible string. His sudden tirade had awakened a few of his followers.

"Be quiet, you son-of-a-whore," one snarled, re-rolling himself up in his sleeping cover.

The shape of the hill above them had emerged into a grayish slope. A pair of unseen birds began an antiphonal question and answer.

"Should the Grail heal me," Gawain told him, "I'll let you have it to carve the whole world up with, John-the-priest."

John was flapping his mouth and jerking his limbs like a carnival puppet, caught in the crashing torrent of his vision, spewing words (Gawain thought) the way a mule pisses in thick, dark, erratic spurts:

"Parsival will yield up his secret. He will join our cause or die! I spit on his vaunted strength!"

Gawain sat up: shouted at the sleepers who'd somehow managed to sink deeper despite John's harangue.

"Arise, you shit cups!" he yelled. "We want to beat the sun to the castle."

"With the power of the Grail sword the world will kneel and a new age begin!" He jerked left and right as he held forth. "This is the final year!" Next ends the world! With the Grail sword I can save the chosen!"

Gawain had heard it all before.

"You have more wind than the sea," he told him. "And who said the Grail was a sword?"

One of the men actually threw a fist-sized clod of dried mud at the wobbling priest. Missed.

Gawain stood up. Stretched his limbs. Yawned hard.

"I will hail the gatekeeper myself," he announced. "Call out Parsival." Shut his eyes for a moment. "He will help me to the Grail," he murmured, "and I will drink from God's cup and be made whole again." Nodded. "Then let ends end."

Should it prove to be a sword, he thought, as thinks that loon, *I'll jam it in his southmost hole...*

Behind the cursing, groaning, spitting and rustling as the men stirred, he heard a long, lucid, lyric bird suddenly trill in the distance. He took it for a sign, a murmur from God.

Book I: *999 AD*

PARSIVAL

The grass was fresh-looking as the dew burned off in the morning sun. The hot beams had just cleared the tree line beyond the open area that surrounded the little castle. The hillside sloped smoothly away down to the streak of whitish dust that was the valley road. Beyond it were dark, sod-roofed serfs' huts and fields.

Parsival stood there, nude, leaning on a jagged-tipped spear, watching Gawain, in his green and battered armor, leading his sorry-looking lot of predatory foot soldiers back down the slope. He rode his thick-legged charger in a kind of furious slow-motion. He was followed, at a little distance, by the second mounted and armored man: the fanatic John of Bligh, who had wanted to kill Parsival after making rambling speeches about visions of the future and what he would do with the power of the Grail. Yet another madman, Parsival noted, on that markless and meaningless quest.

He took a deep breath. The summer sun was pleasant on his skin...The day promised to be less humid.

So I really am going to live after all, he thought.

He glanced up at the battlements. Several of his men were still staring down at him from that helpless distance. Others were just pushing through the partly opened gate. They would have been too late, in any case, had things taken a worse turn. He'd been surprised while drunkenly making love to his guest's chunky wife on the long grass in the dark before dawn.

He was found at first light, the dull gray melting into deep, dark red. Gawain and the others couldn't believe their luck: he was not only outside, essentially alone; but unarmed and stark naked. For a moment Gawain thought maybe that bird *had* been Heaven's messenger.

It's always a woman brings a man low, he thought, watching Parsival, startled, pulling out and back from the kneeling lady who, seeing the men, stifled her gasps of pleasure and crept backward on hands and knees until she brought up against the castle wall. They'd been closed in with nowhere to run.

John the ex-priest had demanded the Grail while Gawain sat silent with visor closed. John had bobbed, fomented, fumed, gesticulated, weaved, threatened, promised, pleaded and waved a knife in the knight's face then pressed it to his neck.

Parsival couldn't oblige, as he had no idea where to locate the Grail so with death's blade literally at his throat, the sun coming up behind the spiky hills, he suddenly (inexplicably) felt filled with light and lightness and sweetness as if he were a cup and that benediction were water overflowing him infinitely....His eyes followed a bird soaring, very high, catching the first rose-gold beams of the rising sun and, for a measureless instant, as in a dream, there was no distance between them and he seemed to be looking down on himself looking up....

So he'd asked, begged for his life for the first and only time; without fear, just so that incredible bliss and wonder would not be cut short:

"Gawain, please don't kill me!"

"Then lead us to the Grail, Parsival, my old companion."

Parsival had laughed and shook his head.

"Yes," he said, "but I have. I'll show you."

"Is it here?"

"Yes. Exactly."

"Inside?"

Gawain leaned his blank faceplate closer and Parsival could see his own reflected face distorted: too long, eyes too big, chin coming to a point. The others closed around, scarred, grim, mangy faces dulled by hardship, disaster and routine cruelty. Most were former soldiers gone brigand. A pitiless audience for a strange sermon.

"Yes. And outside too, my friends. Anywhere you like. Like seeing something in the night, the more you look the less it shows."

"Arr," said one, with a slit nose and one eye, "he's mad." Raised his spear to kill him.

Gawain had warned them not to try it and said they would learn nothing from a dead man, even if they, somehow, managed to slay him. Two weren't convinced.

"The Grail is moonshine, anyway," one-eye said. "Let's kill this pretty swine and roast his liver." His missing eye was a raw socket, gaping, myriad tiny muscles flickering whenever the good one moved. "I'll skin the bastard!"

He thrust his jagged-tipped spear and the tall, pale, naked man instantly burst the ropes on his wrists, effortlessly disarmed his attacker and, cracking his head open, dropped the fellow flat on his face in the loose-lying wheatgrass. The rest were persuaded to leave by reason and instinct. Gawain was amused. He'd warned them.

"Violence has no meaning," Parsival explained, as they left, heading back down the slope. He shrugged and turned back towards the castle. Sir Gaf's round little wife had run away after picking up her clothes. "No one wins a battle," he murmured. "Save, maybe, the dead."

The moment he'd believed the one-eyed man was about to cut his throat, it was as if he'd died and his soul had been shaken awake. He stood there now, trying to understand what had happened. Like a threadlike rill of purity winding through the world's stale, lifeless muck, he thought he saw all he'd missed and lost in his life and might discover again.

Frowned now, a mere quarter of an hour later, because there was nothing to remember but the facts. The light (or whatever it was) that had overflowed his soul was gone. He was so tired his stomach cramped and his eyes hurt.

An image from childhood came to him: he was eight or so, alone in his sleeping chamber, kneeling on a worn wooden bench under the long, narrow, glassless window where thin, clean spring sunbeams sprayed softly over him. He saw again the smoothly carved bench back; remembered tracing with his finger the whittled scriptural scene of a big-leafed tree (he couldn't know was a palm) in the center, a round-faced angel in angular robes jabbing a sword point at the naked man and woman who seemed to huddle away into the rougher carven cuts where wild beasts and monsters crouched among harsh stones, all fixed in the wood of themselves forever, and it wasn't until that moment in the present, leaning on the spear and remembering, that he realized the image had been Adam and Eve.

He shook his head, amused, thinking how children could look at something again and again without having to form associations. That was better than talent, to have no compulsion to insist on meaning.

He had liked sitting or kneeling there and looking outside at the castle wall where the tops of distant hills and open fields just showed above the crenellations. At certain times of day the sunbeams, angled through the window, would catch lines of dustmotes in golden fire. He remembered trying to catch the shining specks where they winked into brightness like points of magic – but whenever he'd open his hand he could never tell if there was anything in his palm....

I have been doing practically everything wrong since I was six years old, he decided.

He stood there, muscular (with a recent rim of softness around the beltline) scarred, tall, leaning into the spear he'd propped into the soft summer earth, blond hair stirring in the warm, morning breezes. The dew on the blowing grass sparkled as it vanished.

His wife, Layla, had just come to the battlements with the servant who'd shaken her awake, crying: "My lady they're slaying Lord Parsival!" She'd rushed through the dim, cool hall, grey robe swishing around her, bare feet padding, rapid and soft, over the smooth stones and occasional napless rug, flicking past narrow windows full of brightness until she was outside, squinting and blinking into the risen sun. And now she was thinking (because he turned out to be safe): *One day I will come and he will be dead and I will be 99 years old...or more likely he'll live to miss my funeral...*

She turned her attention back to her nude husband posed like a bony-kneed archangel, craning his head around as if searching the sky. The bird was gone.

"I thought you said he was in difficulties?" she commented.

"So it seemed, my lady," said the servant.

She sniffed.

"There's the usual result of my husband's troubles," she said, looking at the angular, ill-armored man sprawled face down and silent on the wheatgrass. Even at a distance she could make out the red shock of blood around the balding skull. "A dead man other than himself."

She knew it should have meant more to her but it didn't. Where Parsival was concerned she felt a grayness, most of the time, except when he exasperated her into actual anger or outrage or despair.

She sighed and tapped her short, shapely fingers on the gritty stone. Why didn't he go away again? He was always going somewhere. He lived a life of pretexts. Once that had bothered her. Right now she was hoping all her guests would leave too. Even her lover, the Greek knight, Sir Constantino Gaf.

His prickly beard is always in my nose, she thought, irritated at her passivity. She was tired. Her eyes were reddened and the sunlight hurt. Too much wine, too much last night…always too much and too many….

She stared down at her husband. He seemed entranced or maybe sodden with drink.

"Where are your clothes?" she called down, not really caring; curious. She had an uncle who'd taken to strolling around the family castle nude, going to the bathroom anywhere he pleased until they locked him in the tower. "Are you drunk?"

GAWAIN

Gawain and the odd monk, John of Bligh, had led the brigands, promising booty and calling it the Grail. Gawain sometimes believed the Grail might restore his ruined face – for want of something else to hope for; the men wanted plunder and women; it was never clear what John of Bligh really wanted, other than to turn the world upside down whenever he found a handle to lift it with.

Gawain had watched from his horse, visor closed over his mutilated features where a sword had chopped the left side of his face away. Watched, half-listening, while Parsival made no real answer.

Watched, as Parsival casually disarmed the one-eyed killer and cracked his head with the spearshaft. Watched and asked himself what he was doing there, feeling disgust and dull depression while Parsival tried to communicate something none of them could follow; not even himself.

In any case, Gawain knew the men-at-arms would soon have the alarm and be spilling out of the castle to save their lord. He shrugged.

What a sad, stupid business, he said to himself. Wanted to lose them all.

PARSIVAL

Parsival watched them go, turning after a moment and leaned on the spear. He looked up and saw Layla at the parapet.

I need to talk to my son, he thought.

"Are you alright, my Lord?" a young groom panted, having sprinted from the side gate, followed by half-a-dozen men-at-arms, in a straggling line, incompletely dressed and armed.

Parsival noted the sallow-faced boy whose hair fell in greasy, uneven bangs. He felt nothing one way or another, at the moment. He'd inherited these vassals and he found them a motley lot – underfed and inbred. He treated them well enough and was known as a fair, if uninvolved master. He was known as moody, a fool for women, a knight who'd lost interest in performance and battle but was too sophisticated for rustic retirement. Since he'd come home, all agreed, everyone ate better because he harried the serfs into working harder and protected their fields; and for reasons he never expressed, he'd freed them and turned them into dependent peasants. He'd been heard once to remark that man had no real property, everything was borrowed and that even his horses and mules were mere responsibility and possession of land was a jest of time. Nobody was sure what he meant and he chose not to elaborate. Layla always believed he tried to live according to some idea he had of how life should be and, as a result, there were no real feelings behind many of his actions. His son, Lohengrin, had vowed never to be like his father because he was sure Parsival took no more pleasure from his passions than from his skills.

"Am I alright?" he belatedly responded. "I have to do something...something..." he murmured again; then to the lad, "Bring me a robe, will you, sirrah?" The men had taken his clothes, naturally.

The youth, at once, stripped off his linen longshirt and handed it to Parsival who tugged his wide back and shoulders into it with some effort. It covered him to just below his butt end.

He waved up to his wife.

"Good morning, Layla," he called, not quite loud enough for her to hear distinctly. She didn't reply, if she'd heard.

He was now looking around, squinting his tired eyes, to see what had happened to the chunky, soft-bodied woman he'd been with last night. Just as those men had surprised him he'd been on his knees with her facing away, "driving her to market," as the villains called it.

He wondered if she'd fled back to her husband's bed in the guest tower and disturbed Layla. The idea amused and annoyed him. What a life.

We are all come to depravity, he thought. *And it is so ordinary and dull, after all...*

"Were you injured, my Lord?" asked the captain of the guard, Lego of Stillwater. He was a solid, high-shouldered, lanky, grizzled, graying fighter with a hooked nose and eyes like ruminative drops from a pond.

Parsival was still thinking about his way of life. He didn't like what he thought.

"I intend to reform a few things," he said.

"Did you suffer a head blow?" Lego asked, concerned. He saw no blood, however.

"What?...Ah, no." Parsival gestured. "Changes. I mean to make changes."

"But my Lord," Lego was concerned, "how could we have known of your plight sooner or come a step quicker, once we did?"

"What troubles your mind, good captain? I don't mean to change my men. Just myself, I think."

He was heading towards the main gate which now stood open. The men moved together, more or less flanking him. He stopped just under where his wife was looking down the sheer, gritty wall.

"Layla," he said up at her, "are you well this morrow?"

"What mischief have you just made?" she wanted to know.

He smiled. He felt fine. He was alive; sober, cleaned-out, ready to make vows.

"Where is my son?" he called up to her.

Just her head and neck showed, cut off by the smooth, weathered stones. The angle made her long face longer. Her dark, back-length hair was billowing out, riffling in the draughts.

"By St. Anne," she called down, "and you take an interest?" She looked around in mock wonder. "This is a holy day."

"I wonder that your tongue does not slice your lips," he said, not loud enough for her to hear because there was no point. "A blade like that would shave a *wudewasa*," which meant a wild man of the woods.

"Behold." she was elaborating, "This is a day of marvels. I see an ox in the field driving a villain in traces."

Parsival was paying scant attention. He pondered his faintly baffled men.

"Who has seen my son?" he asked.

No one had. His wife said something else, lost now in the background, then she withdrew from the wall.

"Mayhap," the captain of the guard offered, "he has gone off again."

*Run from me again...*He knew it was partly true. *Everything's partly true sometime or other,* he quipped to himself. Then sighed.

He kept walking, using the spear like a prophet's staff, holding his improvised tunic closed with the other hand, feeling the first twinges of a headache as the excitement wore off and his body reacted to the strain of a sleepless night and the rest of it.

"I'll talk to him later." he said, as if the bemused, sleepy men-at-arms really cared. They passed through the gate under the wall into the yard and he saw his son's black charger, Firetail, being groomed at the stables. The boy hadn't left this time, not yet, anyway.

The captain kept pace alongside him. He spat thoughtfully into a muddy wheel rut. Patches of weedy grass grew here and there on the hoof-and-foot-chewed earth. The sun was still below the wall and the air was dewy gray, the sky pale rose.

"Aye, my Lord," he agreed, glancing back now and then as if to assure himself that the brigands who'd trapped his master had not reappeared.

"Well, Lego," Parsival said, "Do you think me a poor father too?"

"All a man may do is try, my Lord."

"It's the general opinion that I'm a stinking father."

Lego shrugged. Spat again. To their left women were dumping out old, dried and befouled leaves and branches that had been used to sweeten the castle floors.

"Ask me about a horse, my Lord, or a sword and I'll speak out a view. Or a bird, for that matter. Or food." He shrugged. "Ask me what I can pretend to know but not of women and children."

The breeze shifted and they could smell food cooking. "Ask me about breakfast," said Parsival. He aimed his bare feet carefully to miss the fragrant "meadow muffins" left by the cows.

The castle folk were starting to bustle around. Some noted his odd garb: naked except for an unbuttoned shirt that barely covered his privates. A cook's boy snickered, pausing by the well to stare, bucket in hand...He had puffy red cheeks and oversized hands. His younger sister hopped and spun up to him.

"Mama said you'd better hurry," she informed him.

"Plug your ugly face," he retorted.

While she wasn't lovely (nose too long, chin too wide) she wasn't unattractive either.

"Plug your own with dung," she suggested.

The boy didn't react, still watching their lord pick his barefoot way across the ruts and muck of the shadowed yard towards the main keep.

"Look at him," he said. "They say he's a mad one."

She looked so-what at her brother.

"You talk like the hen about eggs," she said.

Without a sign he suddenly lashed out with one long, skinny arm. His open hand just missed her head. She ducked back and stuck out her tongue.

"I'll crown ya," he said, "Lady Dungface."

Lego glanced at the children and then away. He was uncomfortable. Parsival always made him uncomfortable. He never knew what to expect.

"Contrary to the general opinion about me, I won't dispute with my betters," Lego declared.

"Your lord isn't necessarily your better, captain. We all bleed the same red."

Lego responded carefully.

"I hope you're not about to preach a rebellion of dung-squeezers, my Lord."

Parsival grinned.

"Any minute," he said.

He said nothing more because his son had just come out of the main door, looking at his father without expression. His hair was jet black and tight curly. His nose was a fine hook, a falcon's beak, those who liked him said.

Contrary to common gossip around *Ville* and castle, Lohengrin had friends. He was proud, sarcastic and moody and could be mean but (his likers said) he was clever, brave, skillful and loyal, in his fashion. His father had once declared that his son's emotions ranged from surly to furious.

I swear but he has the face of a passing Jew peddler, thought Lego, half in jest.

In truth, though he had no serious doubts about his parentage, Parsival sensed that the lad's looks added to the distance between them.

"You think what you do doesn't matter," Lohengrin said.

"This is your good morning? Don't you say: 'I'm pleased you escaped with your life, father?" said Parsival. He instantly regretted it because the response was automatic. He knew he had to be more patient but they instantly slipped into their familiar roles.

"Good morning? I only get to say farewell to you, father. Was your life in question?"

He watched him, dark eyes showing nothing. Parsival sighed.

"How old are you now?" he asked.

"Know you not?"

Parsival heard Lego mutter something under his breath.

"What am I, a calendar? You are of age to bear arms." Parsival said. That was fourteen.

"But not to bear my life." the boy said.

"As I was. Bah," he said. "Mine were not footsteps to follow but a track to miss." He shrugged and sighed. "Bear what you may."

"You are a great knight, lord." Said Lego, stolid, sullen. "All men know it."

"And how as a father?" inquired the hawk-nosed son.

He finally had Parsival angry. It usually came to that.

"You task me too far," he said. "I want to bring peace between us, Lohengrin. I want to help you become a full man."

"Like you? Full of what?"

Lego cleared his throat. He would have liked to have struck the youngster. He thought about what he would do if he were Parsival.

The parent tried, he went to his son, up the four stone steps. Lego hoped to witness a round blow box to the arrogant child. He was surprised to see his lord, in his odd outfit, take strong young Lohengrin by the shoulders and just hold him. He thought of the biblical story of King David and his son Absalom. The local priest had worked over the tale a few weeks ago. He recalled being strangely moved, almost to tears by the words spoken when the unhappy king of the Hebrews faced the messenger from the battlefield where his furious and rebellious son was trying to overthrow his own father. The messenger gave him the worst news a parent can ever dread and: "When David heard that Absalom was slain he went to his chamber and wept. And thus he said: "Absalom my son would God I had died for thee."

"I have much to repent of as a father and husband," the knight was telling his child. "Pray you allow me to do so."

Lohengrin started to reply and then didn't. That was new. He was actually surprised. He didn't pull away from those almost delicate, hard, well-shaped hands that could have practically twisted the head off a bull.

Parsival had no more to say. He stared into Lohengrin' s eyes, wondering how to express to him the strange truth he'd just been touched by. Lego sighed a deep breath.

Parsival had done Lego a service in the wake of a minor battle between King Arthur and some rebellious Baron. Parsival was looking for any of his wounded or dead they might have missed. Dusk was coming on as if it flowed subtly from the rills and stones and sparse, harsh highland trees themselves. He heard shouts and a clank of arms nearby.

He'd been crossing a stony, smooth hilltop. Down in the shallow valley a row of huts smoldered, the dark smoke streaking the warm dusk. He could see the baron's castle set well up the far hill-slope. That lord and what was left of his forces were sealed inside, repairing themselves and eating bitter bread and turnips, hoping there would be no siege. The fields beyond the huts were littered with their dead.

Parsival had followed the sounds over the reverse slope and found a posse of some of Arthur's hired men-at-arms (the sort who blurred the boundaries of banditry) had trapped and disarmed a man who'd been wounded in the thigh and deserted by his companions. They'd looped a rope around one armored ankle and were having sport dragging him over the rocky ground.

Parsival hadn't approved. He was able to accept his way of life only by being as fair and decent as possible. He was always bothered by the memory of times when he had showed no mercy.

"Every time a man is cruel," he liked to say, "it leaves a dead spot in his soul."

Like a callus that can never be smoothed from the skin.

So he shouted:

"Hold, you base oafs!" He cantered into the thick of them. "If a man be down let him lie, by Christ."

The soldiers had scattered like schoolboys caught at a prank. At a little distance two had paused and turned around.

"Knight," one cried, a potbellied man in ragged leathers, "Why do you help an enemy?"

"Let the fallen lie," came the answer. "We are not cut-throats."

"Lohengrin," he said to the boy, "if I could tell you...."

"If you could tell me," his son said back. He noted what seemed tears in his father's eyes. This was odd. "What?"

Parsival had dismounted and stooped beside the wounded man who looked up at him with gratitude and a wry smile that Parsival instantly liked.

"Arr," he grunted. "Chivalry. I have lived to see it."

"May you live to see more."

"Something often talked about." He winced and caught his breath.

Parsival looked around. The soldiers had all re-gathered now at a little distance.

"An enemy is usually an accident," said Parsival.

The fallen man shut his eyes and sighed from his wounds.

"I ask a boon, chivalrous knight," he whispered.

"Which?"

"Leave me a leather of water."

"I'll do better than that." Parsival cocked his head, thoughtfully studying the man. "Friends should not be an accident."

In the following years they had become fairly close. Lego had become Captain Lego and a loyal vassal. Although he was from the lower nobility (a younger son and so not heir to anything but his brother's whims) and entitled to knighthood he refused to be knighted. He was like a modern Sergeant Major who rejected not only the responsibility but the very look of being an officer. Also, though not technically a peasant, his mother was not highborn.

"What have you from me, my boy," he asked Lohengrin, "beyond power and rage?"

"A broken wit, father? A lying nature? A cruel indifference altogether?"

"You had better hope your lance will match your tongue," Parsival said, "or else you will talk yourself into death before you have twice shaved."

His son yawned and rubbed his eyes, looking up at where the far wall cut across the pink and blue sky. He was enjoying the clean morning air. His father's reddened eyes disgusted him; and why was he half naked? He refused to deign to bring it up. He'd been out drinking and had made a fool of himself, obviously.

"I want to be knighted," he said, seriously. "I mean to start shaving this morning."

Lego guffawed.

"Ah," he said, "How can you hurt those little hairs?"

"Are you then prepared to serve and study arms at your uncle's?" Parsival wanted to know.

Lohengrin was still studying the sky. He was thinking about breakfast and hunting later. The peasants and serfs had been complaining about boars in the fields.

"I want to be knighted as you were," he said. His eyes said something else. He was thinking it was time for him to leave that place and go and do the secret thing he'd planned since he was nine years old. The thing he never mentioned. He was sure it was now time...Then they'd see something. Then his father would see something.

Parsival shook his head and tossed his spear into a muddy rut, in disgust. The shaft quivered and rippled the puddle.

They now went into the castle together, into the cool dimness, the daybright still shimmering with each eyeblink for a few steps.

"You think you are part of a tragic tale, Lego?" he asked wryly.

"Not yet, my Lord."

"Not yet."

"The...what-do-they-call?" Lego frowned his eyebrows. "Before the play..."

"Aye. The prologue."

His shod steps echoed as they entered a large chamber; Parsival's bare feet were virtually soundless on the cool flagging.

"I mean to make it right," he said, "if I can."

"If you can."

"With my wife, as well." He sniffed out a chuckle. "Her ladyship."

Lego showed no reaction.

"I see," he responded neutrally.

"I mean it."

"I said nothing."

"You said nothing. Yet you disapprove."

"What right have I to such a position, my Lord?"

They stopped by the table that was still being set for breakfast with bowls of fruit, mugs of weak beer, trays of roasted eggs, toasted bread, strips of salt and smoked meat and fish plus trenchers of mash and wild honey.

The servants seemed unshaken by their master's odd garb, which left most of his legs bare. Castle folk were used to seeing one another in various states of undress. Some of the girls who'd heard talk about Parsival and Sir Gaf's wife, traded looks.

Parsival and Lego stood there and began eating. The semi-dressed knight was pondering a bowl of berries when his wife's voice caught him and his stomach sort of winced.

"Ah," said she, "you break your fast ere your guests have stirred. You and your precious lackey."

"He's a captain, not a lackey," Parsival responded, not looking up, sighing, because what was the point? With women facts were futile since she wanted him to feel something and the means to feeling didn't matter. He knew that. "And you call them *my* guests?" He put a strawberry into his mouth, savoring the cool, almost over-ripe richness. "Well, has not Gaf had his host's best?"

Lego didn't quite smile.

"He likes your jibes," she noted. "My husband was not once called fool, for small cause. He wants but cap and bells."

She crossed the chamber. She'd changed into a deep rose, silken robe. He didn't look directly at her. He was hoping no storm winds would stir.

I need to try... he thought. *A new approach...or....*

He drank from a cup of thick, spiced buttermilk.

"Maggots are guests too," he couldn't help but say, "feeding on what's dead."

Lego imperfectly stifled a guffaw

"Good fool," Layla said. "Now sing a song for your food."

Parsival felt his captain tense beside him.

"Were it your wife," he commented, "you would, I imagine, kick her like a snapping cur."

Lego shrugged. Said nothing. Looked nowhere.

"Kick me," she sniffed, just standing there, hands lost in the deep, sunset-colored folds of silk. Daylight was fuzzy brightness at the huge, open main door.

Parsival set down the cup and looked at the floor before his long, pale bare feet.

"I have, myself, let the wine sour," he pointed out. "Whom might I flog if my head aches from drinking it?"

Here they come, he thought, glancing across the room where the visiting family was just coming to table: Sir Gaf, round, wheat-haired wife and dumpy, jowly, moist-faced mother. Gaf (Layla's momentary lover) had a roll in his gait and ridiculous (Parsival thought) confidence. *In a fight he'd soon be kissing the ground....*

Not that he was normally jealous. He didn't feel his honor was bound up in Layla's chastity. Sauce for the goose was sauce for the gander, too. This knight was nothing if not even-handed. But Gaf's obvious misapprehension of his strength and skill was annoying. He felt a warrior ought to be realistic. And, too, there were rules of courtly love, written and unwritten: some held that husband and wife could never be true lovers since love was the heart's wild freedom and might not be tamed by law.

The dark, short, stocky, slightly bowed knight swaggered up to the spread and nodded at Parsival with slight contempt. Lego bristled, at once.

"Some as are haughty," Lego said, to no one in particular, "is like the mouse that scratched the cat."

The blocky knight paid no heed but his mother, picking up a hard, green pear, reacted:

"We start our day with proverbs from a peasant? And view the bare behind of our host."

"Ah, ha," said the host's wife. "he's a very courtier, for style."

The son took notice. Scratched under his beard with a thick thumb.

"Is it not an insult to have us break-fast with a low-born dog?"

"Cats, mice, now dogs," said his barelegged host, staring out the door into the day's hot, rich brightness. "What about goats and cows? Is this a castle or a farmyard?" Looked back into the relative dimness of the room, more or less at the family, blinking at the purplish afterimage of the door. "A farmyard," he said, judiciously and Lego guffawed, again.

Layla didn't like that.

"My husband keeps low companions," she announced, "to assure his own stature."

Chunky Sir Gaf rubbed and scratched his curly beard, again. His mother crunched into the hard pear, then poked a short finger into her mouth and worked a loose tooth. There were stools but no one but she was sitting. She put down the fruit and tried a slice of pork.

"Mayhap he is too deep in the habit and has become low, himself," Gaf pronounced.

Parsival touched Lego to check his response, saying:

"Ah." Took a bite of sweet, soft cheese. "Your wit soars like a clipped falcon. Or those wingless, trudging birds of legend."

"Clipped?" put in the lean, long-faced captain. "I'd say feathers of lead, my Lord."

"Silence, churl," snarled Gaf, stepping over and snapping a backhand with his wide fist at the soldier's face. Missed, as Lego slapped the corky arm aside.

The furious knight snatched up a knife from the table and hooked at Lego's lined, insubordinate face.

"Hold," said Parsival, effortlessly catching the thick wrist in mid-cut and tugging Gaf off-balance, driving his hand down so hard the blade broke off in the table, snapped tip quivering.

Gaf then, foolishly, drove his fist at his host's fineboned features; met air as Parsival leaned away, then countered with a terrific kick to the knee that popped something and dropped the knight on his side, cursing fluently. His mother was howling, meat filling her mouth.

The wife looked away, embarrassed. Layla, incensed, flung a ripe peach at her husband and hit Lego in the chest.

"You bastard!" she cried. "Go away like you always do!"

"What did I wrong?"

"Some say this is the last year of the world," she said. "If I am so misfortunate as to meet you in eternity, husband, there will be time to tell you."

"You've hurt my boy," the older woman almost howled, on her knees beside him, wiping pork fragments from her lips with the sleeve of her dress and holding him.

"Ought I have let him kill me? Boy?"

"There you stand," Layla continued, "with your balls and dangler in the wind and your arse for all to see."

Parsival raised both hands over his head, in frustration which made things much worse as it raised his shirt several inches more. The wheathaired, bubble-shaped wife looked back, now; her mother-in-law shook her fist; Gaf clutched the table in an effort to rise; Layla rolled her eyes.

"Are you now a pagan wrestler?" she wondered. "What a display."

Lohengrin was just coming through the sunbright door in his black tights and red and white, loose shirt. Out of the corner of his eye Parsival saw him and shook his head. Nudged Lego.

"Retreat," he said. "The enemy has the field."

Sir Gaf, partway up, lost his grip on the smooth tabletop and fell blockily back on his mother who gushed out wind from his weight in a kind of belch and outcry. The round wife finally got up to assist. She stole another look at Parsival whose arms were back at his sides. Layla just stood there. A woman servant came back with a mug of something and took the scene in as one who'd seen the play before.

"Leave it and go," Layla told her. "Bring back a sack to cover my husband. Or fool's skins."

"Trust me," the bearded knight hissed, "I shall slice out your liver and roast it, you damned cuckold!"

"Enjoying break-fast?" wondered Lohengrin, sauntering up, grinning.

"Don't involve yourself," said his mother. Then to Gaf: "And you, have a care what you utter."

"Sounds like a quarrel in a stew," put in Lohengrin. He loved acrimony and, especially, to see his father under fire.

With help, Sir Gaf got up with his stout mother, but his leg buckled, again. His eyes bulged with anger. He leaned, heavily, on the table full of food.

"Stench and cuckold!" he went on. "Coward!"

Parsival, moving away towards the hall and stairs, started to raise his hands, again, then checked himself, grinning. Glanced back at Layla and shrugged.

"My Lord," said Lego, "he hath called three times now. Should not his meat be served?"

"He has enough to digest," his lord replied. The woman had come back holding a bright yellow robe. He shook his head at her. "Not my color," he told her. "Anyway, I'll leave as I came."

"Just so you leave," snapped Layla.

"Cuckold," repeated Gaf.

"Mind your mouth, oaf," Layla recommended. She suddenly had no notion of why she'd let him in her bed. A silly, self-righteous, selfish man.

I have no judgment, she thought. *I let asses mount me….*

"We must fly this den of murderers," mother Gaf said.

Lohengrin was delighted at the break in monotony.

"Father," he called over to the retreating knight. "Why do you creep from the fray?'

"I'll fray you like a worn sleeve, my son," he snapped.

"Ha," reacted his son.

Parsival spun and went for the boy with his open hand drawn back. The boy didn't flinch, still enjoying himself.

"Now strike down your son," Layla said, heading over. She always got between them, sooner or later.

"Accept my challenge, you stinking bastard," blustered Gaf, leaning heavily on his mother and the table. "Meet me on the field of honor or be known a coward, hereafter!"

Parsival shrugged and, on impulse, raised his arms over his head, exposing again what ought to have been private. The mother covered her eyes. Gaf's bovine wife stared, as if to recall something. Layla sneered. Lohengrin laughed, actually taking his father's part, for a change. Lego, in disgust, went to the door and out into the morning's dazzle.

Not an hour since, Parsival was thinking, *I was breathing bliss that makes air coarse and hearing the musical sighs of angels past the dull ear's utmost capacity....And now I am back with my family....*

With a movement so swift and economical that it seemed a blurring swallow's flight, he glided three steps to his son and, even as the boy tried to duck back (finally afraid he'd pushed his father too far) caught his two shoulders in that incredible grip and lifted him, effortlessly, off his feet.

Layla was still coming to intervene, slippers skidding on the smooth white tiles – then she stopped, surprised, because her husband suddenly, fiercely, kissed his son's lips and then released him.

"You are all ridiculous," he informed them. "So am I. But I love you, Lohengrin, despite what you choose to believe. And your mother, too."

And then he padded, barefoot, across the hall in silence until Sir Gaf cried out:

"On the field of honor, coward! On the field!"

Parsival went up to his second-floor chamber. He was weary to the bone. His stomach and nerves shuddered with exhaustion. His eyes were sore. His thoughts dragged through the molasses of his mind.

He went straight to the big bed and threw himself down on his back. Covered his loins and legs with the silk sheets. The feel was cool and soothing. Sunlight creased in through the slit windows.

Without energy to move much, he tugged some more sheet over his face, rolling partly on his side. He lay for awhile and slowly felt the tension melt from his limbs.

"My son," he muttered, adjusting the material so his nose was clear. Yawned and rubbed his face. "My wife...."

Noises in the castle yard kept him from dozing off completely. He'd drift for a moment, then snap back to his headache and sore joints.

Dozed and was instantly in a field of golden flowers that seemed dense and, somehow, heavy with color, set on either side by massed, rich, deep green trees in a perfectly straight line to the horizon and he understood, dream-like, this was what he'd always wanted: follow the straight line to the end, into an epiphany of summerich light because his life had been nothing but twists and turns....

He blinked himself back. The sheet had shifted from his face. The light at the windows hurt. His left eye throbbed. He tried to relax his forehead by gently rubbing it. Covered his eyes again and heard himself start to snore...was running straight and gently upslope between the flanking walls of trees, through the ankle-deep and knee-high flowers as if his body were dissolving into light...running behind a nude woman who moved just ahead of him in blurred perfection like a roll of wind forming shapes in the golden blossoms...and he needed to touch her and end the reaching...closer, she seemed to have been formed from the flowers, a living hush flowing...reached and ran and reached as if he might be wafted into her glowing substance...reached....

"...and if you do, I'll crown you with this jug, you bastard!" a reedy woman's voice was scolding, outside. A man muttered something back and might have spat. They were close under his second-floor window.

In a lull he went under again and this time he was in a tunnel, smoothly carved that almost melted into black, unreflecting stone. Pitch dark, yet he could see. Sensed he was down deep and that mountain masses of rock lay above him. The tunnel twisted and bent back on itself like (he dream-thought) the intestines of some stone behemoth...then a dead end where a niche had been hewed into the black wall, a ledge with something like a vase or jar there, a shadowy blurring in a gout of darkness.

Sensed menace and power all around and that the container held the heart and soul of the darkness which pulsed and spread its lightless beams out into the eternal stone night, beat steady and yet measureless...sensed a watcher watching as he reached for what he now dream-perceived as a fat cup with holes to grip; he gripped and realized he held a living black skull because the mouth bit down and held him fast....

He woke in soundless screaming and just lay there, sweating in the twisted covers....

Always dreams come back, he said to himself.

The man outside snarled something at the woman. Parsival dozed again. Came back. The woman was saying:

"...the world ends, ya old fool...."

He dozed. Shuddered awake, to hear:

"...this is the last year...."

The man (probably the husband) said:

"You're as mad as that priest who says such...."

Heard that much rebuttal but was out again when the woman said:

"The Antichrist is everywhere. Water will turn to blood...."

Asleep, Parsival was seeing rivers, lakes and seas all staining red with naked corpses bloating in the waves.

"...we must flee to the Holy places...the Great Whore is already among us," she went on, reedy, penetrating.

The knight was awake again, panting. Felt numbed, as if drugged.

"What?" the husband's voice cut through the murmur of outside sounds, "is ya damned mother come again to stay?"

Parsival's laughter finally fully woke him. He stared straight up at the low, vaulted ceiling. The quarreling voices faded as the couple moved off.

Outside there was suddenly noise and banging and shouts. Horses and armored men, he realized. Because of the dreams he kept his aching eyes opened and listened:

"What?" a voice cried.

"Where is your lord?" another, deep, irritable, demanded.

"In heaven with his holy host," said the first he now knew was Lego's.

"Mind your mouth," the irritable voice advised.

What is this? Parsival wearily wondered.

"It seems more like you must mind, my Lord knight," Lego responded. "you are, after all, within our walls here."

"Think you churl," was the retort of a new voice, cool and logical, "that your walls will long stand one brick on another if Arthur the King willed it otherwise? Call your lord."

By now Parsival had dragged himself to the embrasure and tilted his head far enough out to look down into the dusty yard where the high sun now beat hot and steady.

He blinked, saw Lego in his leathers, leaning on a staff, saw the open gate, and the castle people gathering, the soldiers alert: the three armed, mounted knights reined up at the main steps about fifty feet to his right. One was drinking from a pot of water held up by one of the castle grooms. They sat with their helmets on their laps.

Parsival leaned out far enough and called down:

"Here I am without my choir of angels."

They all looked up.

"Parsival?" The rough voice said. It belonged to a balding, bearded, middle-aged knight who seemed familiar.

"For the most part," he called down. "What do you want of me?"

"All of you, save your jibes," the logically-voiced knight said. He was long-limbed, hair dull red, nose long with an uptilt. The blunt sunlight flashed on his mailed hands as he gestured with near delicacy. "For body and soul, as we know, are you not vassal of your master?"

Parsival took that in. The sun was hot and felt good on his face. He shut his eyes to soothe them.

Vows, he thought, *are cheaply broken though dearly sold.*

He said:

"I'm hoping to sleep. Unhorse. Lay aside your gear and troubles. Rest. Eat and drink. Later we can parse body and soul." Parse. He liked that.

Back to bed, he thought. Considered going out and napping on the hillside under the lime trees. Nothing felt better than a doze in the sun and cool shadow.

"Do you object to my point?" The long knight, the leader, wanted to know.

Parsival was annoyed. He'd had his fill of trouble, when you counted the plates.

"Rest and we'll speak later," he called down. "Else you may object to *my* point."

He meant his sword. They got it. He smiled, because he was, after all, their host.

"Give me your message," he said, "from my sovereign liege. Then wait upon yourselves."

"We expected a more gracious-" one began to say. Parsival cut him off.

"Enough of this babble," he snarled, "my head aches with it."

"King Arthur calls you to service," the red-haired, long faced leader snarled back.

"Ah ha. For my singing?"

"Will you say nay to him?" the burly one wanted to know.

"I agree to attend upon the king and sing holy chants. My fighting is off-pitch these days." *Out of the mode,* he thought.

He pushed back from the deepest windowslit and let himself sink back into the bed.

*The next thing Layla will find me here and my torments will mount...I need no summons to spill blood. Yet I'll go to him and speak it to his face...*He yawned and rubbed his eyes. *I'll strike only who first strikes me...if I cannot run away...*Shut his eyes and tried again to concentrate on what had happened that morning.

"First I was fucking that lady and she made sounds like a pig which is what I've come to," he whispered aloud.

My life is a barnyard...

He lost focus. Sleep lapped at his thoughts and there was a flutter of darkness, a lapse of sound and time...and then he tensely jerked awake again.

"Christ," he whispered, "fucking and then set upon by Gawain and those witless…" Sighed, feeling sorry for Gawain. Sighed again, feeling sorry for everybody.

When I sleep all is real, he thought, *when I wake all is real…what would happen if they came together?*

He brought himself back again to the point where he'd expected to die and tried to recapture the…what? The floating up? The widening? The blast of light? Tried to bring it back. Held his breath. Imagined his soul was soaring among the angels…was that dreaming? Was it both?

He was still just lying there with a headache. Tried to calm himself deeply, asked God to bring that lost moment back. Prayed with all the humble sincerity and simplicity he could muster. Waited…fell asleep again…shook awake with a worse headache.

He sighed.

"Everything slips away," he told heaven or just the vaulted ceiling.

The way his childhood had slipped away. Which he really always missed the most. Maybe he'd lost the Grail, maybe he hadn't; but he knew he'd lost his childhood and that had been the most real of all places, in his memory it was all one seamless summer, dappled fields awash with pure dazzle and the scent of rich, ripe sweetness…endless time…energy and interest without bottom…as if he'd wandered in and out of time like a wounded angel.

He shut his eyes.

I don't want to be young again, he thought. *I just want to find those days again and walk in them now…*

Opened his eyes. Sunbeams slanted across the fine dust in the air giving the light golden substance. He imagined the fanning brilliance was a bridge and that he could make himself small and weightless and ascend that span of light and follow it to mysterious golden realms. A daydream. But it hurt. Because he remembered lying there thirty years before watching the dustmotes. He believed there were small, misty, effortless beings who fed on sunlight. He used to imagine their world where clouds were solid as earth.

By Saint Stephen's nether eye, he thought, *I cannot rest...*He blinked and the chamber was just dull stone and sunlight again. *No magic kingdoms of air....*

He heard a footstep outside the room.

"Who's that?" he demanded, afraid it was his wife. A neutral female voice responded:

"Marga, my Lord."

He pictured her: young, slim, freckled, nervous.

"Marga," he said, "go and fetch my man Captain Lego. Tell him to ready two good horses. Tell him to cinch and bit himself for a long journey."

"Yes, my Lord."

He had the idea and instantly approved it: get away without having to deal with Arthur's emissaries or his family.

He was out of bed and getting ready in one movement. He splashed water on his face, took a drink from a mug of honey wine he kept in the niche by his bed. It had to be nearly noon now, he decided.

He could reach the broken hills by sunset this time of year. An easy ride. Just himself and Lego. Men without women. No apples to bite; no sweet fruit of doom.

"Now where are you off to, you bastard?" Layla inquired from the doorway. She wasn't shouting anymore he noted, just simmering ferocity. If he didn't stir her, he hoped she wouldn't boil over.

"I must heed my liege lord's summons," he lied.

"Ha, ha," she said in that tone that was not encouraging. "Why do I doubt you?"

He paused, halfway to the doorway, watchful.

"I will return as soon as I-"

"Spare me the list of foods I never eat. Return when you will or never. You are no husband to me."

He brushed past her now, heading into the corridor. The air was cool there. He didn't want to leave on a bad note. He tried again:

"I would like best to be a good father."

"You were too late to the feast," she said.

"Yes, but I've come," he said, pausing in the dimness, looking back into the room. The sunlight angled behind her, falling just short of where she stood so that she seemed a dark outline, depthless as a distant shape in the evening.

She was shaking her head. She was thinking about how three months ago she had been ready to fall in love with him again.

It was the spring, she thought. I can't help being a fool in the spring...

They'd gone to the little lake and swum and made love despite the nightchill. Talked about taking a trip together to the seacoast with their daughter...let themselves dream a future for a little while; then Sir Gaf and his family arrived and settled in and the weather went cool and rainy and the mood got lost somewhere...

She sighed.

"Too late," she said. "Too late. I will not trust you again, Parsival."

"Let me teach my son to trust me," he said. "Let him attend me and go where I go for some days." He was thinking out loud.

"And even though you tied him to your mount," she said, from the depthless image that was herself, "I ween he would chew himself free from you like a snared wolf."

He considered that. A feeling sank in him that almost forced tears from his eyes.

He swallowed, without a voice from the moment, Layla knew she'd hit home and said nothing more.

LAYLA

Next Morning

In the first grayish vagueness of pre-dawn Layla awoke because the bed sagged and a man grunted and breathed too hard.

For a moment she thought it was her husband and was mildly annoyed, thinking he'd come to try and apologize once again. She was curled to one side; felt a hand stroking her bare belly under the light summer satin coverlet. She brushed at it and twisted away.

The hand followed and next a wiry beard was pricking her neck and she inhaled Gaf's sour-milk smelling breath.

She pushed him off as she sat up, big masses of pillows behind her. When they moved the thin canopy poles swayed. The bed was old, she tangentially noted, and needed some repair.

"What do you want here?" she asked, almost snarled.

He knelt on the fluffy, crackly mattress wearing a puffy, dun-colored robe. Where it parted she could see his genitals, swaying. She'd seen them before. With the sun coming up, she had no desire for the view in blunt daylight.

"I want what you have granted me before," he declared, voice thick with (she thought) either drink or heat. His member seemed, she noted, uncertain. She remembered him topping her two nights ago, crushed down under his weight, feeling him poke at her until he found the place, at last.

"I'll grant you leave to go," she said.

"Aha," he said. "Come to me, my sweetness." Knelt himself forward, tipping the bed like a boat.

She got out on the far side and tossed the sheet up over him. While he lashed at it, struggling to get free, she simply left the chamber, saying, over her shoulder:

"Return to your wife and mother, Sir."

"Bitch dog," he called after her, catching in the sheet so that he knelt out of the high bed, cracking both knees on the tiled floor, the thin rug offered little protection so that the hurt Parsival had given him was doubled into blinding agony. He yelled, without words this time. Layla was gone.

HAL

An hour later, the sun streaming in everywhere, King Arthur's three emissaries were washing their faces from the bowls held by servants in another wing of the medium-sized castle. The slit windows faced east and looked across the morning fields that seemed to shimmer in sheer freshness.

Sir Gaf hobbled in, leaning on an undrawn sword for a crutch, darkbearded face sweaty with pain.

"The great coward has fled," he announced, too-loud. "He fled me and you as well."

"What's this?" wondered the red-haired, long-faced leader who stood shirtless, water dripping from his face. "Who fled?"

"Great coward Parsival," Gaf snarled and winced. "The cuckold has run."

"Cuckold?" the stocky, olive complexioned knight said, looking up from where he was rinsing his mouth and spitting into a bowl.

There were two servants attending, both male and about fifteen, pages-in-training loaned to Parsival's household by a noble neighbor some ten miles south. One was small with a deformed upper lip and slight limp; the other was stocky, strong, flaxen-haired, blue-eyed and murmured to the other, smaller fellow:

"There be more cuckolds in this castle than flies on cheese."

The other smirked, bobbed his head, nervously.

"Aye, Henry," he whispered back, "and this one's the captain of them."

"And Parsival the King."

At the same time Gaf was saying:

"Track him and kill him, as I will myself so soon as I am healed of my hurts."

The stocky knight made two fists and stared at his leader.

"You see, Alinn," he said, "we should have gone straight to-"

"He cannot have gone far," Sir Alinn of the red hair cut in. "Dress and we'll eat as we ride." Looked at Gaf. "Look you, fellow, say cuckold all you please, for any man may be deceived; but say not coward of a knight second only to, maybe, Lancelot. Pray you never meet him in anger."

Gaf glowered at him, then limped out, sword click-clicking down the stone corridor, echoing as he struggled away in silent fury.

"Must we slay him?" the thin, third man asked, from where he was now urinating into a copious bedpan. Sir Alinn was rubbing his long nose, thoughtfully.

"His Majesty wishes us to give him every chance to see reason," he yawned and said. Belched. "And killing such a fellow is not lightly contemplated."

"Well then?" asked the stocky, dark knight.

Alinn shrugged.

"We follow," he said. "We keep talking sense to him."

"And finally," the third said, "we talk with a mace blow for I fear his ears are stopped."

Alinn sighed and shrugged again, gesturing to the pages for the jug of buttermilk Henry the blue-eyed Saxon held. Took it and swigged, staining his chin with the pale richness.

"What think you of your lord Parsival, boy?" He wanted to know.

"A famous knight," he replied.

"Ah, yes. Still, why do you imagine he refuses his service to his liege lord?"

Henry shrugged, uncomfortable.

"I know not Sir Parsival's mind, Sir," he said, creasing his wide, normally smooth forehead. He was looking at the buttermilk left in the bowl Alinn still held, absently. "I know it is a great offense to refuse service."

The knight nodded. Noticed the young man staring covertly.

"Would you like some? he offered the bowl which Henry (or Hal as friends called him) took at once, without ceremony, and gulped down major swallows, amusing Alinn and the others. "Don't they feed you here, boy?" Alinn asked. "You seem stout enough."

Coming up from air, Henry answered:

"Yes, Sir. Why they set a good table here." The three knights were grinning now while the other page rolled his eyes. "This buttermilk is rich and tangy. My friend Lohengrin likes to say I have an understanding of food."

The stocky knight guffawed.

"If you ever come to be knighted," he said, "on your arms you'll wear a goblet crossing a stuffed goose."

They laughed and then Alinn commanded:

"We're off within the hour so ready yourselves." To Hal: "Pack us food for the road and mind you, eat it not before you deliver it." Grinning. "Not even a mouse's nibble, do you hear me, boy."

PARSIVAL

His armor was packed on the mule tethered to Lego's saddle. The beast swayed reluctantly behind the mount.

Parsival rode in front at a walk up the twisting narrow trail. He felt neutral. He planned to stop at the top and nap for an hour. The rocking of the big dappled gray horse was soothing.

A wall of huge clouds was slowly starting to cut off the sky. The sun was arching down at two o'clock and would soon be swallowed by the massive greenish dark thunderheads. He could see distant flickers of lightning around the immense bases. They were still too far away for the atmosphere to tense yet. He reckoned they were still hours away.

"My Lord," Lego said, behind him.

"Yes, Lego?"

"Why did you bring your knightly gear?"

Parsival didn't look back, replying:

"You mean if I intend to retire from the field?"

"Aye."

Lego could have happily dispensed with the balky, stumpy mule.

"Mayhap," Parsival said, "I will offer my steel to the saints."

*Or maybe I mean just to do something dramatic...*he thought. *I have to be careful of that, of mere gestures...*

"To a new life."

"I have not worn out my old one, my Lord."

"My new life. You are to be a witness." Parsival glanced back. "Then you can go home with the testimony."

"My Lord..." Lego began.

"Yes?"

The captain brooded now. Reached back and jerked the mule's halter.

"Stinking dung!" he said without venom. "My Lord, you ought to have ..."

"Yes? I ought to have struck my son?" Parsival looked back at his companion. He respected Lego very much and was willing to consider any advice, at this point.

"Maybe," Lego knitted his thick eyebrows together. "Yet the beaten horse but strays the further."

Parsival nodded.

From here he could see the long valley and his home in the distant mist. He thought he understood why monks choose high places; not so much as to see God, but to escape from men. He already felt the events of the morning had happened years before, and were melting into memory's mists...

"You're just a witness, Captain Lego," he reminded him. "Once you've seen what you see, you will return alone."

"Hah. Give your sense to Frenchmen, jokes to Germans, calmness to Italians." He thought a moment. "Soap to the infidels."

Parsival smiled appreciatively.

"What's this advice, Captain Lego?"

"Only give to those incapable of receiving."

Parsival chuckled.

"If they tried to take, Captain Lego," he added.

Lego smiled and spat into the dust. He had two daughters; no sons. He scratched around his beard. Went back to thinking about getting the youngest married. At fifteen she was ripe, he thought, for trouble, and she ate too much. Always chewing down bread and honey. He always said she should have been a nobleman's child. As soon as he came back from this expedition he would look into the situation. He nodded to himself.

He might have thought it better to have had sons except for his lord's example.

To get his mind on something else, he asked:

"Where are we bound?" Because Parsival had been so mysterious. He seemed to be dodging Arthur's emissaries but there had to be more to it.

"These seem dark sayings," the soldier observed.

"But dawn will come apace," the knight told him.

The hilltop was rocky, barren except for stringy bushes and pale, spiny-looking flowers. Parsival realized just how elevated his castle actually was because they hadn't climbed more than a mile and suddenly they were above the tree line.

The monastery was just ahead. It had massive walls and timbered roofs. The stones were grey and wet-looking. A strange silence, Lego thought, seemed to infuse the place. No chanting, no bells, no barking dogs, no voices on the breeze.

"My Lord," he asked, as they dismounted in the courtyard and watered the horses at the trough.

"Yes, Lego?" Parsival was scanning the building, the slit windows showing nothing but shadow.

"Do you mean to enlist here?" Lego wondered.

"I mean to ask a question," was the knight's reply. "What I do depends on the answer."

Lego rested his arms on his mount's saddle. The late sun was still hot on his face.

"Mayhap, you will speak to the stones here, my Lord," he offered.

Parsival went to the door. It was iron with brass overlapping straps. Slightly polished and rustless. He pushed hard. It stood solid. He drew his sword and knocked with the hilt. The door must have been hollow because it rang like a gong, rich, resonant as if the whole dull building were ringing sweet and deep.

Parsival just stood there, leaning into the sound. His memories were haunted. Pictures came: a field of bright misty-silver grass and milky flowers like recrudescent dreams. And across the gleaming field, a wall of translucent stone and a crystal gate that was just opening; movement beyond a haze of gold, figures that might have been dressed in golden armor moved and seemed somehow portentous, mysterious, profound...He shook his head as if to clear it. The sound was dying away now.

"Well," said Lego, "that bell should stir them. It would bestir the dead."

And then the door swung silently inwards and a little monk with a narrow, reddened face like (Parsival thought) a ferret, was tilting his neck around the jamb.

"May you speak?" Parsival asked.

The monk shook his head, and motioned the knight inside. Parsival followed him.

"I'll wait for you out here," said Lego. "I have little taste for the monkish mysteries."

The knight followed the monk down a high, narrow corridor that suddenly sloped steeply upward. There was a single step so high they had to half climb to gain the incline.

It must mean to have a humbling effect, he thought. The monk bounded, silently, up the extreme slope. Parsival followed feeling the strain in his legs.

At the top they entered a square, windowless chamber. On what the knight took for a carved stone coffin sat a man he assumed would be the Abbott: bold-faced, middle-aged fellow with short arms and a razor thin nose. His eyes were lost in his cheekfolds and squinted brows.

"Do you speak?" Parsival wondered.

The face was a strange combination of ascetic and worldly: The full, purplish lips, contrasting the edged nose; the fleshiness of the face against the bony head and sharply pointed jaw. *A fat-thin face* the knight decided.

"I speak," the monk said, his voice high-pitched.

"Did you expect me?"

The Abbott smiled, for Abbott he was.

"Did you say you were coming, Sir Knight?"

Parsival smiled, scratched behind his ear, and took the situation in.

"I expect mysteries," he said. "Perhaps too often. Perhaps I miss them too much."

"Man is certainly a mystery. That such a divine and marvelous work should sink so deep in self-made mire."

Parsival sighed and nodded. He looked and there was nowhere to sit unless he were meant to perch on the coffin or whatever it was.

"I despaired of my life," he said. "I lived sealed behind a fortress of errors."

The Abbott nodded brightly. He seemed to be enjoying himself.

"That is a good beginning," he said. "You've got to remain despairing for much longer, however, if you hope for results."

"A mystery?" Parsival wondered.

"Hardly that, my son. You clearly want to repair your life, not wash it away in a sea of prayer and meditation. But only when the tooth rages do we seek to pull it out."

Parsival thought about that. He scratched behind his other ear.

"You may be right, Father," he said. "And afterwards I may swim. Isn't that so?" The monk smiled. He tilted his head to one side.

"You might," he agreed. "But you might merely drown."

"Do you have any suggestions?" Parsival wanted to know.

"You came here for suggestions." It was a statement to the possible question. Parsival nodded. Shrugged. Scratched again.

"You had better start over, Sir Knight, don't you think? You clearly missed your way."

Parsival nodded. "Yes, I took a wrong turning twenty odd years ago." He closed his eyes to collect his thoughts. "I saw something, just this morning."

"Saw something?" The Abbott reached down into the seeming coffin, and Parsival realized it was hollow and open, the monk just braced on the thick edge. He came up with a small loaf of bread and golden goblets.

"Maybe it was a mark on the trail," Parsival continued.

"Here," said the Abbott. "Are you not thirsty?"

Parsival went over and sipped the wine. It was sweet, red, scented with a spice. It burst with slow heat in his belly. "What signpost did you see, Knight? A vision?"

Parsival shook his head. Had another sip. It seemed to strike him softly behind his eyes so that his sight was blurry and the windowless chamber, lit by oil lamps seemed suddenly brighter. The

Abbott lost his outline, for an instant, and seemed just a softly covered shape without sharp features or certain edges. It was interesting. It was pleasant. He liked the wine.

"No," he replied, "not a sight...it was a feeling...something perfect and beautiful – a great solitary power filled me..." He drained the goblet. The floor seemed to tilt like the deck of a ship in a slow swell. He wanted to say more. The wine made it very easy and poetic. "What have you given me?" he wondered.

"What have you asked for?" the Abbott returned.

"Nothing yet...but to be resolved in my mind..."

"The mind teases itself to confuse you. That is not what you are asking for, Sir Knight." The depthless outline seemed to gather the unsteady shadows into itself so that the Abbott appeared to be a human-shaped hole in the dim chamber. "The mind can never, of its own working, be resolved."

The warmth stayed even as he swallowed more wine. The stone flooring remained tilted but didn't shift.

Strange drink, he thought. *This is somehow like the mysteries of my younger days when I would wander into and out of portents at will....*

"I think I really hoped," he said, expository, because there was no connection personally with a shadow, "I hoped that ...somehow...I would find my way into a place without death in it."

The Abbott (such as he truly was) may have responded; he couldn't be sure for a moment because of the strange drink and the tilting and the dimness.

"What?" Parsival asked.

"If I were you, Knight, I would try again." said the Abbott sagely.

Parsival nodded, half-hearing, setting down the goblet on the stone with a faint clink. He sighed and turned away. Shut his eyes. Felt what had to be the priest's hand on his shoulder although he hadn't been standing that close to him. Then felt what he was certain was a soft, deep, heavy blow in the center of his back that seemed to stun his heart. Frightened, he tried to open his eyes...couldn't. Tried to move; couldn't. Couldn't feel the floor or his feet....nothingness...

His mind was fast, lucid though he couldn't feel his body...next he was standing on a fog-shrouded beach of chill-looking, gray, gritty, glassy sand, ice crusting the shoreline with massive, freezing surf crumbling just behind him. He felt nothing. The mist billowed and shook in the windblasts.

What desolation, his mind said.

Found himself moving inland though he couldn't actually see his body, as if he were merely floating eyes. There were little creatures, furtive shadows in the mists, seemingly armed and savage...he had an impression they were, somehow formed from the fog and ice. He glimpsed their faces: long mustaches and oblique eyes which seemed to glare, reddish, feral...they moved constantly, seeming to melt in and out of substance as the fogs filled and shifted...

Mist creatures? his mind wondered.

He drifted inland, steadily as if the wind propelled him and he kept passing over the little creatures without really perceiving any purpose to their activities...he paused over a pit that seemed slashed from the harsh, frozen soil. Glimpsed three mutilated bodies laid out head-to-head at the bottom.

Then the fog was gone and there were green fields all around: bright, tiny blue flowerets; clumps of spiny, twisted trees...he was rising now, soaring into a clear sky.

He saw a line of people in mixed dress led by a single knight in red armor, too high to make out features, moving in single file, twisting, zigzagging as if following some unseen and needless path on that perfectly flat plain. He had an impression the leader in red was reading a map.

Rising higher he discovered this was an island, vaguely rounded or heart-shaped: foglost shore, a green band surrounding the center that was just blurring, no cloud, no surface, as if his eyes simply failed to focus.

Higher...higher...the isle was a spot on a vast, shrouded sea...a speck...gone...

His eyes popped open and he was staring straight at the vaulted roof, flat on is back in the stone "coffin."

What? asked his mind. *What?*

He sat up. Then stood, as if in an empty bath. The monk was watching him. The floor seemed level again.

"What happened?" he wondered.

The monk was across the room by the entrance.

"You lay down," said the monk.

Parsival blinked. His sight was clearer. He could see the round, thin-featured face quite well. The floor was firm. He heard a fly buzz near his ear and flicked his hand at it.

"I thought I'd come here and be told something," he murmured, climbing out of the tub-like artifact.

"Told what?"

"I don't know." He felt sober. Dull and sober. "I don't really know why I came here." Rubbed his face. "I just had a dream."

"Well, sleepers do dream," the monk said, without emphasis. "Are you now awake?"

The tall knight went over beside the little man. At the doorway he stood at the too-steep ramp. He had an impression that if he slipped he'd slide to the bottom like a child on a slicked board.

"I suppose I'm just running away again," he murmured.

"Go back the way you came," the monk said, as if giving casual directions.

"Back home?"

"No. The way you first went. Go back that way. It won't be the same."

Parsival wondered if the Abbott meant he wouldn't be the *way* he was when he first left his mother or if the road would now veer differently. Or both. Or neither. He reached for the man's arm as he asked the question except the fellow had moved, slightly and silently, like a shadow. In the dimness he seemed to float back across the room to the coffin.

Parsival felt too weary to follow or even go on talking. He turned towards the stairs. He didn't want to look back and find the mystic had disappeared or shifted shape or something….

Hours later Parsival and Lego were working their way back down, facing the sunset. The horizon hills cut a wedge into the speck of hot sungold that burned into the gathering clouds.

"Aim always at the sun," he remembered and smiled. Lego noticed it.

"Something, my Lord?"

"My wife's father once gave me advice. An age ago when first I met her. I took it."

Lego grinned. He considered the matter.

"Always a mistake," he said.

"Nay. It led me in circles. Her father told me to ride always into the sun and so I went east at dawn and west by dusk." He chuckled and shook his head. "My error was finally riding straight. I came home and fell into misery."

"It is easy to find the lumps in the bedding," Lego said, "but a man must make the best of his life. It passes like piss in a stream."

Parsival was looking at the sun. It was so perfect, he felt, beyond thinking. The way the colors toned and blended, melted the clouds into a twilight mystery of light and dark.

"Bad cheese, my Captain," he said, "is still bad. There's no way to keep it on your stomach."

I'm going to do it again, he thought. I'll get to aim at the sun again....He noticed something: a puff of dust down where the trail flattened into the valley itself. He read it at once.

"Ah," he said, "here comes the other side of chivalry."

Lego frowned leaning up toward his horses neck.

"I was taught," he said, "to heed the proverbs of the serfs but otherwise to keep my distance from them."

"And to be courteous to all." Parsival added, grinning. "To trust no one. To break open heads. To defend the helpless. To war for the good to the gates of the Holy City itself."

"The proverbs never failed."

"Here's one," Parsival responded, watching the horses coming toward them out of the hoof dust. "trust not Greeks bearing gifts."

Lego pondered this. A Greek merchant had sold him a saddle once at a very good price. He supposed that could be like a gift.

"Why not?" he wondered. Parsival shrugged. Considered.

"Know you not the tale," he replied, "of the knight Ulys who hid in a horse?"

"Nay."

'A horse of wood. I heard it of a minstrel at court. Sir Ulys and his men hid in the horse which was left at the gate. When his enemies dragged it into their castle out they leaped and slew the lord and most of his men."

"Out from a wooden horse?"

"So runs the tale."

"It was hollow as a cask?"

"I imagine."

Lego turned over the idea. A few points occurred to him.

"How long were they within the horse?" he asked at length.

"I know not."

"Were it overlong, they'd have to void piss and shit within."

Parsival smiled and agreed. He was watching the riders come.

"Tellers of tales," he commented, "often leave a few pegs out of the bridge."

"What a stink that would be," Lego posited, watching the riders. "Are these Greeks coming here?"

"No. Knights of Arthur's table. They intend to practice chivalry on me, I think."

"How do you mean?"

"They'll tell me if I say no to the king-which I have every right to do-great sorrow will be my fortune."

"Well, we all have had the lesson: be courteous to all, but fear everyone."

The riders were close enough to them now to see the glint of arms and armor. Between the heatshimmers and the dust the men seemed to be forming their substance out of some vague, intermediate stuff.

"I have a proverb," Parsival said. "If they press me too closely: Be not the lamb who bites the wolf."

Lego nodded and chuckled. He appreciated that.

"They'll shortly be nipped, my liege."

"Nay." he said. "Not nipped."

Because he knew what he was going to do. It was suddenly clear. Mad, but clear. He smiled at himself.

It was mad. He watched them coming and considered it. He felt a rush of laughter bubbling up within him instead of cold rage. He shook his head and kept grinning as the three knights reined the bulky chargers up in a jingle, clip-clop and clitter of arms.

Parsival and Lego had already stopped. Captain Lego watched as his master dismounted, stood there and began stripping off his clothes and tossing them into the bushes until he stood in what amounted to a loin cloth.

The mounted men opened their visors. The leader removed his helmet and set it over his saddlehorn. Lego saw that, indeed, these were the emissaries sent by the king. The lean, sour-faced, red-haired leader looked puzzled but determined.

"Parsival," he said, "what does this nonsense mean?"

"It means I am mad," the famous knight returned, "or a fool."

He kept on his sock-like buskins. He fell on his knees in the dust.

"Are you angels of God?" he demanded.

The leader raised both eyebrows. He didn't like this much. He glanced at the other men.

"Were we such," he replied, "we would call you to heaven instead of to his majesty."

"A shrewd answer," said Lego.

"I don't recall the rest," Parsival said, standing up again.

"What say you?" the knight wondered.

"You're made of shiny stuff," Parsival told them, half smiling. "You must be angels after all."

"Enough of this," said the wider knight. "Will you come to your lord or no?"

"What makes a man a knight?" Parsival asked. Deadpan. He heard Lego guffaw up behind him.

"Honor." said the leader. "Have you forgotten, perhaps?"

"Who makes a man a knight?"

"The king to who -" started the second man then caught himself in fury. He didn't enjoy being baited. Who would?

"If you be not a knight within yourself, none can cause it from without," overrode the leader of the three. "Do you mean to mock us Parsival?" Parsival shook his head. He wasn't quite smiling. He looked past them now at the sundazzle on the fields where the dust of their passage was still puffing out steadily and thinning away.

"Nay," he answered him. "I mock nothing. I will start afresh. I want the king to make me a knight again, from without. Perhaps it will take away the curse of the first time."

"Curse?" The second, the wide one said. "The pride of heaven, a curse?"

Lego chuckled, looked down and couldn't believe what he was witnessing.

"That's good," he said. "The pride of heaven is good."

Parsival remounted. He kicked his horse lightly and rode past them without looking back. Lego followed. The knights watched them go, dustgouts spurting under the hoof impacts.

"We will follow at a distance," the leader said.

"I think he's mad," said the second man.

The third, short and wide with a bull-like face, had another view:

"It's his cunning and craft. No more. He means to deceive us."

"What matter?" said the leader, thoughtfully stroking his long nose with his forefinger, squinting. "He's no man to provoke. We'll follow at our leisure."

GAWAIN

He watched the backs of the mismatched men at arms and bandits marching behind John of Bligh who was now riding a dull gray, one-eyed, one-eared horse that he'd decided perfectly represented the half-blind, half-deaf Christian churchmen of the world. He'd announced this, greatly to Gawain's amusement and the men's incomprehension.

They were several days march away from Parsival's castle (where they'd left him standing naked, holding the spear with their comrade sprawled at his feet); but still way up in the rugged Welsh highlands, following the road to the sea and the only settlement resembling a city north of England itself. It was perpetually misty here. The last two days it had drizzled steadily and was chilly as autumn. The men were unhappy and getting hungry. They'd been promised loot and fresh converts – which meant women.

Here the fog was rising and thickening as if the earth were coldly smoldering.

Looking from the rear, John on the gray horse was no more than a bulging and thickening of the mist itself and the men seemed to be following him into increasing insubstantiality.

Disgusted with them and himself, Gawain was half inclined to just turn back the way they'd come. There was no way to ride very far from the road here on that jagged mountain ridge so you only had two choices of direction. He decided to wait until they reached the lowlands. He knew his hope was probably vain. He'd always been a realist – until that terrible wound had cut him off from life and love, not so many years ago. It had taken months for his face to heal as much as it ever could, and before he left to ride off into brooding fury and isolation, he'd curse those who'd saved him.

He'd lived like a bandit after that, almost never letting himself think about the part of the past that hurt the most; so that only sometimes, while dropping, as drunk as possible, into the feverish dreams that usually waited at the end of his consciousness, sometimes he'd see the woman he could never know again...there was no way to control it as real memories would seep into the nightmares; remembering her was the worst. The name he never let himself say: Shinqua, exotic and passing beautiful, goldendark skin, eyes like shadowed, distant places, a velvet touch, a heat and natural perfume that stopped his breath and heart...

After being challenged by a young knight, thirsty for reputation, in an inn, he'd gotten the notion that the Grail Parsival had been so obsessed with, might be the miracle for him.

At that time he didn't have the famous wooden hand yet to replace the flesh one he'd lost along with half his face. He'd learned to fight shieldless, one-armed, one-eyed, depending more and more on craft and speed. He'd knocked the lad down without much trouble in the muddy yard near the horses. The peasants and one other knight who'd been sleeping in a chair by the fire came out to watch. It was a cool, autumn twilight. Stars were showing.

Gawain, wearing his monk-like cowl and a mail shirt, had one foot on the fallen knight's sword arm and his blade at his throat. The boy groaned: the flat side of the blade had banged his head, leaving a massive, bleeding lump that probably wouldn't prove fatal.

The average-sized, balding but still young knight who was watching from under the timbered, dirt-floored overhang, squinted into the grayish dimness at where Gawain's hood had pulled back on the good side of his face.

"I know you," he said.

Not turning, Gawain said: "I know you, too, Erec."

"When you never returned, it was said you went in quest of the Cup of God, as have so many."

Gawain stepped back from the semi-conscious boy. Sheathed his sword. Started for his horse.

"Farewell, Erec," he said, not looking back.

"So it's true, then?"

The other knight followed him across the dimming yard as three or four of the peasants were carrying the loser out of the mud and back into the inn.

"True? You don't want to see what's true, Erec."

"Where are you going?"

Gawain stood by the horse, his hand on the saddle, brooding, remote.

"Back to the Kingdom of Nothing," he said.

And it was then that the idea of finding the Grail occurred to him.

Better than nothing, he'd joked to himself.

Meanwhile, he stood there because he really wanted to ask and was hoping his fellow knight would bring it up first. So he waited.

"You were injured," Erec said, looking at Gawain's left arm where no hand showed at the bottom of the loose sleeve. "Do you mean to return?"

"What is there for me? I belong to Nothing."

The other man got it, and said:

"She ran away to find you. Her husband brought her back. She has given birth to a male child." A pause. "Will you return?"

"A child," Gawain murmured. His life had run out and away, in a moment, like spilled water, with a single swordcut from a dying adversary. What was the world where children played, to him, now? Or the world where she mattered? Or anything mattered? No more than water spilled and gone forever mattered. "What belongs to nothing must to nothing go."

He flung himself upon the horse and sat there. The only meaningful light now as the firebright in the inn windows. Everything else was drained and vague.

"The black woman spoke of you," said Erec.

"My Lady, you meant," Gawain said, sharply. "For she is my Lady."

"So please you."

"What does the child look like?"

"Like any other."

"Not striped dark and light? Or a sullen mixture?"

"Like any other."

"There's some lesson there." He squeezed his good eye shut and open. "Tell her, I charge you..."

"Yes, Gawain?"

The eye wept and, he knew, with a sick despair, that the torn blind socket on the left side wept too, in sightless grief.

"Nothing," he said. "Nothing."

Spurred the horse onto the road and was lost in the night. Sir Erec watched him go, glint faintly once or twice as his mail caught the last flicks of firelight, as if he were riding out of the world like a phantom into the land of death....

PARSIVAL

Now it was dark. The sky seemed encrusted with the stars. There was no moon yet. Lego was saddlesore and baffled.

"My Lord," he asked as they were moving beside a stream, palely phosphorescent, hinted in the forest darkness. Lego could smell the water, mud and wet green.

"Yes, Captain?"

"We must have passed the castle in the dark."

"I meant to. I mean to go on alone, Lego."

"Nay, my Lord. I have my duty to your person."

Parsival was a blurred shape moving just ahead of him. The air was warm and comfortable. He re-dressed himself from a saddlebag. He was wearing a sleeveless leather vest over a buttonless linen shirt. He'd put on Saxon-style sandals that tied around the calves plus breeks that amounted to shorts. A short, thick-bladed dagger was strapped to his belt.

"I release you," Parsival said over his shoulder. They moved up by a deep curve in the stream where the trees closed massively in overhead. "In the morning you return."

"But where will you go?" Lego asked, as, after dismounting, they watered and tethered the horses.

"To the king, Captain. But I expect to get lost along the way."

Later, lying on the soft grassy earth beside Lego, listening to the man's gentle snores, Parsival reviewed the day. He sighed and stared up into the dark blots of the branches overhead, where here and there a piece of sky showed with a little star spark. He remembered the intensity, the urgency of the morning when he was about to die. He tried to recreate that moment. He couldn't. He tried to somehow reach himself up into the darkness, into the vast night sky that rolled in perfect silence over him. But nothing happened. He sighed again.

"It's wanting a thing," he murmured, "that drives it off."

He shut his eyes and let blankness come. He needed blankness. The earth was soft and the blanket he'd spread beneath himself was a real comfort...

He opened his eyes and the world was now a ghostly, dull grey dawn. He glanced over and saw Lego was sleeping, curled on his side.

Ah, he thought, *rest easy, good fellow...I will journey alone, again...*

He moved quietly and unhitched his horse. He'd strapped the armor to the flanks before turning in so the mule could be left with Lego.

He led the horse in near silence along the dew-wet grasses into the misty obscurity of pre-dawn.

I'll stop to wash and piss and chew some loaf after the sun is fairly risen...

It was still grey an hour later (he was mounted now) because the wooly fog had rolled up from the sumpy area he was just skirting.

He was aiming at where he knew the sun would be rising, though it was still invisible. The fields rolled smoothly here and only now and then did the thin line of trees (long trunks, a cluster of branches high in the vagueness) loom up, mysteriously.

It's foolish, of course, but I've got to go a little mad or there's no hope for me at all...since I can no longer even pretend to fall in love...

His horse paused at a crease of streamlet that gleamed dull grey in the mistlight.

He frowned and then smiled, suddenly remembered his mother. Another lifetime ago.

She gave me advice, he thought, *and I really should have heeded her: "Cross not streams at dark fords..."* Smiled. *We'll start with that again....*because she'd never said how big the stream had to be, just dark.

He urged the charger forward but didn't cross the thread of water; instead followed it as it looped down country in easy, wide curves. Trees, sparse at first, gradually thickened in around the water. After awhile, the horse had to work to pick a steady way.

Perhaps a mile further on, the trickle simply folded into a cluster of golden flowers and was gone into the earth.

The mist was burning off, now. The fist clear sunrays lanced into his eyes. He blinked and squinted. In the dazzle he thought he saw a woman in a bright gown standing in the clearing, a sky-colored tent behind her.

A moment later he realized the field was empty. It was an impression rather than a hallucination. The effect was like an image.

"Spirits?" he asked aloud. "A vision?"

The woman had seemed stunningly beautiful: tall, hair a dark rush, long exquisite limbs. *A trick of the eyes,* he concluded – except he knew it meant something. *Like a dream, or a memory, or a vision...are they trying to come together?...will the world become a blur of dream, madness and solid earth?*

LEGO

Lego sat up suddenly. He'd been dreaming something violent. The pictures faded quickly. Smoke and smudge and swords, darkness lit by tortured flames...something in black and glowing armor, with red eyes like coals. Terrific unsounds that burst his ears.

He realized at once that his lord had left him behind. He'd expected it. Parsival was moody, even melancholic these past few months.

Troubled in mind, he reflected, *but does he think my oath so light that I will kiss the wind and depart?*

He yawned and stretched and scratched. Who could blame his master? What a family life he'd had. Lego shook his head.

My own life, he thought, *is far from perfect, yes. But my Lord has been chewed like a rabbit in a nest of weasels...*

He thought about a number of things standing there, taking in the situation, letting himself fully wake up.

I need a woman again, he thought.

The last one had been a peasant girl he'd seen working in a field as he rode by, marching his men-at-arms on the way to battle. How long had it been? Over a year, he decided.

They'd camped near the village and he'd slipped away at dusk.

He'd found her eating a bowl of salted peas and pork, resting barefoot, against a haymow as the shadows went darker and depthless, the sunset draining away like water into a dry field. It was a rich moment. He'd felt strangely, intensely alive. Maybe it was the prospect of a battle the next day. He'd felt that strange fear and anticipation a young man feels (though he was nearly forty at the time) realizing, without putting it into words, that the power of women is in the power of refusal because the only thing men really want from them couldn't be raped into possession. So they had to give it willingly and could withhold it in a moment. Any of them had the power. Otherwise all you had was the body and a sheep would do as well.

They hadn't had to say much. He'd squatted on his hams close to her and nodded. Probably he'd smiled. She'd nodded back, sucking the grease from her hands. He'd liked that. She was dark-haired, full-lipped with smoldering eyes. He'd been hit at once.

She'd offered him a rib bone and he'd chewed, thoughtfully, watching her eyes watch him.

"Well, your lordship," she'd said at one point.

"I am not a lord, girl."

"You be not a miller be you?" She'd said smiling. Her teeth weren't bad, he noticed, pleased. She'd licked her lips with a red, pointed tongue. "Or a reeve?"

He'd chuckled and had shaken his head, liking her. The tension of anticipation had been strong but not unpleasant. Not the way it would have been were he actually a young man.

Age has the advantage, he later reflected, of permitting a man to enjoy certain of his discomforts; like an old cheese, where the mold becomes satisfaction.

"It's an honest trade," he'd said. "Miller, at least."

"Aye. There be no end of honest ways to go hungry."

"Well," he'd said, "you've eaten."

"This week." She'd stood up and cocked her head toward the hut. "There's nobody about. Come on then."

He stood there in the misty morning, blinked and remembered that, for some reason: the rankness, muddy, sour hay smells, spicy smoke...the crush of straw under them, her strong yet sweet sweat, powerful calves rocking, locking down his legs, the hot shock between them.

He blinked and blocked away the memory, now.

"No good thinking that way," he told himself. Not when alone, with no woman in sight.

By the time he'd mounted he knew he would simply follow Parsival. After all, he was a vassal. What child had not been told the tale? How the seneschal and his wife, who, when their lord's castle fell and he was killed, and as the victor was about to slay the infant son of that lord, he being a male, the vassal and his wife cried out that it was their child dressed in the noble robes to fool the enemy, and so they were forced to stand by while the baron discovered their own child who was the same age, and cut his head off on the spot. They'd saved their liege's boy. That was the point. Lego knew perfectly well he could not have done such a thing, but that was the ideal. He was far from ideal, he realized, and wasn't sorry.

He smiled at the thought. He believed the tale overdone but it rang true enough in spirit: you are supposed to be loyal to the death. It didn't matter if the lord was insane or cruel or foolish; you were supposed to be loyal.

PARSIVAL

Parsival had dismounted and was poking around the glade, as if to find something tangible where there had only been an effect of light. The sun was hot now.

Bees were stirring among the lean, blue, thistly looking wild flowers.

"This feels familiar," he murmured.

He was thinking it had to be a place from his childhood. He looked around, trying to recover an image. Nothing came to him.

What am I looking for? he thought, *A ghost of which mistake?* Because they had all been errors except among the errors, false starts and hopeless endings, as, among thorns, exquisite flowers have blossomed, so there had been other things, moments rich in life and joy...other things...

He remembered. There had been a tent. There could have been no trace of the tent, even a week later much less decades. But he remembered now, how he'd wandered into a lady's tent (wearing a fool's ratty hides that his mother had covered him with in the forlorn hope of keeping the world from wanting him) and how he'd kissed and fumbled in his almost supernatural teenage ignorance...kissed and fumbled her into total ruin in the end, by accident.

Ah, but what is pain? he asked himself. *Only the mind which holds on to shadows...*

He hadn't thought of that woman or that business in years and years and now, suddenly, the memory was a vivid stun and he saw her, her lovely, pale breasts naked on the sleeping silks and furs where she lay waking into fear, startled by the strange beautiful young boy crouched over her.

"What was it?" he murmured. "What was the name?"

Jeschute, he remembered. That was it. It all came back to him: her husband, the mad duke black bearded, vicious, unforgiving, after tormenting his wife, finally falling to Parsival's lance; and later, to his own insensate, self-consuming fury: actually chained to his horse because his back was broken, charging Parsival on a narrow trail, missing and wedging himself between two trees, raging, demented, helpless and doomed as the (then) young knight rode away....What was it, fifteen years ago? He never found out what had actually happened to her back in those torn, firefilled, bloodsplattered, tormented days. Days when he'd lost every trace (or so he believed) of his youth. He frowned now, troubled, thinking about it. He was drawn by a strange retrograde current that was sucking him back into past shadows...Why? Why now after all that time?

What happened to her? he wondered. How many causes had he set in motion to effects he knew nothing about. It would be good to find out...Yet it was absurd, he knew, though it followed from everything else, because absurdity was the soil in which his garden grew.

Perhaps I'm going to find out what became of everything I touched and so I'll owe nothing to God or to man when I'm done – I'll *have forgiven myself, been purged of consequences...*He recognized that this was already an obsession. He was caught because it wasn't just walking over the same paths (if indeed they were) of his youth, it was living it again.

"This time," he said, "If a damned door opens I won't let it shut. I'll jam my head in and let it be crushed."

He kicked the earth. He stared at the grass.

It was here, he thought. *I know it now...*

There, in the misty morning of the last day of his childhood. There...

If that woman be alive then I must right the wrong I did her, he thought, calmly, like a man about to undertake an all consuming feat. *There's my repentance. There's my expiation...*

He understood it was a vow he was making. And like anyone making a vow, he felt instantly better, as if something were already accomplished.

He found it important to speak aloud now: "I'll find her, and save her." As if he believed it. As if she might need saving. It didn't matter. It was his impulse and could guide his life through what might otherwise be a pathless trek. Because if he meant to drop his past purposes he certainly needed new ones.

LEGO

At the same time, a mile or two away, Lego was riding and brooding. He followed the river and hoped for the best. The sun went higher and higher and the heat burned towards afternoon like an open furnace door.

He rode steadily, squinting across the general dazzle. He picked up Parsival's tracks without much trouble and he sat with one leg across leaning on the horses neck, watching the steady flow of matted grass and dusty earth rhythmically marked by the puckered broken circles of unevenly printed horse hooves at once alike and yet as various as snowflakes...it was hypnotic...

So at first he didn't realize the fact that there were too many prints, suddenly, and it hit him just as he looked up and saw three riders cresting a grassy rill perhaps a mile ahead. He squinted at them across the lush valley. His stomach clenched at once. He spurred the big roan forward.

Would I were going to the sea shore to rest in the sun and row a skiff, he thought, *yet, instead, I ride on the road of troubles....*

LOHENGRIN

Lohengrin had left that morning. He'd made up his mind to get away while his father was absent. He'd planned it for weeks. The young squire, Henry called Hal (whose family had sent him for training, as was the custom) had agreed to go with him. Lohengrin liked the fellow just enough. He thought young Henry of Aud stiff and stuffy, even somewhat foolish; he assumed he was brave enough.

Because of the season Lohengrin strapped his light armor to his horse and rode in leather shorts Firetail; Hal wore fighting leathers, long pants and tunic. Both carried swords and daggers.

"Why wait and suffer what they tell us." He'd reasoned with the lad who was, in fact, a year his senior, at fifteen. "We'll strike out for ourselves. Win our knightly spurs in the old style."

Lohengrin liked the idea of the old style. He liked stories about more lawless times than theirs. He liked the idea of knights banding together against the world and winning riches and honor and various unclear glories. Mainly he liked the idea of being free to come and go as he pleased and fight whom he chose. He'd been well-educated for a youth of his class; Hal not so much.

His eyes were dark, intense, magnetic, persuasive. His tongue was precocious and convincing and so the two of them had slipped away just before dawn and by mid-day found themselves miles down the valley on the main south road, roughly paralleling the direction taken by Parsival and Lego, and indeed, Arthur's emissaries.

The sun seemed to impact the dust flat on the hoof-chewed surface.

Lohengrin was sweaty. He hated hot weather. Both of them rode with their armor and fighting gear strapped to the horses' withers.

He opened his loose, linen shirt to the navel. His dark, surprisingly thick chest hair showed, matted and wet.

"Now I have misgivings," said young squire Henry.

"What?" wondered Lohengrin. "Are you a girl-heart?"

"Nay, as you might know. But will they not send after us and bring us back in shame?"

Lohengrin spat past the horse's shoulder. He smiled faintly without humor. "Hah," he uttered. "You will not find me a light burden to carry in any direction. There is no dishonor in what we do." He wiped his eyes. "I think my flesh will melt to the bone. And sweat to me nothing."

Henry took this in. He stared across the lush, rolling fields, serious, uneasy. His face was roundish, with wide slightly protuberant eyes. He didn't look like he battered his brain with violent thinking; the few ideas he had, however, were nailed down to stay.

"How will we eat?" he wondered. "After a day or two our supplies will be gone, I think."

Lohengrin smiled with real amusement this time. He shook his head in disgust. He realized why he liked having Henry with him: because Lohengrin loved to mock and stir things up. Even if he liked you well enough, he still enjoyed pricking the needle in.

"You eat beyond what is human," he commented. "Maybe your grandfather was a horse."

Henry's brown, small eyes looked seriously at his companion. He had no sense of irony or sarcasm. Many of Lohengrin's sayings, consequently, were lost on him.

"I am well proud of my blood," he said stolidly, "and the deeds of my forbearers."

Lohengrin almost laughed. He looked sidelong at his companion with a provoking air. "I am proud of Lohengrin," he said. "Let the rest be fucked in their ears and asses."

Henry said nothing more. He looked contemplative and uncomfortable. Lohengrin always made him uncomfortable. He was about to ask himself if indeed he had not made an error in joining him. "Surely," he said at length, "we will come to a village before long."

Lohengrin looked uninterested.

"Do you long so for the company of villains?" he asked Henry.

"No," responded his companion, "but base folk make some excellent dishes."

He nodded thoughtfully. He remembered things. "Some nobles think only the dainties from Italy are worth swallowing." Lohengrin seemed incredulous.

"You concern yourself with such things," he wondered.

"Naturally. I think the foods of our country are greatly underrated. Did you ever have flatfish and thistleweed stewed with clams such as the peasants eat at my manor?"

Lohengrin chuckled. "I'll drink salt water and chew dry oak leaves," he said, "in trade for one of their choicer wenches."

"What's that? You'd mate yourself with a serf sow?"

Lohengrin shook his head. Henry was hopeless.

"What have you fucked above a sheep or two?" he wondered.

Henry was offended.

"Do you think me unnatural, Lohengrin?"

"A wench with a bath is a clean hole," Lohengrin said, "but a sheep dripping Arabian perfume is still a foul beast."

Henry was agitated. His eyes flashed.

"Why do you link me to such Godless practice?"

Lohengrin guffawed. He was really enjoying himself now. He shifted around in the saddle to better look at his victim.

"Haven't I seen you rightwise linked?" he snorted. "Linked to a sheep's arse?"

The strong, stocky Saxon youth stood up in his stirrups. "Cease!" he cried, baited, furious.

Lohengrin couldn't control it. He was shaking with laughter.

"What a sight," he said. "Fear not, I'll not reveal your vices to your lady."

Henry sat back down, looked uneasy.

"I have no lady," he said, nervously.

"Ah, have you not?" Lohengrin cocked his head to the side. "Come now, Hal."

Hal was sullen. "I have not."

They were just entering a thick, dark wood of mainly saplings massed together. The thin trees made a soft-looking grey wall.

"I know her well," Lohengrin said. He did. His aunt's daughter. A slightly thick-waisted, but pretty-because-young flaxen-haired girl, a year his senior. "I had her kiss me stick," he said, breaking up.

Henry's eyes flashed. He'd had just enough.

"You lie," he cried. "she never-" then cut himself off, realizing, finally, he was merely being provoked.

Lohengrin squinted ahead across thickly bright green, overrich, almost spoiled-looking fields and rolling foothills. He felt confident. Life would be his. He stretched and cracked his finger joints. He felt good.

"You want serf's pasty bread?" he asked, rhetorically.

"I-"

"I mean to make war, like any other lord. I have an idea of booty." He looked quite cold, his eyes suddenly dark and still. Henry didn't say anything watching him, uneasily. "We'll raid and we'll rule," Lohengrin assured him. "I've made my plans." Which was true. He'd sketched them out during long, dull afternoons in the castle yard, in his chamber, or riding in the neighborhood. They were crossed between the just possible and youthful daydreaming.

"Plans?" asked Henry.

Lohengrin came back from the cool distance of his inner vision.

"We're heading to the seacoast," he informed Hal. "I've thought it through. We'll gather foreign and masterless men about us."

Hal blinked. "Gather men? What men would follow two boys?"

Lohengrin didn't quite smile. But he was amused. He felt the cold spring of strength rising within him, in his belly and head, and almost ecstatic power and confidence.

"You'll see who follows," he said, quietly, "and who dies." Because he felt, in fact, that no one was better. No one who sat in large castles with small armies at their disposal, yes, not even the king himself, would have any more claim to glory, or power than Lohengrin of Wales. He saw his future. He would have women for sport, hounds past counting, an army to rip and smash whatever stood between him and...but the thought was really only a feeling and the precise final goals were still vague outlines of battles and big fortresses and triumphant processions...

"You'll see well who follows," he repeated. Because he'd kept his real purpose, the one that was clear to him, private; although now he was content to tell Henry, now that they were on the road. "I mean to win where my great father lost," he said. "Then we'll see."

Henry nodded. Frowned.

"Win what, Lohengrin?"

The dark-complexioned young fighter stared straight ahead, not looking at anything.

"When I was small he'd tell me the things he told no other," he said.

Hal nodded again. Shrugged.

"Fathers share their wisdom with their-"

"Bah!" Lohengrin cut him short. "My father had no wisdom I ever noticed. Better to take the advice of a chirping bird."

Hal shrugged again.

"Well then," he said, "what is your import?"

"He told me many times, the story of how he tripped over the Grail Castle."

Hal looked as thoughtful as he ever did.

"But you always say –"

"I always say my father was stupid. But he almost found something that might, like Arthur's Excalibur, give a man power in this world. I mean to succeed in taking hold of this Grail that all men desire."

Now Hal was amused.

"Ho, ho," he emitted. "And you a boy will succeed where the great Knights of the Round Table all have failed?"

"We'll see who's great, Henry. I have a map."

"A map? Let me see –"

"Hal, you are precious," Lohengrin cut him off yet again.

PARSIVAL

Parsival remounted and rode across the glade into the harsh looking woods beyond: The trees were very old and gnarled here, and bent thick, branches twisted close to the ground so that he had to work around them and stoop constantly. "Even if I had a destination," he muttered, finishing as a thought: *I'd be lost in an hour...*

The heat was oppressive as the sun mounted into bronze, blazing noon and broke through the leafed interstices in burning spears and boiled a hot steaminess from the damp earth. He was glad he'd stripped off his armor and the leather vest. He just wore a loose, linen shirt, and his bare legs were comfortable.

He kept slapping at insects, sweaty and miserable. Enough was enough. He contemplated turning back. And then he heard the steady whoosh of running water and he aimed towards the river, well downstream at this point.

The trees arched away here so he decided to follow the curves for awhile. The river was wide and not-too-deep.

"What vile heat," he told the day.

He halted the horse and dismounted. Leaned down and dipped his face and hand in the coolness. Nothing ever felt better.

He blinked and stared. Sunscatter created bright greenish, golden fannings of light. He remembered, as a boy, staring and imagining that strange fairy-like beings lived there among the fluid fronds and mysterious rocks and shadows.

A flash of silver as a fish winked suddenly into a lance of sun and hung there. He was tempted to draw his sword and impale it because it was so elusive, so momentary – like, he thought, all the bright things that eluded human grasp.

He leaned back from the water and cocked his head. He heard voices: a shout and a high pitched cry.

"What's this?" he wondered, aloud.

"You pig!" a woman cried out. "Curse you!"

He stood up and headed for the sound: downstream, close. He went around a sharp bend. A man was raging in wordless fury. A woman had just fallen half into the water on hands and knees. Her clothes were ripped. He saw bright blood spots on the white pebbles.

By the cut of the man's stained, ripped clothing and the quality of it, Parsival took him at once for a well off townsman.

What a world, he thought.

He rushed forward the last few steps and got between them. He had a feeling the man was about to deliver a blow on the light haired woman's head. He kicked the fellow in the side sending him into the shallow water flat on his back.

"You bastard," the man cried, in a somewhat high pitched, raspy voice.

Though the woman was obviously low born too, Parsival instantly helped her to her feet, as if she'd been a lady. That was his way. She stood there blinking, startled, breathing hard. One eye was bruised and her lips were cut, fine nose intact. Well, peasants are always fighting. But these both, he had already noted, seemed more refined that the usual run.

She's a beauty, Parsival thought.

Meanwhile, the now dripping wet man scrambled to his feet, clutching a big smooth stone in each hand, eyes slits of fury, thin chin beard plastered to his cheeks.

"I will break your head, you bastard!" he raged.

Parsival glanced at him and raised an eyebrow, speaking to the woman:

"Is this your husband, who so abuses you?"

She looked weary, haunted, but furious. Her eyes were dark blue, face freckled and pale, hair a reddish brown.

She wiped her lips with the edge of her hand and smeared the blood. She cast a fierce look at the man who edged closer, cocking his arm as if to throw one of the stones, obviously worried by the virtually unarmed man's total indifference.

"The priests joined us indeed," she said. "At the very door of the church."

"Mayhap I ought not to judge this knave too harshly," Parsival reflected, "since two and a hundred times have I longed to serve my own wife thus."

She paid scant attention to his ruminations.

"Loan me your dagger, fellow," she said, "and I'll sever the bond."

He noticed she was well spoken. Not unheard of in a peasant but really rare.

The man finally kicked his courage free and whirled the stone at Parsival's head.

The knight nodded just to make it whiz past his ear, not really looking away from the woman.

"Repeat that folly," he told the fellow without turning to him, "I'll send you on a dark journey."

"You pig!" she said to her husband. "You dog's stool...."

"You whore!" he interrupted. "How curse me when you dipped your head over that pardoner's prong! While I—"

Parsival was both bored and amused. He accepted the contradiction without analysis.

"I might as well have stayed at home," he declared, "to hear such discourse."

"Ah, did I indeed?" she wondered, standing, wide-legged to face him. "At least he had a bone and not a boiled sausage!"

Parsival raised an eyebrow and nodded.

"That's plain talk," he commented.

"Yer a slut!" the man declared, raising the second rock. "Yer twice a slut."

Parsival wagged a finger at him.

"Mind," he warned. He noticed the fellow's eyes were reddened: maybe drink or recent weeping. No doubt he had cause for either or both, Parsival thought.

"He is a man," she told him, as if they were alone at home bickering among the turnips, Parsival thought. "Not-"

"Boiled sausage," Parsival put in. He shook his head, grinning. "For Godsake, no more of this. Have I just come to another room in my own castle?"

"Ya great ass," the man addressed him, "ya fancy yer indoors?" Shook his head still holding the second stone at his side. "He's a fool."

Parsival sat on a fat rock, under a sweeping willow tree. The shade was pleasant and the smell of the water was cool and refreshing. His horse had finally come up and was waiting, nuzzling the surface of the stream.

"There's no sense in fighting," he told them. They both just looked at him now. The woman plastered back strands of her wet, disheveled hair.

Really very pretty, he noted again where her traveling dress was torn and hitched up, the long graceful sweep of pale leg held his eye. *More than pretty...*

"Are you a disguised priest," she wondered, "come to make peace between us?"

"There'll never be any peace, you bitch," said the man.

"Eat dung, Hubert," she recommended.

Hubert's mood suddenly changed. He dropped the stone and went and sat on the bank.

"Go with him to his castle, Katin," he suggested to her. "He looks a right lord."

She studied the horse, saddle, clothes, light armor.

"It's a knight's gear," she pointed out.

Parsival realized he should just go, he was watching himself begin the process of acting silly because it was a female, and he'd soon be inventing, he realized, reasons to linger.

"Where are you bound?"

"Where indeed?" she replied. "Ask the donkey there." Hubert the donkey didn't look up. He spat towards the water.

"Women," he said dully, "take out the heart of a man."

"Ha, ha," Katin said. "What might you know of men, Hubert? Or hearts, for all else?"

Parsival tried again. He really did want to leave. He felt a strange obligation to do something. This was life as he knew it.

"What has brought you here?" he tried asking.

She was now kneeling, washing her face in the stream, cupping the water to her hurt mouth.

"I rode a mule named misery," she said.

"Be not so harsh," Parsival suggested. "You seem not provisioned for a long journey. Is your village close?"

"We have no village nor no course," Hubert declared, bitterly. "So that leaves us no distance to go."

"Ah," said the knight, "here's logic at least, but what drove you here?"

"Troubles," the woman said, standing up and facing Parsival. She was bold-eyed, strong, with a slim, very good body. He almost knew how she'd feel naked in his arms: strong, nervous hands; the smooth wiry back and shoulders; the pressure of hip and thigh….

He blinked the thought away; rather, tried to blink the thought away.

Didn't quite meet her dark, knowing eyes. She understood. She was almost sure already, watching him from under her eyebrows now as if she actually could read his thoughts. It rarely took women long, he knew. He tried to stay cool and remote with the usual success. He avoided looking down at her legs. That was a start.

"I came form the land of dullards and cruel, useless men," she said.

Ever I am drawn, he thought, *to the same slim beauties with needle tongues…*He blinked. *Still, she's well spoken for a peasant wench…..*

"Well," he offered, "we may all journey together for a time, towards better places."

The man, Hubert, didn't quite look up, sitting with his arms on his knees brooding, sullen.

"Do so, by all means," he said, sourly. "She'll lie flat in the field for you at the point of your lance, the slut."

Parsival didn't get it at once because he was only half-listening. He was wondering if he should bother at all with this. Twice, now, is a short space of time, the world had dissolved: first the blade to his throat, then in the monastery…as when you lay sick and feverish….

"But I don't battle women," he protested. "Even were she armored *cap a pe*, bearing sword and buckler. Anyway, I gave up my lance."

"Were a woman hid in armor," she said, thoughtfully, "how would you know if you battled her?"

"Bah," muttered the man, "you'll thrust into her, never fear."

"Oaf," she sneered, not looking at him.

"Come now," Parsival said, "I am not that sort of fellow."

He felt faintly like an ass, saying that: under certain conditions he was exactly that sort. "Anyway, you're in luck because I'll journey with you for a time." He smiled. "But you must give me your oaths to make the peace between you."

"Ha, ha," said the man, scornfully, "we're in luck, as you are, yourself, if you meant to travel with us and hear every oath ever framed."

LEGO

Now, Lego came over a knoll into denser forest. The tracks were still plain and overlaid his lord's. Were these the knights sent by the king? He had to assume they meant harm. It was prudent and natural.

Each time he passed through a deep tree shadow the coolness was a shock. The hot, thick, wet air; and then the coolness. He urged the horse on into a canter. When all this was over, he decided, he'd ride to the village of Arsra and see his 17 year old daughter. She'd married a man of law, a pardoner. He was thin, dour, with a sallow complexion. He did his duty but no more, not by a hair. Lego didn't exactly delight in his company, but he enjoyed her wit and the way she looked at life. He missed her. He nodded to himself, thinking that, watching the roots and leaves and sun and shadow flick and flow past.

LOHENGRIN

Lohengrin and Henry "Hal" were not too far ahead of Lego but angling away, following the twists of another valley trail that intersected the course of a sluggish creek branching off from the main river. Lohengrin vaguely remembered this was a shortcut to the seacoast. The mountains were to the right, tops craggy and dark above the trees.

The black-haired young fighter squinted his, still, jet eyes into a sudden break in a nearly solid wall of forest.

"What's this?" he wondered.

Hal blinked; followed his companion's gaze.

"A tent," he observed.

They reined up. Lohengrin looked calculating.

"Not just a tent," he commented. "This may be opportunity."

"Nevermind that," Hal said. "I mean not to plunder like a base-born robber."

"Suppose there's roasted chicken to be had by plunder? Good game pie?"

He loved the fact the savory images gave the appetite driven young man pause.

"There's no right in such things." He shook his big head, solemnly. "We will ask for food but do no dishonorable thing."

"I am fortunate to be in such chivalrous company," the wry, swarthy young man said. "You give me as much pleasure as a stone in my shoe."

"I was taught a knight's armor is like a mirror. If it be stained or blemished in any part then the picture it shows is false."

"I am glad you are not pompous."

"I mean what I say."

"And I say what I mean." He chucked his horse to a walk, heading for the large, cylindrical, red and black tent. "We'll be lovers yet. There are women here, my ponderously moral friend."

"Can you tell?"

"Smell the perfume? I ken roses where none are growing. Wait here and I'll say a greeting."

Hal sat his horse, crossing a leg over to ease his back and hind end.

"So you do none harm," he said at Lohengrin's back, "who merits it not."

"I'll come back with bacon and cheese. Content yourself with such thoughts." He was looking around carefully, alert for trouble. No horses. No smell of horsedung, either. Just green earth, a faint scent of rotten grass and the odor of distilled roses. He twisted around to say: "I'll share equally, always. The women for me; the victuals for you."

"Still your talk, Lohengrin."

"Have you never fucked aught but a sheep?" Lohengrin asked as he passed under the trees into the clearing. "I wonder not at your love of mutton."

The little glade was a sunny hush, walled in by dense thornbushes, heavy with the dark red flowers, purple, swollen, ripe; dripping petals. Though he really didn't react, he was vaguely conscious that the place was strangely over-rich for the border of the Northern highlands. Even the leaves seemed too large and palely, almost biliously green. Here was the source of the faintly rotten smell.

He halted the horse in front of the silverblue, silken tent that shifted delicately in its guys. The stillness was strange – dream-like. He decided he might be a little giddy from the sun.

He was a moment from turning back except the fabric's sheen wavered and parted and a woman who might have seemed (to a more poetic eye) a very exhalation of bright afternoon's sweetness stood there, just inside, the perfume (hinted soured roses) faintly stung his eyes.

Her gown was the rich ripe color of the heavy, winedark blossoms and shimmered like dim gleams on twilight water. Her face was pale, oval, exquisite as carved cameo. The lower half was covered by a soft, silken mask. Things she'd seen showed in her eyes; things he was too young to perceive as contradictions. He was hit. Stunned. He understood no better than a tomcat comprehends the pull of the moon and the scented ferality that burns and fills him.

The effect was raw and total and drew him so that he was already dismounting, walking at her before he really realized he'd moved.

Here's an opportunity....how silly Hal can be...

"Er," he croaked.

What's wrong with my voice...

She just stood there, not coming out past the parted flap. Her face showed nothing. He stopped himself from touching her.

"Are you unattended?" he asked. Imagined he felt a tingling from her that crackled like clean, brushed hair.

"For the nonce," she replied. Her voice was dark silk, too.

He felt soft inside and silly.

"For the nonce," he pointlessly repeated.

He wondered if this were love. Most songs and poems were equally about violence and love. He had never felt the things they described.

"Young warrior," she asked, "are you unattended?"

He liked that.

"I have my best friend with me."

"The shy fellow in the road?"

"No," he said, "my sword."

She wasn't quite disdainful. His giddiness gave the impression the world was slightly tipped towards her so that it was partly gravity bringing them together.

He kept imagining her nude: pure, pale, cleanly scented. It was like hunger because it was taste he wanted. An urge to kneel and somehow feed on her flesh. This was something new.

As if she read his thoughts instead of merely knowing them, she faintly smiled and gestured. He went inside; bit his lip. Couldn't focus on anything but the knee-weakening hunger.

"I..." he began.

"Come, boy" she told him. Her robe had parted, calves and bare feet visible.

He hadn't been this tense when he'd lain with his first woman. Thirty-odd old, husband dead in battle, a friend of his aunt's. They'd met during a feast at home while his father was typically away, about two years ago. He'd been surprised how well it went once he got past the first few moments. Undressed, they'd embraced in a dim upper story storage chamber on bolts of satin and linen, raising a fine dust when they moved that hung and held the dimming, deepening bloodred beams that came in almost flat across the sill of the tiny window a vague streak in the shadows.

At first he'd tensed, chilled as if the energy pressing through his loins withdrew from the suddenly heavy, awkward flesh. Felt nothing there....nothing. Then her hand (at first seeming knobby, rough, harsh) as he lay athwart her, those fingers, somehow kneading the energy back out until he arced and ached to press himself into her.

Or that same year, finding himself with the fifteen year-old daughter of a physician by an abandoned outbuilding where he'd agreed to meet her after, in church, she'd passed him a pale scrap of parchment inked with symbols that made no sense to him. He was always pressured to go and sit, recalcitrant and bored, hoping the priest would trip on the altar steps, again, and spill the wine...

His unwittingly cool lack of response had finally driven her to boldly invite him to what he didn't yet know was a liaison. He'd really only cared about fighting. Even falconry bored him. He enjoyed pig-sticking more than stag-hunting because he liked being in on the kill himself and not, as he put it, watching a pack of dogs do his work for him. "Why not," he'd told a knight, "fight a joust by having a gang of soldiers drag your opponent from the saddle ere you come to grips with him." He enjoyed the last moments when the quarry was out of resources and room, trapped and fell to the hunter's will.

Lohengrin studied people trying to understand things they seemed to feel that meant nothing to him. Eventually he was as a sharp as a Borgia in reading the human motives and weakness he generally didn't share. He tended to judge love by his parent's example. So he'd gone to his liaison non-quite-sure why. He'd gradually exasperated the comely miss with the redgold "Viking" hair until she finally led him by the hand to the adjoining garden on that unseasonably warm, pre-spring afternoon, sitting in the yellow-brown grasses where a few scattered, pale-blue flowerlets specked the earth. The sky was leaden and when she finally sat on his lap and put his hand where it mattered he understood and was instantly straining at her like a bar of iron. It started to rain (as if on cue) and they went inside into a musty, disused room which still held a strange, faintly sour scent from when they'd used to hang and bleed game on the hooks set into the masonry wall. It didn't bother him. Why would it.

"Ugh," she said, wrinkling her nose.

Lohengrin knew what to do with the same precocity he brought to fighting. Unlike his sire whose strange, fluid skill always left the impression that his victories simply revealed the ineptitude of his opponents, Lohengrin practiced with total intensity to beat his enemies at their best, meet their strength and bend it back on them.

He worked his way into and under her garments, wildly excited by the first smooth, amazing touch of bare flesh, running his hands up and down, not so much in awe and excitement as basking in possession as if he were molding her into a form for his pleasure; not that he actually conceived these things but that the inner map of his being demanded it.

So he opened and spread her, made love with suppressed fury as if he'd mounted to joust, rocking himself down into her until the girl, through spurts of passion and pain (back getting battered and scraped raw as he rode her across the floor into the wall) cried out – he didn't notice she was resisting and, at the end, pressed her shoulders flat and bowed himself into and arc of victory, spending her soft sweetness and seat and fear as if ejaculation were a coup de gras...

He blinked the memory away, so to speak. He followed the woman inside the tent into a warm, rich, thick musk of spice and scent so intense that for a moment he felt his nostrils might close. It was somewhat difficult to breathe.

Took another step, blinking as the dimness tilted and, in the velvety red blurring he was stunned by a pale golden flash: she was instantly nude, magnificent, eyes remote in mists of strange, sweetened wickedness that no man might ever call her back from; coppery hair like dreamflame, spilling and folding over her shoulders.

"Kneel, boy," he thought she said and he never knew if he'd obeyed or had simply toppled forward in vertigo onto the perfumed, almost foamy masses of cushions and silks. A part of him was enraptured; a part was furious. "Pay homage," she commanded.

She stood over him where he crouched on all fours in the uneven softnesses, furred pillows crackling with spice-stuffing. He cricked his neck looking up her incredibly long leg and then her toes were lightly brushing his lips. It was strange: the tips and undersides were perfectly smooth (he thought of polished alabaster except they were warm and soft) and he couldn't help but move his lips back and forth as if her foot was formed of sugary stuff, not mere flesh.

What is this madness? He tried to think. He found himself eagerly licking, lapping as if expecting honey, then sucking as a baby sucks the rich syrup from the charged breast.

His body was excited, heart thumping hard.

"Good boy," she said from her remoteness far above him. "You will serve me well."

"Yes," he heard himself agreeing. "Yes."

She was far, far above him, a goddess towering into the smoky, rose-red, perfumed atmosphere. Time had gone somewhere else...dreaming had leaked into waking and dimly inhaled the crush of odors and tasted the sleek sweetness cramming his mouth.

He moved and she moved, at different points...his mouth traveled and tastes sharply changed. He licked and sucked whatever presented itself...lost track...lost himself, spent and stifled by the mass of musks...tried to wake up until he realized he wasn't asleep...intended to get up soon...

At some point he began working very hard, straining, holding his breath until he forced his eyes open. It seemed someone had poured jelly over them. He blinked but all h e could do was shift the blurrings around.

And there she was: golden-pale, tall nude, towering above him, endless legs curving up into the reddish dimness.

"Up on thy knees, young knight," she commanded. "Training continues."

He twisted around and was looking right at it, eye-to-eye, so to say. Her fingers gripped his head like tongs and brought his face where she wanted.

He intended to struggle. What she wanted suddenly nauseated him. He had no say. She planted his face there and again he was amazed by the sweetness and silky textures. Thought of the most succulent peach he'd ever tasted. Then she moved away.

Nothing but this could be important. He slipped back into the strange torpor. Had to reach that perfect goal. Rolled with great effort…half-knelt, half-fell his way over to her. She was on her back, legs effortlessly wide. Crept toward her as if she had a gate there that went somewhere and he had a destination….

"Drink deep," she admonished, "from this holy cup."

He did. It was sweet. He was as lost to time as a suckling babe. He sensed (somewhere in himself) this might be wrong. But who could be sure? Wrong in war was the loser. Who was the loser in love? The one fucked or fucking?

PARSIVAL

Midday. The sun was a whitehot hammer on their skulls. Parsival, Hubert and the wife were following a twisting road; the trees didn't overhang very often. Parsival rode with the woman sidesaddle in front while her husband stalked along through the yellowish dust. The untilled countryside tilted wildly there, rising and falling in short, sharp swells.

Her scent was strong, musky but pleasant, the knight decided: flowers and sweat. Her hair right under his chin, smelled like hot, dry wheat. He liked that.

I'll never reform, he thought. He went back to his interview with the abbot, the blurry conversation in the burial chamber (or whatever it was) where the holy man had been perched on the side of what seemed a stone coffin. *Never….*

The couple had begun wrangling, again. He hated it. Really sickened him.

"Too hot for that," he told them, wiping the fresh sweat from his forehead. "Christ's feet!"

"Hubert were born cross," she said.

A pun? Parsival wondered.

"Oh, hear how the whore uses me," cried Hubert.

"We travel but a short time on this earth," Parsival intoned. "We ought to enjoy one another's good points."

"Had he any," she said, "I'd revel in them."

Parsival shook his head, chuckling. He kept staring ahead, unfocused, across the brilliant afternoon as they tipped up and then swayed down roll after roll of road.

"Have you ever tried to pull up the roots of your disputes?" he asked them, thinking of himself and how he never had.

The askew-looking man tilted his head around and just missed being struck dumb by wonder. His wife gazed up at the blue, blazing heavens as if to draw strength from above.

"The roots," she said. "That's good."

"I'm serious," the knight told her. "I've been pondering many things." He shifted to the side a little to ease the growing numbness in his left leg. His body's memory of a forgotten wound. "I war at home more than ever in the field. What folly! We repeat ourselves until we're dull as dead men." He bit his lower lip, narrowing his eyes. He wished, just for a moment, he could feel that vast, clear otherness again that would have filled out his words with a power beyond mere sense. "Dull and dead...and so we die long before our time and our world shrinks to a small and bitter knot."

She twisted around to see his face. She wasn't mocking him, saying: "You be an odd figure of a knight. Mayhap you should make poems."

He nodded.

"That would surpass what I've done," he agreed. "Nay, but I want peace...peace at home, first, um...." He gestured, inclusively.

She got it.

"My name is Katin," she told him.

"Peace at home, Katin."

"Ha, ha," put in Hubert. "Then slay your wife."

"Slay yourself, you wormy cheese," she sneered and recommended.

"I'm getting seasick on this horse," Parsival said.

The valley was narrowing now, steep bluish hills closer. She sat quietly, thoughtful. Hubert spat in the dirt and marched along, up and down the sickening rills and ruts.

"Be you truly a knight?" Katin asked, looking straight part the mount's neck.

"Not so truly as once I was," he replied, shrugging. "There's everything wrong with it."

"You're the first to say so," she said.

"Yet it's but the fool in the armor," he reflected, "so it's the same as all other work I suppose."

Hubert was weary and irritable. He glanced over.

"Why do I doubt you?" he wondered. "Do you really believe this fellow?" he asked her. "I take him for a fraud. Where is your knight's stuff?"

Parsival was amused.

"It weighed me down," he answered.

"Aye, as you fled from battle?"

Parsival nodded. He liked that idea.

"I suppose I am fleeing from battle."

"What is your famous name, then? Some fine knight. Bah." Hubert spat into the dust and watched the spittle roll into little balls. "Fly shit."

"You guessed right," Parsival said.

"He seems a knight to me," Katin put in.

"Oh, aye, to you he would. And he can do great deeds and then come back and stick it in you."

She tossed her head.

"Pay him no heed," she said, "he be low and dark as the Devil's shit."

"Which famous one be you?" queried Hubert. "The great Lancelot or the mighty Parsival?"

"The mighty Parsival," the knight declared, grinning. "And Lancelot the squat? I fought them both. Parsival is easy."

That was too many for Hubert and he shook with chuckles, dropping to one knee.

"Oh yes," he got out. "To be sure...and you still alive and unbroken..."

"It's a living death, fellow."

They were passing a crumbled hove near the road, the first sign of habitation in
some time. The roof had fallen in and birds perched on the crossbeams.

Parsival squinted through the sagging doorframe into the inner dimness. Leaks of light hinted at lost shapes of long-lost life....

Everything seems strange but familiar, he thought. *Like first love....*

They'd gone on. The forest had closed in almost completely there and the road was fairly level, though twisted and seemed to be succumbing to the undergrowth in places.

Everything seemed to remind him of long ago. Everything was like the sights of childhood, suddenly fresh and charged with gathering promise; promise without a cause or purpose....

He pulled himself back from his reverie and decided to try a new tack. Not that he had to try anything; he could have booted Hubert in the hind end and chased him. But he knew women enough to think she might have left with him; wasn't his style, anyway.

"Look you Herbert," he began.

"Hubert," corrected the man.

"Pardon me, I..."

"There it is," the man interrupted.

"What is?"

"A knight begging me pardon."

"It's just words, you ass," she said. "Some lords are like that. It's the training."

"Look," the knight went on, "it doesn't much matter what I am. Let us pass on our way in peace." He nodded, satisfied with his point. "You, Hubert, what is your trade?"

The man had stooped, picking a few from a red scatter of wild berries he'd spotted by the road; straightened, kept walking a little behind them, now, nibbling, staining his fingers and lips.

"Don't offer none such," she commented.

"There's scarce enough to plug the bung of a bug," he returned.

"That's his true trade," she said, "pluggin' bungs."

"Oh, hear her. You had yours plugged aplenty." He chortled. "Well sir It-Don't-Matter-What-You-Be, I'm a bailiff, or was, more properly."

"More properly," Katin muttered.

A bailiff was the highest rank of peasant, a man privileged to take meals and sleep in the lord's manor house, steward of his lord's affairs and property when the master was absent. Years might pass without a noble paying a visit if he happened to hold many villages, which was common enough, so long as his profits were collected and passed on to him. So Parsival assumed, at once, that this fellow had probably tithed himself a little too well and drew unpleasant attention.

Still studying the brush for more berries, Hubert had drifted behind to the edge of earshot.

"Well then," Parsival said, "I can imagine what befell."

"The reeve was a thief," she told him. The reeve, among other things, collected and tallied for the bailiff.

"I believe that to be common," Parsival said, judiciously. Actually, his knowledge of manor affairs was sketchy, like most fighting knights. His seneschal did most of his business and he held only a single fife, in any case. His wife had much to say on that subject since he'd rejected holdings in the south offered by the king for his war service. Parsival didn't want to feel beholden because he always meant to quit fighting. After lust, this was his favorite inner conflict and self-indulgence.

"My ass of a husband had to bear the blame," she said. "So we were cast out." She seemed amused but with a bottom note of hysteria. "Vagabonds..." Bitterness, too. "Who could have foreseen this day?"

Parsival took this in. The road twisted sharply back and forth. The trees were massively old, densely green with humped, gnarly roots.

"He was fortunate not to have gone into the dungeon."

She sniffed.

"The reeve went under the castle, as the saying is. God curse him. Now we wander the cold world like Tom O' the hedges."

"Your husband knew not of his crimes?"

She laughed. Her hair flicked across his chin and cheek.

"He is the bird who let the snake warm her eggs." she said.

Parsival was considering the case when something caught his attention: a glint of metal among the branches. He squinted, leaned closer. From a middle branch a rust-rotted chain hung straight down, suspending nothing but an iron collar. Convicts were often hanged that way after a slow death elsewhere. He sucked his lips, feeling it somehow meant something.

He vaguely hoped her husband would sort of somehow fade away, because she was leaning back into him. His nose was full of the scent of her sun-heated hair and the rich, soothing smells of the hot earth. She was slender but he had a feeling that her body would be a surprise. He kept trying to picture her naked...would have liked to run his hands under her clothes and feel the sleeks that always took his breath away.

He sighed and rolled his eyes. Tried to concentrate on the weaving road and cool silence under the trees.

"Nothing new," he said.

The road was suddenly paved with wide stone blocks. He realized that was as far as the old builders got. He was used to coming on roman handiwork left over from the centuries –ago occupation.

We all only get so far, he thought, *on any road we build or follow...*Snorted at himself, his strangely reflexive, didactic mind. *Should I have been a priest?* The idea was troubling.

The hooves clunked dully on the stone.

"Bound to be a village ahead," he said needlessly.

"Or a castle town," she added.

Because the road showed use; the grasses were crushed down between the blocks and worn to dirt in places.

So he was busy studying the surface as they rounded yet another sharp bend, still following the course of the now, unseen, river. He was startled to see the horseman sitting his motionless mount as if he'd been waiting for them.

The red armor surprised him. The branches parted there and the hot hard sunbeams sprayed around the figure.

Parsival blinked and squinted, automatically easing the woman down from the saddle in case of a fight.

"Wait," he told her, glancing around for her husband who hadn't turned the bend yet. He edged his mount closer to the knight whose visor was down.

I am on the road of ghosts, he thought, remembering the day he met the Red Knight, Sir Roht, whom he eventually killed for his armor. He was young then, younger than Lohengrin.

He eased the horse a step or two closer, into a splinter of sunlight. The armor wasn't really red, just totally covered in rust.

"Have you never heard of grease?" he couldn't help asking.

The visor was closed, flat and dented. It looked like it couldn't fit over the man's nose.

"You come," the metal-muffled voice commanded.

Parsival thought about that.

"I come?" He lightly touched his chest where the pale linen shirt fell loosely open.

There was an overgrown, mossy wall just in the underbrush. Perfect cover for an ambush. He wondered if they'd all have rusty armor and would the joints stick when they struck blows?

New idiots, he thought. *Always new idiots…..*He estimated the distance to the wall. Scoop her up and ride.

"Come closer," he murmured to her. "Nonchalant."

"How?"

"Slowly."

"She die," the armored man declared.

Parsival couldn't place the accent.

"No doubt, but when?" he asked.

"You come or she die." Gestured with his rusty head. "Follow, unbeliever."

The woman was close to the horse's flank. "Unbeliever" made him hesitate. He'd seen bowmen from the Holy Land. The range was hopelessly close were there any behind that wall.

"Mount up behind me woman," he instructed. "Nonchalant."

As she did, a row of heads popped up behind the wall and he saw the short, deadly bows. Not Muslim but nomad. He'd seen those too.

"We come," he said, soothingly.

"What does this mean?" she wondered. Glanced back, looking for Hubert.

"We're making new friends on the road." He felt her fear.

"Will we be slain?" she asked. "Will I be raped?"

"The infidels I knew hated women," he said. "You may be safe as long as there's a loose goat."

Unless they *were* nomads. But how did they get to Britain?

They came over the wall and out of the bushes. There had to be twenty or more, dressed in rag-tag fighting gear.

Parsival had the feeling they'd looted a long-deserted castle or a mass grave on some battlefield to judge from the condition of the gear. He supposed they were in disguise. He wondered how many blind beggars they'd deceived so far. The men were mostly dark with oily-looking hair and beards.

The leader in rust-red eased his pony backwards into the brush where a narrow trail intersected the paved road.

The swart men fell in all around and Parsival nudged his mount forward. The leaves flared greenish-gold in the hot sunbeams. A sweet breeze cooled the sweat from his forehead.

"We go," he muttered. "If they meant to kill us," he went on, "they'd have tried already. I wonder where the bailiff is got to."

Suddenly he felt a strange, old feeling attached to nothing, or something lost...long ago...lost meaning from lost years....sense of strange peace unconnected to this moment. He remembered stumbling across grass on infant feet in a warm dazzle of springtime light and enriched air, drinking in life unframed by any thoughts....

He shook his head; he was becoming detached from his immediate surroundings. His life had been poured into a cracked mold. He was suddenly afraid. He shuddered slightly and she felt it.

"Do you fear, Sir Knight who has not named himself?"

He was alarmed. She obviously was depending on his coolness.

That's sooth, I haven't, he thought.

"Call me Sir Discontent," he suggested. "Yes. I fear."

Afraid to pass through the door. Afraid to stay inside....

He wished now he'd kept his armor. Wished he'd gone left instead of right...wished....

GAWAIN

By the time they'd reached the lowlands he'd decided to stay with raving John and his motley men. Until he solved the Grail problem, one direction seemed as good as another. He believed Parsival wasn't lying when he said he didn't have it, but sensed that he was afraid to look again.

Now I'm as big a fool as any for the Holy Lie and emptiness, he said to himself as they slowly topped a bristly hill on the wide, well-worn road to the city. In the middle distance, stood an old-style wood and rock castle (just one huge central keep with a low wall) a fat column of smoke rising almost straight up into the hot, bright, windless, midday summer sky.

They made way for several wagons loaded with cloth and rope, heading away from the city out towards the fiefs and fields. The sight of the evil-looking crew of unhappy, dusty, sweaty, partly-armed and armored rogues marching behind the little man on the one-eyed horse, made even the roughest carrier lay hand on dirk, stick or club for reassurance. When they saw cowled Gawain at the rear in well-worn mail and a priceless charger, they held out little hope for themselves and blessed Mary and the Saints when nothing untoward happened.

Admirable madman Gawain considered, *he believes he will conquer this place with his ravings....*Shook his head.

From the hilltop they could look down on the hundreds of mud and thatch huts, dozens of scattered two-story part-stone buildings and the big church which stood a few hundred yards from the rocky North Sea coast where awkward-looking too-high ships were moored while barge-like boats rowed to and fro. One sailing ship sat in the offing, motionless on the glassy water, sails flat and lifeless in the prevailing calm.

I'll go to the whores and keep my face covered, he thought. *Yes...and not think of her...*

"Ha, ha," he said, not laughing. The nearest man turned his raw-looking, reddened, too-long face around to study the knight.

"Eh?"

"I'll not think of her," he snarled at the man who, like most, believed Gawain both mad and deadly as a viper.

"A' course," the man said, uneasy. "That's plain."

"Am I thinking of her now?"

"Ah," the fellow sighed. "There's that."

He squeezed his sole eye shut. Didn't scream out the answer.

What else do I think of?

"Fuck you," he said to nothing.

The man turned and concentrated on walking while Gawain's troubled thoughts roiled on.

Parsival...I'll find his path and be healed....

He groped back in his mind, looking for clues in the times they'd been together...the last, prior to the confrontation a few days ago, came back to him, about 15 years ago....

Fifteen Years Before

Moonlight had lain softly on the pale road Gawain followed without a particular purpose. He'd skirted the main battle lines where the massive fight between Arthur's army and Clinschor's black armored mutes had finally wound down. He wasn't running; he wasn't seeking combat, he simply didn't care.

He'd heard that Lordmaster Clinschor had come from Sicily, Africa or some such place of darkness to despoil Britain and possess the Grail he believed was hidden there by one of Christ's disciples. He believed it would make him immortal. Another damaged brain, Gawain had concluded, leaking nonsense like a cracked cup.

There were lines of refugees along the road. To them the knight seemed a phantom, taking shape from the ghostly, silvery glow. Some crossed themselves. Gawain reined up when he faced another horseman (he didn't yet realize was Parsival) blocking the road.

"You mean to challenge me?" he asked.

"Nay," Parsival answered. "Do you know me?"

Gawain raised his visor and let the moonlight angle into his face. Turned the horribly slashed side to him.

"I don't care a shit if I do," he said.

Brought his eye to focus and showed his good side too. Even in the softening moonlight the effect was hard to look at.

"Gawain," Parsival said, voice choking a little.

"My friend the fool."

"I hope I'm your friend."

Now Gawain kept his ruined side turned away. The handsome profile looked pale and mysterious in the subtle light.

After a few moments, he said:

"You're changed."

Parsival agreed.

"Yes, Gawain."

"Thinking I'm changed as well."

"Well, time alters all things."

Parsival was being careful. He shifted on his horse, looking around into the softly gleaming knight, half-expecting to see Clinschor's killer mutes closing in. Gawain gestured with his right; chuckled, mirthless.

"That's good. This is nothing, my friend. None still dare come at me from his side." He shook his fist. Parsival waited. "So you think you know something now?"

"I heard the fighting is done."

"No," Gawain grunted. Parsival noticed the sour wine-reek on his breath; could see he was a little unsteady in his saddle. "You never stood up to me, you pretty little by-blow." Dropped his hand to his swordhilt. "I've lost count of all I've sent on their fucking way." He snarled with sudden, empty fury because he was breaking his rule and thinking about her; thinking, too how this still young blond knight could kiss and fondle and ram himself into his lovers as he pleased. "Or the bitches I've pried open."

He turned his nightmare side back to the young man who wouldn't look directly at it and shifted, uncomfortably.

"Yes," Parsival said, quietly.

"I'm still a man. Think you are old enough?" His eye came back to Parsival and the two sides faced him together. "Want to try me?"

He kept thinking about her. Over and over. Saw her face, too.

Parsival shook his head and the eye looked somewhere else as the tortured knight cried out in pain the younger man mistook for self-pity.

"God curse it!" he was breathing as hard as if he'd been fighting. "God of filth and swine, curse it?" Drew his sword and ripped it through the night air, slashing at nothing. Parsival, reflexively, leaned away.

Gawain slammed down his visor and shouted something muffled. Parsival stared at the sudden, slivery blankness.

"Gawain," he started to say.

Thinking about her, seeing her, Gawain shouted what seemed a wordless cry of pure suffering. They were words but they were his alone.

"Oh, Gawain."

Gawain was past listening or speaking. Kicked his charger into a canter, thudded and jangled past his old companion and the attendants and refugees along the roadside, riding, Parsival felt, not just away but out of the world entire....

In The Present

Gawain kicked up the pace of his horse and rode past the column as they now were plodding down the reverse slope into the city itself. He paused, briefly, beside John of Bligh and his one-eyed, one-eared mount.

"Where will you and these dullards encamp yourselves?" he asked. "In case I decide to rejoin you later."

John seemed surprised by the idea.

"We're not here to camp but to raise an army," he responded. "Ere the worlds fails and falls entire to the Antichrist."

Gawain knew the story by heart: John was persuaded that Clinschor was the Antichrist promised in the scriptures and that, as the world was poisoned, boiled and broiled in the coming year, he would rule with magic and inconceivable cruelty. John believed that the wizard had retreated to an underground fortress. Only the Grail Sword, wielded by himself at the head of a host of transfigured believers, could cut down the Antichrist and his fell defenders.

"Still," said Gawain, absently retightening his wooden hand in its screw socket, "even while saving the world, men need rest."

The smaller man cocked his head up at the knight, rocking as his unsteady mount clip-clopped along the (now) pebble-paved road.

"You mean to desert me? Here, in the shadow of doom?"

"I owe you no service, Lord Madman. We're on the same road, for the nonce."

He chucked the horse ahead. There were carts and mules and burdened peasants coming and going.

"There is only one path for everyone," John called after.

"Being so," Gawain responded, not looking back, "nothing can part us."

Later

Cowl in place, horse in a barn, the sun setting in a rapidly graying sky, Gawain stalked along what passed for a main street, stepping over offal mounds and reeking puddles. He'd had directions to a drinking place from the bearded, toothless, one-eared hostler at the stable.

The inn sat (or rather, sagged) in a pool of stinking mud and was accessed by a duckboard that squished and half-sank as the big knight crossed to the door. He hesitated. Almost went away in a spasm of self-disgust.

"Be fucked," he said to the door; kicked it open.

It got the patron's attention. Both of them. A fat bald man sitting on a stool in the middle of the dirt floor and a stringbean with orange-red hair at a tilted table bent forward to suck beer from a clay bowl.

Seeing it was an armed knight (or armed somebody) they watched and waited. He sat down, laid his scabbarded sword on the table. The host came in from the other room and bowed, slightly. He was round and smiling. Kept licking his lips as if some sweet taste lingered there.

"Yer honor," he said.

"Bring me a whore."

"No drink, me lord?"

"Bring one hemlock and a whore."

"What?"

"Ale."

"Ah."

"And a whore."

"Yes, me lord."

And I'll be content as a man with lice on his balls...as a man with a bee-stung prong...a fishbone in his throat...content...

The innkeeper brought him a leather jack of drink and a few minutes later, a tall, tense, lean, dark woman barefoot in a shift came into the cave-like room, shielding a candle flame with her cupped hand. She came to his table and set the candle down. As she approached he'd been a little surprised by how good she looked. In the dimness her age didn't show until she was close. She had high cheekbones and a faraway look in her eyes, hair touched with gray.

"G'day, me lord," she said sitting down. He liked her voice.

"Yes," he responded.

With his head tilted inside the cowl the place was too shadowy for her to really see his features. When she moved the candle closer he pinched out the flame.

"Sir?"

"Our business wants no light, woman."

He'd already changed his mind. Quaffed the ale in a long steady swallow. He already liked her.

"We can go out in back," she suggested.

He shook his head.

"Is he your husband?" Gestured towards the innkeeper who was slicing some cold meat and cheese at the far end of the low, smoky room, covertly watching him.

She made a disparaging gesture.

"I've borne him two sons and two daughters."

"That's near enough," Gawain said. "Does he whoremaster your daughter as well?"

She creased her thin, long lips in a knowing smile.

"So, that's your pleasure, me lord?"

He couldn't read how she felt about it.

"If they look as you must have," he complimented, "they are rare beauties."

She had no expression, saying:

"The eldest be seventeen and married to a good fisherman. The other fourteen and not for sale. But there's a hag two doors down who'll serve ya her babes."

"Will she throw in breast milk?"

"Her dugs give old cheese," she replied with a faint smile, this time.

"So he whores just you?"

Though he raped in war and had done violent deeds without count, the idea of the man selling his worn, pleasant, dignified wife bothered him.

She shrugged.

"There's others as work for him," she said, expressionless, again. "But yer a fine gentleman knight, so he offers you his best."

The ale was working in him. He gestured the man over. He didn't quite scurry, holding a fresh jack of ale in one hand and a wooden trencher of meat, hard cheese and dark bread in the other, which he banged onto the battered table. He was sweaty and smelled of stale food and drink.

"Yer grace," he said, round, reddened face uneasy, knowing and sly.

Gawain felt like breaking his head with his wooden hand. His mood baffled him. Why should he care? What point? But, as he sucked down more ale, he found his cold anger growing.

"Grace? I'm no Duke or Bishop, but I have gold," he found himself saying. "True royalty," Lying, "I crave your youngest child. Name a price, innkeeper."

"Oh," mused the man, uncertain but engaged. "Well…."

"No," she said: bitter, furious, controlled.

"Come, come, peasant, you know I could take what I please if I pleased but my pleasure is to bargain. A price, I say."

"A price, yes," repeated the man, clearly lost in calculation. "But sire, with no disrespect, we here as knows how to defend ourselves. This ain't the countryside."

"No, I say," she snarled, standing up. "You filthy, lying..."

Her husband cut her off with a casual backhand which staggered her and left the fine nose dripping a thread of blood. Gawain had what he wanted.

"She's a perfect little beauty," the innkeeper said, "all fresh and untouched."

He must have gestured in some way because the other men were on their feet, both holding a long stave. "Worth her weight..."

"You pig!" she cut him off.

He just ignored her this time.

"As I'm sayin', yer honor," he went on, but this time Gawain who'd noted the two armed peasants with cold relish, spoke over him.

"Nay," he said, "as you seem worth *your* weight in shit, I want you. I long to probe your south-most hole with my stiff dangler."

The innkeeper's face went flushed and wild.

"Unnatural knight," he cried, "begone from among us."

His cronies had moved in on either side of the table, rather smoothly, he noted.

"To lose your company would be like losing a bad tooth," he told them. "Don't send me away."

"Go from here and find your own kind," said his host.

His wife now got Gawain's point.

"Be still, ya fool," she advised, "lest this fellow kill us all."

"Not all," the knight assured her, standing up as her husband drew a chopping knife from behind his back and, simultaneously, both his fellows swung their staves. They'd done this before, Gawain realized, as he instantly countered, cutting one stick in half and stepping back away from the other as the woman screamed and the innkeeper surprised him hurling the heavy, semi-square blade with terrific speed and force, point-blank.

There was no way to avoid it. A death blow slicing into his cowl that his reflex twist barely moved to the left of his nose. The fellow had a special talent for murder, it appeared. But that inch to the left sent the blade into the space where his face didn't finish.

They were all stunned when the cowl was ripped back and away and they saw bare skull and teeth. The woman gagged and fled, thinking her husband had cut his face in half. The others froze in shock and terror long enough for the knight to chop down the two of them and then go for the red-faced man who bolted for the back room.

Gawain was incensed.

"Wait up, whoremaster," he pleaded, charging after him, leaving the other two in a welter of blood and pain.

The pimp didn't wait; so sore afraid he actually ran through the side wall (loose fitting planking) into the alleyway, squatly ploughing through mounds of refuse knocking man and animal aside until he finally fell flat, exhausted, safe behind a maze of twists.

Except Gawain stopped two steps outside. The stink alone, he later said, had been enough discouragement.

"So much," he muttered, "for the pleasures of Eros."

He went back in and found the ale cask. Dipped a fresh jack and drank deep. Began eating some cold meat. One of the wounded men had crawled away somewhere; the other had been hit in the head and wasn't going anywhere.

He didn't realize the woman was still in the room, crouched behind an overturned table, watching him. She stood up.

"Well," he said, "what's this, woman?" He instinctively turned his good side to her.

"I'm used to ya now," she told him. "I've seen worse hurts and them as was born looking like a trod worm."

"You relieve my mind," he remarked, mocking.

"Did ya kill'm?"

"The world's fastest fat man? Nay. He rolled from my sight like a kicked ball." Drank some more, keeping his head turned, after trying to readjust the slashed hood.

"I'll mend it if you like," she offered, coming closer.

"That pandering, fat nastiness just had me nearer death than any knight in twenty years." Studied her, from an angle. "Mend what? My torn heart?"

"I see yer too much alone, sir knight."

"Fine," he snorted. "How much for mending?"

She touched his face in profile to her. Her hands were cool, stonehard but smooth. She gently stroked his cheek. He felt it melting him.

"Just yer word on a thing is me price. You tell the word here that if he does any hurt to me or the children you'll return."

"Sorry I didn't slay him," he said, nodding. "He was too quick." Still amazed. "He nearly had me."

She was close against him now and her hands went here and there. So he didn't bother to reflect on how he might have been better off if he hadn't ducked aside; for once, he was satisfied to be alive.

"Come up the ladder," she breathed into his ear, "to the sleepin' loft."

His knees went a little soft; throat felt choked.

"Yes," he managed to agree.

LAYLA

She shut her eyes and reopened them very slowly. She knew it and she knew she knew it.

Stood in the sharp shadow of the thatched hut, the sun a whitish-yellow dazzle in the dusty yard, the bright green furrowed fields of early wheat rolling up the rounded slope towards where the castle sat. Men and women were out in the fields in gray, red, brown, some men stripped to the waist, most wearing turban-like hats or hoods.

The old woman came out into the hard-shadowed doorway. Her eyes were lost in squinted lines, dress a shapeless grayness. She was holding a heavy clay pot in both hands.

"You need not show me," Layla said. "I knew in my heart."

"Aye," said the crone. "The seed did sprout, lady."

Layla was staring across the sharp, wooded hills to the empty sky beyond, shimmering in heat haze, the powdery blueness of midsummer. She sighed, not knowing how she really felt.

"No," she murmured, unconsciously touching her belly, feeling a strange, annoying tenderness for her husband. It welled out like water through a clenched fist. Hating it, she remembered the first time she'd touched him when he was a strange, clear-eyed, too innocent teenager sitting in an oaken tub in her family castle. He'd stopped there, she thought years later, like Paris tripping over Helen, playing, she'd thought, at knight in borrowed armor. The herb-strewn water steamed around him while she and her sister (to show their father's *courtois*) scrubbed him with perfumed soap and she'd learned her own deep weakness and need when she gripped him under the water and shocked them both into one...for a seamless moment and a broken lifetime...

*What nonsense...*She sighed, standing here in the golden, mellow August light, staring, she imagined, like a snared bird in a fowler's trap. *I have birthed two and lost another and by God I'll lose this one too since my soul's already on the list of the damned so what's one more stain of darkness?*

Just the memory of him in the tub, her desperate wanting, as if she were dying of thirst and he a full skin of water. *Except it wasn't he,* she understood, *because I got my wish and felt only worse....*She'd touched between his legs, startled them both and in his perfect eyes she saw his need waken. *They were so blue...like broken jewels...*

Over the years the soaring promise had fluttered, spun and finally hit the bitter ground like a stricken angel. In that fateful bath she'd gripped his innocence and never forgave him for being the mirror of a magic he never actually possessed...

"My lady?" asked the old woman, cocking her head to one side.

"Bring me a ladle of water, will you?" Layla asked, staring.

Both gone, she thought, meaning son and husband. *No more men...*Pictured her last mistake, Sir Gaf, the Greek, and reprised his wet kisses and itchy beard; his insistent but short-lived member. *They all* *have to tell you how the other man is a weakling yet the wrong word at the wrong moment and their fine club becomes a willow wand....*

The crone came back out of the cool interior holding a wooden bowl of water. Layla took it and absently drank. It was warmish and satisfying, tasting of earth and stone.

"No more men," she told the hag. "May God damn them!"

"Hah. The fox had a full belly ere you feared for the goose."

Layla handed back the cup and left the yard. Mounted her palfrey by the sagging gate, and sitting astraddle, man-wise, let the horse amble up the hill. She didn't actually look when a horseman clattered from behind the last hut in the village and reined up close to her.

She'd just been watching a big ram with dirty, yellowish fur and one gimped leg, clumping and skidding awkwardly across a walled-in muddy field in hot pursuit of a long-legged lamb who kept just ahead with gangly effortlessness.

She grimaced, recognizing Gaf.

"Still around?" she asked.

She was wondering if she could keep her daughter from all the twists and hurts of growing up; all the phantom joys and hollow nights that attended love....

"I have come back," the knight said. He wore mail armor but no helm. His beard was trimmed to a close-cropped point. Maybe, she decided, he thought it made him seem French.

"I can see that," she said. Urged her mare ahead, glancing back at the enclosure where the ram seemed to have finally cornered the lamb. The hill beyond which reached up to the square castle silhouette, was just being slowly covered by a cloud shadow. The sun still beat hard and steady where they were. "Why?" she wanted to know. "You ought to make haste back to your sweet bride and mother."

She was mildly annoyed to note that he was keeping pace with her. She felt sweaty and grouchy with no desire to deal with him.

"Spare me your barbs, Layla," he told her. "I'll not leave you with that fool and coward."

"Which one," she wondered, deadpan, "particularly?"

"Indeed, which one."

"Do not mistake him," she warned, wiping her brow and eyes with a handkerchief.

Why doesn't he go away?

"I will have you to keep, Layla," he said. He seemed, she decided, more tense than usual.

"Why?" she asked, quite seriously.

"Life, in other wise, holds little joy for me."

She didn't quite laugh. She wasn't amused, for one thing; and for another, she'd been brought up to take romantic declarations seriously since so many knights were willing to be maimed and die for the sake of such notions. But she was closer to laughter than awe, at this point.

She squinted at his face in the dazzling sunlight.

"I'll tell you what," she said, "ride with this token-" She held out the damp handkerchief. "-and return with a dragon's head and I am yours for eternity."

What, she thought, *are we children still to follow nonsense like a spellbound moth the shifting and inconstant flame that drops him scorched to oblivion in the end...not likely, Sir Gaf...*She was furious now. Thought about the new child one of them had left within her.

"Do not mock me," he said.

She smiled without humor.

"So you've cropped your beard to come and win my heart," she said. "Bring me back the head of a pig, or failing a pig, the head of your wife, and I'll..."

He went red in the face and leaned over to slap her but she leaned away.

"Evil-tongued slut," he snarled, exasperated. He shout-whispered: "Heed me! Mistake not my resolve."

She was a long way from the safety of the castle. She knew she should have dissembled until she could slip away. The idea of appeasing this selfish, pompous bastard (as she now thought him) disgusted her. The memory of his distracted caresses, perfunctory kisses had little appeal. She was amazed at how she'd once been eager for those contacts.

An then I have to lie on my belly and him above and it's no more use than a glove without a hand in it..

She had to get away. Fast....

LOHENGRIN

He felt dulled, drowsy, enervated....He could barely open his eyes and what he then saw was all bent into blurs.

He felt he didn't belong there, that he ought to get out but time and the past seemed to be melting away....

He kept considering crawling across the silk and velvet floor to the tent opening – except he wasn't sure which way was right. To his blurred sight the interior seemed a seamless dimness.

"What has this witch done to me?" he murmured. The air was suffocatingly close, hot and densely perfumed. After what seemed ages of stagnant time he managed to roll over onto his back. "Have I been here for days?" He tried to recall when he'd eaten last. He couldn't tell if he were hungry or thirsty.

*I never believed in witchcraft...*He feared he'd be spellstruck forever, prisoned in fairy twilight like a fly in amber. He'd heard tales of supernatural races that hid behind screens of deceptive magicks and might madden and obsess humans.

He closed his eyes again (or thought he did) and seemed to dream that he was lying enchanted in the tent and he told himself he was dreaming and then reopened his eyes (or thought he did) and was still nude lying in a strange, gray world of slow-flowing mists where shapes stirred almost into forms but never quite revealed themselves...and there was one, a shadow that might have been cast by some remote, gigantic statue (he sensed that much) that yet lived and had a message for him which made him feel that he would, somehow, be made into something as powerful, massive, enduring as stone and that his life would be monumental...

And next he blinked and was looking down across his belly at the top of her head where it was wedged between his legs and felt that her mouth was drawing all the strength out of him, like a pool draining away, being drunk away. It had to be a dream: neither pleasant nor unpleasant.

She seemed to drain him until blackness flowed in and filled the almost empty pool of himself and then he was gone...

And then his eyes popped open again and a bright glare burned into them and a voice nagged and he winced.

"Rouse yourself from this pitiful torpor," the voice was saying. "I have waited an hour or more for you. My guts are hollow. I was in a way to chase a rabbit with my sword when I bethought myself: yonder lies a tent and there must be victuals within." Big Henry was looking around the silk and satin interior. "No doubt you have eaten and forgot to call your companion."

Lohengrin just looked at him from under his black, thick eyebrows, his eyes like dull, burnt coals. He wondered who this clumsy-looking, pout-lipped oaf was.

Where is she? he wondered to himself. *Do I sleep or wake?*...

He suddenly sat up. The light from the parted flap was blinding. He held his temples under the matted, curly black bush of hair. Henry was still saying things. Lohengrin remembered who he was now.

I feel better...As if a spell *had* lifted. He stood up. Swayed slightly but that was all. A few blackish dizzy spots holed his vision but that was all. One, as it was fading and his sight cleared, gave a fleeting impression of a graceful female body topped by a skullface...and then there was just the sting of factual sunlight.

"Where is she?" he wondered.

"What?" Henry was still poking around the tent.

"The woman."

Henry liked that.

"Ahha. So this is what reduced you to ruins."

Lohengrin grimaced, wryly, looking down at his naked body. He found his garments here and there and began putting them on.

"How long were you outside?" he wondered.

"Some little time. I saw a woman come out. And then I came in."

Lohengrin looked at him while sitting there, tugging on his metal-studded, pointed, low boots.

"She was a beauty, eh?" he said.

Henry shrugged.

"She had red hair," he said. "She went into the woods. I didn't see her face."

Lohengrin was staring again, as if rapt.

"It seemed a long time....." he murmured.

"It seemed forever to me," said his companion. "When you're waiting to sup, the sun stands still in the sky." He was poking around now, lifting cushions and what not. Wrinkled his nose. "It reeks in here like a Sunday mass between the scented smoke and the old women stinking of flower-water. And you say you found no food?"

Lohengrin stood up to strap on his sword belt.

"I have to say I did not look, Henry." He headed outside into the green and blue brightness. "Mayhap I fell into a sick dream when I went within. The close air..."

It seemed possible now, out in the blunt daylight. Anyway, that was better than being mad. He finished dressing in the hot sun. The tent was empty. There was no witch, no woman even. The whole business meant nothing and didn't bear thinking about.

He squinted up into the trees, not looking back, even when his starving companion came out of the tent.

"We go forward," he said, as if to Henry, "on the road to destiny." He liked saying that. He'd heard a tale-teller tell it.

"The only road I seek," said Henry, "is the road to roast meat."

As he braced and swung his leg up over his horse's back, and Henry mounted beside him, Lohengrin thought:

It was no dream......it was not a dream at all....

LEGO

Lego was following the river trail about an hour behind his lord. He came to the place by the wall where he noted many sets of hoofprints coming together. He dismounted and studied the signs: Parsival's horse joined the rest and cut through a break in the wall into the forest.

No marks of a fight, he thought. It was hard to imagine Parsival being taken against his will. *odd…..odd…*

He remounted and followed. A short distance in, the trees opened into a little glade where the sun lay in hot, mellow brightness on the wild grass and stony earth. The air was heavy with afternoon heat; grasshoppers flipped semi-sidewise like chips of brown wood or flickers of grass; bees stirred in the bushes; birds twittered and the day murmured in a way that made him long, suddenly, to stop and stretch out and sit in the shade like a day-dreaming child.

A few yards later, just before the forest closed in again, he heard the snarl of flies in the brush. He twisted his mount aside to see what was dead because he noticed the horse snort and shy slightly, as horses will when they smell blood.

So he wasn't too surprised to see the dead man (he didn't know was recently Hubert the Bailiff) lying on his back with his chest cut open, both eyes wide, stunned and glassy. The bush's shadow hid the worst of his wound but blood fresh enough to be still red was spattered around him like dew in the relentless sun.

Lego unconsciously touched his swordhilt and squinted hard into the waiting tree shadows. The hot breeze plucked at the grasses and ticked the heavy leaves. He felt watched. He sneered, without knowing it, breathing carefully. He liked being alive. He suddenly felt there were so many things still worth doing. He hoped his lord hadn't been killed, somehow.

"Come on if you're coming," he whispered, waiting while his horse jogged its head and snorted, nervous, uncomfortable, flicking its tail and ears at the stray flies that drifted from the feast. "Let's have it now."

Nothing. Just the buzzings, whooshings and general murmur of the afternoon. So he drew his blade anyway, rested it across his armored lap, and urged the horse back along the trail into the trees.

PARSIVAL

They came out of the cool trees into an open place that was almost perfectly squared off as if the pines and other trees had been chopped to frame a barren, stony rise that wasn't quite a hilltop. A dark, muddy trickle of stream pooled and puddled its way along the shallow slope.

The woman immediately noticed the bugs: the air was full of nasty, tiny midges that went straight for the ears. She grimaced and kept slapping at them. This spot seemed far more humid than the rest of the forest. And there was a foul odor. Parsival realized (with revulsion) they'd been using that sluggish little stream as a latrine.

"Christ's eyes," he muttered.

"Who are these creatures?" she asked.

"They seem like infidels from the Holy Land."

"Why came they here?"

The tall knight shrugged, running his fingers through his long, brown and copper-streaked blond hair.

"Maybe to rescue us from the grip of Jesus," he remarked, wryly.

The leader came out of one of the sorry, stained, ragged tents pitched along the near wall of evergreens. He sported a red, greasy turban and ragged robes over the same light, rusty chainmail favored by most of the others. A scar sliced down his forehead almost vertically and virtually divided his wide, flat nose before ending in a pucker at his upper lip.

"What is it to be?" Parsival asked him.

The fellow responded in damaged English.

"You are knight?" he said.

Parsival blinked.

"I am sunset," he said, staring at the little man.

"We bring knights to someplace," the fellow elucidated.

"Wonderful," Parsival told him.

"We look for king."

"Your king is missing?"

"You know where is king?"

He tipped his head and blew out one of his nose-halves onto the ground and wiped the nostril with the back of one hand.

"Your king?" Parsival reiterated, trying to decide how seriously to take this talk.

"No our king. KING." He waved his arms around, inclusively.

"King Arthur?"

The fellow scowled and rubbed his noses.

"Bah," he said. "Great king. King of allbody."

"Ah," said the tall knight. *That* one. No head."

The woman poked at Parsival.

"What is this madness?" she wanted to know.

The two of them stayed on the horse who was just dipping its head to lick a fetlock. The ragged-looking troops had gathered around them and were silently, avidly watching. Parsival felt somehow that he and the woman were giving them an appetite. "They look live wolves," she concluded.

"I'm no lamb," the knight said. He let himself center within, not focusing on anything, waiting for the crisis. He'd decided it would be an interesting fight.

"King," the leader demanded, shrill, tense, "where is king?"

"Which king?" Parsival wanted to know. It struck him this was a formula, somehow like a ritual because the fellow didn't really seem that interested in his response; he rubbed his strangely split nose with his middle finger, then drew his curved blade with a jerk and gestured at the sky.

"Tell or die!" he screamed. "Tell or die!"

Parsival nodded as the woman shrank back against him.

"Very well," said the knight, holding her shoulders with one hand, and, with the other, brushing his long, blond bangs away from his eyes. "I'll reveal all." He pointed. "Follow the sun for seven days and nights. Especially nights. When you come to the river of blood, swim or sink, as you will. On the far shore you come to the king's kingdom." He smiled with half his mouth. "You'll know it by the stink."

"You jest with these?" she ask-whispered, afraid.

He shrugged. He realized the oily-dark little man hadn't paid any attention anyway. He'd sheathed his blade and was snarling commands at some of his men.

"Jest?" replied Parsival. "For all I know its sooth and a half."

"Will they kill us now?" she asked.

He shrugged.

"Who knows? They seem right mad."

"I'm afraid."

"Don't fear yet."

"Will they slay us?"

"Not all of them. Only a few, if any."

"Why is that?" She twisted as if to look at his face.

"I will kill most of them, if it comes to that." He brushed at his hair again and made a mental note to trim it soon. "Maybe all."

She didn't drink the whole cupful because she said:

"Am I a babe to be soothed by a tale? She sniffed. "You're not even armored."

"You err. I am armored."

"In madness?" She watched the leader who was now squatting on his hams, having a bite of dried meat with his scimitar in his lap. She kept studying his scarred, divided nose, wondering where his breath went.

"No. It's a skill I have no pride in," the knight told her.

"You are that strong?" She twisted around to glimpse his face just above her own. The ragged troops seemed to be gathered, waiting for something.

"Other men are, often, that weak."

He stayed centered, looking at the treetops interlacing a rich blue edge of sky. He didn't see any birds. He was wondering if every time someone tried to kill him he might have a mystical vision. The burnt hay scent of her hair was a distant distraction.

The leader came close and peered up at them. His expression wore a kind of permanent fury. Spittle flew in a fine mist from his mouth when he shouted and Parsival could smell the strange acridity of his breath.

"You ignorant," he cried.

"And you annoy me," the knight said. "Everyone always liked to tell me I was ignorant. My wife still delights in it."

"We want king who dwells under earth," the leader said. "We look." He moved his arms, significantly. "We seek…we make sacrifice to him…we ask…we follow…we pray."

"Quite a full roll," Parsival commented. "I commend your energy if not your demented purpose."

The warrior screwed his face into a scowl that twisted his divided nose as if he had two faces trying to form a double fury. He swept his arms to include his men.

"We are one!" he cried. "We will find lost king!" Then, apparently, shouting the same sentiment in their common tongue, they all clashed their weapons and chanted for a few moments.

"Let us part now," said the knight, "and we will look too. And if we find your king I'll come straight to you."

The little man smiled. The scowl (Parsival thought) was better. The lean, contorted face was close to the horse's shoulder as the beast drifted a step or two, nodding into a clump of grasses.

"He, ha," the dwarfish leader said. "You no go."

"Ha, hoo," said Parsival. "Say you so?" To the woman: "A fine lot of trolls."

"You learn soon."

Parsival tried one:

"Why do you seek this king-in-the-ground?"

The face was right under him now, looking fiercely up. The knight resisted kicking the pointy chin.

"He holy man. He will take…"

"Take?"

"What was stole." The face was grim. "Enough. Now come or you die."

"I love a choice," the tall, wide-shouldered knight replied as he freed his foot from the long stirrup and flicked a kick that should have dented in the little fellow's ear. Except he was snake-quick and ducked and snapped a cut at Parsival's near leg so fast it was almost sliced.

With cheers of pleasure half-a-dozen more warriors charged forward, circling to enclose the riders. The woman started to clutch at his legs so Parsival shoved her forward into what resembled jumping position, face close to the horse neck.

He needed a sword. He drew his long dagger and deflected the next slash from below.

"Christ!" he hissed, seeing that more little men were coming from all sides. "This is no jest."

"I thought you were going to flail them all like bunches of grain," she reminded him.

"That's not a quote," he responded, turning the horse hard and fast, looking for a gap to ride at.

With an ululating wail the line of wild-looking, scruffy fighters charged, scimitars chipping the hot summer sunlight.

"Oh, God," she said. She shut her eyes.

"Here come more madmen," he said, wheeling the horse, then breaking it backward, high-stepping hooves spatting mud as he withdrew across the sluggish streamlet, stirring up nasty clouds of nipping black bugs. "Always madmen."

The attackers spread wide to cut him off, as he'd expected. He shoved her forward once again onto the beast's neck to give himself striking room.

"Hold fast," he said.

"Can we escape?" She shut her eyes.

He aimed the horse suddenly on a slant (now that he'd spread them out) wrenching violently around so that he was now rolling up their curved line.

"Can they?" he replied, setting his teeth for combat, dagger held along his thigh, as his mount's chest and legs were knocking the first two down. The rest circled to close again but he twisted violently the opposite way and broke free of their net.

He felt the strange, hot, high excitement of combat. His concentration was tight but fluid. He saw everything without really looking. He was aware that there were bowmen coming into it now. That wasn't so good. Short bows. Handy in thick underbrush.

He stopped the horse dead so that the nearest man could cut at his side. She screamed. He kicked up into the fellow's armpit, whipped sidewise and grabbed the thin wrist. By breaking the force of the stroke he was able to twist the curved sword free as he backed and whirled his mount around again and looked for another thin spot in their line.

One little fighter with scattered stubs of teeth in a distended mouth darted close to snatch at the reins near the bit and stab the horse in the throat. Parsival lifted him by kicking the mount into rearing and before he could drop back and escape the knight's blade poked into his ribs and he went down with a curse and scream.

"God save us!" Katin gasped.

A moment later the first arrow whizzed under his chin. He was impressed by the instant accuracy.

"Piss," he said.

He wheeled so that his back was to most of them, to cover the woman a little. He didn't like the situation, but didn't want to quit yet. Cut the animal left, right, left, right, left, left, right...

Another near miss and a few wild shots scattered into the trees. He needed the trees badly. Crashed across the mucky stream at a canter and cut in among the pines. Altered the horse's gait now: slow...slower...fast...stop...back... up...forward—fast, keeping the tree trunks in the way.

She clung to the animal's neck and gasped and reeled with the intense movements. The knight was good; very good. Had he been armored he might have slain most of them, as he'd told her.

He couldn't lose himself in the trees because the foot fighters had been scattering around him and infested the bushes and shadows. The sunbeams flicked and flashed through the branches. His sweat beaded his face in the hot air.

Arrows banged into wood and skittered through leaves.

"Piss," he repeated as one bare-topped little fat belly burst from behind a fallen tree trunk, wild moustaches flying and stabbed a spear at Parsival's side.

The tall knight parried with the scimitar, then skidded the blade down the haft and chopped wristbone. The infidel yipped and rolled under the fallen tree to escape another awesome counter-stroke.

A ricocheting shaft hit Parsival in the back and the almost spent shot nicked a rib.

"Wormy bastard clods!" he yelled, yanking the horse hard left and down a sudden slope where the trees were suddenly gone. He slammed through a last screen of high berry bushes and realized the little devils had driven him where they wanted because suddenly there was loose, dried-out clay and dirt and the hooves were skidding and slipping down a suddenly too-steep drop that ran in a huge circle: a pit, with worn crumbled ramps corkscrewing down. He realized it was a long abandoned excavation. An open mine.

The infidels (as he thought them) were turning up all around then. Working, scrambling down the crumbling ramps to get at him as all he could do was hold the reins and Katin (who was now screaming) as the horse slid almost on its rump down and the sky and the rim of the pit leaped and rocked with each wild careen and bump as they hit each narrow ramp too fast to stop.

There was going to be no way to ride back up the huge spiral even if they weren't spilled any second: bowmen on top could skewer half an armored army trying to fight their way back much less one gearless knight and a frightened woman.

They've got me this time, he thought. *Like a pig in a sack.......*

And then the straining, outstretched forelegs caught behind a stony ridge and Parsival cursed as he heard the awful snap of the bones and horsebleat, the woman's shriek and felt himself and her sail out and down with at least fifty feet to go to the bottom; a sickening space...then a semi-soft but solid wham as the earth seemed to punch him with a vast, dull fist and he went from bright to instant blackness...

Lego had come out of the trees into the squarish clearing at the far side from where Parsival and the woman were crashing across the mucky stream into the dark pine shadows with the whole crowd of smallish warriors fanning out, dodging close, then back, actually driving the knight towards the abandoned mine working just beyond the wall of trees...

Lego recognized his lord, stood up in his stirrups and drew his sword, cantering fast in pursuit. A bowman took a running shot at him and missed. Then he was in the thick trees and bush, cutting left and right to find a way, slowed like Parsival so that he couldn't really gain much on the men. He rode down a straggler and had the satisfaction of seeing him bang off a tree trunk and spin down flat.

Sweating, kicking, yawing hard, he came out of the trees onto the sudden slope in time to see Parsival and the woman go skidding and scrambling down. Lego shouted, as if that would help. It was not so steep where he was and he managed to halt his rank-sweating charger sidewise, horse and rider tilting, trying to inch back up on the best angle possible.

He dismounted, sword in one hand, and leaned into the reins as the big hooves scrambled in the powdery soil. It was hard going and he was panting by the time they struggled back to the more level tree line.

Half-a-dozen bowmen were waiting: small, dour, dark. He sighed, dropping his swordtip and leaning against the heaving flanks of the almost spent, blowing animal and took his own deep breaths that might prove to be his last at any moment....

LOHENGRIN

Lohengrin and Henry had come to a miserable village. The thatch and log roofs were broken and the few cows and horses scattered in the fields were bony and torpid-looking, not moving far or often. The heat was heavy, steamy. The place felt like a bog, Lohengrin decided. Even the grass and breeze seemed somehow exhausted, barely stirring. For a moment he had an impression the whole was embedded in foggy crystal.

He was still groggy from whatever had happened to him in the tent. The sun rang his head like a dull bell. He understood he wasn't himself. He had no focus, he was neither annoyed nor impatient; he just wanted to be quiet and not have to deal with anything for a while.

Hal kept commenting on this and that but Lohengrin hardly paid attention. He was vaguely anxious because he kept worrying that he was, somehow, going to be drawn back into that state or spell.

Because the path kept tilting like a slow swell in the sea, the sky and trees stayed blurred and he felt the heat was making his stomach churn. He needed to rest. His companion's voice blurred into the hot drowse of afternoon. The hot breeze rattled the thick leaves and the birds, insects, a soft rushing of water- all became a soothing, hypnotic hum……

So that he blinked several times when the young peasant said something to them from the side of the road. The fellow was actually squatting on his heels on the low wall of a stone bridge that crossed the winding river – the same one they'd all been independently following.

The peasant's feet were bare, reddened and bony, giving Lohengrin a fleeting impression of lizard-like toes and a long V of a face with tiny eyes lost in a network of creases. He wore baggy, sack-like, dun-colored clothing. Both long-fingered hands cupped his chin, pointy elbows on knees.

Lohengrin reined up. Rocked slightly in the saddle.

"Churl," he addressed the fellow whose head was patched with unseemly bald spots set off by tiny curls of red hair glinting like dull, uneven flames.

"Where do you wander, knightlings?" the fellow asked in a high voice that wasn't quite as disrespectful as his choice of words.

"To glory," Lohengrin said, hand on hip, sarcastic.

Out of the droning, soft rush of afternoon he didn't quite catch Hal's comment.

"Well then," the disturbingly misshaped fellow said, raising both fire-tipped eyebrows to reversed V points, "stay on the path that dips steady. You'll find such glory as will content you."

Lohengrin cocked his head. He was debating where to kick this apparition to best pitch him from his perch.

"Are you a prophet, ugly one?" he asked. He felt vaguely dizzy again, suddenly.

"Eh?" Henry said. "And you but bend your stare on nothingness and speak to birds?"

Lohengrin swayed and blinked and rubbed his face. There was a bird on the bridge wall: a frowsy-looking crow with one toeless foot hopped unevenly, flicking its quick, dark bead of an eye at the two horsemen. Its feathers had a coppery tint in the flat, hot sunlight.

Lohengrin grunted.

I was poisoned, he told himself. *It will wear off...*

He looked straight ahead now, past the arched, nodding horsehead at the twisted, shadowlost road that rose and dipped in an almost choppy effect that made for hard and somewhat giddy going.

The trees had closed in here and the way was getting gloomy and often overgrown. There couldn't have been much traffic out there. Henry was complaining (his companion felt) as regularly as the drip from a water-clock.

Lohengrin was trying not to really notice anything or think too much. He wanted to avoid talking to anymore birds.

"We're lost for certain," Hal was saying. "Night will find us nowhere."

Lohengrin looked around. The trees virtually walled off both sides of the road. The heat stayed oppressive even in the shade. There were bare and broken limbs everywhere. Only high up did thick, dark green overarch and block the sun- which, to judge by the thin, stray beams that worked through the cover to the forest floor, was certainly angling down to sunset.

Lohengrin felt more alert now, as if he'd dozed off just enough back there. Nothing weird had happened for a couple of hours at least. Maybe it was all over.

"You're worried about supper," he said.

"Yes."

"How did I divine this?" Lohengrin grinned. "But what's this now?"

The road (if you could call it so) rose and twisted up a rocky slope. The air was thick with no breeze at all and a smell of earth and faint rot. The way forked here.

They halted horses. The stream had veered off someplace behind them. The left direction seemed less rocky and cluttered. Lohengrin thought the trees seemed like they might open out a little past the first visible bend.

"Let's try it this way," he decided. Booted his mount lightly in the new direction. Sure enough, it was immediately smoother, wider, and seemed to gradually descend.

"How do we know we won't get lost?" Henry wondered. He followed a horse length behind.

Lohengrin peered ahead as they rounded the bend and lost sight of what was behind them. He smiled. There were paving blocks here, wildly overgrown on the edges but set (by whatever pioneering Roman engineers centuries before) so close together that only sparse weeds forced their saw-edged-harsh-green-hardiness up between the cracks and joints.

The trees fell back and they found themselves heading for the sunset, the sun a fat, reddening ball settling into the end of a long, straight valley.

"A bird told me," Lohengrin answered, at length.

This new, solid road ran almost straight down and across open fields where the dusk seemed to wash in and pool like a soundless tide.

"There have to be folk down there in such a place as this," Henry thought. He was thinking about coarse peasant loaf and hung sheep milk cheese and ale. "It stands up to reason," he concluded.

LAYLA

By sundown they caught up with his family and retainers, camped with some hide-covered wagons and half-a-dozen horses.

Layla had given up arguing and berating him, for the moment. Her back was sore from banging into his armor for hours. She was more frustrated than nervous. She blamed her husband, naturally, but only to a point; after all, this idiot had been poured from the same mold of selfish, jackass men. She saw the campfire about the same time she smelled the roasted meat.

"Well," she asked her ex-lover, "and what will your mother think of this?"

"My mother," he said. "Ha, ha. That's good."

"Did her husband keep two wives?"

"My father? Ha, ha."

"Flawless dolt," she said, "Will you tell her you're so mad with love for me that you stole me away?"

She longed to smack his bearded face but that was impractical at the moment. They were among the tents now. She thought what a charming outing this was going to be.

"Mad for love?" he wondered. "I want your husband to come fetch you. He has insulted me and thinks himself safe. He thinks."

"Something you spare yourself as much as possible, Gaf," she said. "Listen, how will Parsival divine that you've made away with me? He will consider I've run off for spite, if ever he comes home to learn I'm gone."

A man stood up from the fire and moved towards them. He held a spear like a staff, leaning a little. His outline was just a blot against the warm flamelight as the sun went deeper red, becoming just color now and even that starting to drain away as if the horizon clouds actually sucked up the light

"I left word," her captor assured her. "He'll learn. He'll learn. He'll be brought to heel like the hound he is."

She twisted her head to look back into his bearded, shadowed face, the eyes unwinking glints.

"I cannot believe I let you have your way with me," she sighed. Shook her head.

"You liked it well enough," he grunted.

"Do I like an itch because it feels pleasant to scratch it?" she asked.

"You itch? Did a bug bite you?"

"You were but the tree stump the dog rubs his hind against."

"I begin to understand your husband," he snorted.

"Good," she responded. "Then why not be like him and leave me at once?"

He reined up by the fire, his man-at-arms holding the horse while he half-lifted Layla down, dropping her so that she hit the earth hard enough to stumble. His wife was there.

"Good even my Lord," the soldier said.

"Have any passed this way?" Sir Gaf demanded.

"None, Lord, save a mendicant monk and a charcoal burner."

Sir Gaf dismounted, heavily, favoring the leg he'd hurt in his breakfast brawl with Parsival. It reminded him. He glowered and spit with spite.

"You never bucked me off," Gaf said, defensive and clearly insecure. Gestured at his wife. "Or either of you him." Meaning Parsival.

Layla liked that.

"Never bucked is right," she said, "We hardly felt the riders."

His wife giggled at this racy pass though her face stayed expressionless.

"Feed yourself and be still," said Gaf.

He handed her a seared rib. She took it but didn't bite yet.

"Your husband means to draw mine by using me as bait," Layla told her. "That's like setting out a pot of honey to catch a toad."

Layla bit the rib. Wrinkled her whole face this time.

Gaf stood there. He was now spilling beer from a jug directly into his throat, head backtilted. He paused long enough to say:

"I'll clip him close when next we meet."

"If you don't free me," Layla said, "I'll clip *you* while you sleep." She turned to the wife who seemed unmoved. "You astound me," she told her.

"I?" asked the woman.

"You live with this man and yet...have you never tried to slay him?" Layla queried.

The lady shook her roundish head.

"I do not grasp your import," she said. Her husband was now ignoring both of them, absorbed in his beer.

Layla's face seemed to keep changing expressions in the uneven firelight.

"Ha," she said. "I bring nothing from across the seas but I'll import some advice from the Italians: Better a short life than a slow death."

PARSIVAL

He and the woman had rolled to a stop together on one of the circular ledges about one third of the way to the bottom of the spiral pit which must have been the entrance to a mine, he concluded.

"Have you killed most of them yet?" she wanted to know as he helped her up and out.

He sighed. Whenever he'd brag at all...

"There are a few left," he admitted.

The soldiers were riding around the spiraling roadway rather than attempting to cut across and be spilled like Parsival had been. It would take them time to circle down.

"Now what?" she asked.

"Come on," he said, taking her arm, helping her climb to the next level.

"You want to reach them sooner," she wondered.

"I do," he replied.

He was timing it, so by the time they scrambled up three levels all but one horseman in the posse of seven had passed them. Now they'd have to come back uphill which would allow their quarry to run lower and evade. The rest, were on foot and, of course, were scrambling down the sides from level to level.

"I'm good at this business," he told her. "I've tricked them."

"Yet we still seem surrounded."

The last rider had just come up, reining back and raising his scimitar, shouting incomprehensible words that clearly meant, "Stop!"

"I'm not bragging," the knight assured her.

He stepped close and gripped the man's calf just above the pointed boot, forcing him to slash straight down wildly whilst he yelled in agony as the terrible grip closed. Parsival leaned under the stroke, took the sword and tossed the little man down to the next level.

"There," he said. "Come."

Mounted her behind him on the armorless pony these Mongol-like fighters favored.

Headed up the spiral towards the next clump of opponents, foot-soldiers who came running, leaping and skidding from several directions. He brushed them aside: banging, kicking, cutting. No bowmen yet. Kept climbing.

As he came over the rim he saw Lego coming out of the trees. Reacted to his loyalty once again. The next thing he noticed were the arrows zipping and hissing out of the woods at them.

Lego got his shield up fast. A couple sparked and skidded off the steel. Then he saw his lord actually deflect two or three shafts with the edge of his open hand. He realized the woman had been hit. Then he was trapped.

They wheeled their horses and crashed back along the forest trail to the main road. They reached it at the same time as the three knights from Arthur's court who'd been following at a distance. Their visors were open.

"That's enough," commanded the lean, red-haired, long-nosed leader. "You have defied your king long enough."

Parsival shifted the slumped woman around to the front of his saddle. She groaned. He'd been afraid she was dead. He was trying to get a look at her wound, which was the reason it was Lego who saw the sideblow swung by the burley, big-jawed knight. Lego lunged nearly out of the saddle in a hopeless effort to block the stroke that laid the flat of the blade alongside his lord's bare skull. Even so, Parsival's reactions were so quick he actually rolled a little with the blow as a tremendous, red/black blotting soundlessly burst in his head and seemed to push him face forward onto the rutted road.

"Ahh," he whispered, rolling to his knees, holding both sides of his head as if to keep it intact.

The little fighters had already swarmed out of the woods and surrounded everybody. The split-nosed leader came panting up, on foot, yelling both his language and crippled English:

"You stand still! You caught! You stand still!"

The three knights didn't: they charged instantly, in unison, swords ready, shields up. Parsival was tempted to follow them, except his legs weren't part of him yet. The woman lay sprawled in the dust.

They reared to a sudden stop as a wedge of mounted "infidels" rose up to block them. Parsival's head felt like a broken bell.

"Well, lord," Lego said. "Gone but a day and I find you with a woman."

Parsival went on his hands and knees to her and carefully ripped the fabric away from the arrow wound. A strand of blondish-brown hair unwound down his forehead and he shook his head to keep it out of his eye.

He saw the arrowhead had penetrated her ribcage and the pain and shock had knocked her out. He realized it wasn't deep enough to cut her lungs, but there would be no way to push it through: he'd have to pull it straight back the way it had come.

Lego was watching the three knights circling their horses, looking for a weak point; there were too many warriors now. He was waiting a chance to strike down the one who'd hit his lord.

Parsival took a careful grip on the shaft, deciding to take advantage of her unconsciousness. He braced his left hand on her breastbone, held his breath and pulled with a steady wrench.

Praise our lady, he thought, because the head was small, narrow and oval with no reverse edges to stick between the bones. So it popped free, followed by a gout of blood. She groaned and thrashed for a moment.

"Get the medicine bag from your horse," he told Lego. He'd pack the wound with a field poultice before binding it. He knew that more wounded survived who were treated by fellow soldiers than those who fell into the care of professional surgeons.

At the rim of his attention, he saw the foreign warriors had shut them in; but if they'd meant to kill they'd have already done it.

Lego came back with the bag. He was looking at the newcomers his lord hadn't seen yet. Parsival found what he wanted and started dressing the wound, aware of the clash and jangle of horses and metal looming over them. He assumed it was Arthur's men. The sun was low and right in his eyes where he faced southwest on the road so it was all shadow and dazzle and he didn't understand what Lego was talking about when he said:

"These are strange knights."

"Aye…and days, my friend."

Parsival squinted and shielded his eyes, looking up not at Lego, but into the silvery facemask that was now close to him. The rider leaned down.

What? he thought. *What?*

Because it was a skull face with blood-red fangs; the distorted, furious grimace of a demon in deep black armor, darker than the shadows themselves. And he was shocked because he knew them, twenty years ago, while escaping from the madness, plague, fire and famine of those days, returning home he'd been tracked by twelve of these black armored killers, the last (he'd believed) of the dark army whose lord and leader Clinschor, the eunuch, devil, wizard and fiend, had unleashed on Britain in an effort to conquer the land and possess the Holy Grail.

Parsival, weak and weary, far north and near his home, had been caught up with on a white pebbled dry-wash that served as road in the Welsh highlands. His memory was true: the steep banks, violet highland flowers on the rocky, scrubby hills; the black knights: with their carnival facemasks charging him again and again and again. Him: striking, blocking, twisting, ducking, blacking out, the world spinning gray, bright and dark...finally the earth slapping him flat on his back and it was over, and when he returned to consciousness he found he was the only one left alive or unbroken......

He'd been a boy then. The boy who'd found the unfindable Grail Castle, by seeming chance, and then left, and lost the way back forever.......a fierce, hopeful, dreaming boy with a fighting talent that seemed to possess rather than obey him. A skill that was poetry and pain. A violence cursed with elegance.

He remembered in a bright link how he'd lain there in the white pebbly wash among the dead and dying Black Knights – sleeping, half-waking, shivering with fever from his wounds, the mist-paled Northern sun seeming to appear then flick away into moonless night. Eventually, he'd wakened and healed.

Those killers had followed him for literally hundreds of miles. They'd been sent by the tyrant Clinschor to take the Grail from him.

This mistaken belief had become his life's chief curse. The Grail, he'd said, was like a tin can tied to a cat's tail that drew all the dogs to him.

Absorbed in the memories, he touched his head where the flat of the sword had just hit. Winced. There was blood and a bump. When he stood up to face the Black Knight who was regarding him from horseback, reeled and staggered forward, groping to hold himself up on his horse that suddenly wasn't there...falling...bracing himself to hit the ground that wasn't there either...nothing under him but nothing...darkness....

LOHENGRIN

The wide road tilted steeply down and ran straight into the valley where the shadows were gathering, filling the rills and clefts with an almost tidal rush as the sunset died into livid purple and deepening red.

Young Hal looked up, frowning, watching the crescent moon blotted out as a vast hand of cloud clenched it. The horses were uneasy, feeling the tension of the coming storm. Lightning flashes jumped, shifted and wildly shadowed the underbellies of the thunderheads.

"Now we'll be soaked," he complained.

Lohengrin cocked his head, concerned with the sudden straying of the road. The horses were bracing back to keep from skidding on the pebbly surface.

"There's bound to be a village along such a broad way," he assured Hal.

"Yet do I doubt you," Hal responded. "Peradventure we should camp and take shelter."

"Where? Here? This is like a child's slide." Indeed, the horses couldn't help accelerating. The hooves clacked and scraped as the slope dropped away. "Who could come up this stupid road?" The two of them were tilted hard back in their oversized war saddles. "Goats?" Faster and faster down now, approaching a gallop. "Christ!" he cried as they plunged into a sudden mass of trees, the road purely theoretical now. The night had closed in and under the clouds it was as dark as a closed room except for the shudders of oncoming lightning.

The first winds ripped around in the upper branches, swirling leaves loose.

"What a place," Hal complained, in a gasp, clutching reins and saddlehorn as they crashed down far too fast.

Under the massed, creaking branches the darkness was now total. The wind puffed and strained, violently. Even huge trees groaned and crackled. Unseen dust and dirt whipped into their eyes. Lohengrin cursed in short, furious barks. The horses were terrified.

Then lightning hit a tree nearby, so close the sound was more pressure than noise and the flash shocked their eyes, the afterglow a blinding greenish-red...and the bolts in the air everywhere so that the forest flung wildly in staccato convolutions.

And then suddenly they were at the bottom trying to slow the totally spooked mounts. The flashes showed they were still on the wide, straight road. When another big bolt blasted a nearby tree to flaming splinters, both horses reared in panic. The young men barely kept their seats.

"You shithead," Lohengrin snarled, kicking the beast forward savagely.

And then the rain finally came scything down like knuckles on a fist of wind. At least it was warm. They struggled into the stinging gusts that clittered and drummed on the shields and armor strapped to the horses as the light and shadow twisted around them.

At some point the road must have turned and they didn't because they were suddenly out in the open again. The wild light showed twisting downpour empty fields around them and mist that boiled across the fields as if the clouds had been driven into the earth. Hal was shouting something off to Lohengrin's left. He wasn't far but his voice was sucked away by the storm. The wind shook them in their saddles.

"Christ," Lohengrin said. "Christ."

In the leaping stormlight he glimpsed a metal gate in a wall of shadows. He took it for a trick of the eyes. Squinting and shielding his face with one hand he forced his mount for it, flanked by Hal, who'd fallen back somewhat. He had an impression of a long, low castle wall, strangely folding back into itself as if the wildly shifting shadows were part of the structure.

He was thinking they could shelter from the wind a little there. In the flashes it really seemed to be physically moving, the gate jumping forward, back...to the side. Suddenly it was right in front of him, glinting. He had an impression it was set in the inner crease of a V formation of dark stones that had once been part of a great, structure, now shattered and jumbled.

Leaning back and forth in the saddle against the blasts of mists and wind that let up slightly as he entered the open end of the V. He saw the gate was perfectly intact: a doorway, he thought, into rubble.

The broken stones on each side of him were ten or fifteen feet high. As he went deeper into the narrowing area (that must have been a courtyard), the gale puffed overhead, roared and whispered; but he could sit straight now and the horse settled down a little.

He stopped in front of the perfect arch and massive portal. Dismounted and secured the bridle to one of the arm-thick bronze bars close to the hinge. Then he gripped the double handle and braced to pull. He was surprised, staggering back, because there was no resistance: it swung open as if the pins had been oiled that day.

Hesitating, he looked back for Hal. The open triangle forming the entrance was maybe thirty feet deep. He could see no more than forty, when lightning permitted and then just billows of dense mist and downpour. Shouting would have been futile so he shrugged, gave the horse a pat and a word in its ear, and went inside, leaving the gate open behind him.

He hoped to find enough roof intact for a night's shelter. He was surprised to discover a sudden, steep tunnel cut through the stone and then dipping the way, after the arch of the mouth, the throat suddenly drops down - except, balancing himself at the brink, he discovered neat stairs cut wide enough to make descent acceptable if nerve-wracking.

Adjusting to the flickering flashes from the doorway he went down a few steps: too fast. It was hard to stop. He leaned backwards and just caught the sides of the shaft with his outstretched hands. About five feet across. He paused. The wind and thunder was a distant hollow pulsing here; and the flickers from above barely broke the darkness.

How deep is this? he wondered. Twisted his head around to look up where he'd come. About twenty feet. How did I get down this far already?

He didn't want to go back yet. There was nothing behind but the storm, finding Hal and hearing him complain. He had a vague idea there might be something valuable below - a treasure or old weapons....He didn't really believe it, but his recent experiences reminded him of minstrel tales where anything was possible.

In any case, he carefully descended, keeping both hands stretched out to the walls, into darkness that had become thick enough to sit on.

This is stupid. There's probably no bottom and what's down there? He had no means of making a light. This is a fool's enterprise fit for my father... I'll wait at the top....

Even as he twisted around to climb he realized he should have just backed up because his foot slipped immediately and skidded. Even as he cursed he was sliding down on his belly feet first, chainmail surcoat streaking sparks as he gathered speed over the stone steps.

"Holy Virgin!" he exclaimed.

He gave himself up for dead as he protected his face with his forearms and sickeningly accelerated. The steel was already burning hot from the friction.

What a stupid death! he thought.

And then there were no steps; nothing under him and he dropped, spinning slowly end over end into total blackness. Then, inexplicably, he felt as if his body had dissolved and there was only a tiny point of himself left in a vast, lightless silence. He relaxed, strangely.

His mind automatically insisted it had to be a terrific uprush of air cushioning him. He couldn't tell if he was still actually falling.

And then an instant impact: crunching, grinding, powdery crumbling through what seemed unseen brittle layers of lumps and sticks or loose straw which gradually slowed him until he finally stopped, buried in a heap of scratchy fragments of what he decided, deep breathing himself back from shock, might be kindling wood.

I could have broken my neck, he pointed out to himself.

He sprawled there, several body-lengths deep. He had a sense of being at the bottom of a well. Wondered if the stairs came all the way down.

He half-climbed, half swam to the crumbly surface. Struggled, kicked his way to the back wall and groped around it. It was square and wider than above. There were no stairs. He couldn't stand upright because of the brittle stuff he rested on so it was a little time before, groping higher, he found space behind what he'd assumed was the wall of the well. Apparently he'd dropped into a bigger chamber from a hole above.

This could be good or bad, he thought.

He clambered up and over and was now outside the square full of whatever had cushioned his otherwise fatal plunge, standing on solid stone flooring. He stood a moment, brushing chips and splinters from his hair and mail surcoat.

He stared up the shaft and imagined he saw faint winks of the lightning outside. Maybe just his eyes reacting to total darkness. He shrugged. Now what?

This is my father's type of nonsense, he said to himself. *I can't believe this....Still, if there's a way in there usually a way out....*

Lohengrin wasn't given to panic; but this was pretty much whistling in the dark. Then he realized something. He leaned over the lip of the square enclosure and picked up a long stick from the heap. As he felt it carefully and knew he was right: a human bone. An arm or a child's leg. A pit of bones.

Mary's sweet milk, he thought.

He tossed the bone aside and drew his sword. He felt better holding it. He groped forward, using the blade like a blind man's stick. The metal clinked on the stone flooring. The air was damp but not unpleasant.

It turned out the square charnel pit was set in the center of a square room.

Who was collecting bones he wondered? A troll? They'd obviously been dumped from above. But they were old, desiccated....

"Alright," he murmured, after going around the chamber twice, touching the walls, "there's no door. Or it's hidden or subtly set and I missed the latch." He sheathed the sword.

He made another circuit, reaching as high as he could, running his hands over the smooth, ancient stonework. By the third futile pass he was nervous and tired enough to sit with his back on the wall, facing the bone pit.

He breathed steadily to calm himself. Told himself he'd try again. Shut his eyes. He had no idea what time it was. Tiredness softly pulled at him. He felt leaden.

He went out as if he'd dropped into another well except this one had no bottom. No shattered bones—nothingness...

And the women were all beautiful. He counted eight of them. Their bodies were full and golden, trimmed with rings and thin gold chains that covered nothing. Their naked bodies were sleek, stunning lines and rills, shadows and archings; the bare feet had bright rings on each toe.

There was music and they danced. Reedy music with bright cymbal clashes. He watched as if nothing else had ever been.

As they swayed and spun closer to him he noticed each girl had at least one blemish on her body: reddish black blotches that suggested swollen birthmarks. He was attracted and nauseated at the same time.

"Who are you?" he heard himself saying. "What is this? What is happening here?"

A perfectly formed, nude girl with exquisite features, long hair the color of hot embers, came and knelt at his feet. Her eyes were amber, haunting. She put a finger to her lips.

"Shhh," she murmured. "You ask too many things. Ask nothing and you will get everything."

"No questions," he snorted, "even in my own dream."

"You have been chosen for the gift of power."

That was nice. He accepted that he was asleep or had a fever, but was enjoying himself. He became aware of the chamber suddenly:

garish gold and red. If he tried to focus too long on any area it blurred into a dark hole.

Now a stooped, hooded man in red and gold robes came toward him. He hadn't noticed him before. The robes wavered like a shadow. He was holding something out in front of himself with both hands.

Lohengrin tried to see what it was but when he looked directly it dissolved into a head-sized blot that seemed a hole in the dream he assumed he was in. For an instant, through the hole, he thought he glimpsed a landscape: a vast view of ragged stones and distant, sharp-edged mountains under a sky of wild, black clouds and deep red as if the atmosphere itself were dully burning.

The scene was compelling and seemed to draw at him. He had an impression that if he somehow let go he'd be sucked through the hole into that forbidding yet fascinating world. He sensed (but didn't see) life there: strange, dark and powerful.

Then the hole became a blot again and then a face because the bent little figure in the redgold monk-like hood was suddenly standing over him. The face swam in shadows. He kept trying to focus on it—except it wasn't a face, it was a skull-shaped goblet. Looked like reddish black metal.

Silly nonsense, he thought.

He was supposed to drink. He felt that. The girl's muddy gold-colored body was close to him. Her too-short fingers were intimately soothing and stroking him as the hollow-topped skull bumped under his chin.

Drink, she soothed, somehow in his mind. *Drink and become the great lord.*

He liked that. The great lord sounded good.

He reached for the cup. Why not - it was only fever-dreaming. Looked into the hollow. The same hole again: window into a barren, dark landscape under the bloodred smolder of sky that seemed depthless.

It was like a well. He didn't want to fall. He could see and sense things out there where far and near seemed strange. There were human-like beings standing or floating (he couldn't be sure) on some flat, jet black clifftop and the one in the center echoed the gesture of the cowled cripple except his head wasn't a skullcup, it was swollen, all huge mouth gnashing long teeth opening wider and wider -Lohengrin felt it pulling at him.

"No, no, no!" he insisted. "What is this place?" He was suddenly shouting and the woman seemed to cry:

"Be still!" Her voice becoming an echo that repeated and overlapped itself until there was only the darkness again, the wall of the pit and himself yelling over and over:

"What!? What!? What!?"

GAWAIN

He woke up after midday, surprised by what seemed a din outside the dim, comfortably cool place where he lay, naked, on his back on a blanket laid over clumps of hay. The smell told him it was a barn or stable. The noise reminded him he was in the city: voices calling, talking; shouting children; bells ringing; carts banging; music and drums in the distance....

He reached for the woman. Then sat up, looking for her. He'd left the wooden hand screwed in with the joint wrapped in a silky fabric. He was in a hayloft in a stable, as he'd thought. No animals present either, he noted. But it was in use, you could smell the dung and horsereek.

He remembered being led here by her, struggling up the ladder, spilling half a jack of ale over himself and her and finding it very funny. Remembered fragments of the night: her strong, smooth, long limbs, tender breasts, her mouth all over his body...It was the best thing he'd known in so long, he'd almost forgotten reality....

Of course, she was gone now, he told himself. *She woke sober and saw my face. Likely she's still in flight...*

He started when he heard her sudden voice at the foot of the ladder:

"So ya finally stir yerself," she called up. "I've got hard-cooked eggs and mare's milk." Her head and shoulders now showed in the loft as she paused there on the steps. "And yer hood be sewn."

He grinned, turning his face away so she only saw the strong-jawed profile and long dark brown hair almost untinted by gray.

"Am I in the same world I fell asleep in?" he asked. "This seems a pleasant place."

"Yu've earned some respite," she told him, kneeling up beside him, now, barefoot and naked under a loose, fresh white linen shift that probably (he later realized) was her best that she'd gone home to put on.

Though he'd lain with noblewomen in finest samite gowns, sporting fair jewels and traced with rare perfumes, he was as touched by this as by Christ's parable of the widow's mite, whose gift was greatest because she was poor and gave, with her mere pennies, all she had.

"I thank you, woman."

"Me pleasure, Sir Gawain."

She laid the cowl over his lap where he sat, cross-legged, and gently touched his shoulder.

He nodded. He felt good; yet his eyes were teary - and not with self-pity.

"Yes," he said, thickly. "I do thank you. Yet, I disremember your name."

"You never asked, me lord."

"Yes?"

"Enea," she told him.

He adjusted himself into the cowled cloak, still sitting.

"You need not cover for me, Sir Knight."

"I know," he said. Quaffed some milk. It was warm, musky, rich. Offered her a sip which she took. "Where is your excellent husband this morrow?"

She shrugged.

"Somebody took away dead Tom," she said. "I don't doubt it were him sneaked back." She took a bite of egg and handed him one. "I don't doubt he's hiding and watching to see if you be gone. In fear, he'll be."

He took her by the shoulders and squeezed, tenderly.

"I -" He began and stopped.

"Aye?"

He realized he wanted to take her with him; tell her that. Where? On the road with the madman John? Why would she want to?

Ice or fire, he decided, *uncomfortable either way....yet, might I linger here?*

Because it was nice to make love, again. In any case, he couldn't bear the idea of seeing Shinqua even if she'd actually accept the horror of him.

This one was smiling, faintly, just looking at him.

"Had no such humpin' ere this,' she told him. "You was as loved by the great ladies, I trow, as salt peas by pigeons."

He liked that. Grinned and let himself relax into feeling good. Why not? It would soon pass.

"Savory comparison," he reflected.

"You be a humorous sort," she said, chuckling. "In yer own style."

"I laugh like a priest prays: in fear and doubt."

"Fear not ne doubt," she murmured, reaching down his crotch with both hands and following with her mouth. He was surprised and stiffened at once into the world's sweetest discomfort. Sighed and hummed, reflexively.

Her mouth worked him, held him so that when she broke contact the cool air was a cold shock and her absence an ache. She knew it.

"Why did you stop?"

"So you'd remember what yer missing, me lord."

"As though I knew not," he said, rubbing his hand in her hair, gently trying to shift her head back where it had been.

"I hope to grip ya to stay," she told him. "As yer a wanderin' man."

"Well..." He gasped as her intense mobile mouth came back to cover and soothe his need, again. "...take over your husband's ...business..." he joked in ecstasy... shut his eyes... lost what he'd meant to say. "Ahh...mmm...."

LAYLA

She was brooding in the tent by the light of a wan oil lamp, bare feet on the rug floor. She was in her shift with a traveling cape over her shoulders for a robe.

She had just washed her face and hands for the night and was waiting to get sick again. That was the first thing she hated about being pregnant. There were others.

She sat there, torn, because she couldn't help an underglow of tender warmth that diffused within her as if from the seed itself while her mind kept saying:

Not again, not really ... Jesus and Mary, not again....

She barely glanced up when the flap parted and Gaf's dour mother came in and stood there. When Layla didn't react, she said:

"Well, whore, I'd hoped we were rid of you and your delightful family."

Layla was scraping at the cuticle of her little toe, waiting to get sick. She didn't look at the woman. Tried to decide if her feet were already ever-so-slightly swollen.

"I'm not here by choice,' she responded. "I wasn't missing you and that hairy sneak so much I couldn't stay away."

The Lady Gaf tilted her short neck forward and stamped her heel into the earth floor.

"You led my son into sin," she declared, bitterly.

"Oh, surely," said Layla, done with the toe now. "As the fly led his mate to dung." Smiled, almost looking at the stout lady.

"What is that?"

"That is this," said Layla, "flies love shit and need none to guide them to it."

"Well," said the other, "you are both fly and shit together."

Layla liked that idea.

"Like the mystery of the Trinity," she reflected, "vinegar to reason but honey to faith." She pulled her sock-like buskins over each long, pale foot. "Why don't you help me escape?"

"Would that I could," the mother muttered.

"Ah, but your son's in love with the dung."

"He's a fool."

"Not a fly?"

She thought about the seed again, the spot of life and heat that had been jammed into her most intimate recesses. She felt the strange anger and tenderness mixed again. She couldn't decide which father would be worse.

Because she'd slept with Parsival within a week or so of the other. They both had been sodden with wine: blurry, edges softened, sleeping awake...instead of fighting that night they'd gripped together in a burst of reluctant joy, not kissing, like two shipwrecked strangers clutched together in the heaving of the sea....

Later, lying side-by-side, neither wanted to talk; afraid to talk. She'd felt him waiting for her to fall asleep so he could get up and go prowling.

The older woman stared at her.

"You bring trouble without profit," she said.

"I bring? Ha. You came to my manor with that prize son of yours. He took advantage of my drunkenness." Like my husband, she thought.

"Ah, so you say," the mother cut in. "Yet you were half-drunk each day between matins and vespers. There's no taking advantage if that's your natural state."

"I wish I were half-drunk now," Layla said, bitterly. "Meanwhile, I was merely captured and dragged here, as you must know. I have no wish to spend another hour with your mulish sod of a son, let me say-"

"You are as bad a guest," the mother snarled, "as you were a hostess."

But she was cut off: "Guest? Guest?"

She remembered lying next to Parsival that last time, realizing she didn't care where he went or what he did. She'd wanted to tell him "Go, go!" except then he probably would have stayed, just to prove something. One of his noble gestures.

She sighed. Looked at Lady Gaf.

"Listen," she suggested, reasonably. "Why don't you help me leave? You are not happy I'm here."

"My son must have his reasons. He rightly seeks justice for your husband's insults."

"That's funny," Layla said, mirthlessly chuckling. She refocused her attention on her toe. "Your son is a prince of pigs. Justice for him would be to slice bacon from his flanks."

Lady Gaf sat on a stool, her back very straight. The weak glow from the lamp filled her face with pits of shadow.

"Say what you please," she commented.

Now Layla was thinking how it might be the son who'd made her pregnant What an idea. She didn't look up, saying:

"Listen, woman, if my miserable husband actually takes enough interest to come after me, your lout of a son would find himself knocked flat as a cowflop." There was little doubt of that. She shook her head. "When it comes to breaking heads he doesn't disappoint."

Madame was unimpressed. Her small, dark, cold eyes were moist-looking like stones in a stream.

"I was born Italian," she announced. "In my country we have learned one need not always stand up to fight."

Layla raised an eyebrow.

"You think us clods?" she wondered. "Think you'll poison all your enemies in the field? I warn you, beware of Parsival." *Poison his cup,* she thought, *and he'll spill it by chance. Put a viper in his bed and he'll fall drunk on the floor that night....If he showed up angry, they'd all be in Hell before breakfast.* "Fornication might get him," she allowed, "if you could find a pretty woman with the plague."

"He's not the only warrior in the world."

He'll come to get me out of duty and kill out of duty but without honor, Layla thought *He'd rage if I said so but with him it's duty without honor. He'd tiptoe past the bedchamber where I'd be deceiving him, I think, and not care who knew it, yet if the same man who cuckolded him, cursed me or showed my disgrace in public he'd drag him to the lists and batter him to pulp....*

She sighed. Because she believed all he wanted was his freedom to do what he pleased and his conscience demanded that she also could do what she pleased so he might think himself just.

The whole point is I wanted him to force me not to do what I pleased, she thought. *The fool...*

"Invite him here, Italian, Greek, what ere you be," she said. "It will be as much sport as watching hogs butchered."

Her mind wouldn't stop: *I'm going to have another child...I'm going to have another child...God damn them...God damn them to the Devil's deepest shithole....*

LOHENGRIN

The blackness made Lohengrin feel like a speck because the only things that existed were the things he actually was touching. His hand hurt. It was stretched up over his head as if in blind Roman salute to the stone wall where he knelt. His knees hurt too.

"Fine," he whispered or thought; he wasn't sure. "Fine...."

When he tried to lower his hand he discovered it was stuck in a hole in the abrasive stone. Caught as if in some monkey trap.

He eased himself upright and gingerly moved his hand. His fingers were caught as if in rock jaws.

I must have put my hand in there and then the wall slipped...or something....

He was afraid they would clamp down further and crush his bones. In a near panic he jerked free, ripping the skin. Most of what had held him crumbled.

"The wall bit me," he murmured. The idea was, somehow, funny. Because there were actual teeth gripping his knuckles. "Christ..Christ..." Part of a jawbone. There must have been a skull entombed in the wall and he reached in while asleep. That was his best, unsatisfying idea.

He slammed the bony fragments against the blocks and yelped when it bit him again as it shattered. He felt blood on his hand.

Madness, he thought, *do I die down here?*

His fingers were numb. They tingled as he rubbed them. Holding down serious fear, he moved almost frantically around the inner perimeter again except this time, in mid-stride, he tripped over what proved to be a raised landing for a set of stairs.

How did I miss it before?

He went up one step, another...another...up...up...he felt a draught.

Impossible, this wasn't here...the hole in the wall must have opened it.... He imagined the space where the skull had caught his fingers was some kind of door latch.

He groped and stumbled up, panting, touching the walls on either side, thinking, as if it meant something:

I've been bitten but not eaten... bitten but not eaten...they let me go...they let me go....

Then stopped, staggered, because the steps had ended and he kept trying to climb. He was outside, the wind gusty, cool, damp and sweet. He realized he'd only gone up maybe 30 feet.

The storm was still in full fury and the reflected lightning flashes showed he was under a massive overhang at the base of a cliff. He'd obviously descended it through the steps and well inside and came out at the bottom, here. Hal was way up at the top.

He was sheltered here from the rain and wild storm blasts. The thunder and wind were greatly muffled.

Examining the rock face he discovered he'd stumbled out through a sprung iron door that had sealed shut behind him. As if he'd want to go back.

They didn't like my taste, he thought, *so they vomited me out...*

He moved to the edge of the overhang. Rain whipped into him. The landscape bounced and seemed to spin as the lightning ripped and spasmed. He saw only mist and blots of trees.

"Where in Hell am I now?" he wanted to know. "Where's my horse?"

He knew the horse was on top. There had to be a way around and up. He started working his way along the cliff, still partly sheltered by broken talus rock and the overhang.

First the witch, he thought, now this....I'm cursed...that's it...I'm cursed... under a spell....

Except he didn't believe in spells.

"Fuck the Devil and Heaven too!" he suddenly shouted at the storm. "The Devil —"

"-Has heard you," a woman's voice said behind him, from closer under the cliff. "Who's there?" he demanded.

"What a fool you are."

He squinted and groped back. In the shifting flashes he could see she was behind a steel grate set in a niche in the wall.

"Fool?" he said, staggering slightly in a gust that stung his cheek. "Who are you, woman?"

He went over and gripped the dull, black, solid bars.

"All the power you wanted is here," she told him.

"Where did you come from?"

"Where are you going, boy?"

"Away from dullness," he answered.

He leaned closer to see her face. In the flash and shadow her features changed expression and form: she seemed fierce, then tender, then distant; sharp featured, then palely gentle....

"Who are you?" he wondered.

"A prisoner of this rock."

Lohengrin touched his beaked nose, as if in thought, then suddenly stabbed his hand through the bars to grab her. Talk never satisfied. She evaded him or he misjudged. She was further back now and the reflected lightning showed less of her shape.

"Don't go," he said, face pressed to the square space in the grating. "You're not a spirit. I don't believe in spirits."

"Do the spirits care what you believe?"

"But you're not."

"So please you. You belong to my master."

He was young enough to be more annoyed than curious.

"I have no master," he said.

"All men have masters, boy." She seemed amused. "Men are ruled by mine, yet few serve him."

She was closer again, though he hadn't noticed her move. The light and shadow winked over her face again. The nearer she was, the more changing and unfathomable she became.

"Is this a nunnery?" he wanted to know

"All kings serve my master," she explained. He winced with irritation. Wanted to try and grip her again.

"So it's just God," he said, harsh, beaked face showing impatient disdain. "I'd hoped it was the Devil, for the sport of it."

"Name him as you please," she whispered, words almost lost in the wind. He had a random feeling that she, somehow, might dissolve in the wind herself and blow away in mist.

My father would be certain it actually happened, he thought. *And would discuss the mystery of it at dinner....*

"How about I name him Lord of the Dunghill?" he suggested. In the shifting light her wrist looked close enough to the bars to catch. He moved the way you try to get just a little closer to a deer you've surprised. Breathless, infinitely slow.

"You may serve my master," she whispered. "He is eternal. Come back and embrace him. Take the ice and night into yourself and you will live even in death."

Lohengrin liked this bizarre exchange. It had the effect of bringing him back somewhat to the everyday world. "A riddle," he said. "Your sire is death, himself."

She spoke past him, pleasant, meditative..

"If you become one with him," she said, "his strength is your strength. You will love and live with him. He will protect you from all error." She paused and moved closer, right to the bars this time and he could see her pale, sincere, pretty face. "He will nourish and feed you." Her eyes were closed.

He was impressed. The flashes and thunder were rattling towards the horizon, now.

The shadows barely shifted on her face. Impressed, but not convinced.

"I'll feed death," he told her, "until he feeds on me. But I don't promise to love and wed him."

In the time it took a fading flash of lightning to glint on the dull bars, her slim hand shot through the bars and with fingers of steel and ice locked on his throat, yanked and slammed his face into an iron crosspiece. The next flash was pain in his skull.

I must be sick, he thought. *I'm so weak...these women...what is it?*

First the witch who'd sucked him dry; now this.

"I yield," he grated into the choking fingers. "I yield."

His famous cold fury was filling him. His forehead was rubbed raw.

Enough, he thought, and slammed his thick forearm up into her wrist hard enough to snap bones or bend metal.

He wasn't sure which was worst: the shock of pain or the fact that her grip locked on unshaken.

"Surrender to the truth," she cried, singsong, rocking slightly. "Let the cold fill you and become one with dark." Her eyes seemed to flash or mirror the faint lightning. "You will now be made a knight, undefeatable. Fulfill your quest and you may return here to join the kindred."

She released him and he staggered back a step. His nose was bleeding. He was too impressed to be angry or even apprehensive.

"Amazing," he said. "Will I learn the secret of that strength?"

"All the kindred have great powers," she explained, still singsong and swaying behind the grating. "You will become a knight inestimable, colder than ice, harder than stone, with fists to burst walls and break plate!"

He raised both dark, wet, bushy eyebrows. Maybe he was becoming a believer.

"A joy to ponder," he said. Rubbed his face. Felt groggy, as if waking up. Smiled. Maybe he wasn't becoming a believer, at that. Not altogether, anyway.

She paid no direct attention to him.

"You may, if you succeed, become lord of this land in the name of our Master."

"My rise is certain, then, witch?" He cocked his fierce head to the side. "So long as I surrender? I'd believe you better were you less sweet to see."

She shifted, gracefully, along the bars.

"The hemlock flower looks pleasant to the sight," she said. "Yet to taste it is death."

He nodded.

"Which is what you are offering."

"There is ordinary death," she said scathingly, "and there is the joining."

He was focusing, amused.

"My father," he told her, "whom I little respect in most matters, would probably ask you how, in this, you differ from all other women?"

Her voice had altered and seemed a man's.

Mayhap I were but feeling weak and she were not so strong as it seemed....

Her voice had suddenly changed, was shrill but, unmistakably, a man's.

"Youth," it said, without inflection or feeling, no more personal, he thought, than wind blowing through a pipe, "go next to the ruler of this land. There you will be given power in trade for a service worthy of you. Heed this and remember all you have been told. Thou hast been chosen. Do not ponder why. You are young, yet you may be found fit to bear my authority over all men." Suddenly she opened the gate, and still in that shrill, inorganic voice, said:

"Enter!"

He tried. He felt stuck in stone. Felt he was losing his wits; certainly he was sick of witchcraft.

"When next you come you will enter without effort," she assured him, in her natural voice this time. "You will soon be shown the way to what you need."

Suddenly he could move again and he stepped forward as she slammed the gate shut with her effortless strength. In the last flickers of lightning light he was left with an afterimage impression that her hair was bushy and moving as if in an electric wind or, somehow, independently alive, a sense that her face was wide and flat, depthless, eyeless, awful....

And then there was just the wind, fading rain, coolness and relief....He started walking, still groggy, out from under the overhanging rock ledge.

Where's my horse? he asked himself. *Where's Firetail?*

He felt vague, weighed down by a vast, massive softness.

"He's on top of this damned cliff," he muttered, "that's where."

It seemed infinitely high and far. He wished he could fall up, for a change.

There was a clump of pine trees alongside the clifface. They swooshed soothingly in the dying wind. He was so spent he could only think about being tired. He went under the massed branches into a peaceful silence. The air was rich with clean scents as he waded into dry fallen needles. He had to sit. He sat. Then stretched out. Then was gone from everything....

PARSIVAL

There was no dawn from the darkness he lay in. And it had to be a dream because the island was back, a mile below his point-of-view, the island he'd seen when he'd gone blank after sipping the drugged wine with the monk and woke up in the strange open stone coffin. He saw again the obscure center that his dreamsight couldn't penetrate; the icy beaches where the dense fogs smoked; the clear inland plains that ended at the impenetrable center.

He dropped down at sudden dreamspeed towards that dome-like blurriness, covering the seeming mile in a seeming instant. As he hit what seemed the surface of the dome (if dome it was) he had an impression of beings and towering structures—and then something like a giant hand batted him aside as if he were an insect.

The blow actually woke him up. His head hurt, eyes unfocused for the moment, so the late afternoon was a blur of sky and treetops massed together so the world was only a general brightness which gradually resolved itself into a graceful movement, a flowing soar that seemed inexpressibly perfect, a harmonious pulsing that lifted him up and up with it until, a few eye blinks later, his eyes reverted to normal focus and he realized it was a white dove beating across the clearing where he lay on his back, still surrounded by the lean, blade-faced warriors....

He grunted and moved his head, tentatively.

"How are you, my Lord?" Lego asked beside him as Parsival sat up, straining because his arms had been bound to his sides as were those of Lego who was standing between two of the small men.

"Where's the woman?" he wanted to know; couldn't see past the circle of small, oily little soldiers crowded close around him. Even in the open, he noticed, they smelt strong and strange. He decided the odor was like horses in a barn.

Is it what they eat, he wondered, *Or what they are?*

"They took her," Lego said. "I know not where."

Parsival shrugged to test his bonds. They were tight and his arms were stiff and sore.

"Where are the noble knights?" he asked.

He meant the ones King Arthur had sent to bring him back to Camelot.

"They fell or fled," said Lego.

The rust-armored leader strode forward, bumping his men aside and scowled down at the captured knight.

"Shutting up!" he cried. "No more talk!"

Parsival looked at his eyes to read him, if possible. They were dark, depthless, filled with unfocused fury.

"What did you do with the woman," he asked him, thinking he'd been to enough trouble over her to have earned a right to know. He knew this fellow was a nasty, deluded, dangerous son-of-a-bitch driven on by winds of nonsense. He expected to be killed, though he really never believed it would actually happen. He always seemed to find room to wriggle and fight free. Yet...

"Soon you know, dog," was the promising answer. Then, as a form of grammar, kicked Parsival in the ribs with his leather-wrapped foot.

He didn't wince. Lego snarled and tried to kick the man.

"Shitwit," Parsival commented.

"No talk!"

Tried another kick, but this time the knight twisted aside and locked both legs around the man, chopping him flat on his back. He cursed in whatever language he spoke, rolled free like a ball of wire and made to slash the bound man who'd come to a squat, ready.

The little killer wiped his lank moustaches with the back of a hand and glared, barked something, and several warriors rushed up and dove on Parsival who might have rolled and kicked them around for a while, but it was pointless to be banged unconscious, again. His head still rang, he thought, like a dull gong.

"Now you see," shouted the little leader. "Now you learn!"

They kicked and shoved the two Britons forward through the crowd of armed men. They went back to the strangely squared-off clearing where the ragged tents were pitched.

At the moment two of the foreigners in spiked helmets were dancing around holding up the ends of a big banner of torn black silk. A huge face was painted on it in the color of dried blood. The features were thick and a fat Mongol-like mustache drooped to the heavy chin. The mouth seemed lipless where it showed; eyes dark pits staring straight ahead. He wore what might have been a crown or a turban. Parsival couldn't tell.

All the men began shouting, chanting, leaping and saluting the image with their weapons.

"Ai ai ai ai-eeeee!" it sounded like to Parsival and Lego. Then they began howling a name – or what seemed a name. "Mmm'a'das-sss! Mnn'a'das-sss!"

Maybe it wasn't a name. Now they kicked the two captives' legs out from under them, forcing them to kneel on the soft earth.

"Bow!" yelled the leader. "Bow down! Bow down to him!"

They were shoved and kicked forward until they nearly toppled into a pit that had to be ten feet deep and at least that wide.

Even as Parsival's sight adjusted (the sunbeams fractured by the tree-line were needles in his eyes) he heard Lego gasp, choke, gag and curse so that he basically vomited the word:

"Shit!"

Because it was too horrible and Parsival felt his heart and stomach bump and sink together so it was pure fear before it became even anger and madness, before disgust, then slow seething outrage.

He was about to go berserk except he couldn't win yet so he shut his reaction down into black, bitter ice, locking his teeth and looking at the sickening violation with stone eyes: the naked woman with a naked man on either side (he recognized two of Arthur's knights who'd been sent after him: the olive-skinned strong one and the red-haired leader) all on their backs, a round stone placed under each forcing them into an unnatural arch, mouths open in soundless shouts of blood.

That was bad but bearable the rest was no good at all because each had been slashed open from navel to sternum and in the blackening mess of blood and stuff in there Parsival could see that the hearts had been torn out. The three organs had been placed in a row at the bottom of the pit like three strange redpink squash.

He blinked with his whole face.

"Sweet work," he said, toneless. Anyone who knew him well would have known that toneless was past the limit. Toneless was death itself swooping in with scythe cocked to cut. "What sweet work you creatures do."

He shut his eyes. The leader's voice went on, sing-song, cold, almost hysterical at times.

"The Master eats all enemies!" he yelled in the infidel tongue, then back into fragmented English: "All enemy. We are doom! Master is king! All kneel, all kneel!" His men now whirled in mad circles; scraped and beat the earth with their blades.

"Eat enemies!" they cried in their own tongue. "Eat enemies!"

Lego couldn't look away; Parsival refused to open his eyes.

The leader wasn't spinning. He tore off his leather and steel armor and stood there nude except for leggings. He was wiry and complexly tattooed as if a long, symbolic history was engraved on his dry-looking flesh. Lego had an impression of a burning city covering the yellowish, papery skin of his flat chest, the smoke boiling into a mass of storm clouds, tiny figures fleeing, two huge cloud masses looking like clawed, bestial hands clawing at them....

"These things they do in God's clean sunlight," declared Lego.

Because the nude one had hopped down into the pit like an obscene frog while the others chanted and kept spinning all around, reeling, jerking like murderous marionettes on unseen strings, while the tattooed, wiry one knelt over each body and took what seemed symbolic bites out of their flesh.

"Filthy scum!" Lego yelled, unaware that he was making any sound at all, voice dry and raw. "Devils of filth!"

Parsival opened his eyes in time to see the bony, yellowish gnome pop the three hearts into a sack, licking the blood of the three victims from his lips. He was pulled out of the pit by three of his fellows.

Parsival wasn't shocked. He'd long since seen too much. He was going to wait until he was able to kill them, if at all possible. He was wondering what he and Lego were being saved for. Could it be worse than this?

These are no followers of the prophet Mahomet, he thought. *Though they resemble them in form. These turds have been scooped from Hell's rankest cesspool....*

Yes, he'd seen many things; but this was bad in a special way. He heards Lego's emotionally overloaded voice scrape away to a gagging whisper.

And then they were jerked upright again and driven forward to where a blackened kettle sat steaming on a heap of embers; on the slope here where the puddling, stinking, discolored stream oozed turgidly downward.

Parsival's mouth seemed to cloy with foulness. He was looking at the leader's bare back where the tattoo seemed to depict a line of people (suggesting thousands), arms raised in what could have been pain, despair or supplication, unbound, unguarded, walking into a huge, smiling mouth as crammed with teeth as a shark's....

The leader emptied the bag of hearts into the cauldron.

"Sickening witchcraft," whispered hoarse Lego.

"Dogshit," said the knight.

The chanting became a howling. The spinning a cyclonic insanity, the fighters careening and bouncing off one another, circling the steaming pot where the tattooed leader with the scar-divided nose shouted in snatches of French, English, and his own snorting and guttural tongue.

He brandished a dipper, now, which he plunged into the kettle and held to his lips.

"Fuck thy sister," Parsival said, toneless, "and thy mother too with a burning brand."

MIMUJIN

Later, Sunset

The tattooed little leader was nude, squatting on his heels over a pot of cool, mushy food which he ate with his hands. He faced west where the sky was a deep red wall behind the trees. His people's campfires were a little distance away.

A tall woman stood facing him with her back to the black and red intensity of sky and shadow. The outline of her garb made her seem a nun. Her face seemed to gleam unnaturally in the ambient light, like metal. She stood very still, arms close and composed. Her voice sounded bored, faintly mocking, remote.

"Mimujin," she said, in his language, "I care nothing for your rituals. Or your revenge."

He looked into the pot. The sunset tinted his face so it gleamed like a dull coal.

"Woman," he responded, "when your people have suffered as have ours, then you may understand the word revenge." He took some grayish morsel from the pot and put it to his lips, saying: "The Great King, blessed be his name, saved our people. Smote out oppressors. And we became his sword." Ate, as if everything he did was ritual.

"Nor," she said flatly, "am I interested in the history of your wretched tribe. We have a bargain. I will guide you to your king. You will continue your good work in this land."

He looked at her, tall, still, the darkening red behind like clotting blood in heaven as the twilight gradually seemed to absorb her form into the general dimming. It was clear he'd like to have struck her down and knew he couldn't; had already tried that.

"Sorceress," he said, flat bitter, furious, "we do what we must."

She felt a pause, a question.

"Yes?" she urged.

"Why do you hate your people so much?"

She was amused.

"Do I?"

He shrugged. Only his eyes gleamed at all now; she was just a vague outline, the red almost all black behind her, as if the night had tried to take shape and was just dissolving back to emptiness.

"You give them to us," he said. Shrugged. Ate another bite from the pot full of darkness.

"When a man is wounded," she said, "and his wound rots, what do you do?"

"What? Why we burn it with hot steel, and if that fails we cut the limb off."

"You do this to save him."

Mimujin nodded, invisible now in the pooling night.

"Well then?" he wondered, curious.

"When a people rots," she explained, "one must do the same."

He grunted. The idea impressed him.

"So our hate for your people may save them?"

She agreed:

"A wound may also be cleaned by maggots. The maggots feed and are content. The victim is healed."

"You call us maggots?" he wanted to know, carefully adding each offense she gave to his collection.

"I call you healers," she said, invisible now as the tide of night had covered them both.

LOHENGRIN

The next morning he opened his eyes and thought they were still shut. He blinked, rubbed; then closed them one then the other.

Am I struck blind? he asked himself. Because there was only grayness everywhere until his thwarted focus found the shadowy outlines of the massive pine trees that surrounded him. The sweet, rich damp smell was a tonic in his lungs as he finally came fully awake.

He ached; but he was young and it was alright. He sat up squinting into the fog at the hints of forms that melted to vagueness a few feet away. He decided even his bones were damp; the good news was today promised to be as hot as yesterday.

By the time he stood up, rinsed his mouth with water and then sour wine, ate hard bread and salt meat and "went to the bushes", the mist had turned steamy and was beginning to churn under the sun's pressure.

He mounted, helmet hung at the horse's flanks; rubbed his head violently. As he'd expected Firetail had been waiting up there on the high ground.

Poor Hal, he thought, had he no better breakfast than this he'd count himself close to death….

He had a vague urge to go and look at the strange stronghold he'd escaped from. He remembered fragments of the past night: the dream-like girl, the pit of bones….He wanted to look for Hal but the visibility prevented even a poor guess as to direction.

The thing is to go downslope, he decided.

As he went he discovered the surface was grassless, covered with small smooth stones that gave the impression that this had once been a watercourse.

This mist should burn off soon, he thought.

He really wanted to find Hal again, wanted to tell him about the strange adventures that had been crashing over him like a wave of madness; but for the thought of trying to struggle up or around or whatever to find him.

So he went down and it *was* a dry riverbottom, twisting and gradually steepening. At first he thought it was a road except the horse was already leaning back to resist slipping on the seethe of pebbles that clicked, skidded, and scraped under the backpedaling hooves. It wasn't long before it was just a long, twisting slide down a dry mountain riverbed, the horse slipping to its haunches.

"Piss and shit," he said, leaning back, clenching the reins, trying to will traction for the skidding hooves as he hooked around a sudden, tight bend. On the left he heard a roar and then saw, between the thinning trees and lifting mist, churning rapids: grayish-white foam and dark rocks like fangs and broken teeth. The fog was unwinding up the slope like a heatless fire. Now he could see on the right an embankment too steep for either horse or man.

"All I've been doing is falling," he gasped, again wishing he'd stayed home. He had a stray idea that it was no wonder his father was so odd, having been out wandering and questing into and out of madness for so long. He felt an abstract sense of sympathy for the man he so resented. *Maybe there's no bottom to anything,* he finished as a thought.

The mist was bad because it kept billowing up into his face. A Latin phrase that his tutor liked to quote whenever he came into the study chamber for a lesson (which wasn't often) kept repeating in his mind as the horse staggered and struggled and skidded down and down and he could only see in brief gray flashes: *"Qui similis bestia"* Over and over.

At any moment he might career into a tree, a wall, over a cliff into God-knew-what abyss....

There was no stopping: faster and faster....he was tempted to just roll from the saddle but felt that would accomplish little more than leaving him rolling on with a shattered limb or two.

"Shit," he said.

Their speed was amazing. In the blurring to his right, he thought he saw a fallen man with a woman standing over him gripping a sword that she'd either just plunged into his breast or was trying to remove. Her expression, glimpsed in a flicker, could have been fury or grief....

What was that? he asked himself, leaning back in the deep bowl of the saddle.

"Blood shit!" he cried, because suddenly they'd skidded to the brink of what had to be a waterfall (when there was water) and they went end over end. "Oh, fucked turds!" he yelled.

In strange slowed motion, he kicked himself free and away from the horse, dropping into clouds of mist and he had a sense that this might be a very high dried-up waterfall with the stony bottom a long, long way down....

LAYLA

She just sat there in the stuffy, hot tent, watching the flap, dreading a visit from any of the Gaf family or retainers; but mainly the dumpy wife. The woman was dreary, nasty, sullen, stupid, and cruel.

Those are her best points, Layla joked with herself, *imagine her defects....*

She sat on her litter-like camp bed in dim, orange, unsteady light from the single oil lamp set on a stool-like table. She decided to try and slip away just before daybreak. Even the dogs, she remembered, seemed to share the same general dullness as the rest of them. She doubted they'd even bark, much less pursue her.

Not that I'm so anxious to go home, she thought. *If these dolts had anything at all to recommend them I might journey with them until someone actually missed me...Holy Mary, what a life I lead!....*

She heard what sounded like singing chants outside. Some man seemed to be shouting in a resonant bass but if the words were English or Latin, she could not make them out. She hesitated, then went to the entrance and parted the flap just enough to fit her eye. She was shocked.

Where did all this come from?

Because about fifty yards away at the far end of the encampment, there was a big bonfire, maybe ten feet or more of flame. There was a cross set up with a naked man hanging from it. For a moment she believed she was having a vision. There were at least a dozen more naked and half-naked men and women clustered at the foot of the crucifixion, kneeling, rolling in the dirt, crying out while a cowled monk scourged them with a flail. Her captors were all an audience, on their knees, fully clothed and (she observed with disappointment) not being beaten. The other disappointment was the fact that the guard was still on duty in front of her tent, leaning on his halberd and watching the religious show.

Now the Monk paused in his flagellations, panting a little, and addressed them. From where Layla looked the fire at his back turned him into a two-dimensional outline without feature or solidity. The voice was hoarse but strong. She could only make out some of what he was saying; based on that sampling, she didn't much regret what she might have missed.

"...end of days...only through pain...God will choose...follow...only a few will be..."

She went back inside. She'd seen and heard enough.

I forgot, she thought, *next year the world ends...I should recite this every day at Matins....*

She sat back upon the bed. Thought about Sir Gaf, her ex-lover and present captor.

That stupid, scratchy beard, she thought. *He hath on his face the same fur as his asshole...Ugh, I refuse to be pregnant....*

"I'll sit on a sharp stick," she said aloud. "I'll go back to the witch."

The tent flap fabric rustled and she assumed it was Gaf coming to claim her favors or whatever.

"Get out of here," she said, "you Greek cowflop."

She folded her arms and sneered at the opening except it wasn't he, it was half-a-dozen of the naked and bleeding pilgrims preceded by a stink that hit like a solid wall. She wondered if they'd been bathing in a pit of shit.

She leaped up when they immediately tried to drop a sack over her head. She ripped her nails at them, tearing flesh and fabric.

"You must be saved," one shouted.

Her head was in the stale bag. She struggled, choked, tore at it, freeing her arms for moments while they reeled around the interior: banging off the tentpole, toppling over the cot.

They're killing me, she thought.

In total, suffocating blackness, the world spun and tilted around her. Sick lights flashed in her head.

Far away, muffled, she heard a woman's scream that was not her own, and what sounded like a hammer driving nails. Before she could have an idea about it, she went over the edge and dropped into a bottomless dark like a stone into a well....

MIMUJIN

Mimujin, the chief of the wandering fighters who were a shattered remnant of what had once been a great horde was entertaining a guest. A single oil lamp hung in the center of the rank-smelling, round hide tent.

An even smaller, quite round priest of their god sat crosslegged under the lamp facing Mimujin, who stood with folded arms, wearing only a loincloth and chief's body tattoos.

"Battle leader," the priest said, "the people are troubled."

"Because we do the work of the enemy witch," he anticipated.

The priest lifted a just smoldering straight wooden pipe to his lips and sucked in cloying, sweetish narcotic smoke. Exhaled, and said:

"Because we have only your word, Mimujin, that she will show us the way to Him."

"You have only my hope, Tarkas. And we have little else." He began to pace around the tent.

Priest Tarkas knew he was dangerous when he moved restlessly. He'd been known to suddenly strike and slay. "You want proof? There is no proof." He shrugged. "When there is no water in the desert, a man looks for the signs. When there are no signs, a man can only look."

The priest puffed smoke. The dome-like space was filling with the sweetish, stinging vapor.

"You say, this witch has a map that shows the way?" he asked, not looking up as Mimujin paced and brooded.

"Bah! I have not seen it priest." He was angry; but not to kill. "Yet another thing I must believe." The fumes were affecting him slightly. The drug was a relaxant. Tarkas liked to use it during tense meetings. "And what would prove, to see it?"

"My chief, the people say we are warriors. They ask, do warriors collect the dead and poison the land?"

"Warriors do what they must," he said. "We are broken and despised in this miserable place." His deep, jet-black eyes were cold, furious."We have no home whence to return." His split nose gave him a demonic cast in the wavering, dull reddish glow. "We need an ally."

Tarkas nodded, puffing. The smoke seemed to be subtly soothing the chief.

"So the woman is our ally?"

Mimujin shrugged. His eyes were now more thoughtful than angry.

"She is what she is," he said. "We will find the Great King or perish. Then we will see what befalls our friends and enemies alike."

The priest offered the pipe to Mimujin, who took it and sucked smoke gently.

"It shall be seen," Tarkas said. "Or not seen."

"The witch is wise." His eyes were just cold now. "I trust her as the snake trusts the scorpion. She plans cleverly."

Tarkas nodded.

"A new plan?" he asked. "Do we now eat our own young to please her? What new enormity, O chief?"

The fury smoldered in the coal eyes again.

"What young, O priest? Where are our women? Taken as slaves. Dead. The youngest child still living among us has seven years. Hear me, we will perish and be no more, save we gain strength enough to do better than strike from the shadows and shit in wells!"

Tarkas nodded, this time. Sighed. Thoughtful. They sat in silence for a time.

Allow the great knight to escape, he thought, remembered. She'd wakened him at dawn sleeping in the midst of his men and none had stirred. Oh, she was a witch for certain. Again, he struck at her, thinking she meant to kill him. He was fastest of his tribe. His curved dagger split the air in a flicker and, somehow, missed her throat though she seemed not to have moved. She'd held his knife hand with a soft strength beyond his understanding. She'd told him freeing the knight was essential to their purpose. What could he say but yes?

"I will tell them," the priest said, at length, "Mimujin is a wise chief and a father to his people."

PARSIVAL

The cart bumped along under a lightless, overcast sky. A fine, misty drizzle gradually soaked them. Humid, thick air. The road was ruts and rocks. The bumps hurt the knight's sore head.

"They want us for something besides a snack," Parsival said.

"Mayhap they aren't hungry yet. As the farmer lets the pigs live on in false hope," Lego offered.

"I'll make chewy bacon."

The loud straining of the cart was a background sound almost drowning out the steady *scree* of insects.

"Somebody warned me not to wander with you save I craved adventure," Lego said.

"No doubt it was I warned you. Or Layla."

"No. Some man." Shrugged.

"Well, most men crave adventure. Few crave it's miseries." He grunted and braced as they whacked over what must have been a log in the road.

"Christ's hairy wens!" cursed Lego. "Aii! I hit me fucked head!"

"In a word," Parsival said.

By the tilt you could tell the way was steepening down; though they were pretty much in the lowlands already. The dark was solid.

"Are they bats," wondered Lego, "to find their way in this blackness?"

Parsival smiled.

"Maybe moles," was his view.

We're probably about to enter some bottomless hole, he thought.

They went on. Somehow, despite the bumps, tilts and twists, and general discomfort, Parsival dropped into and out of sleep; tortured twisted sleep. The rain picked up to a steady, muted whooshing and tepid drops began pittering steadily over the cart whenever the trees opened out at all.

The air seemed to thicken and make the wet heat worse.

"Aaah," grumbled Lego. "How pleasant. Still, better be rained on than pissed on."

"Better to be dry," said the bound knight.

They jounced steadily down...and down, the lukewarm water gradually saturating their garments. Parsival kept his shoulders braced to keep his head from banging and tried, grimly, to doze off...Now and then the rain would instantly stop and he'd be out for a moment or two. Sometimes it was mere blankness; now and then a vivid dreamflash so he knew it wasn't real when he saw a roofless, vast, shadowy hall where a palely phosphorescent knight whose body looked half-consumed by the palpable darkness, spectrally gleaming spiked crown on his skull, leaning back on what seemed a sharp-edged iron throne, a young man (who reminded him of his son) kneeling as the king held out a cup of blackness as if inviting him to drink or maybe fill it with something....then Parsival shot straight up into the dark shaft at impossible velocity for what had to be miles, rising, finally, out and up and the strange island was under him again, surrounded by icy seas and freezing fogs and the blurred center that defied focus through which, it seemed, he had just shot too fast to note anything.

And finally the rain was just gone and the wheels no longer bumped, just rumbled smoothly, still downslanting.

Parsival was awake for a few seconds before he realized that they were rattling along inside someplace that echoed. He was fuzzy, sore, sick to his stomach, and miserable. He almost didn't care that they were inside some sort of paved cave – but why pave a cave?

"They must be bats, these miserable cannibals," Lego decided. "That in this hole they use no torch."

Parsival backed himself higher on his raw elbows. From there he twisted himself up to sit crosslegged.

"Mayhap," he said, "to them dark is indeed light." He kept remembering the woman he'd meant to help: the obscene mutilation...but it wasn't just that, because he'd seen worse horrors. The terrible part was that it was a form of worship, that there was prayer in it. Murder and madness was one thing; holy worship, however narrow and misguided, was always lit by compassion.

The infidels, whom these resemble outwardly, he said to himself, *pray for Allah's compassion above all else...the Hebrews, the*

Greek, even the Roman killers all asked mercy and prayed for the love in Heaven they could not express on earth...

"Only in blackness," he said, "can they find their way to what they adore."

"I fear," said Lego, "that we'll soon come to the place where they roast our gizzards to make the Devil smile."

LOHENGRIN

The drop was about fifteen feet in fact. He hit (what he didn't realize was water yet) with a splash and hung suspended in a sudden, soundless shock.

Where's my horse? His mind asked. He was upside down, spinning, sucked away, surfacing (despite his gear) catching a breath, hearing the instant, terrific smash and hiss of the rapids. *I'd rather be home....*

He went under and up, whirling, losing breath and orientation...time came and went with his rare gulps of breath...time was how long it took his lungs to starve. He'd hang in a motionless universe then rise and roll past edged rocks and just under the surface he'd stare up into the glare of day like a fish....

Then he was sucked deep into dark currents where he was bumped and dragged through webs of weed.

I die, said his mind.

Body spasmed, struggling to claw out of the iron shell (he wasn't conscious was his armor) that was trapping him. He clawed, twisted, tore, bent and felt himself kicking free while his lungs seized up with agony and he desperately thrashed up and finally broke the bright surface and found himself treading water still as a pond; the downcrashing torrent back behind him, muted, steady, distant and blurred....the water was bright blue under a seamless sky.

No more fog. The air was lucent, breezeless, warm. There was only a slight current as the river debouched into a long, wide lake surrounded by low, bluegreen, round-topped hills.

He felt he walked to land though he knew he was floating. The forest grew close to the shore and even unpoetic Lohengrin was moved and stunned by the rich, sweet masses of flowers that choked the tree trunks in redgold clouds.

As if the sun had bled onto the earth, he thought, reaching the shallows near the shore and really walking now. He'd just realized, though the sky was blue and bright, there was no sun visible! It seemed just fine. *Is this fairyland?* he wondered. He may have been walking but he felt he drifted into that sweet shining hush. Still the work of that witch, whatever-geas she may have laid on me….At least it was pleasant.

And then, as if the flowers had exhaled their scent and that sweetness had coalesced into human shapes, there was a misty ripple and suddenly, seven nude women, perfect and graceful beyond imagination, seemed to take form. He felt pierced and shocked by what wasn't even desire yet.

Their eyes spoke somehow clearer than words, promising sweetness without end and he perceived himself like a bee swimming in a sea of flowerscent, sucking his way from bloom to pollen-gorged bloom, sucking infinitely from infinite flowers….

Their message was he could stay and lose himself forever in arms that were exhalations of perfume and bodies that were dream breezes….

He asked with soundless words:

"Will I ever be able to find my way back here, if I leave?"

Their composite dreamvoices answered:

"This land is hard to come to. Bright island in a dark sea. Harder to leave than find. Once left, few return."

"I would stay."

"Hardest of all is to stay."

"I would stay." Wanted to catch one or two of them and do a little sucking of sweetness. He felt more himself, suddenly.

Everything was thinning. He could see through them, through the trees and flowers and hills themselves.

"Where is it?" he demanded in his actual voice. "Where? Tell me which way?"

Too late. It was all fading fast. Lohengrin tried to move, to enter the now shadowy outlines of the magical forest. He felt as if his head and body were going to split in two, as if half of him belonged to what was fading away.

"It were easier to tread out your days," a voice seemed to say that might have been his own mind, "had you not seen what you saw."

He tried to move, seemed frozen while the strange tearing in half seemed to continue....

PARSIVAL

The cart suddenly stopped. The driver, whom they could not see, got down silently and walked away. They could hear his padding, animal-like footfalls.

"Do we wait here for the cook and butcher?" Lego wondered, twisting around, staring into the pitch darkness back up the tunnel.

"We're leaving before the feast," Parsival told him. "I know what I have to do now."

"Yes?"

"Go far away and never come back."

My life is very stupid, he thought. *My life makes completely no sense....*

He was disgusted, discouraged, bored and empty. He was also much stronger than he appeared. He was stronger than anyone suspected. His power came into him like water; flowed into his arms, wrists, hands, fingertips.

The tight, waxy cords that had been binding him stretched, then gave. He sucked air into his lungs like a bellows. Grunted, strained until his eyes swam with flashing lights of dissolution. Blood welled from his wrists. He kicked his legs, puffed...then the bonds burst with a crack.

He raised his agonized hands in front of him, gasping. Lego was amazed.

We're leaving this...charming...pit," Parsival said with broken breath.

He freed his legs and then Lego. They went on up into the driver's seat. Lego took the reins and turned the cart around in the tunnel. Their eyes had adjusted and they could dimly make out the smooth floor and walls.

"My Lord, why did they just leave us here?" He thought for a moment, listening carefully for anything. "Unless it were to fetch the greens for soup."

The knight wasn't really paying attention.

"Soup?"

He chucked the team back up the slope the way they'd just come.

"Sir Parsival and Captain Lego soup," was the response.

"Soup," Parsival repeated. Grinned, grim and alert. He felt something. Clenched and unclenched his hands. He had no weapons.

Not this time, he vowed. *Not again.*

The cart creaked up the smooth stones, hooves scraping and clicking. Parsival rubbed his sore wrists where the ropes had cut into him.

"They'll meet us at the gate," he said. "I'm used to that."

Next the lustrous starfield was partly blotted and they could hear the grate and scrape of feet and rattle and creak of wheels.

"I might have known," said Lego, "there must be a hundred of them ahead."

"We'll have to delve deeper into this rat warren," he decided.

They got out of the wagon and started back down into the deeper darkness. As they went quickly, they discovered feeble torches set well apart casting wan flutters of light and showing only patches of shadowy stone.

He kept swinging his arms. The numbness was just a tingling now.

"I feel like a sheep," Lego said, "being driven from the pen to the knife."

Parsival was sure they couldn't have planned this. They could not have expected him to break his bonds. They were probably supposed to be picked up by these coming behind.

Except there wasn't a turning or a break. The tunnel stayed wide, straight and downtilted. The sounds behind them kept pace at about a fast walk.

And then they hit a wall of smell. Both men winced.

"Corruption," Lego gagged. "Is this the bottom of a toilet hole?"

"Save your breath for vomiting," Parsival suggested.

He pressed his sleeve across his nose. Excrement, he verified, was only part of the stink; the rest was decaying dead.

There was a sudden turn and then there was so much torchlight it seemed blinding for a moment.

Enough darkness makes a candle like the sun, Parsival thought.

The first impression suggested pictures in churches depicting the horrors of Hell; heaps of dead and dying; demons with weapons overseeing; lost souls tottering in flame and poisonous shadows.

He dragged Lego down behind a pile of broken timbers just to the side of the tunnel.

A good spot to wait and watch.

As their eyes adjusted, they could tell what was going on in the big pit-like chamber – which was as bad as Parsival's first impression.

"These people," Lego muttered, "what are they?"

Each thing they do, Parsival thought, *is worse than the last...*

At the bottom of a kind of bowl hollowed out from the living stone maybe three hundred feet across filled with heaps of obviously dead bodies and tottering, clearly starved or ill men and women loading carts with corpses.

They're all dying, the knight said to himself.

The little killers goaded them on. Looking more closely, they could see that even the not-yet-dead were being lifted into the wagons. The stink was palpable as miasmic fog.

The group that had been behind them arrived: the empty wagons and a dozen or so soldiers.

"I want to squash these little turds," Lego ruminated. Gagged again and spat.

Parsival noted how the torchlight fluttered and smoked constantly which meant this was no cul-de-sac. He squinted, trying to focus past the hellish flapping of flamelight and shadow.

Then he saw a fully-loaded wagon being driven into an opening on the other side that was an obvious continuation of the tunnel they'd descended.

"As I said, Captain Lego, we are getting out of here."

Lego rubbed his nose and eyes.

"How? By dying?"

"More or less," the knight agreed.

Lego got it at once.

"My Lord," he hissed, "those people have plague."

Parsival nodded.

"When I was a boy," he told him, "I stacked heaps of them." He shrugged.

"There's been no outbreak in twenty years. Where do these come from?"

And then the question was answered because another wagon came in with men, women and children bound as the two of them had been. The cart was tilted up and they were dumped into the heaps of dead and dying.

"That was to be our fate," Parsival said. And then it hit him: he was nothing special to them. Just fodder for a grotesque and stupid death. He realized he'd assumed he was somehow the center of some complex plot to use him to find the Grail or something...

They were just going to kill me like a chicken for supper...

"I don't get in a cart full of poisonous dead," Lego insisted.

"That's not the plan, exactly."

"Eh?"

The tall knight gripped his arm and the captain winced.

"They sold me too cheap," Parsival said. "I want to dissolve into perfect love." He shut his eyes, flashing back to the moment again, the blunt blaze of total light that had, for a moment, in the perfect peace of morning under the walls of his castle, dissolved him into (he believed) mere, luminous air. "But I'll have to postpone it." He felt something, not fury, but rather a sense of power and justice like a wave heaving up somewhere deep within himself. He felt it lift him. He felt indestructible. "Follow me," he said.

They charged around the woodpile. They'd each, automatically, snatched up a club. Parsival's was about five feet long and thick as a young tree. He was going forward, exploding with the wild joy of combat he hadn't felt since he fought the tyrant magician Clinschor's black-armored knights some twenty years before.

"My Lord," cried Lego, "there must be twenty of them!"

"Feel no pity," Parsival snarled.

I've no woman on my lap, this time, he thought.

The small scimitar-wielding fighters turned and watched the two ragged, filthy wildmen charging them brandishing poles. No wonder they paused and wondered – which was a mistake because Parsival was very, very fast on foot (from a childhood spent chasing game in the woods) and closed on the first five or so guards with nearly the speed of a horse.

They slashed and stabbed at him. The impression Lego had (lagging some twenty yards behind) was that they stumbled and staggered trying to cut down a blurry shadow and then began falling as if struck by a thunderbolt.

He'd never seen his lord at full fury before. His attack was like the beating of supernatural wings whose invisible winds sent his opponents flying and falling. As he drew closer he could hear flesh burst and bones shatter

As he reached that spot, his lord had already ploughed into the next group of soldiers who were, noticeably, less quick to engage him. The knight was working his way around the rim of the bowl and obviously meant to fight them all.

Just then two new infidels came up from behind to attack him and he had all he could do to beat them back.

Meanwhile Parsival had smashed another half dozen down like stuffed dummies on a training field. Lego ran after him, jumping over the fallen, some writhing and groaning, others flat and still.

He stooped and armed himself with a scimitar and tossed the stick aside. Parsival, he noted, was using his long club like a yeoman's staff, holding it in the center and swirling it in all directions whenever he closed on a new group of opponents.

Lego really had no one to fight as he followed in his lord's wake. They'd reached the far side of the rim where the arch opened into the other tunnel where the loaded carts had been exiting.

Then one soldier who hadn't been really hurt suddenly popped up and tried to slice him down the back. He pulled aside and cut back, taking a chunk out of the man's side, which was enough to put him back down again.

He came up to Parsival who was now alone in the archway standing by a wagon whose driver he'd just laid out.

Others were coming from the far side of the hollow full of horror. In the blurry confusion Lego had the impression the warriors in their spiked helmets were condensing out of fire and shadow.

"Come on," Parsival ordered.

Lego shook his head to clear it, and followed, breathing hard, feet sore and getting numb from pounding over the stone flooring.

"Yes," he gasped.

They mounted the wagon and headed into another downslope, steeper than before. They could hear the hoof clacks on the cart ahead of them.

We're at the bottom of the toilet hole, Parsival said to himself.

Then they were suddenly outside in the middle of the night. No moon, just brilliant masses of stars and (Parsival recognized) the pale, greenish, flickering planet Saturn nearly straight overhead.

They were on a road that leveled off and twisted into the bulging shadows of dense forest.

"Let us follow the wagons," the knight said.

"Do we care?"

"Didn't you ever wonder," Parsival said, smiling grimly, breathing steadily and slow from his exertions, "where the dead go?"

MIMUJIN

Back up in the plague chamber, chaos swirled like a wind as Mimujin came crashing in on his panting pony, skidding to a halt, taking in the terrible scene: captives fleeing, some being cut down by what remained of the guard; dead and wounded scattered around the central pit full of plague bodies and sufferers.

He was so angry he was weeping.

"Fools!" he cried.

At first he assumed Parsival was slain and that he would have to answer to the witch. Then, as he slowly rode around the stinking pit (she had showed them this cave complex, in the first place) he realized the truth. He felt sick, now, and a little afraid.

This dog must be dropped by arrows alone, he thought. *Father of my people, am I?* he mocked himself. Headed into the downward tunnel, without hesitation. He knew he'd have to slay that pale demon himself. Nothing less would answer. So many of his men fallen. There was no excuse and he made none. *Witch or no witch,* he thought. *We will succeed or perish without this terrible white devil...he'll serve us only destruction...and could not this be that pale, plotting red-haired bitch jackal's purpose too?...*

His virtually pathological distrust of other people was now red and raw. Only blood could soothe his icy fury now: his own or another's made little difference, just so there would be blood.

A warrior holding a shattered arm, sweating in silent pain, stood by the tunnel entrance. Mimujin paused by him:

"The white dog went this way?" he asked.

"Yes, lord Mimujin," the man responded, eyes rolling back in agony.

Others had come. One or two unhurt men who'd reached the fray too late.

"See what was done," one man moaned, beating his chest. "So many slain."

They saw their chief was weeping and were amazed. His eyes were terrifying.

"Bring me a coal of fire," he commanded, as more men arrived, retaking the captives. He looked around the smoky, bloody chamber.

"No more of this. No more do we work for the treacherous witch!" he commanded. "Tell Tarkas and Arunijen, my dearest captain, no more playing with the dead. Move through this cursed land and slay and burn until we find the witch and her map. Make their deaths terrible until we are shown the way to the Great king or all die here!"

The men around him shrieked approval, clashed their weapons. One came up holding a coal in a blackened tongs.

"Here is the fire, my Lord"

"Blow on it," the leader said. "Tell them I bear the guilt alone. Tell them I go to slay the filth who did this." He jerked up his left hand, some of the men already yelling: "No, my Lord! No!" and sliced off most of the pinky with his blade. Blood spattered. He took the tongs and jammed the coal into the wound. He snarled and sweated and didn't move. The men began to chant his name. He pointed at the captives. "Eat their hearts and pray for victory. I apologize to the people."

And then, half-fainting from the pain, he rode into the tunnel where Lego and Parsival had escaped.

LAYLA

"No, no, no," she said, and dove for the back of the tent, clawing frantically, digging, scraping, burrowing under the thick, harsh fabric, on her belly in the dirt scrambling under and out.

I'm not going to change hands again! She insisted.

She was vehement. Her body was vehement. Before the first spike-helmeted fighter ripped through the tent fabric sword first behind her, she was gone into the darkness. On under faint starshine, through dips, curves, rills, brush and scrub tree branches that plucked and tripped her...falling, getting up...she went on, not even considering the possibility of capture, hearing nothing but her own breathing and sounds of flight.

"Never," she would mutter. "Never...never..."

Until she could pause and the screams and clash had died into the soft winds and drone of summer night-bugs.

LOHENGRIN

He opened and shut his eyes and shook his muddled head. He was on his hands and knees as if he'd been vomiting onto the weedy, rocky soil. It seemed he had.

"By Saint Jane's left teat, he swore. "How vile..."

*I'm sick of dreams and weakness...may I gag up all such...may I spew up the whole week...*Burped and sucked in his breath. *I'm getting up,* he assured himself.

"And going on..." he didn't move. "Any time now..."

For the first time since he was a toddler, living in the nursery with other castle children, as was the custom, home seemed a good thing. He wanted to go home. Even the boring fief, his semi-anonymous father, martyred and sharp-fanged mother and all the dull characters from Hal (whom he actually missed) on down seemed just fine right then. All those whom (he believed) wasted their lives in those bleak and stupid northern hills a world away from greatness, ambition and opportunity; the tasteless cousins and crude guests (like Sir Gaf and family) not to mention the occasional wandering, second-rate knight who came to try and learn the art of murder from his father.

He was coming around and felt a little better. Thought that maybe he'd go to London Town instead. After all, he was young. The stiffness was already easing.

Find a horse...poor Firetail...and find gear....

With only a tunic and surcoat, weaponless he felt bare, exposed.

There was a long, straight slope ahead. The road zigzagged through the sparse, second-growth trees. There'd obviously been a forest fire: all the vegetation was new.

He went on in a kind of steady stagger. He was determined to go on until something made sense. Why was the road, for instance, zigzagging on a virtually unbroken surface? And the road was clearly used: hoofchewed and footbeaten.

There'll be a village or something ahead...I'll ride a mule or pig...find something...even a woodcutter's ax would do....

"Stupid road," he muttered, striding faster now around a zig or zag when he tripped on a stone and went down flat in the dust. "Shit!"

he snarled, jerking instantly up to his knees. Paused before getting up. Then stared in shock, because, beside the road stood a naked man wearing only a steel helmet with closed visor (a knight?) pressing his short, stocky-squat, muscular body rhythmically over a pale, spread-eagled woman or girl who seemed to just lie there, motionless except for his impacts.

Why fuck by the side of the road? He wondered. *Is she asleep, in any case?*

If he was a knight, he'd have to have a horse. A mount, he thought, other than the woman bouncing stiffly under him.

Lohengrin's crafty nature stirred. His armor had to be nearby, as well. Probably strapped to the animal.

So he crouched to his feet and quick-stepped into the underbrush which filled in the thin woods to about man-high.

Closer now, he could hear the man grunting and thrashing. The sun was poking and spearing through the hazy cloud trails and Lohengrin realized it was early afternoon. He felt there was still a lingering, faint, charred smell in the earth. The air was warm and a little humid.

"Keep humping and bumping, fool," he whispered, now spotting the light-dappled, golden flanks of the saddled horse just ahead through the screening brush.

Armor too. A mace was strapped to the neck, a sword to the flank.

He has what he wants, I have what I want...

He prepared to mount, making soft, soothing sounds – except, like something from a mad mystery play, the naked knight suddenly popped through the bushes.

"What, done already?" quipped Lohengrin. He coolly freed the mace from its thong and tested the heft, cocking one bushy black eyebrow at the ludicrous apparition. "Why hide your face? Looks it like a dog's arse?" His witticism soothed him.

The otherwise naked man (stocky, scarred, and knotted-looking) stood there, bushes still swaying behind him, breathing hard inside the helmet that was adorned on top by what the young man took for a brass mouse.

"Ho, ho," said the man, voice tinny, muffled and very deep.

"Ho, ho?" echoed Lohengrin, studying his genitals: the receding penis and shapeless sac. "Fellow, you should wear a helm over your dick, as well, the sight of which diseased and misshapen stub would revolt the devil himself."

"Ho, ho."

"Again? Now I see why that girl was asleep under you. Your wit stunned her like a blow between the ears and what followed left her undisturbed." Lohengrin forgot his anxiety and discomforts while jibing. "Spare me another 'ho, ho.' "

"Cowardly thief," the man rumbled. "Name thyself."

"Lohengrin of Wales who will cut your head off second. Your nether parts being unbearable to view a moment more."

"A dangerous boy to a man unarmed."

Lohengrin grinned and cocked a half-nod at him.

"I'll perform a service to mankind...nay, womankind," he said.

"Let me have my sword and I'll serve you as you merit," the man suggested, voice deep enough to vibrate in the earth.

Lohengrin touched the swordhilt poking up on the other side of the horse. A sword was his preferred weapon.

"Ho, ho," he said, preparing to mount. "Next time."

"Hold." The man came closer. "Hear me, she's a rare beauty, lad. Wish you not to enjoy her ere you depart?"

The young man leaned on the horse, one hand on the saddlehorn, the other gripping the mace.

"To have one you'd touched first would be like eating the cheese where the rat has bitten."

"Were you hungry enough, you'd eat the rat along with it, lad. This one is honey to the senses, not yet sixteen. No peasant slut, either. Child of a noble family. Sweet and soft and will deny you no pleasure." His deep, deep voice was a soothing persuasion.

"I'm not yet sixteen myself," Lohengrin told him. "And I'll enjoy spilling your polluted blood if you step nearer."

"She says no to nothing, whatever you wish of her. I have seen to that. She is a perfect woman." He inched nearer but Lohengrin read no menace, now. "You're a stout lad. I like you, I who hate all men. I'll teach you pleasures you cannot conceive!"

"What fortune that I happened on you," Lohengrin said, spinning the mace effortlessly in one hand. "Now my life will take shape, at last."

The bizarre knight headed back into the brush.

"Come with me and find life's sweetness, lad." He didn't look back. "Unless you enjoy men or beasts more than woman's love."

Lohengrin smiled.

"That's my weakness," he said. "You have me." But he was curious. An idea was forming that involved taking the girl with him and exploring her charms along the way. He was already following, mace over his shoulder.

Shortly, he was standing over the red haired girl. Her beauty choked his breath. The outspread legs; the reddishgold tuft; the length and naked impact of her. He was instantly excited and now felt she'd been drugged. The idea of her utter helplessness drew at him. The image of how she'd just been vigorously fucked.

He knelt, keeping aware of where the naked knight was, and gently poked her cheek.

"She's dead," he exclaimed.

"Go on! Go on!" cried the knight, hopping from foot to foot. "She is perfect! She is sweet…So sweet…Go on! There's nothing here but your pleasure, boy. No resistance, no discussion…nothing but pleasure…"

Lohengrin lost his erection at once in a spasm of fear and disgust. He'd been so blurry with desire he hadn't noticed she'd been strangled: livid bruises on her throat, blood on her lips. And the too-deep, dull voice was still inveighing him to mount her and give himself up to exquisite, mad, dark joys.

"You…you fuck a woman you kil…"

The word was cut off by a tremendous blow that imploded his chest. His breath blew out. His lungs felt flattened. The other man had delivered a kick that lifted Lohengrin and dropped him on his back four feet away.

Despite pain, suffocation, light and dark blotches clawing at his consciousness he was, after all, Parsival's natural son and grandson of the mighty Gahmuret, so he still gripped the mace.

The naked, stocky knight (or whatever he was) went around the horse and drew his sword.

"I'll put you both together," he said, in his tinny, dull, deep voice, "one atop the other and I'll fuck you both till you start to stink too much and then I'll keep your skulls to piss in." Laughed. "As you rot you get softer and sweeter, at first." He suddenly jumped up and down crying out incomprehensible noises as if in the grip of demons or a fit, Lohengrin thought, with a detached part of his mind.

He could only lie there, arms at his sides, the one on the far side from the killer holding the haft. The man was a blur looming above him as if he lay underwater, fading in and out, still airless from the blow. Whatever he was saying had no more content for Lohengrin than the rumble of distant thunder. The flashes in his head could have been lightning.

"Do you know what number you are, boy?" the man was blatting. The boy didn't understand. His detached thoughts kept going over the fact that he'd been taken like a fool. "I need a monk to inscribe my deeds in a book and keep the count." Flat, blatting laughter. "You are number—"

But he never finished because the teenager told his arm to strike from that impossible position and he arced the heavy weapon across his body as if it were a willow wand and managed to take the murderous man's leg from under him just below the knee.

The answering swordcut just dug dirt and the ruined man toppled sidewise in a spray of blood and curses. Lohengrin was just wheezing his first actual breath into the white-hot agony of his chest.

He paid scant attention to the man's thrashing and blowing as he struggled to open his faceplate — as if that would help. He rolled through a puddle, pounding his fists, splashing mud and foam.

The young man heaved himself to his knees. He'd never done anything harder. He was finally breathing and wondered which ribs were broken.

Holy Mother, he thought.

And then he got up, still holding the mace that was smeared with mashed flesh and bone from the blow that had half-taken off the killer's leg. He watched him bleed and stop trying to open his helmet. He lay flat in a spreading puddle of blood and muddy water. He was just moaning now.

"One sneak," said the boy, "met a better sneak."

The other whispered around his moans:

"I slew…I slew…ah…I fucked…ah…"

"Turn your mind elsewhere," Lohengrin suggested. "You're done with all that."

"Fucked men…women…beasts…ah…ah…the pain is…is…"

The young man rubbed his beaked nose-edge. He touched his ribs next and decided maybe he'd be alright. He found the maniac interesting.

"And there you lie," he said.

"I…have known…ah…pleasures…"

His voice was draining away into gurgles. Lohengrin was thoughtful – by his standards. He watched the man dying. The big leg artery had been smashed apart.

"Why did you not seek fame and power in battle?" he wondered. Squatted down by the man's concealed head. Worked his helmet off. Nothing special, which surprised him. No demon's dark and twisted visage: just a plumpish, pale face with small, colorless eyes. "How strange you were." The man whispered something as he drained away. "What's that?" Lohengrin bent closer, alert for a possible last attack. "Speak up."

"Taste her," the deep, dying voice managed. "No…one…can stop…you…"

Lohengrin stood up, annoyed. He looked at the victim and her beauty stunned him again, dead or not. She looked sweet and soft, outspread and waiting.

What's wrong with you? He asked himself. *She's not willing, she's a corpse...why did he waste her like this? Why sleep with the dead? He makes it sound like paradise...taste her...*

A spray of small, white butterflies were collecting and recollecting on the bushes among small, bloodred flowers. The young man noticed a fat, black weasel a few feet away mixed in among treeroots and shadows. The dark, bright eyes were alert and deadly.

"I'm alone here," he said, "but for bugs and animals and a dying madman." He chuckled. "I'm not alone at all."

But he knew he *was* alone. He wasn't directly facing that fact because of where it might lead his mind. He could have gone on but he looked back at the nude girl. It was true, you could do anything you pleased with her without discussion, consent or force...and none to know.

He rubbed his face violently.

What thoughts are these?

It was like, when he was twelve, finding a dim, musty, remote spot in the cellars of the castle and, stripping off his clothes and lying nude on a blanket he kept there, thrilled and afraid, taking out the stocking he'd stolen from his mother's lovely attendant whom he thought and dreamed of ever since he'd seen her in the bath, rubbing the stocking on his body, touching himself rhythmically, and, as his passion pyramided, sniffed, inhaled, then, arching in childhood's first sweet sensual dissolution, crammed into his gasping longing mouth, bit down, sucked, cried out overwhelmed by shame and joy...and then rose, dressed, put it all away and refused to think about it until the hint and titillation, as a day wore on, drew him inevitably back to his secret place...

He'd stopped and forgotten all that two years later after having actual intercourse – though the pure erotic darkness of those moments of strange surrender would haunt his entire life.

"Bah," he said, because he'd just remembered the silky, pungent perfumy stocking. "Let's mount and begone."

Mount her, he reflex associated. Rubbed his face again. Didn't head for the horse. Thought about things he'd never done with a female. The memory of the stocking and the woman he'd been obsessed with plus the sight of a beautiful naked form before him conspired to pump an unbidden throb of stiffness between his legs.

He was alone there. That was the troubling point. He could do whatever he wanted. And, at his age, he could have sex with himself or another 10 times a day. He knew he came from an excessive family.

"I have a horse and weapons. I can rub my stick later."

He started to walk to the waiting steed. Found himself turning in a hesitant circle and was looking at her again. Had some vague idea that he ought to bury her or at least cover her. After all, he was a near-knight. So he went back thinking about what to cover her with.

Christian burial, he thought. *If I'm indeed still a Christian...*

Religion was nothing to him. He was distracting himself again from the blot of darkness he wouldn't look directly at.

He looked at the dead or still dying man again.

"You turd," he snarled. "I'm immune to your talk."

He considered piling stones over her. The idea of covering that exquisite body bothered him.

What would dead nether lips taste like? His mind asked. It seemed a reasonable question. Who would know?

He suddenly stepped between her splayed-out legs and began to unbutton his breeches. Then caught himself.

"What's wrong with me?"

He turned and half-ran for the horse. With every step he wanted to go back. As he was riding away he wanted to return. He rubbed himself forward and back on the saddle.

LAYLA

I'll find a crone and have this baby out, she was telling herself.

She'd been walking steadily on through the deep darkness among the vague shapes of trees and massive glacial stones, heading steadily, but not steeply, down.

"I hate them," she whispered. "Oh *how* I hate them," meant men.

The starshine showed just enough to keep her from banging squarely into anything but she still tripped and slipped, now and then.

She didn't realize the dawn was close until, almost imperceptibly, pale mistiness began to blur the heavens and the landscape started to materialize and show edges and differences.

She'd determined to walk until she found running water to wash in and drink and then follow down to the eventual and inevitable village where streams always led.

But suppose the old woman was mistaken and she really wasn't pregnant? She hadn't shown the appetite yet. It had to be very early on. She might have missed last month's bleeding just reacting to suddenly having sex every day after months of nothing. That kind of thing had happened before. Maybe it had been so slight a staining that she'd just missed it...

Vain hopes, she thought.

The trees were getting sparse and the land was leveling out, though still rough and stony. Not farmland yet, she noted.

Ahead in the subtle exhalations of first light she saw what seemed a long, delicate spire wavering up into the sky's softly crumbling darkness.

Where there's a church there's a town...

As she came closer and the light incrementally intensified, she started to think it was a ruin with just the spire itself left standing. And there were no other buildings visible yet.

She decided she could at least shelter there and there could be a well.

Closer now, she saw there were no huts, not even the burnt-out husks she'd started to expect. Just a tower, poked into the earth with no trace of a church either.

Most odd...why build so far and just stop?...

She was now crossing the long grasses that surrounded the place. There was enough light now and colors showed: pale greens, powdery blue and rose sky; the dull, rough grey fieldstone of the tower.

She could see, as she circled the strange edifice, there was no sign that anyone had ever even intended to erect more than the tower because it was closed on all sides, plus no door. Yet there were slit windows, too high to reach.

"Where's the cross?" she murmured. *Never got even that far?*

The clouds were pink now. A flight of crows broke over the near treeline, wings loud and sudden; circled the tower once and then went on across the already hot, steamy morning. Watching them, she nearly fell into a pit.

She caught herself and dropped to her knees to look; it looked more like a short tunnel that went under the tower wall. She hesitated. Shrugged and climbed down. At the bottom she had to crawl on hands and knees.

Inside was hot and smoky and surprisingly bright: hundreds of candles lined the intilting walls from the floor all the way to the top. Her first thought was how much work it must be to keep replacing them.

Most of the smoke went up through the steeple tip which was open. She hadn't noticed the smoke. Smoke instead of a cross.

At first she didn't notice someone was sitting on the floor in about the center of the room. As her eyes adjusted to the crisscrossing candlelight and shadow, she saw he was bent forward, seemed fairly old, and wore only a loincloth that left his big, round belly and thick arms and legs exposed.

She decided he was either lost in contemplation or asleep. Maybe a hermit.

He looks like he's never too far from food, she thought. *If he's a true man of God he's bound to have drink too...*

Being Layla, she went straight up to him. He didn't stir or look up.

"Pardon me fellow," she said. "I-"

But he cut her off:

"These are the latter days?" he said, not looking up. His voice was ordinary save that his inflection made every statement seem a question.

"Are they? Why ask me?" she wondered.

The shadow shiftings made them both seem to blur into and out of substantiality.

"Would you be saved?"

She looked around, hands on hips.

"I'd be fed, good sir," she said. "Who lights all these candles?"

"The living who were the dead?"

Again, she took it for a question.

"I don't know. What do you think?"

"You are of the dead?"

"I will be if I fail to eat and drink soon."

"Eat as you please," he said. "There is food here to feed the still dead?"

"Fine," she said. She stared up at the rows of candles circling towards the steepletop. "I'm afraid to ask where the food is." *Where's the ladder to get up there?* "Are you here alone, sir?" She sat down in the dry hay. Decided her appetite was a sign of pregnancy. Considered starving herself for spite.

The hay had no particular odor, which she might have found odd had she noticed it. The place seemed strangely sterile. The only real scent was waxy smoke.

"There is bread and salt meat in the cask by the wall," she was told. "And beer too, if you thirst for it? Sleep where you please?"

"If I please," she said. "Are you innkeeper or priest?"

"Well asked," the pale, round, swollen-looking man said, still not looking up. His thighs were bowed and immense. He suddenly stood up. The soft, changing light made him resemble a wax figure, melting slightly. "I keep this inn for wanderers?"

She shrugged, taking it for a question again.

"Don't you know?" she asked.

She got back up and started looking for the victuals.

She kept half an eye cocked on him in case he should turn violent.

"Yes," he declared, "innkeeper I am?" The days of this world are nearly done?" He folded his arms. She thought them thick as hamhocks. "Death has been seen on his stark white steed? The fell hooves are heard?"

"So you're a priest after all," she said, still circumnavigating the interior. "I have found no food yet."

"The dead don't feed?" he seemed to ask.

"Not that I've noticed. Or are you just telling me something?"

"I have seen the shadow of the angel's wing? In his hand he held the vial to pour upon the waters?"

"Ah ha."

"To turn the seas to blood? I have seen the angel of the seventh seal who will bring silence in heaven?"

She had just tripped over the cask. Inside there was cheese and bread. The bread was still moist as if fresh-baked; the cheese dry and hard but very good.

She sat and ate. He sat back down and contemplated the ground again.

"I have seen the star Wormwood?"

"I can't find the beer," she said.

"The world ends in the year one thousand?"

"I don't know," she answered what hadn't been a question, chewing and rooting in the cask for something to drink.

"The beer is in the jug?" the seer said, not looking up.

"But what of the unbelievers with different measures of time?"

"Their reckoning is false? As is their vile faith?"

She nodded.

"So we say," she replied. "But mayhap the world ends only for Christians?"

"Salvation is only for Christians?" he told her – or asked.

She found space between candles and sat down, leaning her back against the intilted wall.

"Lucky for us," she said, chewing bread. "I better make sure I'm sitting under a cross on January the first."

He shook his head.

"Neither cross," he intoned, "nor the blood of God will avail thee aught unless thou be reborn in his light? *'Unless thou art again born, thou shalt not enter heaven's kingdom'* " he said in Latin.

Now she sipped a little warmish ale from a clay pot she'd turned up. It was delicious. In those days every village had local brewers, usually peasant women with husbands in the fields. Sometimes the results were very good. In this case, it was more proof that there were monks or priests involved because they were, generally, the best brewers.

"And the babe born today or -" She did a rough calculation of her probable term. "—next February? Might as well never come out? Doomed?"

Touched her belly, thinking:

So now I'm just accepting it again...I'd be most blessed by blood between my legs, let alone God's...

"Woman," he said, "I speak not of birth in time and pain?" He pressed his short, fat hands together and lifted his face up towards the peak. "You must be reborn into true knowledge? The Antichrist is hard by the door and enters without knocking?"

"Is that why you have only a tunnel into here?" she asked to mildly mock him, now eating cheese with her ale.

He turned and looked straight at her for the first time.

"You did not find this place by chance?" he told her, looking surprised. She was getting used to his rising inflection and resisted answering the non-question. "You show quick wisdom? The knowledge is to find the womb? To find the *place* of salvation?"

"Find my mother's womb again?"

He suddenly hurled himself flat on the straw-covered floor, face down. His voice was muffled and gave the impression the words were coming up from the earth.

"The tunnel reminds us of our first birth? You must find the second way?"

She sighed.

"It always comes back to *you* must find," she said. "No one ever seems to have a map of anything."

"Map?"

She took another long pull of the sweetish, satisfying brew. It got better with each swallow. She found herself taking the conversation somewhat seriously, after all.

"This tower is a lighthouse," the muffled, earth voice said. "As when a ship is lost from port and the steersman sees the brightness in the distance over the storm waves and crushing wind and knows home and safety lies there?" He sighed, or was it the earth, she wondered, half-serious.

"As when the once-holy Jews were led through the desert of death to the land promised of God," the ground resonated as he shouted now. "We have the cloud by day and the pillar of fire by night, and you can be brought to safety? As when the blood of the lambs, which was even then Christ's blood, was smeared on the Jews' dwellings and the Angel of death passed over them, so have we the sign and place of safety and we will guide you to this place and you shall be saved?" Paused. His voice croaked again. "Yes, there is the map?"

She was lightheaded, both from drinking and exhaustion. Wanted to sleep.

"Will you?" she asked. "Will you, indeed?" My life's miseries have grown from week to week and year to year until to live my life, take the pain and blood, you might as well try to shit out a ten-pound stone from your bunghole. Will you save me, fat monk? Why do I doubt it?"

He shouted so loud the structure seemed to shake.

"Doubt or not, we will lead you there, foolish woman!?"

She nodded, angry and disgusted.

"Men always know what's best for me," she snapped back.

"You will be saved?" he bellowed into the earth. Croaked again, a froggy bleat that seemed like a spasm. "We will pull you back from doom as one pulls a foolish child from the path of a charging horse?" The candle-lined walls actually trembled, this time.

She nodded again.

"Of course," she muttered this time, "Whether I like it or not." Finished the pot of ale. "Fine." Looked at him lying flat on his face. With the hay around it his rear end rose like, she thought, a barrow from a wheatfield. All it lacked, she decided, was a circle of Druidic standing stones around his bunghole.

PARSIVAL

They stayed in the caravan of death after they left the cave and set out through a misty valley behind the ragged hills. The road was beaten deep and rough by hooves and sliced by wheels.

At each fork or crossroad a cart loaded with plague bodies would separate from the main way for several hours; they were the only two left by the time they finally came to a village in rolling, lowland country. It had to be well after midnight under a mostly clear sky and setting half-moon. No one was stirring.

They stopped by the town well. Parsival assumed they'd drink and water the horses. He pulled up beside the other cart. The driver was British; the other wore a turban but no armor.

"Ar, Jack," the driver said to Lego, who was closest to him, "this one's ours."

"What's this?" Lego responded. "We can't have a drink?"

The fellow laughed.

"That's good," he said. "Why don't you wait till we've done here, you'll enjoy it more."

This tickled him so much he shook with laughter. He and the other man got down from the seat.

"Well," said Lego, "go first then, if you're so thirsty."

He looked at their empty wagon.

"Yer done anyways," he said. "You better go back fer more or you'll find some trouble."

They went around behind the vehicle and started unloading the corpses. Before the knight and the captain could react, they were dumping a naked plague victim into the well. It was half over the rim by the time Lego and Parsival stormed down.

"Anointers!" Lego cried. "Anointers!"

There was a popular theory that plague was spread by monstrous men who anointed places and people with polluted holy water or foul tokens of plague. To be accused of anointing sealed your summary doom.

"Be quiet ya fool!" The Briton hissed. "Ye'll wake the town!"

"Die, Anointers!" Lego snarled, laying on with his captured scimitar. The turbaned man drew and struck before the Briton even reacted and would have sliced Lego's arm if the tall knight had not bumped his captain clear with his hip and simultaneously chopped off the top of the turban.

"Pig-eater!" was the infidel's first comment.

"Here, now," said the Briton, backing around the well where the deadly dead body flopped, head down in the hole. "Here now..."

Lego chased him, cutting furiously.

"Traitor!" he said. "Devil!..." Cut, cut, stab. "Anointer!..." Stab, then a scream from the Briton as the razor tip nicked his breastbone.

The foreigner was very fast and slippery in the cloud-dimmed moonlight. He ducked under the cart forcing Parsival to chase him around the other side while the little man chopped out at his legs. The knight dropped to his knees within swordreach and faced underneath. He could hear Lego fighting as his opponent backed away down the road, insisting they were on the same side....

Normally, when Parsival fought, his mind was silent and he simply followed events as if he were the enemy's shadow. But this was distracting. It was almost silly. Villagers were coming out of their homes. Candlelight flickered into a longhouse.

Lego came back, panting and unsatisfied, dabbing at his chest cut.

"He ran...the bastard..."

Parsival stood up.

"This rat's in his hole," he said. "Let's leave him to the cats."

As the peasants came up, armed with sticks and scythes and hammers and stone, Lego told them: "There's a foreigner under this cart. A nasty beast. An anointer we caught bringing the death to this vill. Putting dead in your well, here. Burn all these bodies and deal with this infidel as you see fit."

"Good speech," Parsival approved as one lanky man came closer, holding a staff, yawning.

"Who be you?" he asked.

"Men who fear God and love Britain," said Lego.

We have to get horses, Parsival thought. *We need an army to block the roads, protect the towns and warn the folk...*

"We have to see the king," he said, to himself.

The peasants were getting it and starting to surround the wagon, improvised weapons ready. The man underneath was panting, more from terror than exertion. He heard him farting, as frightened men often did. Lego leaned down, sneering:

"Come out ya windy rat in a hole," he said, poking his sword under as if driving a cat or dog from under a bed.

The man screamed and lashed a cut wildly at the blade and everyone's feet who stepped too close. Two men had already dragged the body from the well, the rest (about eight) were reacting to the bodies in the cart. Some women and older men were coming outside now. The fellow underneath was yelling in his own language which wasn't doing him any good.

One long farmer squatted down to peer into the shadows. The moon had come out of a rill of clouds and the area brightened.

"What use is this?" he asked the infidel, who answered with a slash that cut his cheek.

That was enough. One man had come over with a torch and another with an armful of dry thatch reeds which he tossed under the cart, silently, while the other, silently and instantly thrust the torch and pulled away from the sudden, crackling, smoking blaze. The little man screamed and thrashed around trying to flail away the flames, and then rolled out, clothes smoking. Two other men freed the mules from the traces.

"We got to burn these up, anyways," the long farmer said to Lego, as the villagers closed around the screaming man who, turbanless, was gleaming bald in the moonlight, waving his blade and patting his smoldering clothes.

Parsival wasn't watching. He turned to the farmer and said:

"Keep the other cart and team. We need two sound horses."

The infidel was crouched, trying to shield his head from the stabs and blows raining down on him.

The man's eyes were round and almost frog-like. He studied Parsival.

"Oh, yes?" he responded. "And who be you?"

"Mind yer insolent mouth," snapped Lego. "This is my master, Sir Parsival of Wales."

The infidel was silent now. He just lay there like a heap of shadow as they poked him a few last times. The wagonfull of dead had caught fire and the flamelight showed a spreading pool of blood.

"Where's 'is armor then?" the farmer wanted to know.

"Ya fool," said Lego, ready to punch the man, "yer all farmers here. Do you take yer ploughs everywhere ya go?" Lego was speaking now as he had as a village boy.

They picked up the fallen man, who was close enough to being dead, and tossed him on the cart on top of the heap.

"Get us two mounts, fellow," the knight said, turning to watch the cart burn. "We have to see the king."

"Aye," said Lego. "An I'll pick'm out myself, you churlish, long roll of dung! You'll not palm off some broken bone-sacks on my Lord."

One of the men who'd just dispatched the infidel (who was starting to smoulder with the rest of them), short wide, bearded muscular, sweaty, a bloody scythe in his hand, walked into the firelight and confronted them. He was barefoot in hide shorts.

"What if we say ride off on shanks's mare and be damned to you?" he said.

Parsival gripped Lego's arm to restrain him. He spoke softly.

"We need to see Arthur," he explained, "so this whole land may be saved from poisonous death."

The blocky man rubbed his beard.

"Walk then," he said. "Yer feet isn't broken."

Others had gathered behind him. There were a few chuckles.

"We've got no lord over us 'ere," the long, frog-eyed peasant explained. "This be no manor at all, think what you thought. We don't relish to give up no horseflesh to any as comes by. An' you bear the same foreign steel as that there little bastid who's now a-roastin'."

"Ya ungrateful pigs!" yelled Lego, violently shoving the fellow sidewise several stumbling steps. "We just saved yer filthy little cesspool of a vill and now I think I'll shit in yer fucked well, ya fucked, ugly, dull, foul-smelling piss-pans!"

"Hush, captain," said Parsival, who was coldly angry himself at this point. "You people are behaving with stupid selfishness," he explained. "You will merit the misfortunes that come upon you, I fear."

"What's he sayin'?" the blocky, bearded man wanted to know.

"That yer close to death," answered Lego, "you shit-pot."

Parsival stepped quietly closer to the man. Just in swords reach. The fire was at his back. His shadow was long and shook wildly over the half-circle of villagers as flames billowed around.

"Your garment ill-becomes you," he said.

In a flicker of motion that seemed no more than a stray flash of light, the knight cut at the fellow, turned his back and walked to Lego and the long man. Nothing seemed to have happened; but two steps later the blocky man's hide shorts parted in front along the line of the swordcut he hadn't even noticed much less felt, and then fell, leaving him shocked, scared, and naked.

"Our horses, if you please," Parsival said.

MIMUJIN

He walked his little unshod nomad's pony quietly, alert in the darkness. He heard shouts and clash of arms ahead where across the level fields he could barely distinguish, the outline of the low village roofs where Parsival and Lego had just trapped the little man under the cart.

He sat the horse, totally still in the deeper shadow of a tree when he heard footsteps running, a man panting. Drew his curved blade and waited. As the man drew abreast, Mimujin could see he was too small to be the knight or his companion. He decided to question the fellow before killing him, so he just laid the sword out flat on to catch the light and hissed:

"You stop!"

The man, recognizing the accent, was relieved. Stood breathing hard, hands on knees for a few moments.

"Ah," he gasped, "two strangers...came with...cart...we were dumpin'...bodies..."

"Strangers?"

"Aye...they fell upon us..."

"Who with you?"

"Varin."

There were many voices shouting now and a sudden fireglow. Then a scream.

"You run. He dead." The man understood and instantly twisted and ducked to try and escape the vicious slash that just creased his head in a sear of fire. He plunged on, in a panic. Mimujin drew his bow and casually shot at the man. Missed. Then rode on, not too fast, watchful, patient. He had only one purpose so it all was simple. The pain where his pinky had been throbbed steadily; was a reminder he didn't need.

LOHENGRIN

He rode all afternoon through the flat, sparsely wooded valley. Watching the sun's slow arc, he developed the idea of heading southeast to the Channel; maybe find one of the boatmen who ferried people and animals up and down the coast. He had no clear idea of distances.

Near sunset he came to a wide, gentle river that took big loops as it worked through increasingly forested, low hills. He was on a well-used road now and was just passing through a cultivated area as the sun was setting and the long shadows fused together into general twilight.

He slowed the horse as he came into a village. He was relieved because the animal had developed a slight halt in his gait.

There'll be a blacksmith, he thought. *Or I'll find a new mount...*

Except the place was deserted. As the light failed, he rode through and back again: no people, no animals, no fowls, no dead.

Yet there are crops in the fields, he pondered. He knew enough to know farmers didn't willingly leave good land. Feudal peasants never really went anywhere.

In one of the thatch-roofed dwellings that were partly dug into the earth, he found a side of bacon (was amazed a villain would have left such a treasure behind) and a hard, black loaf.

He cut some bacon and bread and went outside to eat. As he chewed and washed it down with water, he thought about Hal. Rested and let time pass.

Could his adventures have matched mine?

Mind blurred...drifted off into a long nap...went deeper...no dreams this time....

Suddenly back, he looked above the low trees where the waxing half-moon was now rising. It bleached the little town of cave-like houses into mysterious rills of light and shadow.

They all left here together...

No signs of violence either, nothing smashed or burned. They'd gone in a hurry but not fleeing.

Keep on to the sea, he decided. *I've come this far...*

He lay back on the soft earth, hands locked behind his head. Watched the moon. The leaves cut dark, sharp outlines across the bright, whiteblue, halved disk.

His thoughts drifted to his favorite ambition: to gather a band of fighters; find hungry outcasts, outlaw knights, younger brothers dispossessed by the laws of inheritance...

He yawned. He'd inspire them. Shut and opened his eyes at intervals. Without his noticing it, the moon was suddenly straight overhead – which more or less meant dawn was near.

He rubbed his eyes. Everything was a silvery blur. Then a female voice that still seemed a part of a dream was saying:

"It's well I came back, comrade."

"Came back?" he muttered and yawned.

"To see if any were left behind."

She was young and sounded intense. He forced himself to sit up. The taste in his mouth was ugly. It reeked of bacon grease and dogshit, he thought. She stood in front of him, shortish wearing a hood and cloak. The moon shadowed her face.

"I just got here," he told her.

"Well, your good fortune I came," she responded. "You can leave with me."

He rubbed his whole face this time.

"I can leave with you?" he wondered. "At least show your face so I can fairly judge."

She seemed nonplussed

"My face? What matters my face?"

"If you're toothless with a cast in one eye and drooping ears," he said, "that will influence my decision."

"You are strange, young sir. I mean to save you from doom, and you wonder about my looks."

"Save me? Only if you're pretty."

She was amused.

"Myself," she returned, "I'd hold a leper's hand to save my life and ignore a handsome knight who'd lead me wrong."

He was amused.

"You're too wise to be much pleasure," he told her.

He was waking up. Stared into the shadows of her face without much success.

These women I meet...

He thought back to the tall, red-haired, devastating witch whose feet he'd worshipped in the strange tent...then the next, the pale girl behind the bars set in the stone cliff who'd had the strength of a demon and offered him strange immortality by kissing death on the mouth or whatever...then the dead girl...

"Sit down," he suggested. He had some vague idea of pulling back the hood and kissing her neck, if she proved attractive.

Mayhap she is fair and pleasant...

"I came back here to lead whoever was left to safety," she declared. "Not to sit and soon find myself on my back in the clover."

"You're no serf's girl," he said.

She started walking away.

"Come or not," she told him.

"How old are you?" He wanted to know.

"You are a fool, I think," she returned back over her shoulder. "Come or not."

"Nay." He stood up. "You take me for my father."

PARSIVAL

"I know where we are," he told Lego.

They were on a gentle hill, shaped something like a woman's breast, overlooking a long, subtly sunken sweep of clear green, lightdappled fields, crisscrossed by many twisting streams, touched, here and there, by blinding spots of sun reflection.

There were crops and distant, grazing animals. On the horizon, as if the summer haze were solidifying, was a sudden steep hill topped by the vague outline of a huge castle.

Parsival pointed, standing with his legs wide apart.

"That's it," he said.

Lego was just freeing his horse to graze.

"Camelot?" he asked.

"I think."

"Think?"

The knight shrugged. The horses now both were nuzzling the lush, rich lowland grasses. Yellow flowers speckled the slopes. The sun was just past noon.

Lego sat down and rubbed his big, hard sun-chapped hands gently over the rich earth. He sighed.

Parsival folded his arms, brooding into the distance like a depressed archangel.

"It's been some time," he said. "And I hate this place."

Lego looked up.

"This place looks like heaven on earth," he commented. "You hate it, my Lord?"

Parsival shrugged again.

"When I was a boy," he expounded, "I had hope. By the time I left Camelot, my youth was in a coffin and the hole was already dug."

Lego plucked a buttercup and held it next to his palm. The gold reflected faintly on his skin. He remembered, when *he* was a boy that it meant something.

Somebody loves me...or do I love them...

"You make me sad, my Lord."

Parsival looked down at him.

"You have a gentle nature, captain," he said. "You're above all those pigs in armor. You recall an excellent fellow who served my mother. I've never seen him since."

He pictured the blocky, solid almost uniquely literate retainer: big, gruff, bearded, loyal...Lego was much like him...much...

"Last time I came here," he told Lego, "I killed my first man and took his armor and horse." Shook his head, still brooding. "My life proceeded from there, unfortunately."

My first man...yet there must be knights who were killed the first time they fought...I may have slaughtered a dozen such...who knows?...here's an odd career: train a lad his whole youth to ride and war, and then his first day he dies....

Lego lay back, palms down flat at his sides, staring up into the bright blue. The ugliness, death, pits, darkness and poisoned corpses of the past week momentarily dissolved away like fog in sunlight...

"This is such a beautiful place," he said, softly gruff.

A big grasshopper rasped over him, little wings fanning, glinting like metal. Up high, a hawk circled, riding the easy air.

Lego closed his eyes and kept his hands flat on the earth.

After resting they went on across the late afternoon fields. The castle hill was dimming as dense, low rainclouds gathered ahead of them. There wouldn't be much wind, Parsival decided.

By the time they'd come to the base of the hill, it was a dull gray twilight. Fog rolled down the slope at them like ocean breakers under a warm, light drizzle.

"If this fucked mist thickens up," declared Lego, "we won't be able to see the horses' damned heads, sire."

Parsival was looking straight ahead. It was steep here. They'd already lost the trail which would have led to the main road and castle gate. They'd come to a farmer's wall of field stones, just too high to jump going uphill. They were forced to follow it and went left, for no special reason. The billows thickened, as Lego had feared.

"Christ," he said, "you could cut this smoke like cheese."

Parsival nodded. Lego was just a blur to him, maybe five feet behind.

"I can still see my mount's damned head," he joked. "Though, in some ways, I'd prefer to have never met this noble steed at all." The peasants had given them two second-rate horses, insisting these were their best. This one had a habit of suddenly trembling and then loosing low, long farts, apropos of nothing. Lego's would puff whether at a walk or fast canter, as if it had galloped a mile. Neither rider was anxious to overstrain either animal.

"This is some witch's spell, I think," Lego added. "This is not natural fog."

"You think they know I'm coming back, captain?" Parsival smiled. "Better they kept me away the first time."

It was strange, he considered, how being suddenly closed-in like this made grown men as uneasy as children.

"How will we find this castle?" Lego said.

"Well, captain Lego, seeing as how it covers the entire hilltop, need we do aught but climb on? It's too big to miss."

They climbed on after passing through where the wall had fallen away. The trees were sparse here: now and then a couple would seem to suddenly condense out of the still thickening fog.

By the time they'd reached the crest and the hill leveled off, it was night and with only the bright, rising full moon for vague, diffused light, Lego's fears were now justified. The ground was almost completely flat so they could no longer guide themselves by the tilt.

The wind had died away. The two horses were almost touching flanks and still the men seemed more blur than substance to one another.

"This fog seems unnatural enough," said Lego.

Parsival grunted.

"It can't be far," he murmured.

"How far, my Lord?"

The knight chucked his mount along at a very low walk.

"No more than a few hundred yards from the walls."

"It might as well be miles," Lego said.

"Hush!" Parsival commanded in a whisper. "Hark!"

A pause. The mist barely stirred.

"What?" wondered Lego, softly.

"A sound I know too well. The *crick* of an armor joint."

"You are keen, sir." A muffled voice startled them, almost directionless and close in the fog, blurred by what both men knew was a closed visor. They turned around several times but there was only the dark gray wall everywhere.

"How did you find us?" Lego wanted to know.

The voice was amused.

"But who could not have heard your great voices and cloddish steeds?"

"What is your pleasure?" Parsival asked. "We have come to find the king."

Now, a few feet away a knight and charger shaped itself from the cloudy air. Parsival was startled, no stunned: the horse and rider wore red armor.

What? He thought. *What?*

It was the same as the armor he'd won and worn all those years ago, the first time he'd come to Camelot. Impossible, because he'd left that gear hanging in the great hall of his castle. He knew at once it was identical. Impossible...

"I dream again?" he asked.

"You'll find no king, Knight," the newcomer announced, "save you pass me."

"That's simple," he responded. "We'll go on, then. How far past you is the king?"

"You'll go nowhere unless you knock me down, Sir Coward."

"Listen to that," said Lego. "Harken, great knight in red, we are already in nowhere and thus need no permission to proceed. Though, to knock you down seems sport enough."

The challenger drew an extra long, massive, two-handed sword that Parsival instantly dismissed as too clumsy to bother with. He felt the kindest thing would be to simply slice off the arrogant fellow's thumbs with a double cut and leave him to his regrets.

"What do you want of us?" Parsival inquired.

The laugh, inside the heart-shaped visor, was oddly high-pitched.

"I will spare you," was the reply, "but you must enter my service for one task."

Parsival let his steed work a little closer. The armor made him uneasy. It was so much the same as his. Perhaps someone had stolen it for sale?

I'll just disarm this fool, he thought, *and bang him one on the skull to remember me by...*

"Where did you get that armor?" he asked.

"Fight," said the other. "No more talk."

And instantly struck at Parsival from the shoulder with a clean, hard cut. The unarmored knight leaned away and drew the scimitar. The oversized sword missed; but Parsival blundered — something few had ever seen. He forgot the blade he cut back with was a relatively delicate, slicing tool whose quality was unknown. After all, he hadn't taken it from a famous or wealthy knight or solid man-at-arms: just a barbarian knave. So he blundered, making the natural move to strike down on the opponent's awkward sword from above with all his power and knock his hand loose from the grip or even shatter the blade. He'd done it enough times in the past.

Instead, he bent the springy scimitar into a useless U. He instantly trotted his mount into the moon-tinted fog mass to gain a tactical moment and vanished. Even as he took a short circle back to come at the knight from behind, he realized he was instantly utterly alone in the faintly luminescent, damp clouds.

I'll drag him to the ground and disarm him, he thought.

Tossed the useless weapon away. Charged, shouting, "Lego!" for bearings.

His horse glanced off a small tree that seemed to jump out at them as if the mist itself had struck a blow. The fog was in his face like a wall now.

"Lego!" Nothing. No echo, no reply.

I doubt I went above ten yards, he reasoned. *How lost can I be?*

Very lost, it turned out. Stopped and listened.

"Legg-oo!"

His voice seemed lost, dull, stoppered. No response. Then a whoosh behind him, and as he tried to turn, an immense blow struck him across the shoulders. He knew it was the flat of a blade: the Red Knight's blade.

Impossible, his mind said, even as he was sailing from the saddle and aware too that he could have just as easily been hit with the edge and sliced in half. *How?*

The pain was dull and deep and would have left a lesser man down for half a day. It took him a few moments before he got his feet back under him. He knew all the opponent need do was dismount and cut his head off or ride him down and stab him to death.

Impossible, he thought again.

"Very well," he said, wincing and recovering his breath. "Come ahead."

Because he was alone again. Even his horse had drifted away. Calling it would be futile since he barely knew the animal. So he stood there, walled away in the blurred silence.

"Show yourself, back-striking coward!" he tried. He moved carefully to the side until he found a tree and pressed his back to it. Dull silence flowed back over his flat cry.

Then:

"Here am I, Sir Disarmed and defeated," said the Red Knight's slightly reedy and high-pitched voice. The mist seemed to fold into form and the dismounted knight stepped close to him, holding the outsized sword over one shoulder again.

"Do you find me by sense of smell," Parsival wondered, "as would a dog?" He waited, wanting the other to do anything, raise the sword so he could throw him and (furious now) jam the thick blade into his visor's eyeslits and pin the annoying fellow to the earth clean through his face.

The Red Knight responded with highpitched laughter.

"I spared you, oaf," was the reply. "Now thou owes me service."

"I owe you death," Parsival said. "You are no knight but a warlock."

More laughter.

"I swear, before God and the Devil, I am no warlock."

Parsival, like a tight wound spring, sprang from the tree across the perhaps three feet faster than a panther could have, incredibly strong hands clawed to rip the armor from the other's throat and strangle. He hadn't been so consumed by raw rage since he'd gone wild in his first battle and killed an unarmed boy.

But his attack was another blunder because he gripped only mist and went flat on his face again, except this time, there was a steel foot on his spine and a swordpoint pressed into the back of his neck hard enough to draw blood.

"Yield," the muffled, high-pitched voice demanded.

"Ah-ha," the knight said into the sweet, wet earth-smelling grass, "yet you're no warlock."

"That's still true. Yield!"

He exhaled a snarl.

"Be damned, wizard!"

"Impossible. I'll not offer you life again."

"I must find the king," he said into the ground. "There is a threat to all Britain. This is no game or jest, you unnatural fool!"

That caused amusement again; though the blade didn't shift.

"Called fool by the prince of fools," the victor said.

"So you know me?"

"I know you have no choice. Arthur is gone, none knows where."

Parsival sighed. No surprise. He'd been prone to that in recent years.

"Very well," he murmured.

The sword went away. He started to get up.

"Am I to do penance here, wizard?"

Now there was creaking and clashing above and behind him which he instantly realized was armor coming off.

"What now?" he wondered. "Do we wrestle?"

"You put on this gear, Sir Parsival. You then follow the map I leave with you. You will find the king."

He started to roll over. The moment the visor came off he knew it had been a woman's voice, fairly deep. Rich and strong – and he'd heard it before.

"Not a warlock," he said. "A witch."

He now sat facing her: she was tall, magnificently beautiful and nude to her toes. This put him completely off-stride, yet again. He felt he was being played with. She stood at the border of the fog beside the heap of armor. As the silvery clouds shifted she seemed to continually blur and focus.

"I am kin to Ambrosius," she said, "but stronger than he."

"Merlinus?" he wondered. "Kin? Does he yet live?"

She seemed amused. His impression was that her face was not even cold, not even hostile, nor arrogant; just remote as if she were looking through him and all the mists and shadows at things invisible. He felt incidental, somehow.

"If you call his lingering presence in this world *life*," she said, "then he lives. And should you find Sweet Arthur, you may find him too."

"I know you," he half-asked.

"Yes," she said. "And I know your silly son, too. Follow the map and you'll all come together, in the end. You'll have to sail." She smiled, faintly. "The Norse have been raiding again knowing the country to be weakened. Have a care."

"After this I fear only women."

"After this?" She chuckled.

"It's clearer now."

He stood up. His back throbbed. He wasn't angry. The past had come back again...but hadn't he been trying to reprise his life?

Her face had such intense, concentrated energy it was almost repulsive in its stunning beauty; when the mist shifted and softened her outlines, she looked like any artist's vision of an angelic goddess rising from the earth like a sweet vapor.

"Put on the gear," she commanded, stepping back and, in effect, softly fading away.

"Are you his sister?" he suddenly asked. "You're Morgana?"

Morgan-la-Fay. The legendary witch. But, whoever she was, she was gone.

"Lego!" he yelled again, looking at the armor as if expecting it to melt away too.

Incredible, he said to himself. *I'm supposed to put this on again after twenty years...The last time I won this gear...Now I lose and am given it...Somewhere this may make sense...*

He shook his head and sighed. Moved his back muscles, testing: the pain was slowly stiffening into soreness. A good sign.

"Lego!"

MORGANA

Naked, long-stemmed Morgana walked straight back to the castle gate and entered through the portcullis beside the drawbridge.

There was no mist inside, just hazy, dull bright sky above the massive, high walls. The central keep stood thick and massively tall. The former center of Arthur's power was virtually deserted. The inner fields where knights once jousted daily; where thousands of footsoldiers lived in barracks; where peasants held feasts and market. Now there was just flat, weedy turf.

There were no armed men; few men of any kind. As she reached the entrance to the great hall she was joined by several red-robed young women. No one spoke. There was a ritualistic feeling. No one offered her any clothing or took any particular notice.

Inside, lit by high slit embrasures and a massive chandelier, was the round table. All the seats were there. Dust was everywhere; cobwebs sprung from chains to table legs.

Morgana, nude and lithe, ran forward like a dancer and sprung, effortlessly, up onto the immense table and went to the center, stood there with upraised arms, as if in supplication. She was smiling, content.

"O my angels," she said, "we have cast our bread upon the waters and will see what floats back to us."

MIMUJIN

He saw Lego and Parsival blur away into the massed fog that was concentrated around the castle. He was about half a mile behind.

His hand throbbed and he could feel the missing finger. His fury throbbed with it in painful time and dark harmony.

His plan was to charge, in an open place, knowing he could outmaneuver their relatively clumsy mounts and close circles until he placed an arrow in unarmored Parsival; staying too distant to attack.

He was remembering, years ago, before his people had been trapped on the march, the terrible day of disaster, pinned against a swift river with rock walls all around. No room to ride, only to die as masses of European knights ground into the great host and chewed the army to pieces and drove the baggage train, the women and children, into the icy rapids. He relived the terror and pain. Remembered hurling himself, on foot, against a huge, mounted knight, bent on his own death as he killed. He'd been hit in the face (as he stabbed the horse between the armor joints), splitting his nose and knocking him unconscious until nightfall, lying alone among the heaped dead, listening to the sighing, sobbing, groaning dying, mind flowing in and out of darkness in the steady water roar.

So he went quietly into the deepening fog. He followed their track in the damp, long grass. Mimujin was a master tracker. He followed up to where they'd encountered Morgana. At first he didn't recognize her voice. Hung back in the fog-shroud he now believed was too dense to be natural. Curbed his bloodlust, listened and learned. There would be no way to use the bow here, in any case. Close enough to hear, he still could not see them.

"I owe you death," Parsival was just saying. "You are no knight, but a warlock."

Morgana laughed again.

"I swear, before God and the Devil, I am no warlock"

The witch, Mimujin realized. Wanted to kill her too. Counted success unlikely. There was still the possibility she was really an ally of the Great King. A dilemma —he hated dilemmas.

Then motion, conflict, shouts; Parsival and the witch were suddenly out of hearing. He'd now have to circle to pick up the track.

The other man (Lego) was shouting, muffled by the fog. No other sounds. Then a horse thump-thumping to his left, another, a crash of metal in front of him...more shouts and then silence again. As if (he didn't think) the place was haunted by troubled and warring spirits.

He eased his pony slowly ahead towards where he thought he'd last heard them. The trees thinned out which meant he was near the open area around the castle walls. There was still no visibility or sound other than the almost noiseless, unshod hooves of his mount.

He decided his best chance was to wait at the gate, reasoning that if she killed the stinking unbeliever, fine, then he'd see her when she came in; if the pig still lived, they might come together. He'd settle it, either way.

So he waited just where the gate was faintly visible; sat stone-still, thin long moustaches drooping and dripping condensations; waited while the chopped-off pinky throbbed ghostly pain as if it were still on his hand...

A little while later she came back, tall and nude, this time, striding through the gate, a foggy blur.

Did they mate? He wondered. *Is the dog dead or resting satisfied? Bah, I should have shot her now...*

He was torn for a moment: *which way?* Then followed her. A few questions, then see who lived or died...

Book II: *The Cult of the Map*
LAYLA

"The hour is struck!?" the round "monk" had declared, sounding like a question and a croak and driven her back out through the entrance tunnel. She'd had enough to eat and drink and the sweet ale had put her into a general numbness; in fact, the whole thing almost made sense for awhile. She'd slept.

We're off to join the blessed, she'd thought, crawling back through and up the narrow hole, smelling damp earth and cut roots. *All 47 of them...or however many...*She knew the Bible named a number. Some number. Probably more than 47.

As she clambered up into the early morning light it was as if no time had passed: the new day was the same as yesterday. Pale rose and gray. The round one popped out behind her.

Except this time there were about two dozen pilgrims, the men all wearing the same loincloth sort of outfit their round leader (it turned out) wore. The women and girls favored white, rough-cut linen robes. Most of the men were freshly cut and scarred as well on torso and legs by what were clearly whips.

"More mad flagellants," she muttered.

With her luck, she felt, they'd be the same fanatics she'd escaped from at Sir Gaf's camp. And this was a motley enough collection to qualify: a caravan of carts, ploughhorses, donkeys, and a broken-down lot of peasants, about to set off to whatever feverish destination, following a cloud of rhetoric by day and a pillar of nonsense by night.

She sighed, watching an amazingly tall, stooped, scarecrow-skinny man with a chin like a doorstop, bring out, with a flourish, a ragged piece of parchment almost big enough (she thought) to wear as a robe which turned out to be a map. The leader immediately squatted down on his massive, ball-shaped hams and spread it out on the spiny grass.

She went closer.

This must be the famous map, she thought. Sighed. *I'll have to escape again...*

Or maybe it didn't matter. Maybe one place really was as good as another. Except her daughter was still at home. Her son – she winced and shook her head – he was nothing like his father, or her...or anybody else she knew.

Lohengrin...Lohengrin...you were born a stranger...

She stood over the head monk, or whatever-he-was. The sun was just over the horizon, eating up the morning grayness.

"I suppose I'm a prisoner," she said.

The round man didn't look up, absorbed in tracing a stubby finger across the huge parchment that seemed to have been drawn in brown ink or maybe dried blood.

"Sir?" she urged.

He twisted around to look up at her, small eyes lost in their squints and cheekfolds.

"You are a prisoner," he told her, "of truth?"

She rolled her eyes and nodded.

It occurred to her, since this adventure was so patently ridiculous, she might very well cross her husband's path before the end. At this point, she wasn't even sure how she felt about that....

There was a pleasant-looking, blemished, slightly plump girl riding beside her on the back seat of the unevenly-balanced wagon. She kept making conversation. The girl turned out to be an armorer's daughter – which put her in about the highest class under the nobility. Good weapon makers were given land and gold by grateful and competitive lords.

"How fortunate we are," she said to Layla.

Layla didn't quite look at her.

"Don't tell me," she reacted, "the fat priest will bring us to salvation."

"Yes, yes. He has the Holy Spirit."

Layla was thinking how she'd slip away at dusk or after dark and just follow the road back. Something...

"I thought he just had the map," she said.

"Yes," said the enthusiast. "Yes."

Layla sighed.

"You don't think there's something peculiar in following someone Christ-knows-where, just because he has some map?" She sighed. "Why does all he says sound like questions?"

"Ask and it shall be given you. Seek and –"

"Enough, silly girl!"

The girl looked hurt.

"Have you no faith?" she wondered.

"In my wits, girl. In my wits." She studied the banner again; but it still hung limp and told her nothing. "Look you, what will happen if we get wherever-it-is? Will we lie in rosy bowers and suck honey? Will youth never end? Will each of us gaze sweetly upon the other, forever? Will women bleed no more by the moon and lay small eggs at birth instead of laboring in agony? Will death be banished with old age and vile disease?" She pressed her hands over her eyes and shook her head. "You stupid, sad, sorry little goose.

If the armorer's daughter had an answer, she chose to let it pass. She looked away. She looked up. She looked down. Said no word.

Meanwhile the leader on his sagging donkey fired off a peroration, the gist of which was that they were slightly ahead of the following doom and darkness that would crash behind them like a wave as they fled to a land that evil could not touch nor poison stain....

GAWAIN

Gawain was perpetually amazed by the way the runt-like John managed to gather people around him with raving speeches and strange promises. Here they were, hardly two weeks after they'd left Parsival standing naked in front of his castle, and he'd already added several hundred followers to their band with a couple dozen outright whores and camp-followers thrown in, during what John liked to later call his "triumph at Firth Town."

They'd just taken a high noon break. John stood up on a rock beside the dark, dusty road that hooked and curved almost due east towards the water, and shouted out a flow of new promises to those who cared to listen.

Gawain had just dismounted and sat with his back to an oak tree, helmetless, his cowl parted just on the intact side of his face where he ate and drank. He often did his best to ignore his terrible injury. Usually he drank from about mid-afternoon. The drawback was he became mean about vespers, homicidal by eight at night, and passed out by ten, or so.

He sucked sour wine from a Spanish leather flask by tilting it up and squeezing the acrid, blackred stuff into his throat. The best part was feeling the deep warmth seem to spread from his belly through his whole body.

The more of these characters he gathers round, he thought, *the slower we move...after a time we'll just become a great town and stop altogether....*

He carefully didn't ask himself why he stayed with them. Wasn't drunk enough to get serious, yet. Rested his head on the thick bark, lowered his lids and let his eye unfocus so that the raw and reeking armed mob milling in front of him on and off the roadway, eating, drinking, going to the bushes for relief and even (sometimes) sex; the little raging lunatic on the rock, all ran, fused and doubled together in a bright, shifting, misty blur. Felt it was a distinct improvement.

Began to reflexively ponder the Parsival problem again. At first he'd considered just staying near his castle, wait for him to go somewhere and track him. But as John had pointed out, unless he had the Grail on him or was going to it (which they couldn't know), what would be the gain? He squirted another arc of wine into himself.

There are more things wrong with that notion, he thought, *than lice in a serf's crotch...Suppose he never came out at all? Suppose he went nowhere that ever mattered? Suppose...*

"Bah," he muttered. Worked his eye again and watched the blurs stir in a chaos of brightness and shadow. Listened to the steady sputter of voices and shriller cries of the blur above them on the rock, telling the general jumble of overlapping shapes that he, John of Bligh, the chief blur, had deciphered the secret message scrawled by the Last Apostle of Jesus Christ, Joseph of Arimathea, on the wall of the chapel at Glastonbury where (it was said) the Cup of the Christ had been secreted.

He John, scholar and blur, visionary, rebel, etc. etc. had teased out the true meaning of the message. Only he. Gawain was sick of the story. He'd considered cutting off the runt-priest's head, a few times, in a rare spirit of public service. But, on the other hand, the little bastard might be right by accident and, in any case, the knight was on his own. He was, by choice, no one's man anymore; but, not being rich or landed, that meant he had to find his own food and gold – well, pence, anyway. Which really meant, at that time, he was as much a bandit as any other out-of-service knight. He had renounced his claim on his family estate in favor of his younger brother when he went to serve Arthur, over two decades ago.

What none of them knew was that he was in love. Had been for a long, long time. Had spent the best days of his life in the close (if stolen) embraces of his lover, the wife of a Captain-at-Arms. She was not noble (in this land) but very exotic-looking – a converted infidel brought back as whore and servant by a knight who'd been later killed in a pointless quarrel over falcons. Her name was Shinqua.

The color of dark honey, she was full-lipped, supple and graceful. Her mother had trained her to advance herself in a world of selfish, lustful and indifferent men. Her father had been a famous Muslim knight. She was shrewd enough to understand it was better to marry a lesser man and tarry with his betters for gifts and favors. And she'd done that, very well, until she met Gawain. He'd been content with hopeless, poetic love affairs with noblewomen with a few snatched and half-satisfying encounters with the low-born. He was selfish, cynical and (though he never said so) disappointed with himself.

He'd been sent by Arthur to serve the lord of that manor to maintain good relations with a valued vassal. Plus it took care of the knight's upkeep and kept the king informed. He'd taken to this policy with a number of his Round Table stalwarts.

Shinqua had stunned and changed him instantly. Her frank, knowing, steel-under-silk presence; the promise in her look and least movement took him like drugged wine. He put himself where they'd have to meet, talked to her in passing, hinted, teased, or tried to be serious on subjects and petty local events he cared nothing about. Once, when they'd been laughing together over some silly business or other, he'd impulsively taken her by the shoulders and aimed a kiss at her lips; she'd given her cheek instead and effortlessly stepped out of his arms. At that point he despaired of success and began analyzing her and talking to himself whenever he was alone and paid little attention to anyone, in general.

He hadn't tried to approach her at the feast. Once, casually, he'd smiled and she'd nodded. They hadn't danced or spoken. Naturally, he'd agonized over whether to join a dance she was in, strike up a conversation...and thus was generally miserable, pretty drunk, wandering around the two or so acres of carnival...

Intending to relieve himself he'd wandered behind an empty tent at the edge of the woods. The music, fires and revelers were a good way off. The full moon filled rich gleaming around its shadows. Reaching for himself he froze as she came around into the light as if exhaled by the warm, sweet night. Face-to-face, alone, and he felt even worse. He was stunned too, because she looked better than he'd remembered or imagined: the big, deep eyes, uptilted face, remote, somehow untouchable yet yielding expression plus she was wearing a long, loose robe suited to the sleeping chamber, slightly (and it affected his breathing) parted. He was flushed and tense, instantly. Was she there to meet a lover? Just leaving one?

"Ah," he got out. "And what brings you back here?"

She stood now, not too close to him.

"What brings *you*, my Lord?"

He was glad he hadn't already undone the front of his silky trousers and removed his codpiece to urinate. And then again, he wished he had earlier, because the internal pressure from bowls of wine was building and stung now.

She seems annoyed...perhaps because I discovered her here....

The only music left came from a drummer and one shawm – a kind of reedy oboe that sounded like bagpipes, almost two acres away with the peasants.

"Just walking," he lamely replied. "A lonely man under the moon."

He looked up at the full, bright disk, as if that confirmed something.

"Lonely?" she wondered.

"Well, yes, in truth."

He felt like his mouth was full of sand. He wanted to kneel, part the robe, and kiss her legs...and on from there...

"Yet you came never near me?"

"Near you?"

"So I just said, my Lord Gawain."

"Well..."

"Yet not two weeks ago you took me in your arms."

"Well, but you seemed…"

"I seemed?"

"Well…yes…not…"

He imagined the sand was dribbling out between his lips. Somehow she was closer and the scent of her was like a blow numbing his nose and overriding the burning pain and pressure in his suddenly stonehard penis.

"How seem I now?"

The uptilted face was under him and the robe was wide enough apart for all that mattered to be bared to his eyes and the feral moon.

"My God," came out of him. "Oh, my God, Shinqua…Shinqua…"

And he seized her, as if grasping smoke, and felt instead hot, sleek, soft, exquisite flesh…and went down with her, into the silver light and shadow and almost tender grasses, and far, far away, wishing he'd relieved himself because later he'd be in agony…and then even that was lost, flattened like the grasses by the weight and force of love and wildness that took him and moved him like the ragdoll on a puppet master's stick…

He remembered. Half-smiled with his half a mouth at the memory of himself once they'd finally finished, wet with one another, mostly naked, shaking with slow, sighing gasps and painful breaths, drunk with one another – except, once he'd come, the pressure pain from his bladder was like a hot spike driven down the diminishing length of his organ and, against her startled and vaguely protesting arms, he'd rolled to his feet and plunged, stifflegged and doubled, around the curve of tent away from her, whispershouting back:

"A moment, my love…a moment."

From then on they'd met constantly and their affair became notorious. Gawain's present lord (a rich, strong Baron) embarrassed by the complaints from her husband and unwilling to lose his services in the event he attacked the deadly knight and was killed or maimed, demanded Gawain leave off the affair or leave his service. Meanwhile, the Baron asked him to deliver a fee owed to Arthur, which round-trip would take a month or so. Let the embers cool a little, was the idea.

By then, he'd been with her enough to consider a vacation no great matter, after his initial angry refusal. He agreed to go. She didn't like it. It turned out she was pregnant. His argument that her marriage protected her got nowhere. All sound advice about preserving herself and being realistic, not running off with a poor, landless, famously amorous knight, was like mist in the wind of her feelings. Her husband's rage and even pain hit her with the force of a puff of smoke. His threats meant nothing since she knew he couldn't hurt her. And he wanted the baby which could have been his.

Gawain left secretly. The Baron kept her locked in the castle after her lover left. She got wild and refused to eat, saying she'd starve the unborn child unless she were freed. The Baron gave in to his Captain's pleading and released her after a week or so, which, he declared, was far too soon. But the husband could not bear to see that beautiful, silky face rent with misery; the eyes savage with pain; long, tight-curled waves of black hair in filthy knots. She was a beauty that none but nobles normally would have come near, much less possessed; and *he'd* possessed her. And adored her. Every exotic inch.

Naturally, she'd almost immediately followed after Gawain. He'd expected that too and followed, with the idea that at least he could protect her, from a slight distance. The furious Baron, having lost his best fighter, his best Captain, and a vassal woman with child, cursed love and swore an oath that became famous in the land: "If any dare bring such a beauty again into my domain, I'll have her nose cut off and ears slit like a sow!" And he meant it.

Gawain remembered the last time he'd actually seen her. Opened his eye, as if to drive the image away. Looked at the unblurred panorama of grubby fighters, sluts, and malnourished peasants with the Moses, John, perched on his low rock, holding forth as if the wind itself blew the words endlessly from his mouth.

Shut the lid again and risked the pain of the past.

Shinqua had taken her own horse, a slim, short, quick mare, and ridden towards Camelot. Gawain, halfway there, decided to go back to see if she were alright. It was then that he finally completely faced the fact that he loved her, hopelessly, intolerably. Except, the shattered remnants of the defeated invader, Clinschor the Magician's troops, in broken, insane bands were still both fleeing and infesting the countryside. South of them, where the war had expressed its full force, dark smoke still was visible on the mountain horizon from the countless burning villages.

He was passing through a defile where the sharp rocks and massed brush made a wall on each side and the daylight was dimmed when he ran into half-a-dozen of Clinschor's black knights coming the other way. He knew he should have reversed and outridden them. They were terrific fighters, in general and happy, it seemed, to die. Good as he was, there was no sense in taking on a group of them. And they always attacked; showed no mercy. Their only function was to destroy. Whether the cause was won or lost, they tried to kill everything that moved. Some believed they were empty suits of armor full of demonic flame and fell machinery.

But he had a sudden (and unfounded) fear that they'd come from destroying the manor and might have hurt her. He knew it was absurd, but he charged, wielding mace and chain so as to hit the horses too and stop them. He was known for his craft: they could just come at him two at a time and the first was just a shoulder ahead of the second in line, so he swung out to the right as far as the narrow space permitted and drew a sword stroke, checking his horse and leaning away so it just missed him. Like Parsival, Gawain often fought without a shield, depending on his timing and speed. Unlike these fighters, he wore light mail rather than heavy plate. Like Parsival he tended to go for the opponent's hands, wrists, or knees rather than reaching in for head and body blows. They said Gawain had made an army of cripples in his time.

It worked again because he caught the black knight's elbow with his counter stroke and heard him bellow. This let Gawain easily wedge his mount between the wall of rock and the injured man, shove sideways and tilt him over into the second knight, creating a jam so that none of them could quite reach him. His weapon had a flexible chain joined to a long, thick handle. Using the beautiful strategy that had made him famous (unlike Parsival who rarely made any plans going into a fight) he was now able to reach over the wounded man and strike the others, which he did, while the animals scraped and neighed and struggled to get free. Gawain hit very hard and very fast and knocked down all but two in a minute or so.

As he followed, he took off his helmet and set it in his lap, forcing his horse forward past the downed men, so he never saw the last one, headpiece crushed and dribbling blood from the faceplate, spring up as he died, like a trodden snake and strike a last spoiling blow at his head from three-quarters behind.

The blow was blinding, his skull exploded into white fire. He may or may not have screamed before he went down, nearly half his face sliced away.

He'd awakened in moonless darkness, face down, shivering in a pool of blood and vomit. Heard voices and assumed they'd come back to finish him off. It seemed distant and reasonable and meaningless. He'd dropped away again under the terrible pain...

As it turned out, a passing farmer had loaded him into a cart, after stripping the weapons from the dead, and taken him to his village where his wounds were treated and bound in poultices. He recovered and, forever after, wished he hadn't.

He never went to Camelot again though he heard, more than once in days to come, that Arthur had disappeared, left on an unexplained trip or pilgrimage, unattended and hadn't been heard from since.

He never looked for Shinqua. He never knew she'd set out after him or that, in the end, she went back to her husband and had a son she didn't dare name Gawain.

Partly opened his eyes and watched the blurs again. Sucked down some more wine.

"I'll find the Grail," he muttered, "heal myself and find her again."

Or maybe just wait for the return of Christ next year and sing angelic hymns of holy, sexless praise beside her, if, by some grotesque mischance, I should be one of the chosen blest...

Now he really laughed. Wanted to vomit too. Kept his eyes tight shut.

This is my life...why, what a fucked, dreaming fool have I become, merely because my fucked face was chopped off some years ago...merely because my love is forever lost, and, for all I know, fat as a sow with ten sucking piglets at her teats...merely because I follow idiots to Stupidland...O God, please cause these fools to read aright and see this entire stink and puke of a world purged with flame and terror, cindered and gone forever even if I needs must be pitched headlong into Hell for all time....

Except he couldn't ever quite give up. No one who loved so absolutely could ever fail to hope. And, he had a new idea: one of the pilgrims recently joining their march had, according to John's latest vision, brought the final sign from heaven that he, John, had been awaiting. Now their course was clear, the battlefield fixed ahead, the great test just pending.

The new pilgrim was a tall, red-haired woman who wore a golden half-mask and a nun's black and white habit, save for the headgear. She explained that a vision of the Holy Mother had expressed to her that she must seek out the prophet John and bring him God's message. She wore the mask, she explained, because Mary Mother-of-God had told her to cover her face until the second coming of her son. It made, Gawain reflected, as much sense as anything else he'd heard recently.

John was excited and delighted. Here was external proof of his mission. His followers were stirred up, those who paid attention, in any case. She brought a map showing where the enemy was hidden and where the Holy Grail was now secreted - on the isle of Avalon.

Gawain closed his eyes tightly again.

Why not? he thought. *She's got some force about her...all in all as good a lost cause as any other I've come upon....*

Arthur would be there, he decided, if he were anywhere. It would all come together in Avalon. And if there were a Grail he, Gawain, would lock it in his hands long enough to squeeze out whatever truth was in it...

The tall, red-haired, golden masked woman was now up on the rock beside John and suddenly more and more of the armed mob settled down to listen, as the furious little priest indicated her with one clawed hand, shouting:

"Here is the messenger who brought the map! The map will guide us to the Grail! The Grail is the perfect sword with which I, John, will drive back the black doom of the Antichrist and turn aside the fist of death already falling from Heaven to crush all sinners under its hideous weight."

LOHENGRIN

"The fool was my father," he said after her.

The girl kept walking into the moon dappled shadows. She called back to him:

"Is your father *here*?"

"I doubt it," he replied. "But he was famous for it. He was renowned for it." He rubbed his beaked nose with his knuckles, a little too hard, thinking about his father.

He stood up. He could just see she'd stopped.

Bah, he thought

"I think you should follow me," she said. "Why not save yourself?"

"Leaving aside whether I deserve saving, I'll follow. Come and ride with me."

He went over and mounted. Walked the animal over to her where she waited, partly shadowed. She pushed back her hood. The silvery glow sketched her pale, oval face on the deep, mysterious background.

"Fine," she said.

She ignored his helping hand and sprung up behind him with easy grace.

"Welcome to my noble steed." He noted the sweet length of her leg where the dark dress had ridden up.

"Follow the road," she told him.

He kicked the horse into a fast, steady walk. She put her hands lightly on his mailed sides.

"And we'll come to?"

"The others," she replied. "Already have we seen villages and even castles deserted with only the dying and dead within. There are devils loose in this land. There is poison and plague."

Lohengrin nodded, looking at her leg.

"And we will find safety?"

"Your horse tilts," she pointed out.

"I had it of an unbalanced knight. But how will we know the path to safety, if all the world's afire?"

"We have been vouchsafed a map."

"What fortune."

"Yes. Death closes in on all sides. The doom is invisible. No army can overcome the Antichrist any more than we can stab a phantom in its insubstantial form."

He let his bare hand glance along her thigh, as if to stretch. She didn't seem to notice.

"I'm not too worried by phantoms," he said. Wasn't sure just what he meant. "But where is this place of safety?"

"The map shows us."

"Do you have the map?"

She shook her head.

"Our leader is the only one who can read it," she explained.

"So he tells you?"

"You will see when you meet him. You will understand."

"Your father is a knight?" he wondered. She was, obviously, not low-born.

"My father is a dead knight, sir."

He kept thinking about her thigh. Wanted openly to stroke it.

"What is this leader's name?" he asked, just to keep the conversation active.

"A holy man. He uses no worldly name."

His hand glanced down and rested lightly on her knee. She didn't seem to notice.

"What otherworldly, then?" he pressed her.

She shrugged and belatedly brushed his hand away.

"We call him the leader," she said.

"The leader."

They went on in silence. The road was a whitish vagueness that gently rose and fell as they passed under thickening trees. The woods were silent except for breeze rustle and the dinning of insects.

"How far have you come back?" he wondered. He'd assumed, incorrectly, that she'd just left the main body of pilgrims.

"Not far. I waited for a day in the village after they left."

The moon was high by the time they came to open country. He was trying to find a plausible excuse to stop and make advances. They'd been quiet for awhile now. She made him unduly polite, he noticed, and a little awkward. He liked her though he hadn't said so, even to himself yet.

"Why don't we wait until morning to catch up?" he finally asked her.

"I'll walk on, if stop you must," she said.

"That's senseless."

"I must."

"Why?"

"A vow."

"A vow of silliness?"

"I mean to be saved."

"You truly believe the world will soon end?"

In such case, he thought, rehearsed, *we may as well make as much country love as possible...*

"I believe that God has spoken to my leader," she explained, "and taught the way to salvation. And I would save those I can."

The conversation was not going the way he'd have liked. She reminded him of a young nun, a cousin, who used to visit and endlessly try to persuade his father (who didn't care) that the Grail had never been brought to Britain, that the quest was a heathen heresy. She had twisted, buck teeth and a chalk-pale face. His father would stare, faintly smile and nod, meaninglessly, while she went on. As soon as possible, he'd excuse himself.

But what would he have done had she been pretty? he wondered. Except he knew that too.

"I am anxious to meet your leader," he lied.

"Of course," she said. "It will not be long."

PARSIVAL

They never bothered to enter the castle. They never actually saw it. In any case, the fog remained dense as a wall and only thinned slightly as they worked their way downslope. By the time they got to the road, it was dawn and visibility gradually increased as they went back east along the valley.

The day stayed gray all morning, although the mists were gone a few miles from the castle hill. A light drizzle pittered down from the dull sky.

Both of them were bleary, chilled, and tired. Parsival couldn't believe he was actually wearing the red armor again. If it was a copy, it was perfect in every detail, even to rents and punctures he'd had closed by a smith years before.

It's the same, he decided. *Chafes the same...*

They rode until noon, slouched in morose silence. By then, they were out of the long valley again and climbing through a strand of dark pines that blotted the light rain away.

"Rest, my Lord?" Lego suggested.

Parsival nodded and they dismounted on a gentle slope beside the road which, here, had gone back to a scratchy track. They stretched out on the dried and drying fallen needles.

"My Lord," Lego asked, staring straight up into the dim and soothing matrix of limbs and shadow, "where are we now bound?"

His lord put his hands under his head. He wasn't even hungry, he realized, though it had been hours since last eating.

"The east coast, as near we can strike it."

"Then embark for Brittany?"

Lego had been there once. He'd done service for a French prince in a small war. He'd learned that whoever died or was wounded in a skirmish or in a history-changing battle died the same and were maimed the same. A serf, crushed by a runaway cart or stabbed in a drunken melee died the same or scarred the same.

Parsival had tucked the parchment map under his swordbelt. He unwound his arms and unfolded it, rolling on his side to lay flat on the soft needle bed.

"Well, my Lord?"

Parsival shrugged.

"On to the coast," he said. "We need no map for that. Find a ship and head north." He drummed his fingers." Most of this shows the Northern seas and lands unknown. The way points to cold."

"Unknown?"

"Save maybe to the Norsemen."

Lego popped his eyes in mock disbelief.

"To those nasty lands?" he wondered. "Where dwell those crazed beasts who live only to rape and burn?"

"We'll need a few to sail us. Who better?"

"Is that it, then, my Lord?" asked Lego.

"Is that what?"

"You mean to follow this toy?"

Parsival rolled onto his back again.

"Have you a better course?" he asked. "Anyway, I gave the witch my oath." Snorted. "Am I not the perfect knight? An angel pure in my blood and fire-colored gear."

"I follow you, my Lord."

"You need not. You may return to your home; you know that."

"You offer this every seven steps I take, Sir Parsival. I follow you. No more to say. Am I a bird what sings only on sunny days?"

Parsival smiled. His eyes didn't smile because he was worrying about how to find and pay the Vikings he would need.

If need be, I'll pay them with their lives, he thought.

"You may as well offer fresh meat to a horse," Lego was saying. "It goes untouched."

"Good fellow," Parsival decided to explain, "I follow this map because it is, by far, the most senseless quest I've yet discovered." He smiled without really smiling again. "All Britain will sink under plague and other doom while we sail to imaginary lands. Will this not fulfill the purpose I was born for?" He sat up, violently. Clutched a fistful of pine needles and crushed them to pulp in his amazing grip. "Hah. Have I a choice? I wanted to be my old self again and so this fool's mantle has fallen on me. Fitting. Without Arthur, the truant, royal self-pitier, we have no more force than madmen shouting in the marketplace. Even if believed, we have no power to collect his vassals much less set them to war. And how to fight it?"

Parsival tossed the piney clump away and rubbed his sticky hand on the grass. Lego grunted.

"Aye, lord, well reasoned. This is a war without an open army in the field to tilt against." He was sitting up, massaging his stiff left leg, where an old wound had hit bone. "It's all shadow, stealth and poison." Winced as he worked his thick fingers into the scar. "And witchcraft."

Then they were silent, each alone with it; the light rain a distant softness. Lego thought about his family back at the castle. He kept imagining the little poisoners bringing their loads of death closer and closer. The unseen darkness of plague spreading and seeping into the land.

Parsival was thinking about the black knight who'd leaned over him when they had fallen into the hands of the little warriors. Was he one of the tyrant Clinschor's murderous army who'd escaped from their general defeat some fifteen years ago, or just somebody in borrowed armor and silver, beast-faced helmet? None ever claimed Clinschor had died. Some believed he'd fled back to Sicily or the Middle-east. Others felt he was hidden in Britain, waiting his time to strike again.

These midgets could be his men or allies, the knight considered. *This terror his devise...mayhap he even be the "king" they clamored for...yes, he lost his war so now he sneaks and poisons, ambushes and sets shadows on the world, while men fear the end is upon them, the Last Judgment not bursting down from the skies in a rain of ruin but seeping from the polluted earth and tainting the very air...he may well have earned the name of Antichrist....*

He rubbed his cheeks and nose. Blinked hard, as if to clear his mind. He felt a grim responsibility. It was one thing to ride away from his family in frustration and play with notions of retracing his life as if his youth were really important and profound to any but himself; now, his choices were no dreaming game, but might check or free clouds of terrible evil on the world. Many would have gone home and let no strangers within miles until there was sure word the plague was done.

I have no choice now save go forward, as I told good Lego, or flee home…the witch, for witch she was, who set me on this road fools no one…maybe Arthur's own sister or some emanation of her spirit…but she'd want the kingdom intact so it will be her own, and thus far do I trust the whore….

"Bah," Lego suddenly said.

"What, captain?"

"They play with us, my Lord."

Parsival smiled.

"True, captain," he agreed. "The fates and men alike." Squinted one eye. "Yet games and wars are won and lost in surprises. Play on. Play on."

A little later they were back in the saddle again. The trail (were the map drawn true) hooked through a narrow belt of sharp hills before opening into a broad, flat plain that ran to the Channel sea.

MIMUJIN

He entered the center of the castle, close behind Morgana, and was pleased there was no fog inside the huge, practically deserted open area. He saw her just going in the main entrance to the keep, flanked by her attendant women.

If only he could have come on Parsival in this flat space, he considered. He'd have cut around the heavy horses and filled them with arrows. He had no intention of going inside, either. He'd wait, again. He knew how to wait and hate. Kept his bow across his lap with an arrow nocked. Watched the doorway.

At one point, three men robed more or less like priests came out and went by, barely glancing at him. The sun was burning through the hazy sky, now, and felt good on his face. A little later a fat man whose vast belly wobbled him forward, also in vestment-like garb, came puffing across the field, brushing his hand at the tiny flies that were everywhere. He peered at the little barbarian on his pony, shading his eyes with one fat hand, then went up the steps into the keep.

She'll be soon out now, Mimujin thought.

LAYLA

That night they made camp in an open field. No food was cooked. No fire lit. Hard bread and harder cheese was passed around along with water jugs. They sat in a big circle several rows deep on stony ground broken up by clumps of thistles and spiky weeds. The sky was cloudy but rainless. Tiny, unseen, annoying bugs kept flicking into and around her ears. Candlelanterns had been set around the inside of the circle and, in the center, on a sharp edged rock, the round leader perched uncomfortably.

The plump girl was there again. Layla had a feeling she was supposed to keep an eye on her.

"No tents?" Layla commented.

The girl was chipper.

"We want no comforts for this journey."

"God help us if it rains."

"I have a blanket to share with you, sister."

"Sister. Are we nuns now or merely relatives?"

"We are in the family of the saved, praise His name," the girl said, eagerly.

"What great fortune is ours."

"Yes." She leaned close. "Our shepherd has so spoken."

"What fortunate sheep we are."

Layla had another bite of bread because it was softer than a stone; something she couldn't say about the cheese.

"Yes," agreed the armorer's daughter. "He is one with His Father."

That got Layla's full attention.

"You speak of the round fellow squatting like a frog on the rock before us?"

The girl was uneasy again. Layla did that to people.

"The same," she replied, trying for soft patience.

"Meseems his father must be joints of mutton, pies of beef, sides of bacon, bread and jugs of mead."

"What?"

"I believe him to be one with all those and more, to judge by his wholly, round body."

The girl seized on an error - her own, incapable of Layla's pun:

"Yes, you see he is holy," she said, pleased.

The dialogue was cut short by a troop of girls and women, all completely nude, stepping into the inner circle of candlelight and forming another circle around the round shepherd. They knelt and sat on their heels.

Sweet Mary, she thought, *what is this?*

"Ah," said the girl beside her, "a teaching!" She was excited.

Layla finished counting them: a dozen, even.

"Which way do I run?" she muttered.

"Hearken," enjoined the girl. "A true teaching."

He spoke from his inner roundness:

"The Holiness has moved within me this hour," he more or less intoned. For the first time, Layla was sure he'd been a priest or something close. In fact, though she didn't know it, he'd been a monk. A very thin monk, then, who'd discovered "divers prophecies unknown to Mother Church," in his words. He devoted nearly all his time to deciphering these texts, pricked in old script by savants in the Holy Land itself. The authors had believed (as he came to) that these were the secret words of John the Baptist preserved by Christ's disciples. The ideas he absorbed and expressed eventually caused him to be expelled for heresy. He wandered around for a long time, preaching a new vision that, he explained, had been shown him by God direct and thus freed him from the limitations of the Church. As people followed him, he would remain alone in deep contemplation, eating the gifts of food he was brought, always demanding pots and pots of honey, insisting the angels supped with him and could consume only pure sweetness. Whatever the truth, he grew rounder and rounder and said it was the spirit filling him.

Much of this had been explained to Layla by the plump girl during the ride. She told it as if it were scripture.

"Why are they all naked?" she wanted to know.

"To show they are chosen and innocent," was her interlocutor's response.

Layla's appetite kept gnawing at her and she tried the cheese again. Nearly cracked a tooth.

"Who," she semi-quoted, "if his child asks for cheese would give him a stone?"

"What?" the girl responded distracted. "More cheese?"

Now the rotund visionary stood up on the angled rock, barefoot in his traditional loincloth.

"The first child born in the New World," he declared, "must be of Holy conception."

Is he now the Holy Ghost? she thought.

There was a murmur of assent around the assemblage. The plump girl seemed especially stirred. She rocked back and forth on her ample behind.

Layla noted the question-like inflection had gone. Maybe she considered, the sacred prospect before him had overridden it like Moses' speech impediment when God spoke through him.

He sees his burning bush, she thought with a sneer.

"Only the holiness," the bulbous prophet exclaimed, "only the holy will exist in the New World! No man unfilled by the Father's spirit may know a woman, for his offspring shall be demons, subjects and soldiers of the Antichrist!" He paused.

Then: "In these times, the latter days of the earth, all children born outside the Holy Spirit, must be destroyed, instantly. The mothers bearing such must perish as well, for they have had the fiend's spirit quick within them and are now subject to his evil!"

The crowd sighed with what seemed awe and anger.

They're all infected by this, she thought.

"And he's the only one full of whatever he's full of," said Layla.

"Yes, yes," the girl agreed eagerly.

"Yes, yes?" repeated Layla.

"His sons will mate with his daughters," she explained further, "and the world will be saved. We will all bear Holy children."

"He plans to fuck all of you?" Layla said.

"Even you will be blessed, once you are purified."

"What joy awaits me."

"Yes, oh, yes."

He hopped heavily down from the rock and began walking around the circle of nude women. Layla felt ill already seeing what was about to happen.

"Oh, Christ, now?" she said.

"Nay," said her interlocutor, "you are not yet cleansed. You may not enter the circle."

"What?!" sputtered Layla. "As if I'd be fucked by that ball of shit!"

She turned her back when he selected a girl.

Someday I'll be out of madness, she thought. *Someday I'll simply be dead....*

Then she remembered (not that she'd actually forgotten) she was pregnant. The idea was chilling. She looked into the annoying girl's face, profile to her and reversed.

"What do they expect to do with children born from now on?" she asked.

"Are your ears stopped?" the voice suddenly abstractly angry. "They are not babies so born but demons from Hell."

"Of course, that suits reason," Layla said, wondering whether to run then or later.

"Look, look," the girl said, pointing one hand and (to Layla's disgust) thrusting the other under the ragged, sack skirt between her legs. "See how the Holy One mounts her!"

I think I'll run now, she decided.

Stood up and started walking through the circle. She didn't get far, which surprised her. Two men jumped up. They were both pale and skinny; one with a swollen jaw who kept spitting, wincing in pain.

"Ya go noplace," he snarled. Spat.

"Aye," said the other, "ya turn yer back on God's word?"

Layla sighed, almost too weary to think anymore.

"I need to piss," she said.

"Well," said swollen face, "ya wait." Spat. "Until God's business be done."

"God's business," she said. "Still, I need to piss."

"Piss on yerself, then," said the first, laughing. "G'back and sit."

She went back to her place, noting that her plump companion was not the only one touching him or herself. Obviously, the sin of Onan had been forgiven here.

She realized the round messenger of God was on his second Holy Vessel. She just shut her eyes and sat there this time.

I'll sleep and escape tomorrow...in any case, I'll begin then and be gone before these lunatics waken....

She sat there and stared between her feet, listening. The ball of spirit was now grunting as he beat himself into his new vessel, where she rested on hands and knees before him.

If this be vespers what goes on at Matins? she wondered.

MIMUJIN

The little killer had nearly given up waiting and was about to simply ride his horse up the stairs and into the main hall of the castle when Morgana and her ladies-in-waiting emerged. The witch came right to him, the others looked on. Stood looking up slightly at him on the low-backed pony.

"My little demon," she said. "Why dost thou tarry here? More business with me?"

More business, aye, he said to himself. *It will come....*

"Why you set them loose, eh?"

"To do a useful thing."

"Well they do quick," he said, cold and furious. "Or no do at all."

She liked that. Went to his real point.

"Why don't you kill me now?" she asked, amused. "You want to so much."

"Urrr."

"You long to do it like a lover longs for his love."

"You say."

Her entourage came closer.

"I say do not kill them. Follow only - for the time."

PARSIVAL

"Well," said Lego, dismounting and standing at the edge of a sheer cliff on a gritty little trail that ran north and south along the edge, "here's the sea."

There it was, hundreds of feet below, rolling greyly out of fog-masses under a tin-colored sky so low it was like a ceiling where they stood.

"Lifts your spirits, does it?" Parsival said, leaning back in the saddle.

"What does your magical map say now?"

The knight pointed north.

"That way," he said.

"How far, my Lord?"

Parsival shrugged.

"Until we find some Norsemen."

They sat at the cliff edge, eating and drinking while the winds sucked and puffed at them. The summer air was almost cool there.

"What bleakness," said Lego. Nothing on the sea, nothing on the land, all grayness gathering, folding and unfolding. "How far away, do you think, is the closest Viking?"

Parsival shrugged, crushing hard cheese into a bread chunk to make a kind of crude compote.

"What's good about adventures like this," he told his man, "is that they unfold themselves. All you need do is stay alive and keep on going."

LOHENGRIN

He'd stopped so they both could go to the bushes for relief. Since there were no bushes nearby, they went to either end of the horse. Then the horse moved which caused mild embarrassment since he was now consumed by desire for her and kept resisting the urge to embrace and drag her to the earth.

She was still squatting in the vague, silvery light and he was fumbling his codpiece closed. He was torn now by thinking he should open it again and hope for the best.

"Why do you stare?" she demanded. "Have you never seen a woman pee?"

"Not one so fair," he said. He felt thick-tongued and dull as stone.

"What?" she wondered. "You woo me whilst I make water?"

"Shit," he said.

"My God, you are mad!"

"Nay, I but cursed."

She adjusted her skirts and stood up. He moved closer, an impulse that he instantly regretted. She drew back half-a-step.

"What will you now?" she asked.

"The world may end, as you say," he told her. "Why not take some pleasure first?" That was better, he felt. "Here, in the night" he gestured, "under the sweet sky." Even better.

"And, should the world end not, I grow a big belly. I think nay."

He eased a little closer. She didn't move this time.

"That need not result," he explained.

"But generally does."

"There are ways to-"

"Stop, young knight, if knight you be. Even if I desired you, which I do not, I would not submit to your randy heat a minute after we meet like a whore in a stew."

At least she was discussing it. Like catching a bird, you had to move soft and slow, he decided, so much as to seem, often, motionless. He'd had very little experience in subtle seduction; his natural quickness guided him.

"I spoke in haste," he told her.

"And may repent at leisure."

He bowed.

"Because you are passing fair," he said.

She walked around him.

"Let us go on," she suggested. "You may trouble me some other time."

"I have your word on that?"

She shrugged and remounted.

"How can I stop you?" she wondered.

"With your displeasure," he found himself saying. The odd thing was he sort of meant it. He was now troubling *himself*, he realized.

She sat there and stared down at him. The moonshadows merely hinted at her face and gleamed softly in his jet eyes where he looked up at her with the appearance of a strange near-reverence. He hadn't seen her clearly since they'd met and hadn't thought of it; as if he delighted (also unlike him) in hints and pale, uncertain meltings of form.

"Mayhap you *are* a knight in fact," she murmured. "I would not have thought you so *courtois*."

"Nor I," he said, still staring up at the mystery of her face.

It was suddenly important that she trust him. He felt good speaking with her. He felt good looking at her. He felt good being near her. He wanted to be near her continually. He wanted to trap her under him with his body so there would be nothing else on earth to distract her from him. Then he believed he understood:

It was that witch...it was that damned witch who has set a spell on me....that damned witch....

GAWAIN

John's followers now consisted of a pilgrim line stretching back nearly a mile. Like an army on the march - which was how he obviously looked at it. A nice idea, except when Gawain looked at it he saw a straggling line of mismatched, mixed and miserable underclass that might have been scattered by a pack of boys with play swords.

Since the golden-masked red-haired woman had joined them, their numbers had swelled at every village. The death had spread all along the coast and survivors were desperate. The woman proved to be a good speaker and helped persuade the terrorized and scattered people to follow them. The mask covered her features below the eyes which showed pale as water.

Gawain didn't like her; but was impressed by the way she'd simply stand up straight without speaking for a long time, glaring over their heads. Then she'd simply say, in her vibrant, penetrating contralto:

"If you would survive the world's end, follow us!"

And many did. The whole business was madness, he decided.

They'd just entered a town that fronted on the Channel. John and his new cohort rode side-by-side ahead. The sun was behind them and their long shadows wavered over abandoned and burnt-out huts and unburied, stinking bodies human and animal.

Gawain's face ached as it often did. He decided it was the sea dampness. He kicked his horse ahead and then drew up beside them. Studied the woman again: she sat stiffly, as if resisting everything around her, including the motion of the animal. The mask was finely wrought thin gold and looked old and foreign. He wondered how mad she was, on the scale of those around her.

Lunatics, he thought, *spring full-formed from the earth these days....*

"How," he said, in lieu of grunting, "do you intend to ship all these happy pilgrims off to the great nowhere?"

"Knight," the woman responded, her cool, imperious monotone vibrating the metal, "whose face is never revealed to us, perhaps because of a deep oath such as mine?"

He snorted.

"You don't want to see it," he told her.

"That's sure," said John. "Providence has marked him and set him seeking salvation."

"A leper?" she wondered, staring into the shadows of his cowl with her strange, bleached-pale eyes.

Almost like blind eyes, he thought.

"Nay," said John, "a dreadful wound he ought not have survived. Yet he did and now serves a sacred cause."

Gawain snorted.

"Hah," he said. "And I thought my head was but cut in half by some son-of-a-bitch."

"Well," she said, "we will find our way north."

"Mayhap," he asked her, "you have no nose or some wart the size of an egg sits on your cheek?"

"You will see all when we come to the Kingdom of Morgana,"

she told him.

"What? Ought that not be Witchdom?" wondered Gawain, looking back at the endless, straggling line. "I thought we were bound for Avalon?" He was amused. "One imaginary place, I suppose, matches another."

"It is all one, yes," she responded in humorless monotone. "Our destination is not imaginary. Those who come there will be saved from darkness by darkness as fire puts out fire. Preserved from death by death."

Gawain, in his cowl, smiled with the half-lips he had.

"I've preserved many, in my time, with that method. Ha. The more mad the enterprise," he said, "the greater the certainty. Well, I'll make you a promise." And he meant it. "Should you two either err, I'll preserve you well."

John was bouncing up and down in his seat, like, the knight thought, a child with an aching bladder.

"Blessed and saved!" he yelped. "Just so, just so!"

"Lord Death has our lady at his right hand," she pronounced.

"Mean you the Blessed Virgin?" Gawain asked.

"Our lady is no virgin," she responded, toneless. "She has been to the dark place under the earth and returned carrying his chill blessing."

Gawain almost drew his sword and paid his promise in advance. Instead, having learned to adjust his impulses through much suffering, he merely urged his mount forward a few paces so he need not look at them.

"Why are you in this company?" she called after him, in that level, resonant voice with the metallic ring.

He didn't look back.

"I want the magic chamberpot too," he said, straight ahead, "So I can make love again. And take pleasure in meat and drink and all the world's wonders. Unlike you two dancing geese, I know my cause is hopeless."

"Why do you follow it then?" she wanted to know.

"Dull woman," he reacted, "when there are no roads left to

follow, I ride on anyway. Be fucked. Aye, be doubled fucked the pair of fools you are and thank your providence I do not slay you merely out of good taste."

Now there were three shadows, the knight's longest, bending out past the last hut to where small waves broke on a gray and stony beach. In the dying twilight several ships were visible in the shallow cove.

"Behold," John cried behind him, "there!"

"The miracle of the boats," Gawain muttered. "Pray you have sailors among you."

"You are filled with doubt," the woman observed.

"And you are filled with shit," Gawain snapped back.

"Soon we embark," John said, turned and rode back along the line to encourage the followers. "See, see," he exclaimed, "the way is open! Soon we sail!"

LOHENGRIN

By late afternoon the sun was behind them as they followed a well-worn road towards the sea. He was blurry from being continuously in the saddle for over twenty-four hours. She'd leaned into him and dozed, off and on, the whole way.

He really wasn't sure why he didn't just dump her off and take some other direction. What had been done to him? He brooded in his blurriness and became increasingly convinced that the witch (as he had it) who'd briefly enslaved him when he first set out with Hal (where *was* Hal?) was somehow responsible for weakening his approach to women, and impeding seduction. Unless it was the work of the steel-strong girl at the gate to the underground stronghold where he'd swum in a pit of shattered bones.

And were bitten by Death's best companion...if any of this happened at all....

He noted, as they swayed along at a walk, signs of a large group ahead of them: leaving a litter of chewed bones, rags, excrement along with hoof-cut and foot-flattened earth.

"They can't be far ahead," he said.

She sighed awake.

"You see them?" she murmured. Shifted away from him as far their riding double permitted, maybe reflexively fearing the intimacy.

"I smell them," he said.

He came more alert as they were partway through a bend where the trees grew suddenly close to the road. He noted what he took for a glint of metal back in the underbrush. Nice spot for an ambush.

He urged the horse into a trot. Then a canter.

"Hold fast," he told her.

But it was too late. Several tiny men (in rusty middle-eastern armor cut from the same pattern as the ones who'd nearly slain his father two weeks before), no bows or horses showing, blocked him as one (very skillfully) leaped to catch the reins.

Clearly, he peripherally thought, they were tracking the marchers.

He shoved her down into the horse's neck and drew his sword. While not as good as Parsival, he was very good. Youth driven by icy fury and joy in smashing.

He struck with a curse and his trademark accuracy, and left with a pair of wrists dangling from the reins.

"Fucked little shits!" he snarled.

Galloped through swiping and missing the others who ripped slashes at his horse's legs and missed themselves. They shouted things he couldn't understand as they crashed along, raising a spray of dark dust that fell heavily in their wake.

He kept on fast until sunset and they were again in an almost treeless, flat area. Their shadow stretched far in front. He slowed the horse to a walk again. Drew up to study a man by the side of the road; under a net of flies he lay on his back, head broken. A peasant probably clubbed to death by another. His shoes had been pulled off and his traveling sack lay ripped and empty.

"Know him?" he asked.

"No. Why would I?"

Lohengrin shrugged.

Part of your expedition," he explained. "Christ, I'm weary."

Yawned and stretched, urging the horse ahead again. "How were you going to catch up with them without a horse?"

"Someone was supposed to come back to meet me," she murmured, uncomfortably.

"Someone?"

"Yes."

"Good that you found me. You would have been slain or worse on the road."

"I would have waited at the edge of the village. He would have come."

"We haven't met *someone* riding to find you."

She stiffened and said nothing more. He kept blinking one eye after the other. They hurt and his face felt wooden.

"Mayhap *someone* is dead," he suggested. She didn't react. "Mayhap he's taking the long way round." Nothing. "Mayhap he's got his nose in some quim."

"Mayhap you've said enough for now," she suggested. Her voice was dull and she yawned. "You made your stupid point."

He was just staring now out where the point of their conjoined shadows wavered and bent across the earth.

As the night was seeping down through the last, lost blur of twilight they came to a tiny bridge over a narrow streamlet.

They stopped to water the horse and themselves. While the horse grazed and drank, they both stretched out on the cool, mossy bank, side-by-side. He wanted to keep his eyes open. This was a fight he couldn't win. They felt like twin knots. The faint splashing of the shallow water was soothing.

"We dare not sleep," he said. "They'll be following."

She had just snorted a snore. Shook awake.

"You need rest," she said, sympathetically.

"I'll sleep when we catch up," he said, drifting a little. "There may be a horde of the little snakes behind us."

"They seem soldiers of the Antichrist," she said.

He was aware that she was lying close to him and that something had changed in her attitude. He was too leaden to make much of it.

"Antichrist," he muttered, "I'll smite them with a cross, in that case." Snorted.

Has she met them before to know them again? He asked himself, mockingly.

He was flickering in and out of what weren't quite dreams: just faces too close to make out...then there was the red-haired witch who'd enslaved him in her tent - except this time she was holding a silvery, spiky crown in both hands, raised as if to be set on someone's head.

He shook awake as the girl was saying:

"I think I trust you now."

"What?"

"I no longer fear your touch," she said, quietly. He had an impression she'd shifted closer.

Now, he thought from the leaden space he lay in, *that I cannot lift a hand....*

"Yes...good..." he whispered, flicking out again and there was the naked witch or whatever planting a soft, perfect foot over his face. Shook awake.

"Don't let me sleep," he said, struggling onto his elbows, shaking his head.

She knelt up beside him. Her robe-like dress was parted and she put his hand inside, touching her elastic, warm softness, the flicking surprise of her nipples. She sighed and he automatically reached his other hand to pull her down beside him.

Ah, he thought.

"No," he said. "We can't linger here."

She pressed close to him.

"You never gave your name," she said into his ear. Her warm, musky, pleasant breath wakened him.

"Nor you yours," he returned.

"Jane," she told him.

"Lohengrin," he said, groping, heedless now, at her skirts, tugging them up so his hands could roam, licensed, over the thighs and secrets he'd been imagining the whole ride.

She lifted herself and mounted him, stripping away at his codpiece and belt until she found what she sought and gripped it firm.

"Oh," she hissed between her teeth. "How I like this...how I like this...."

"Ahhh," he let out, "fit it within you...fit it within you...."

PARSIVAL

The cliffs gradually folded themselves down to almost sea level as the miles passed. And then, at early evening of the next day, as if (Lego felt) his lord commanded these adventures, they saw fire and heard cries and sounds of combat on the beach maybe half-a-mile ahead. And there were the unmistakable sails and low-profiled dragon ships drawn up to the beach, melting in and out of the smoky mists as the sea wind shifted.

"Well, my Lord," Lego said, "we found them. Pray it's no mistake. What follows now?"

Parsival was running ideas through his head rapidly. So far none felt solid.

"We keep riding," he said, picking up the pace along the sketchy, sandy trail that obviously ran to the burning village ahead.

The knight, when no plan occurred to him, in generally just went into situations and improvised. In that sense he'd never grown up. The fact that he usually succeeded must have meant something, but he wasn't sure what, himself.

"There may be lots of Norse there," Lego pointed out.

"We only need one ship."

Lego took that in.

"Who will sail it, lord?"

"The Vikings, of course."

"I n'ere heard of hiring such devils like London Town watermen."

"We'll win their hearts to our cause."

The wind shifted and the smoke from the burning huts blew blindingly in their faces. The horses cantered over scattered bodies now but they heard no more fighting or shouts. As the twilight went black the firelight showed groups of men carrying booty and wounded back to the longships.

They reined up by the nearest on the smooth, firm, wet sand just above the low breakers. Two bare-headed bare-chested Vikings and one in a horned helmet were raping a woman on the beach while several others were dragging pigs and cattle up a steep gangplank into the ship, blurring away, then fading back as the smoke and fog swirled.

Parsival and Lego both detested violence against women, unlike so many others in a time where chivalry was more a hope than a practice. The big knight in the red armor of his youth, dismounted and fell on the three rapists, wielding his still-sheathed sword with furious contempt. Only the helmeted character who'd been holding one of the woman's legs (she was not particularly attractive, he noted, rather fat) managed to actually stand up and loose his war ax from its shoulder sling before Parsival (the other two were already down flat with cracked heads) simply jabbed the scabbard point into the Norseman's throat and sent him stumbling off, gagging and gasping into the sea. The smoke obscured it from the others.

Lego was beside him.

"Winning their hearts, my Lord?" he asked.

We'll try this, Parsival thought.

"Bring your horse," he said, stepping back and taking the reins in one hand and heading for the gangplank. "We're going to hire them."

"Hire? Have we gold?"

"Better than that," he explained, as seven or eight fighters came to close in around them. "I have the map."

"I doubt they want that map," Lego said, releasing his mount and standing ready.

Parsival didn't draw his sword. He stood up on the gangplank as the men closed in around them with blades and axes. The fog and smoke puffed and filled keeping them at best semi-visible for no more than a couple of dozen feet.

"Who speaks our tongue?" he demanded one hand on hip, obviously relaxed.

"Your language is what the dead speak," a short, very wide redheaded warrior replied, moving closer, war ax ready. He had a slight accent and could almost have been a Briton by the sound of him.

Parsival sighed.

"Yes, yes," he said, "I've been dead ten times this year, to hear others tell it. Hold back your wolves a moment. I have something to profit you."

"Ha, ha. We have just taken the booty of your village. We have profit enough."

"This is not my village. And I speak not of lank cows and pigs, but of treasure ten longships could not bear away."

Lego nodded.

"He speaks true," he said.

That's no lie, he thought, *how can you bear away nothing?*

The Viking cocked his head, pondering.

"So you say," he said, at length.

"So I say," quoth Parsival, "so I say."

MIMUJIN

Morgana didn't quite look at him, still smiling. One of the assisting women handed her a black metal staff which the little nomad assumed was dangerous. He checked the impulse to let fly a quick arrow. Soothed his pony's neck with one hand.

"You follow both of them," she said, in his language.

"Maybe so," he answered.

She carelessly pointed the staff at him. He frowned, expecting anything.

"Do not kill them, yet," she said again. "Wait. Watch. Gather fighters at Channel sea."

Sneered.

"Mimujin not as you, witch," he declared, "in many places at once."

"You are not."

"Follow, how gather people same time?"

She smiled and spoke English:

"I'll cut you in two parts and send each on its own errand."

The ladies-in-waiting were amused.

"Yuh, yuh," responded Mimujin in his English. "Mimujin laugh."

One of the women went over to him. His mind ran, idly, to rape. Briefly pictured riding off together and taking his pleasure before killing her. Wondered if Witch Morgana could read his thoughts. In any case, she clearly knew them.

"Alyal will ride with you," she explained. To a second assistant: "Bring her a swift horse." This girl left, half-running, across the courtyard. "Entrust her with the token you wear around your neck and she will direct your people to the sea while you pursue those you hate."

The little man grunted. His fellows would do what they pleased with her. She was pale, sleek, reddish blond. He imagined her pubic hair. Wanted to see that.

"I go, then," he said, in English.

"You go then," she agreed. "Follow so far as you can, then wait for me."

He shrugged. How could she make him wait? When would he know to wait?

"I go," he said.

"You go," she repeated.

MORGANA

She tapped the staff, watching the little warrior ride out through the castle gate ahead of her handmaiden.

Alyal will not fail me, she thought.

"Leave me," she commanded, and went back inside.

On the second floor the high embrasures were flooded with daylight. Camelot was like a cathedral, in places, lined with narrow windows facing south.

She went to the King's bedchamber. Paused at the massive bronze and oak door, stared as if reading a message on the planks where nothing but wear and time was written.

He still fears my brother will return while I am so afraid he will not. I seek him everywhere....Sweet Arthur, maybe he's found the path to the mystery and now stands with Excalibur in one hand and the Grail in the other....

She pushed the door open and went into a shock of dimness:

the windows were clogged with hangings. Scented candles burned everywhere, cloying, somehow humid. The huge, draped bed where the king had lain with the tragic Guinevere was now occupied by a pale, languorous, naked teenaged boy. His straw-colored hair was oiled and he wore a flower behind one ear. His eyes were restless, nervous. The bed was silken, perfumed and lush.

The time is coming, she thought, *my sweet child and sacrifice...*She looked at his genitalia: pale, small, dusted with light hair.

"How are you, my son?"

"Aunt, is my uncle coming?"

"Nay, Modred. You need not fear. Even were the King here, he could do you no hurt."

"What of his knights?"

"His knights," she said, smiling, raising the staff, "least of all, my son." "Nor Merlinus Magnus, neither. I have taken their measure. You will be king. Your child will rule the earth."

"Mine?"

"Your child."

"Am I to be married?"

"No. Yet you will be well wived."

"Still, Uncle Arthur is a fearful man."

"As was your father."

The boy sat up, unselfconscious. Frowned.

"Who was he?"

"A man much like the King," she told him, "whose bed you lie in."

"Is this Arthur's bed?" Modred was startled. "Will he slay me if he finds me here?"

She soothed him with a kiss and touch.

"Hush, my sweet boy," she murmured, "you have as much to fear from your own father as King Arthur."

"Is he against me, too?"

"Fathers love their sons above all else."

"Will I see him?"

"Mayhap. You are special. Royal and more than royal."

My nephew and son, she said to herself. *I have set the last one I feared to where, if Arthur lives, he will join him...set the vicious barbarian on the trail...all birds in one net save the enfeebled Merlin and one other....*

"All goes well, dear Modred," she murmured, staring into the mist of the future.

And last of all, she went on to herself, *the self-devouring Clinschor...I feel his stunted fury under the world where he kisses death on the lips and strains to claw his way back to the bright earth....*

"So I need not fear?" her nude boy asked, sunk in the sweet, perfumed silks and pillows.

"This world must be heated, hammered and subtly drawn into a pleasing shape," she said distantly, not really talking to him. "Else why live in it?"

His little barbarians will find him for me...their true father...with Excalibur in hand I'll make a vassal of him, too....

GAWAIN

Late morning and Gawain was standing near the pier watching the army of broken-down fighters, peasants and serfs filing into the first ship. The air was soupy, misty and heavy with wet salt. The overcast was smooth and solid.

They were emptying wagonloads of supplies they'd accumulated on the long march from the West Coast. They'd recruited most of the survivors in this town who were nearly all seamen.

The idea was, once all the ships were full, they'd sail up the coast following the map North.

He was less convinced than ever. But what were his options? Stay in a doomed country, fighting to feed himself...wander back to spend a little more time as a bodyguard to a female innkeeper who was sweet to him; but for how long?

Still, it was his best option, because of the sweetness, and he might have taken it...except for Shinqua. She and a spiky fate had turned the once casually brutal knight into an embittered romantic, and a desperate dreamer.

There's no chance there's a Grail at the end of that red-haired whore's map, he thought, *or that I'll be healed....without her it doesn't matter anyway...since I'll never have her again, I might as well die trying...call it entertainment....*

He touched the hurt side of his face with the good hand, as if to check if it were still the same. He always did that. Felt the bone through the cowl.

How did I live? He wondered. Wished he hadn't but wasn't sure he meant it, because something in him never entirely despaired. *Were God truly God, then mayhap it fits some purpose beyond my ken....*

That was another thing: until the injury he thought no more about God than grammar.

As he strolled away from the waterfront, wrapped in his cowled robe, he indulged his favorite fantasy (the old Gawain drank, ate, fought, fucked and rarely even dreamt while asleep) which had him finding the Cup of Christ and baptizing himself with Holy Water and the Blood of the Lord so that the power of He who had raised the dead restored the flesh and bone of his ruined head and, then, riding like the wind to Shinqua and repossessing her. She wouldn't have changed; it would be as if no time passed.

Tapped his wooden hand against his leg where the long chainmail dress-like coat hung to his knees. Grunted to himself to break the spell of his own unwonted imagination.

Went back past where most of the followers had encamped. The area stank of sweat, bad meat, dead dogs, and the excremental stench the westerly breeze eased down from the shallow latrine pits they'd dug just beyond the last hut.

Following the road up onto the rise just beyond the village, he stopped and looked back: the ships in the bay were shadows in the mist; the one at the pier was a flat outline; the huts were soft-looking and even the ragged people were blurred into a smooth gentility.

Hoof beats were approaching on the flinty road surface. A single rider on a heavy horse, he noted.

Could be a knight, he thought, listening for tell-tale sounds of metal.

He watched the big, heavy billows of gray softly flow across the strip of road. Sure enough, a gray armored figure on a lightly armored horse seemed to float up larger and larger into semi-solidity.

Automatically, Gawain loosed his sword in its scabbard. Then, as the curtain of fog drew thin, he saw an extra pair of arms and for a moment imagined a monster or demon approached as four-armed knights were rare, he assumed. Smiled, realizing they were riding double.

Fifty more feet and the bulky, solid riders reined up. He studied the helmetless, bushy-haired young man (looked familiar to him) who tilted his face down to speak:

"Are you one of the world's saviors?" he asked.

Jane slipped down from the saddle and stretched.

"I know your face, young knight," Gawain said.

"I don't see yours," Lohengrin responded from the saddle.

The girl Jane, was stretching her legs and looking over the village at the ships.

"You don't want to," Gawain told him.

"He's one of the leaders," she said. "They call him Gawain."

Lohengrin nodded.

"You know my father," he said, getting down easily and touching the pommel of his sword. "You saw him recently. We may have to fight."

Gawain grunted.

"You don't want to fight me either," he said. "Who is your father?"

"Sir Fool. Remember him?"

"Ah. I did see him. Is he well?"

The darkly fierce-faced son shrugged.

"I know not and care less," he said.

"There is bad blood between you and your father?" Jane asked.

"From his appearance," mused Gawain, "there appears little blood between them." She looked a question.

"Which might explain some things," Gawain considered.

"Is this Paradise, have we arrived?" Lohengrin wanted to know. "Are we now preserved from the end of the world?"

Gawain laughed. He liked this boy. Reminded him of himself past: precociously cynical, ready to kill at a blink.

"Did you two fuck on the way?" he asked. The girl's expression told him. "That's Paradise enough."

"Is there anything to what she's told me?" Lohengrin asked.

"About love?" Gawain wondered.

Scoffs.

"No. About the great seer who will save us all."

Gawain laughed.

"That's good, boy. The great seer is good." He tapped his wooden hand against his mailed side again. "There's a map a dry sort of woman brought to us and is supposed to show the way to God's Chalice and some puissant greatness or other. A fair script for the Miracle Players."

There's new work for me, he thought. *I'm ready for the traveling stage...I can reveal the two faces of Man to applauding morons.....*

"By sailing the sea?" Lohengrin was a little uneasy about that. He had no special love of water. He could just make out the blurry activities at the long wharf as the mists ebbed and filled.

Gawain shrugged.

"You may be my good luck charm, boy," the older man said. "Son of the Grail-finder himself."

Jane squeezed Lohengrin's arm.

"I have to pee," she said. "I'll rejoin you."

"Nay," he said, "I'll go with you."

LOHENGRIN

He walked the horse more or less into the village near the undergrowth where they'd dug the latrines. Gawain ambled behind at a little distance.

Partway there was a smell of roasting meat. Smoke mixed with the fog.

"That's what we need," he told her.

Then a voice:

"Lohengrin, ay!"

Out of the smoke and fog, holding a leg of some meat or other, chewing, came Hal.

Lohengrin was happy to see him. Laughed.

"Good Christ," he said. "You're eating."

"I found my way here," he said. "I met these pilgrims on the road. I thought you might be dead." Took a bite and chewed words. "None I met knew the way home."

"You joined these characters?"

"They seem to know their purpose," Hal replied, offering the meat vaguely to Jane and Lohengrin. "Are you hungry?" He smiled at the girl.

"My name is Jane," she informed him.

"I am Hal," he said, awkwardly holding the meatbone extended.

"Hal the Hungry," Lohengrin laughed. "Let's go sit and have at it."

He watched him watching the girl. He kept offering the food which she finally took as they walked toward the fire.

"Thank you, sir," she said.

Lohengrin was amused.

"Do you know how hard that was for him?"

"What?" she wondered.

"To give up food." To Hal: "You must be love-struck."

The solid, blond young Saxon blushed and muttered, uncomfortably:

"Nonsense, nonsense," he said. "Be still, Lohengrin."

The fire made a kind of tent out of the mist. They sat down on the sandy soil. Gawain watched from a few feet away, enjoying the exchange.

"He's shy," Lohengrin said, fishing a piece of roast meat from the flames with a charred stick. "But be not fooled: he's a mad lover."

"Be you still, I say," Hal snapped.

Lohengrin was partly facing Gawain who was leaning on a tree, looking at Jane and thinking about Shinqua.

Here I stand, he thought, *in an ordinary place with ordinary people...these are not the days of the Bible in the Holy Land where prophets rubbed against saints in the marketplace...no miracles save that I refuse to murder myself despite all sensible encouragement...and here in a poisoned land these three children sit filled with heat and hope and the same desperate need that aches in me...they may drink from that sweet cup...while I cannot...and surely never will, despite the stupid hopes that bubble up in me....*

Lohengrin saw him clench his fist and slam it into his thigh hard enough (it seemed) to break the bone through the chainmail.

"Angry at your leg, Sir Gawain?" he called over.

"Ha, ha," the knight said. "Think you so?"

The younger man stood up, chewing the meat on the stick, and stepped over to Gawain and said to him:

"I know you're a man of sense."

"You know this?"

Lohengrin shrugged and took another bite, bushy eyebrows rocking up and down slightly as he chewed and spoke through his food. Wiped his mouth with the back of his hand.

"Compared to these others I've been meeting, I have high hopes for you."

The older man was amused.

"You have, just now, arrived in the land of the truly senseless," he said. "Prepare thyself for wonders of undreamt idiocy."

Lohengrin liked the idea, the same way he enjoyed acrimony. He was trying to get wider impressions.

"What have you seen yourself," he asked, "of the spreading doom they talk about? I've been only in the North."

Gawain cocked his eye at the young man who was trying to see what he looked like in the shadow of his hood. He couldn't see much, just a hint of a disturbing, too sudden ending of the left side of his face.

"They say," he said, "the South is very bad." Gawain thought about it. "There were no armies in the field. The sun shone. Rain fell. Yet plague spreads and rivers fill with foulness. I've seen this...crops withering...stinking pits forming in clean fields...."

"All unnatural?"

Gawain shrugged.

"Mayhap," he replied. "At least no natural cause I can detect."

"We were nearly taken in an ambush, some miles back."

"Were there many?"

"I had a feeling there were more."

"Soldiers? Brigands? Norse?"

"Looked like nasty little men from the Holy Land."

Gawain grunted.

"We'd better set a watch," he said. "What know you of the Holy Land, boy?"

"Pictures in my father's books. He reads like a monk when home. A rare event."

"You ought respect him more," said Gawain.

"You may do it for me, so please you." Frowned. "Yet I understand him a little better. He wants to flee everything and when he cannot he reads himself away."

"I understand I am as mad and silly as he ever was. You should respect him. I care little enough for the Church but some sayings are sound. Honor Thy father and mother."

Lohengrin sucked for marrow in the bone.

"Now both of them?" he responded. "One is burden."

Flipped the bone into the mist.

The young man took this in. Then glanced over at where Jane and Hal were in close conversation. Hal, he noted, held a chunk of bread in his hand and yet neglected to eat it.

Wonderful, he thought. *A new appetite grows within him...one he'll never satisfy....*

"Meseems," said Gawain, "your lady is beset. Her castle is besieged."

Lohengrin shrugged. He absolutely didn't care. Was amused. He believed he'd never really care about such things. He liked the pleasure, would burn for that, yes, but for the rest...there was no rest....

He studied others to judge their soft and hard places...even to seem more like them. A kind of actor. He loved his skill above all and next wanted to have his way when he wished.

"She defends but weakly," he commented.

Like my unhappy mother....

Gawain studied him even more closely.

"Nay, she is yours. I was like you, lad,' he said. "I cared but for profit...pleasure...and victories - had no more romance in me than a Moor's monkey."

"And now?"

Gawain shrugged.

"Look at them," he said, indicating the couple by the fire. "He longs for her."

Lohengrin shrugged.

"Save I entertain myself by dropping trees across his path," he said, "he'll soon find satisfaction, I think." Narrowed his eyes. "I care not a fart for fame. Profit to me is strength to bid others act as I ask. Above all else I love victory."

The older man put his good right hand on the younger's shoulder. Turned him face-to-face.

"Feel you this living hand?" he asked.

"I must." Lohengrin shrugged again. "As you grip me with it."

"Life longs for life. And he longs for her. Do you see?"

The young man was uncomfortable. Was Gawain cracked?

"I suppose so. He longs for her, as you say."

Up came the wooden hand. The hard, spiky, flexless fingers digging into the bare flesh just below his neck.

"Which touch do you prefer, son of Parsival?"

Lohengrin took both wrists in his hands as if to consider the question: felt the big bone and the yield of flesh and sinew; the smooth, round, hard wood.

"What is your sense, Sir?" he asked.

"I long as he longs. If you never know this, you will never taste life. Do what you will."

"I must long? Should I force myself?"

He kept his grip on the two forearms. The long, thick fingers closed tighter around his shoulder blade and he winced.

"Be not like my wooden hand, boy," the knight almost snarled.

"I see," Lohengrin said, resisting the vise-like pain.

Gawain snorted, furious.

"You see no better than the eye in my ass," he said.

He jerked his hands away.

"What do-"

But Gawain cut him off:

"I am forever sliced away from all I long for, boy. Like an old man cut off by age alone from a love that seizes him too late and can never be." He raised his wooden hand to his face and hooked the carved fingers under the cowl. "A hopeless longing. Out of season. Pointless." His breath hissed in and out. "Be not like my wooden hand."

"Yes," said Lohengrin, wincing under the grip. "I see."

Gawain released him and at the same moment pulled back the cowl and showed his face.

"No," he said. "*Now* you see."

He did. He blinked both eyes a couple of times and then Gawain covered his face again. Lohengrin knew better than to even comment on the ruined features.

"Gawain, I cannot make myself feel what I do not." He was annoyed with himself for trying to explain or apologize.

"No, you cannot," the famous knight said. "But it will come to you too late."

The young man kept seeing the afterimage of that sliced head: the exposed teeth, the halved left eye, the chipped jaw, the missing ear and planed temple; the almost beautiful right side.

"So," Lohengrin said, "you long to be healed."

Gawain shook his head.

"I cannot be healed."

Lohengrin looked back at Hal and Jane by the fire. Jane was looking over at him and Gawain; really at *him*. Hal was watching her, trying to keep her attention, jealous of her focus - only Gawain read it.

"What then?" Lohengrin wondered. Gawain was already walking away from them, heading back towards the village. "What do you long for, Sir Gawain?"

The famous knight made no reply. Walked into the dense sea

mist. Melted away.

In this place, he considered, *a few steps away all are ghosts...like the Greek knight who went to the land of the dead to question shadows and got mist for reply....*

The young man just stood there, staring at the couple by the fire. Jane was smiling at him and saying something. Hal looked alert and uncomfortable and was still not eating.

What is it they feel? he asked himself, probing, thinking about Gawain too. He reviewed things he *had* felt: helplessly aching with need, as when the woman in the tent had him in thrall.; walking around with an uncontrollable erection under his codpiece, looking for a peasant girl or maybe just a shady bush to relieve himself behind; thinking about a woman he really wished he could fuck....*That must be longing....*Unless they meant the Chivalry and pure love people talked about, the worship of women. Some women.

He tried to imagine what that love was about: he loved his mother, he decided, because she was nice to him; his father frustrated and infuriated him so he certainly didn't love him and, anyway, he wasn't a woman.

Frowning and annoyed, he went back to the fire and sat down next to Jane, facing his friend.

"What's wrong?" she asked.

He shook his head. Looked at Hal.

"Do you long for her?" he wanted to know.

The stocky Saxon went bright red under his faded, wheat-colored hair.

"Lohengrin, you great ass!"

"I mean," the hook-nosed youth explained, "is there something you want more than fucking her?"

"What? What?"

Jane just sat there, misreading his meaning.

"Is there some feeling you-"

He was cut off as Hal dove across the fire, flailing his ham-sized fists as Lohengrin jerked back, taking a glancing blow that rocked the landscape and rolled him sidewise into Jane who was tying to embrace and protect him, crying out:

"Oh, my love, my love, you need not be jealous!" Holding him now so that Hal couldn't strike again. They were all tangled together.

Lohengrin looked up past her shoulder, feeling his cheek swell, dark eyes amused, saying:

"You long for blood, which I can understand."

Began laughing as Hal now struggled (in embarrassed outrage) to extricate himself from the unintended embrace they now all shared. Lohengrin gripped him by the upper arms, keeping him pressed against the girl who was trying to push free. Hal thrashing from side to side, the three of them rolling over and over away from the fire across the gritty, weedy sand while Lohengrin, trying to stay on top and pin Hal, laughing and saying, gasping:

"I long...for you both...I have you...love is...triumphant...."

"Diseased madman!" cried Hal. "Unnatural...."

Lohengrin lost his position and went over again, saying laughing, as Hal finally broke free:

"Your wish is granted...why do you flee?"

And Jane:

"Are you hurt, my love? Are you hurt?"

He just lay there now, on his back, Jane in his arms, watching Hal melting away into the mists, not-quite-running. She looked at the lump on his face and kissed it, gently.

"Now," he said, "I have experienced love-longing. At least, I've borne witness to it."

And she, tenderly caressing his bruise:

"My poor love. Oh, my poor love."

MIMUJIN

He retracked back down the long valley. He was thinking about the woman riding the pale palfrey behind him. He wondered if he'd taken some kind of deadly bait. Maybe a witch, too. When they camped, he'd study her. Watch and wait. Question. He was sure his people, would not be deceived.....

His semi-amputated finger was throbbing again. He'd have to make a new poultice soon or risk fever. Frowned, grunted, felt uneasy, impatient. His simple plan to follow and kill already had a knot tied in it. Rubbed his divided nose.

Let his pony drift back until he rode beside her. She didn't attract him, much; he preferred the dark, angled jet eyes and goldish skin of his own women. Her body was rounded and friendly-looking; face pale, lips thin, nose long and edged (he thought) like a blade.

She waited for him to speak first. Her pale eyes were like shallow, grayish water. She wore a rough, gray, shift-like dress, traveling cloak and shoes that resembled half-boots.

"Witch," he said, "my people no believe word of woman."

"I am no true witch, barbarian, sir. My powers are small."

"Hmm. Bad for you. What you tell my people?"

"What Queen Morgana bade me."

"Queen. Ho, ho. What tell?"

"To follow me to the Channel sea, there to join her."

"Bah. Me spit. And what more?"

She looked away from him, staring down the long valley to where the low hills blurred away into grayish haze and fog. The clouds were like a dull wall to the east.

"I know not. Save that from there we will discover the sacred place where the Great King waits."

"*Hooooa. Mn.* Great King. Great King. We see. We see." Muttered in his own (she thought) foul tongue.

LAYLA

They'd been on the road all day and this time, after a meal break, they simply kept on, under a full moon that rose blood-red and then gradually faded to a pale copper. The land stayed flat and she thought, towards midnight, when they finally called a halt, she could smell the sea.

Because she'd tried to escape during the sex ceremony the night before, she'd been forced to walk after the meal. Her ankles were swollen and she wanted only to sleep. The plump girl was still her watchdog and shook her shoulder when she lay down and rolled herself up in a blanket on the grass.

"No sleeping," the girl said.

"Fine, no sleeping."

"You have been called to confess."

"Called?"

"Yes," she almost snarled. "The leader favors you." Her envy was open. "I cannot see why."

"He favors me. What happens were I on his bad side?"

She winced with a sudden abdominal cramp. She vaguely hoped it was her moon blood come round at last. She liked to think this a false pregnancy.

She stared up at the reddish moon, eyes a little blurry so it was a featureless hole in the night, like a dull ember.

"I don't doubt but you'll find that out," the girl said.

She kept her unfocused eyes on the moon: an eye, she imagined, of dull fire. Maybe an omen of the year 999. Maybe nothing at all....

A little later she was called. There was no fire this time. She was walked into the center of the camp and made to face his divine roundness with others, the faithful, in a loose circle around them. They were all chanting something that sounded to her like children imitating frogs.

Brroackbrroackbrroa, she thought.

The chief amphibian came close to her, pale and bulbous under the dulled moon, his loincloth like a shadow under his belly.

If he touches me I'll pop out his frog eyes....

She liked the image. She decided their true goal was to return to some far-off swampy pond where no one would notice or even care if the world did end.

"You know," she said, unbidden, more or less to the spiritual fatness before her, "I went down the hill to visit the wise crone and since then I've been continually abducted. I've grown sick of it. I'm ready to kill and maim. I want my husband to join me for the first time in years. You know how desperate I must be?"

"You'll need no husband," he told her. "You are the bride now of holiness."

"I need my husband to cut you all into fine pieces. He does it so well you'd have to admire him."

"Foolish woman, kneel before the spirit."

She was gripped on both sides by the girl and a skinny, harsh-fingered man and forced to her knees on the stony ground.

"If you pull your frog cod from your frogpiece," she said, "I promise I'll bite it off and spit it back at you."

Her remarks (as usual) were lost on the armorer's daughter and ignored by the leader.

"You," he boomed, suddenly and she now believed his neck really puffed out as he spoke or croaked, "are guilty of the sin of pride and self-love?"

The question voice was back.

"Am I?"

"Silence!" he blew at her. "Confess your sins?"

Standing above her his sleek roundness loomed. She was afraid he might fall on her. She imagined the suffocating mass of his puffy flesh plugging her mouth and nose.

"I confess," she cried, furious, disgusted, "that I slew one of your brothers, not a fortnight past."

"What? What?"

"As he was hopping back to the stream my mare trod him under to a pulp."

"Trod? Trod who?"

"Your bloat green brother."

"I have no brother?"

"Then have I much offended a blameless creature???"

He looked straight down at her over his belly. The plump girl and the skinny man shook her in outrage. She'd had enough by now. Of everything.

She flailed her right elbow into the girl's thick throat and sent her gasping onto her back. She wasn't able to hurt the skinny, hard-handed man who kept his grip so she contented herself with leaning up and sinking her teeth into the leader's bellyfat. He screamed. She held on. The skinny man pounded her head. She held on.

The leader kept screaming and fell sidewise. She tasted his

blood. Fine. She bit harder and harder until her locked jaw ached. She barely felt the blows from the man or the others who ran over, yanking and strangling her until she was almost unconscious, mouth now full of blood and flesh, blows raining all over her and, as she fell into a dark pit with no bottom, she heard him still screaming....

PARSIVAL

Their horses secured in the bow of the longship, Parsival and Lego sat in the stern, backs to the gunwale, watching the fog billow and flow as the rowers rhythmically heaved the ship forward across the grain of the chop, the sail virtually useless at their present angle to the onshore wind. At times, the prow was almost invisible in the dense grayness.

"I hate the water," Lego was just saying.

"Can you swim?"

"Would it matter out here?"

Parsival nodded.

"Good point," he admitted.

"They mean to kill us once we get wherever we're going. How will we get there in any case, since we can't see a pecker length ahead?"

"Much depends on the pecker," the knight said, grinning. "Could be a difference of half a thumb. These fellows, I've been told, find their way at sea like hounds find a rabbit."

"You mean they smell their way? They smell ripe enough themselves."

The knight shrugged.

"They are quite sanguine," he said. "Anyway, we'll try to avoid being killed, if we can.'

"Yes, my Lord."

The wide, English-speaking Viking walked across the bouncing deck to them as if, Parsival thought, he strolled on a garden path.

"Well, Briton scum," he said, cheerfully, "we'll soon see, won't we?"

Parsival was getting tired of him. He cocked an eyebrow.

"I've refrained from killing you," he said, friendly, "but my mood is shifting."

"Brave words." They were on the leeward side so the man leaned up on the rail and urinated into the waves. Shook his stubby pecker when finished. "If you told us a wild tale," he remarked, "you'll find yerselves afloating home like the turds yer are." Chuckled.

"No," the knight said laconically, "more like we'll be alone on this craft hoping the wind blows fair."

"My Lord," said Lego, "Let's let the sailors sail, eh?" He was queasy and the thought of being alone on a ship in the foggy heavings of the North Sea stirred his stomach bile.

"He an't so dumb as seems," the Viking said.

"You don't sound like some Norser," Lego said, trying to be conversational.

"I growed up in Lincolnshire and was took by a raiding party when I was a lad. Raised as one of 'em. I am a Berserker, by Odin, an fear no man or divil."

"Well, then," said Lego. "Very good."

"I've known dogs that feared not wolves," said Parsival, "and died bravely."

He was looking into the mist ahead.

"My master here," Lego put in, "is more or less a Berserker himself, you might say."

As they moved up the Channel they were starting to pick up ocean swells which were getting to Lego. Everything was starting to slowly tip and spin and his stomach was responding. Parsival was generally unaffected. If asked, he might have quipped that he'd spent his whole life at sea, one way or another.

"What truth in your tale?" He sat up on the rail, holding a stay for balance. On board, he had no duty but to fight. "The great treasure ya bent the chief's brain with?"

Lego shrugged.

"There's the map," he said. Closed his eyes. That was worse. "Is it always this rough?"

The Berserker laughed.

"This be dead calm, landsman," he said. "Wait until we're in the Dragon Sea." Laughed again.

Lego said nothing. Sighed. Knew he'd soon vomit.

Parsival was enjoying the ride. He was tired of thinking and planning and fretting and frustration. The die was cast. No back-looking. The world was behind him again. Maybe for good this time. This was what his family disliked about him; but what choice was here? Who knew where his wife was.....probably home, he decided.

This has been forced on me...in any case, I meant to leave for good when I set out...I've been forced into armor...tricked by an unnatural defeat...that witch...I used to follow Merlinus' mystic pointings...I've consulted monks and wizards and fools and visions...and here we are entering the Northern sea of mystery and doom....

"What's your name?" he suddenly asked the Viking.

"They clept me Gralgrim, Briton. An you?"

"Sir Silly," he answered. "Once we land on the island I will show you what must amaze you."

"The amazement is our brave chief thinks ye'll lead him to the sacred land."

"He didn't mention that." Parsival was startled. How would they know that was the secret destination? Their fancy, no doubt: the pursuit of what-you-will mists shaped like what-you-will that they all pursued. "What sacred isle?"

Gralgrim rocked himself back and forth to balance the increasing push of the waves. Said:

"No one says tis an island or no. The land of Thule."

"I've heard of that," Lego started to say but at this point, a slow swell tilted the ship at a slightly steeper angle, and he gagged, clawed around and up the side, got his bilious head over and sprayed all within him into the gray sea.

"Pity the fish," roared Gralgrim, delighted.

MORGANA

Morgana, Modred and their entourage were now on the same road, a day after Mimujin and Alyal had passed. The sky was solid gray. The misty hills ahead were behind a solid curtain of fog.

The boy rode a black charger with a tendency to drool but had a gait so smooth the rider hardly rocked in the saddle. He wore one of the half-masks. His mother rode beside him.

"A castle boy spoke to me," he told her.

"And?"

"He said I could never be a true knight because I was trained by a woman. He said I -"

"This woman could defeat half-a-dozen true knights, at once," she responded.

"But he said I could not be knighted by a woman so -"

"You will be king and dub thyself." She looked around at her women. "We are not bound by forms."

"Aunt, where are we going? I don't like long rides."

"To meet your father."

Ahead was a wall of viscous gray.

"What about the king, mother?"

"Him too, my child as I say."

While the little tribesmen sought the lair of their dark lord she believed was Clinschor, they rode as far north as land permitted, staying close to the coast to avoid the highland Picts, if possible. Morgana didn't fear them, particularly, but why complicate things?

GAWAIN

He went back to the dock area. In the mists ahead, he made out the outline of the woman in the golden mask. She was on the beach in a backless wooden chair without arms, the type used in noble's tents.

The small waves were slapping the beach, unseen in the deep fog. She was alone. After his troubling conversation with Lohengrin he'd had to improve his blackened mood: his mood was improved, for now, by swigs from a stone wine jug. Was feeling the familiar tight alcohol heat suffusion.

He stood over her on the gritty sand. As the fog filled and thinned in the breeze, so at times he could only see her outline. She was facing the water and chose not to turn when he spoke.

"See much?" he asked.

"Yes. Much, indeed."

He stepped around and stood between her and the invisible surf.

Reached for the mask with his wooden hand, not quite touching it. She didn't react.

"You show me yours," he quipped. "I'll show you mine."

"What do you want, knight?"

She kept staring, more or less, at his midsection since she hadn't shifted her gaze when he stood in front of her.

He shrugged.

"Many things," he replied. "Right now, to see the truth."

"My visage is the truth?"

Shrugged again.

"Mayhap, a start," he said.

Now she looked into his hood. The mist seemed to fill it.

"I have no particular interest in seeing you clearly, sir," she said. "You make too much of yourself, I think."

Gawain nodded. He liked her, suddenly.

"Well said," he agreed. "Why are you leading these fools? I'd still like to see what you are hiding."

She looked away again.

"I may be dangerous," she said. "I might have some power to harm you."

He laughed.

"Excellent, my lady. What will you do? Shear my arm off? Cut my face in half?"

She took it in.

"You don't believe in the great goal," she said.

He cocked his head to the good side and lifted the cowl away, showing his absolutely handsome profile, rugged and chiseled. Where Parsival had a magnetic, head-turning attractiveness, his nose was too long, lips too thin and so on; Gawain was perfectly proportioned. Any actor would envy him - half of him, anyway.

Even the masked, stern woman was impressed.

"Well," she said, comprehensively. "Well."

"We'll marry then?" he asked. "Is it settled?"

She surprised him by chuckling. slightly.

"You wish to post banns?" she wondered.

He nodded, closing his hood again. Tilted up the jug.

"I'll get a left mask of silver," he declared, burping, "and we'll clash them together as I hump above you."

This time only her eyes showed amusement.

"I sit on men," she told him. "None top me, Sirrah.'

He nodded.

"I accept your terms, my Lady Mask." He dropped to one knee before her. "How long must I wait before I am sat upon?" he wanted to know. "I am all eagerness. A thirsty horse before water. A starving beggar outside a feast. A-"

Whatever was next was cut off by John of Bligh's arrival. He came up like a gout of fog spilling into small, nervous shape, already pacing before them as he said:

"You, lady, have joined my forces. As much as I respect your wisdom and dedication, yes, yes, because the cause is first and above all else, and-"

And she then cut him off as Gawain let himself sit down sidewise on the sand, chainmail surcoat scraping, enjoying the scene. He set the jug before him.

"You mean to complain," she said, "when you come around to your point, that I have ordered a new ritual to be observed."

John nodded, vigorously. As he paced he kept thinning and thickening.

"That's the way of women," she added in, "undermining a man."

"Exactly," John said, ignoring Gawain. "We must not confuse the people."

"Then," said Gawain, "you should fall permanently mute."

She was, he noted, amused again. He watched her eyes above the carved gold that hid the lower half of her face.

"These people, this army," John went on, "are the last hope of the world. Beyond this there is only-"

Again she cut him off:

"Save your speeches for the 'hope of the world,'" she advised. "Without the map and my guidance, there is no *hope* for any of you!"

She tilted her head up, eyes fierce. John quailed, slightly.

Gawain was delighted. The meadwine had floated him to humor.

"Yes, yes!" he cried. "The map! Don't forget the map! The map inscribed by the wisest Jew of all, great Solom himself! A guide to Heaven, Hell, and Purgatory between, I say. Ah, forget not the map that even Jesus Christ himself consulted ere he dared rise, with the angels, into his Father's shining Kingdom!"

Gawain was laughing so hard, now, that he toppled sidewise and was spitting sand from his mouth.

The map, he thought. *Ah, God's devise....but her mask...I must know...I think I'll possess her if she but have space even for a mandrake root between her legs...even if not, her bunghole alone would suffice for relief....*

"I love you, masked lady," he said, face parallel to the sand, "though you have no nose."

This actually distracted her from the confrontation (one-sided as it might be) with John. She looked down at Gawain.

"What stupid nonsense," she snapped at him. "Unlike you, dull knight, I have nose, lips, chin, both ears and all."

"I mean to marry her," he said to John and the sand and the fog, shaking with silent laughter. "I needed to know if she comes with a nose. Her slitted quim might be stopped or sewn closed...this could I work around...there are other paths or, better, doors to ecstasy. But, lacking a nose, why that's a hard detriment in a woman...or any other, if it comes to that....'

John looked around like a baffled sheep.

"What is all this senseless-"

Cut off, again:

"Be still," she snarled, this time. "I conceal my features to prevent the mad, hopeless love of mortal men from cluttering the path I must follow."

"I knew it," cried Gawain, rolling over on the sand that squeaked under his steel outside. "My future wife is a goddess!"

"Gawain, be still," John cried; then, to her: "We must confer together before deciding-"

And again:

"I do what must be done," she said, standing up and looming over him. Gawain was flat on his back now, hands locked behind his head, enjoying himself. "You are with me or not, as you please."

"Suppose, instead," John railed back, "I cut off your senseless head!"

She snapped out one lean arm and caught his neck in the long, spiky-nailed fingers. He gagged as she lifted him to his tiptoes, effortless, at arm's length, her strength amazing the knight. John flopped like a fish, blood running down into his chest.

"Listen," Gawain called over, "Show me just your nose, to settle my mind, and I swear I'll not drop before you. Surely the sight of your nose alone is not enough to-"

Now he was cut off, or, rather, had not even been listened to in the first place. He didn't care. He watched John strangle and thought how many times he'd almost served him thus.

She dropped him and he fell backwards, gasping, thrashing around, rolling towards the water and almost disappearing. She stood there, dramatically, holding her arm out straight before her, as if in salute to the unseen waves.

"Just two-thirds of your nose?" Gawain asked her. "I promise not to clutter."

She looked down at him. Her arm went back to her side. She shook her head. He knew she was still amused.

"Have you ever surrendered?" she wanted to know.

"Only to beauty."

Meanwhile John had regained his feet, standing, almost invisible, in the fog, raging. He croaked instead of shouting. Frustrated, he picked up something and hurled it at her - except it sailed in a curve and Gawain realized it was a clam shell.

"Traveling with you people," he said, sitting up, reaching for the jug, "is better than a king's troupe of entertainers."

LAYLA

She blinked and tried to resurface. Her head seemed to vibrate like a bell: light and dark flashed with each peal.

There was a roaring sound all around, that seemed like sea or wind; wild wind and voices or the crashing of mad flame and voices...screams...shouts...curses...clashing like smashed trees or voices...voices....

What asked her mind. *What?....*

And then blackness tolled again and she was gone under and away....

JOHN

Racing along the firm, damp sand where the small waves were just curling into foam, charging back towards the waterfront, mind shouting:

We sail at once! ... .At once...once...sail...

He felt all might be lost. Memories kept flashing back from his life, scattered, irrelevant: refusing to study knighthood when he was nine or ten, standing on a trough in the castle yard to face his father eye-to-eye, steady, chill rain coming straight down from a low, tin-colored autumnal sky, drenching them, his bowl haircut plastered flat while he jerked his 14 year-old hands in the air and yelled:

"I hate your life! I will be a priest!"

His father, laughing. His sister, Layla, watching. Both from the shelter of the tunnel-like passage to the gate. She was big-eyed, dark-haired, slim, supple, a few years younger with a quality of petulance crossed with depression. People thought she always looked trapped.

"The priests don't want you. Nobody wants you."

"The Church is corrupt and full of evil! All men are brothers in God yet men are enslaved and trodden down!"

The father looked around, waving his arms in the sheeting rain that blurred anything more than a few feet away as if a large audience were watching.

"See, see," he cried. "I have whelped a mad boy!"

Now, running into the nearly solid fog, other memories kept flashing, unbidden: a few years later, after joining a band of wandering monks who drove him away with stones and kicks when they tired of his trying to convince them to preach rebellion to the serfs and then lead them in a war to overthrow the nobles....befriending a mad hermit he'd discovered in a cave who said He was John the Baptist come again, the pair of them, in filthy rags marching into London Town (still called Lundenwic by some) spewing speeches and diverse prophecies and ending up dumped in a latrine pit from which they were rescued by several obese whores from a nearby stew; after washing John off with a bucket or two (the prophet having fled, terrorized, as someone quipped: "Back to Jerusalem") one dainty delight sat her two hundred plus pounds on him and ground away at his manhood in front of an approving crowd of local color until, red-faced, suffocating, begging, he finally managed to get, what another called, "a hanged man's stiff'un," and spent his seed to great public scorn and amusement....needless to say, this experience had left him more leery of sex than ever.

Suddenly he was splashing into the low tide, shallow water, absorbed in the vivid memories that kept opening before him, unaware that he'd slanted out into the bay and was aiming away from the dock area, seeing (as if reentering the past) the first time he strode into a village, bearded, digging a staff into the road, kicking up a reddish-yellow dust into the rich, summer-heavy air, already speaking to the peasants who were piling and binding early wheat in the square. He'd told them how they'd worked hard and their lord was going to take it for himself, as always, except, this time the people reacted, gathered around, stamped and shouted raw approval....Then they'd followed him, heading for the castle which (in what he took for a special providence) happened to have just been successfully assaulted and half-gutted by Clinschor's warriors. The dazed and wounded survivors fell easy victim to the furious mob who'd been doubly fortunate in that they had crossed the open fields missing the enemy who'd hurried off to their next target. After this they believed in John's special vision and power. The idea spread as they followed behind the raiding invaders like, some said, buzzards and wild dogs....

Now he went out with the ebbing tide, lost in memory-visions that he would only later suspect had been caused by the masked witch. He was following a long strand of damp sand, now, that humped out into the water like the back of a whale or some snake-like sea monster.

Because visibility was near nil, he believed he was following the shoreline near the ships when, in fact, he was running on an angle out to sea, still shouting commands to the followers he thought could actually hear him, voice croaking through his hurt windpipe:

"Cast off! Cast off! We sail at once!"

I'll need no map, his mind said. *God will guide me!*

Except the yelled words were lost in the fog and splashing of his frantic feet and came out sounding more like:

"Broak oak! Broak oak! Wroak ogg! Wroak ogg ogrog!"

GAWAIN

He stood up looking straight at her, the still, hard eyes above the mask, not really amused anymore. The mist whipped around them. He wobbled a little. The tight warmth within had dissipated. Nothing was funny, now.

"You are a delight to know," he remarked. "Most gentle."

"You want to hump me?" she asked, voice neutral. "Is this your pleasure, damaged knight?"

The idea was suddenly sour, unamusing. He shook the jug. Nothing. Tossed it into the shifting, seamless gray that was air and water. Heard the splash.

That bottle, he thought, *has a fairer chance than these mad dullards to reach the sacred goal....*

"What do you really mean to do with these people?" he responded.

"Lead them," she said, eyes showing nothing, "away from their troubles."

"To others worse? Or are you a saint?"

"Far from it."

"As far as reason from religion, I've no doubt. Aye, you act more like a pope. You'll rip out a windpipe to stop an argument."

She stepped closer to him and he waited for those deadly hands to move.

"Fear not," she assured him.

"I don't," he said. "Do what you must." He was wondering if he could rip the mask away before she could react. Doubted it.

"If I show you my face, Knight, you will never leave my service."

"Another *caveat*."

She began walking, slowly, parallel to the splashing surf. He kept pace with her.

Thought he heard John's voice somewhere out in the grayness. He understood she was seriously following some incomprehensible agenda.

"This world," she explained, "has been poisoned and is dying. We are going to a place that is safe."

"Safe. At long last."

"A woman will rule."

"A queen? You?"

She actually chuckled, this time. Took his arm and stopped him. He felt as if her very nearness was, somehow, tugging at him.

"You are better than a jester, Gawain," she said. "Morgana will rule, of course."

"Ah," he murmured, looking almost on a level into the hot blue eyes above the mask. "Arthur approves this?"

"He has deserted his people. He went to seek his dear Merlin. He despaired of ruling, tired of his slut wife and the failure and betrayal of his knights."

"I certainly failed," said Gawain. "I deserted the court for love of darkness. I lost my face and my dark love."

She was tugging at him, without touching. It might have been sexual but he wasn't aroused. They stood there, sealed in the fog without reference of direction or mark of time as if their feet pressed the undefined soil early in creation's first week.

"That is well-known," she commented. "Arthur always forgave love, did he not?"

"It cost him. It cost me...." Grinned with what lips he had. "To lose yourself for love of squat Lancelot with his monkey-long arms. Women have a power to overlook faults past conceiving."

"Else a bony, hairy, crude and awkward beast like thyself would have found few beds to revel in."

She brought her face closer, as if to kiss him. He touched the mask's cool chin.

"These lively lips allure me," he told her, trying to move the mood.

"Be content that I save living flesh for last."

`"You leave things out," he said, as she started walking again. "There's more here."

Something lost in fog; dark and unformed. He followed her, a step behind.

"Of course," she agreed. "Much more."

LAYLA

She opened one eye. Nothing. Dull bright, blankness. Her first idea was that she was dead and in the grayness between worlds. She'd heard about that. Her next idea, blinking both eyes now and realizing she was lying face down with her cheek flat in the dirt, was that she'd been blinded. After that the headache closed in with steel fingers and she moaned and shut her eyes again. Must have passed out because the pain went away to be replaced by a dream, an image, anyway, a pale woman beautiful in her agony, naked in a huge, satiny bed, straining to give birth, a dragon's head emerging from her distended vagina, a clawed forelimb clutching at her thigh, blood spattered everywhere.

"Aiiii," cried Layla, coming to again, taking the spiky pain in her head and struggling to sit up, this time. And still the brightish gray closed in tight around — except she saw her arms and legs this time and knew she was not blind, just lost in dullness.

Sitting up, she realized she hadn't gone anywhere. Remembered the attack, the blows. Touched the swellings and dried blood.

"Holy Mary," she said.

She saw nothing but the sealing fog — then a bare leg, flat on the ground, poking toward her. She strained her aching head and came up with fragments: small, brownish, oily-looking little men dancing, darting, slashing and stabbing, rolling over the believers and their fat leader who'd bolted. She had a flash of him barreling through followers and attackers alike, bouncing, leaping, rolling and shouting in his croak voice....

She had a sense everyone was dead or gone. Silence. She'd, obviously, been passed over because she was already down.

Which way? She asked herself, thinking getting to her feet. *Or does it matter?* Since she had no idea where she might be. *At least no one's going to see me coming or going...maybe I won't be ambushed for a change....*

She stood up. Reeled from the pain.

"Aii," she sighed. "Sweet Mary, I pray my skull's not cracked."

Touched her temples, felt lumps, caked blood. Sighed again.

You don't need a map when there's nowhere to go....

Made herself move, stumble, walk. The circle of blankness kept pace with her. Then she tripped over a headless man's out-flung arm and staggered, then stepped on a girl's hand and stopped. The girl was on her back, too close for the mist to blur much. Her mouth was open and there was a hole where her heart should have been. It was obvious when Layla looked into the gaping cavity. A poet might have made something of it but it was too horrible for her.

She kept going and stopped looking down. The impenetrable darkness stayed closed around her. A poet might have liked that too.

MIMUJIN

Mimujin found the two he followed had ridden straight east along the main road. They'd come out of the low, green, forested hills by sunset onto the flatlands and marshes that stretched, unbroken to the coast.

The sunset was a violet grayness behind them when he stopped to camp. The mists had closed in. The little killer made no effort to light a fire. On the march his people washed down dried food with water, rolled up and slept (as was said) in their own stink; the young woman gathered some wood and leaves, took two flat stones from her kit, struck them gently and almost at once had flame.

He was impressed where he sat, ripping at a strip of dried meat and sucking at a leather of water.

"Witchery?" he asked, in English, assuming she didn't speak his tongue.

"No. Good firestones."

"Fire call bugs and enemies."

She gestured around.

"Fog," she said, "hide us."

She took out her own food: traveler's bread and hard cheese. He pointed south.

"My people that way," he told her. He laughed inwardly because he had kept his agreement with Morgana and showed her the way. "How you find?"

She chuckled

"Oh, assure thyself, I find. I find.'

He nodded.

"Witchery," he grunted.

"If you like. What you understand not, you name ill."

"Eh?"

He was now sure she was bait. Why? To distract him? How could she find his tribesmen? Absurd. A lone female in fog and trackless ways.

"You think I have powers as my mistress hath?" she asked him.

"Eh? Womens talk, water splash. Make sound, no sense."

She very clever, he thought. *Can trick a man. When she sleeps, kill her. She not go to my people, she is dog set to follow me....*

"As you say," she responded, sipping scented, herbed liquor from a silver flask. It was a Druidic concoction: a burst of strength and soothing. "I'll leave you on the morrow."

"That good," he said.

To follow from behind...you will leave, witch woman and go where no path leads back....

MORGANA

She'd turned north and led her group towards the coast leagues above where Parsival and Lego had met the Viking raiders. They'd pitched their tents on the stony beach at the base of the cliffs that overlooked the Channel Sea.

Modred was sick with the green runs. He lay on his pallet in the tent, held his belly and groaned; then he'd jump up and run outside, crying, and squat where the choppy waves broke, sighing, gasping while his Morgana looked on.

The fog had closed in all around, wet, muffling.

"Ohahhh," he cried, the small waves splashing his pale behind.

"Peace, my boy. The potion I gave you will soon bind thy innards."

He staggered to his feet and she helped him adjust his linen breeks around his waist after wiping him with a piece of rag she then tossed into the water.

"You need to clean yourself better," she said.

He groaned and staggered back to the tent. The baby surf broke steadily. She leaned into the wind, listening to the unseen sea, the mist streaming around her, melting and reforming her outline as if she were an exhalation of the billowing vagueness.

"Come inside," he whined.

"A moment," she said impatient, dismissive.

There's the wind, she thought. *There's the wind...it is time...time....*

SHINQUA

I do not care how long it has been, she said to herself. *I do not care what stupid things are said to me....*

She was thinking, as she stretched out on the soft pile of rolled bedding in the back of the cart full of food and possessions she'd packed quietly for days.

The moon was just rising, fat and reddish-yellow. The wheels rolled softly in the deep dust and loam of the pretty smooth road that led east away from the castle. The big glow silhouetted the driver who sat solid, wide, hunched and uneasy at the reins. He kept glancing behind without being able to quite see her, dark clothes and face blending.

Just her eyes and teeth, sometimes, he said to himself. *Can't tell what she's thinking....*In a few hours his wife would know; her husband and the lord too. What a mistake this was. *I had no more than a squeeze on the hand and a kiss on me cheek....*

Remembered the kiss, the wild, sweet scent of her flesh and hair that had left him giddy as she moved back before his arms reacted and came up to hold her.

They were now climbing a shallow slope out of the utter darkness of the valley woods. She propped her bare feet above her head and tilted back, looking at the massed stars, enveloped in the thick, warm summer air.

He twisted back to look at her again. The moonlight only hinted her high cheekbones and deep-set eyes. He'd been smitten and his wife already knew it.

"How sweet is that black whore," she inquired, "that you'd carry a bucket of mule shit for her?"

His wife was small, round and freckled. They'd been working in the stables where he was the lord's Master of Horse, a position about equivalent to Shinqua's husband, the armorer. Valued vassals, social equals – except the African girl's undoing of the great Gawain gave her a kind of legendary status and few friends.

"I did no such thing," he'd answered. Not that it made any difference. He'd helped her clean off droppings from one of his mules that had heaped on the path to her dooryard. While they lived on the castle grounds, both families held land in the village and had what amounted to "summer huts" there with lush flower and herb gardens and serf-farmers to tend the crops. They'd become personally friendly, after that and his wife hadn't missed it.

"Are you alright?" he found himself asking her, half-twisted to try and see her as the cart rocked softly, aware of her scent again.

"Yes, Wilfred," she replied.

He will expect it, she thought. *Like others….*

She knew she'd handle it later. When the time came. She'd ease him past it or, at worst, reward him with a little favor. She curled and uncurled her toes and sighed, relaxing back. Her children would be fine with her mother and sister-in-law. She had no concern there. Later, with her hero, she'd return for them.

Shinqua had little fear. She was strong, confident and had been trained in dagger fighting by her husband and improved by Gawain.

He'd been delighted to discover she could really fight. He taught her to use two blades together and once watched while she stood off a pair of men-at-arms in an inn yard where they'd gone together for a secret night upstairs. She'd driven them back through the gate, blade in each hand, having stabbed and sliced them more than once. "We saw their heels, that even," he always liked to say, afterwards, laughing.

She was remembering him, lost in the stars, still a young woman, still dreaming.

Now, on the reverse slope, they started down into the wide valley that led towards Camelot, the first place to look. Wilfred started. There was a fog below and ahead that seemed as wide and deep as the sea. The risen moon gleamed mysteriously on the surface which lay about 100 feet downslope.

"It's a spell," he said, blurted in sudden guilt,

"What?" she asked, happy with the stars and thinking how stupid the stories were people told about Gawain being crippled.

Jealous lies, she thought.

"To keep us here," he went on.

She looked at him now. Set her mouth.

"Nothing will keep us here," she told him.

She sat up and looked at the silvery mass that lapped like soft surf at the hillsides.

"But see," he insisted.

She knelt herself up next to him, knees on a lump of cloth. Touched his arm with her long, strong, delicate fingers.

"Go on," she said, quietly, allowing him nothing.

"We'll be lost, woman."

"Stay on the road," she said, "and go on."

PARSIVAL

Parsival had dozed, not long after sundown. The last thing he heard as he went under was Lego trying to vomit again for the fiftieth time. When he woke up, it was pitch black and the ship was tilting wildly. Worse, he could barely distinguish the nearest torch in the chill, massed fog.

This was supposed to have cleared, he thought, *according to these experts....*

Lego lay, huddled, by the thwart, half-sleeping, groaning. Parsival listened to the steady bump and scrape of the oars, as the steersman kept the prow angled into the breaking seas. He couldn't see the rowers.

Poor Lego, he thought. Smiled, as he lay back down and tried to get comfortable again. Smiled because this was what he should have expected: just tossed out into the ocean like dice. *Small wonder I don't plan much....*He suddenly had more confidence in the outcome. *Blind and lost, surrounded by enemies, how can I possibly fail?*

"Sail on," he said into the puffing, unsteady, salt-laden wind. "What matters where?"

LAYLA

Eventually there were no more bodies. Her best idea was to not circle. Since there was just enough vague glow in the sky to show where the sun was, she aimed herself roughly north.

Her feet had hardened. She was used to walking, now. She'd been overloaded emotionally so she was effectively relaxed. She still had the sack of food they'd made her carry.

So she rested, ate, went on into the blankness, passing scrubby trees that suddenly seemed to reach at her as if the fog were animate and angry. Several times it started to lift, literally like a curtain rising and she could see wheatgrass, trees, rocks, the gradual slope of the terrain and a sudden brightening which gave her a little hope until it dropped again.

No bird sang that she heard; glimpsed a lone hare that vanished at once; passed deer tracks....

The grade made it easy and she went on until after dark since she couldn't see anyway. She walked into a few trees and tripped a few times before finding a clump of bushes that gave some shelter and settled down for the night.

Asleep, she didn't even dream. Kept waking up and then there was only the damp, lumpy, soft earth...only darkness pressed into her face...going in and out...then waking up, seeing the stars, the fog clinging close to the ground...dozed again and then the even, bright, filtered blankness was back.

She felt the fog was, somehow, like the flood of Noah. She got up, did what she had to do, vomited, as usual, then ate and drank...went on....

"Dear God," she prayed, kneeling. "I confess my sins. I wish not this babe I carry yet I must preserve it if I can. I ask Thee to preserve me despite my most grievous sins."

She rose and went on. North - more or less; locked in her little circle of sight, scared and trapped...went on....

LOHENGRIN

Hal had been gone for awhile and the fog had closed in around Jane and Lohengrin. The fire was crumbling into embers. The banked sand was comfortable and he stretched out with her still on top of him.

She was nuzzling his neck and sighing. In a reflex he was already tugging her loose dress up and running one hand between her legs. Went with it as she sighed and hissed how she loved him.

He let himself get lost in her mouth, shocking sleekness, softness, salty-sweet. Enjoyed the play of her hands down where it mattered. She kept repeating that she loved him.

Her legs came open, loving him, and he found his way between them. It was just that. No great thing, practically automatic. If she'd rolled the other way nothing would have happened. Her passionate whispers might have had no words at all.

He was rocking into her now and her leg came up around him....

HAL

Locked into his little cell of grayness he'd stormed back almost to the dock before stopping, more embarrassed than angry. He felt ridiculous. Rubbed his face and paced around in a small circle, as if the fog actually bounded him physically.

"I shouldn't let his jibes sting me," he murmured. Kept murmuring as his mood and purpose shifted. "I looked a fool...yet, I think she was well pleased with me up to that point...." Kept seeing her face when they'd be talking alone; she seemed interested in asking him questions. The trouble was the questions were about Lohengrin, pretty much. Yet, he'd felt she'd liked him. "It were mere politeness...." He went back and forth with that for awhile. Didn't resolve it. Didn't want to. "We but just met." But then, he'd heard true love was instant, needing no time to grow. "But Lohengrin...could she care for such a...such a...silly fellow?" Went back and forth on that. "She can see I'm stout of heart and not silly...." There was hope.

In any case, I must go back and apologize for my temper, baited as I was by that sharp-tongued Jack....

He turned with sudden resolve and headed back the way he'd come, more or less. He was already planning a speech. He pictured her (with unaccustomed imagination) listening carefully as he explained his emotions, gradually building to the force of his love for her. Heard himself saying:

"I love you, Jane."

Suddenly he was walking into the water. Stopped and listened for voices, looked around as if he'd be able to actually see the fire. Knit his brows.

Should have paid more attention, he thought. *This cursed fog seems unnatural...why did I leave home to wander with that damned, silly....*Couldn't find the noun for Lohengrin. *Save, then I would not have met her....*

It gave him pleasure to say her name.

"Jane."

Tried a new tack, slanting up the beach, concentrating, listening, staring into the cup of blankness that kept pace around him.

He drifted up as far as the road, finding nothing but a pair of goats tethered to a bush; zig-zagged down and nearly walked into a latrine pit the size of a small pond; coming upwind he really hadn't smelled it.

Circled and cursed and sweated: crisscrossed the area until he suddenly heard sounds...voices. He turned, very close now, the wind softly billowing the cloudy stuff around him.

Was it Jane? Heard groaning and gasping and then they were suddenly within his little capsule of mist and he thought she was being attacked, seeing the bare legs kicking and struggling, a wide-shouldered man with his tights tugged down, on top of her as he, still rushing forward, about to rip him away, then, seeing her face as she groaned and sighed:

"Ahh...oh...ahhh, Lohengrin...Oh my love...ahhhh!"

Skidded, twisted at the last moment, stomach sinking from embarrassment, hurt while at the same moment, furious, wanting to kick, cut, kill...anything to release the conflicting energies within him.

Lohengrin, arching back in orgasm, glimpsed the big, shadowy form as Hal actually jumped over them, fell and rolled across the sand back into the blanking fog...rolled, got up, ran, tripped...up again...running, fleeing the actual sound of her voice because he was downwind and still heard her and (now that he knew what it was) each sound stabbed into him.

So he ran in his little gray hole, snapping through, rebounding off thin scraggly trees and brittle bushes, plunging inland, sucking wind and keening under his breath, a sound that might have suggested a hurt dog and a sobbing woman...running, falling into blindness across a treeless field, suddenly following a narrow, sluggish, muddy stream, twisting with it into gray nowhere. Miserable, lost, heart (he believed) torn forever, chasing on into emptiness, having now been in love only once....

LOHENGRIN

Having spent himself inside her, he withdrew and rolled aside onto his back mere moments after Hal had leaped past. He felt that good flow relaxing from deep within himself.

Jane, not finished, rolled back into him, clamping her thighs around his near knee and began rocking, squeezing, gasping.

He peered around, uneasy, wondering who or what had plunged past them.

This is all fine, he thought, *but I can't linger among these weird idiots...Should I bring her? Have to find Henry and soothe him....*

Smiled, remembering the mad struggle over her. His face still throbbed where he'd been hit. Looked down at her rubbing on his leg. Felt nothing in particular. Wondered, vaguely, why it was taking her so long. Remembered other females he'd been with. Drew no conclusions; then, suddenly, a mental image of the red-haired witch woman who'd held him in some kind of thrall.

No, he thought, violently, *that was a dream…I was poisoned….*Sex that went on and on in a dimness that existed without day or night…no true sleep or waking….

Stared around at the gray air.

"Are things well with you?" he asked Jane.

She sighed. Leaned up and kissed him fiercely. When she was done, he said:

"I think you should fuck poor Hal."

"Hn?" she responded, dreamily.

"Poor fellow, he's altogether in love with you."

"Who? In love?"

"Hal. Your defender."

She looked at him, blinked.

"I should what?"

He grinned, scratching his head, the tight, jet-black curls.

"What you will," he said. "Do you like him?"

She climbed up over him, face inches away.

"I love you," she told him, again. Her breath was warm, silky, scented with sex and the crisped fat from their meal. He liked it. "Am I a slut in an inn? I love *you.*"

"You keep telling me that," he said, getting ready to get up.

"And you feel nothing?"

"Nothing?" he reacted, puzzled. "Nay, Jane, I feel many things. I feel you here. The sand. The foul fog upon me."

She studied him, inches from his curved nose that would have suited a Persian lord.

"I see," she said. "But not love."

MIMUJIN

He was furious: the girl had slipped away during the night. When he woke up there was nothing but fog, closed in, it seemed, inches from his nose.

*She follow horse tracks and I cannot see her….*Contemplated setting a trap. *Bah, let her follow….*

Then on the kind of impulse he was famed for he suddenly spun around and charged back along the trail, thick, wet fog cloying around him.

The hoofprints were clear on the softened earth. He backtracked at a sprint for about fifty yards. No sign of her. Stopped, stood still as stone. Watched and sniffed the air for her perfumed scent.

"Where you hide?" he raged. "Foul witch!" Drew his curved sword, in frustration, and slashed at the dull grayness. "I kill and eat you heart!"

By noon he could hear and smell seawater; kept halting to listen; no sign she was behind him.

He could tell by the tracks he was gaining on the two riders, now following the same gradually descending cliffline that Parsival and Lego had ridden down to the beach where they'd met the Vikings.

MORGANA

She still stood at the water's edge, hair and robe whipping in the freshening seawind. Two assistants stood with her. One was short, pretty, round-faced and strong in a tunic-like outfit; the other silver-haired, long and lean with a face like an axehead.

"Feel the wind, old mother?" asked Morgana.

"Yes, sweet one."

"Where we go," Morgana went on, as she cocked her head, "magic will bounce back on the user."

"Do we now take ship?" asked the round-faced girl.

"No, sweet sister," answered the sorceress. "A distance north we shall cross the sea and never leave the land."

HAL

Walking now, somewhere out in the damp silence of a field without bush or tree, following the turgid waterflow upstream along the mucky stream's edge.

All he could see, eyes open or shut, was roiling mist reflected in the water's dull surface and, in the mist, her pale, sweetly shaped bare legs pumping over Lohengrin's broad back as he plowed into her to take his pleasure....

Eventually he just stopped, sat down and let himself be miserable. Sat in a tent of mist. Started talking to himself about what had happened. He didn't realize he was thinking out loud.

"She's not of any quality," he said, "to allow herself like that....." The image of being in Lohengrin's place made it worse. "Disgusting!" he yelled.

LAYLA

Except she wasn't going north anymore. In the mist, the tilts of the ground had sent her into a wide, vague circle. She heard something off to her left...listened...blurred and muffled...a man's voice raised almost to a shout. No answering words.

She let herself drift that way. Even the company of yet another madman might improve on utter solitude. Maybe he could tell directions.

A shout, then silence when she was pretty close. Maybe he was dangerous? She stopped, listened. Heard sobbing. Followed the tears, the broken voice....

JOHN

Was slowing, suddenly up to his knees in gathering waves and realizing he was too far out.

"Cursed bitch!" he croaked in fury and fear. It hurt his throat.

Stopped. Looked around. Panic stirred. The universal clinging chill mist flowed over him and ten feet of visibility was a lot.

Which way? Which way? Which way? his mind asked.

"Where it's shallow," he muttered.

Suddenly he wasn't concerned with the follower or the cause; just wanted to get back. He normally didn't dwell on things past because he'd disciplined himself to think only of the world to come as if imagination itself would solidify his dreams. He wanted to train his followers to forget all that had been. Plough it under. He'd wondered if the witch might know herbs to empty their memories so they could be taught like infants. He'd shared some of his ideas with Gawain who barely resisted cutting off his head to still his mouth.

He knew many thought him mad but (he'd decided) even madness belonged to yesterday with no assurance yesterday's lunatic would remain insane tomorrow.

Still, now, he found pictures from the past coming back...he minced carefully along and tried not to see the images his mind painted on the roiling grayness....Long, long ago, barely out of childhood he saw, again, the bower of yellow and blue flowers and herbs and red berrybushes that his mother had doted on...a sunny morning...his father, the Duke, in his favorite, velvet-cushioned chair the servants had carried out from the castle, his younger sister looking pale and troubled, standing a little apart...his father shaking his head....

He was always like that, he thought, angry as well as scared, now. *As deaf to truth as all these doomed fools.....*

Except doom had closed around him, chill gray and impenetrable.

The scene was vivid and he couldn't push it away: his father toyed with his pointy beard while John yelled and kicked the earth. His sister was in love with some silly boy knight who'd arrived the day before. Young Layla was always in love with someone. He was a priest, then. He'd predicted she'd turn out a whore. At that time he'd just come to believe that all the dogmas of the church needed to be ploughed under by a free peasantry. He'd left home after this argument so he never learned that her lover had been 16 year old Parsival on his opening adventure....

"I have heard all the arguments. When have I stinted on saint's days?" his father had rhetorically asked. John hadn't really listened. His sister was standing under a trellised arch, sagging with roses. She was still, pale and lean, watching them. His father kept talking. "...my serfs are content. Should the mule drive the farmer to market?" He sipped wine from a goblet, staining his white beard. A hovering page dabbed at it with a napkin.

His father said more; his intense son barely followed it, though his tongue found answers enough. He kept watching Layla whom he rarely saw. They argued on; he kept looking at her as if the rich light and shadow had revealed something he couldn't frame in words but sensed as dark, lost, tragic....

All this in a flash of memory...remembered leaving the castle, storming down the road furious, shouting, tearing his vestments off and tossing them into the fields, cursing family, nobility, the Church, stripping down to his loincloth, shouting to man and God that he would find a sword of flame and carve the world into a new shape....

"*Gladius Dei, super terram,*" he'd cried. Sword of God over the earth.

As if he were still fleeing he plunged ahead and was suddenly over his head and swimming.

"Ahiii!" he screamed.

Flailed the water. He was a rotten swimmer. The tide and undertow had him. He was going out to sea. He was, as a Viking might say, on his way to the kingdom of the fish....

LOHENGRIN

He stood up. He felt good, looking down at Jane who adjusted herself and followed suit. He sensed she believed she was bound to him now. He felt a kind of unaccustomed tenderness but, then, the boy loved horses, dogs, and falcons.

"Let's not go to the stupid ships and dim idiots," he declared. "Let's go somewhere else."

"Where?"

He wet his finger and held it in the air.

"As the wind blows," he told her. "I will get back to *my* map." Rolled his head around, stretching.

"*You* have a map? Of what, dear one?"

He smiled at the "dear one." Sort of liked it.

"My father once found a great treasure. Lost it, of course. I mean to find and keep it both." Shrugged, facing the wind that was steady from the sea, now, streaming the heavy mist past as if they were moving forward into the future's inscrutable gray. "I set out with Henry but we got blown off course." Shrugged. "Come," he said, holding out his hand. "Dear." Grinned. He was thinking about having sex with her, again. Later...then the next day. Maybe that was love.

"The way the wind blows," she said.

Looked at her face and liked it.

"Let's find poor Hal. Kiss and make him smile. Better yet, feed him and his gut will digest his heart."

PARSIVAL

Fat, heavy wet snowflakes were slapping into his face as he woke from a doze-dream of a flat, bright-green field with a golden tent in the middle that he kept running for but couldn't reach as the shimmering silk pavilion seemed to shrink and recede.

He sputtered and wiped his eyes. The helmsman was still braced into the tiller. The flames in the sconces hissed and stuttered; the sail rattled and creaked. The Viking Briton was crosslegged on a bench, drinking from an asymmetrical cup.

"Snow?" Parsival called over. "In summer?"

"Hah," uttered the stonehard-looking Berserker. "Do ya fancy we be runnin' south to land of monkey-trees an dark women?"

"Where then, fellow?"

Gralgrim shrugged.

"We follow your course, Briton." He spat with the wind, braced against the vessel's roll and pounding.

Suddenly the longship heeled violently as a massive gust punched them hard from dead astern. The ship ploughed forward, up and over, suddenly riding following waves.

"Ho," cried the Viking, "Thor's wind! The god's favor."

Lego rolled his starey, lost eyes, clutching the thwart.

"Favor?" he wondered, raged. "Favor?"

Parsival braced himself as the hull vibrated and they slid, accelerated. The crew was already struggling to get the oars in the water and shorten sail: the mast creaked, cloth crackled...they scudded, faster and faster. The wind was an immense, throbbing roar.

Parsival shouted to Gralgrim the Berserker from about a foot away.

"The favor increases!"

The Viking twisted around.

"Un?' he wondered.

A cresting wave, almost mast-high, curled over the stern, instantly flooding the deck. The ship pitched wildly. Men shouted and tumbled.

Parse easily held on the side with just one of his abnormally strong hands. The ill Lego yelled:

"Is this an adventure, lord?"

"No," he shouted back. "A disaster."

The oarsmen struggled to find a rhythm; the next wave slammed over them. Parse hung from the uptipped side, then went under the cold thick water as they violently dipped. A cow went past, rolling, eyes popping, silent, over into the pounding greenish darkness, followed by bales of hay, broken wood, a Norse helmet...then they righted again and the rowers got a little purchase; managed to hang on the crest of a mountain-wave, surfing forward, barely rocking now.

Lego crept up and huddled beside his lord, shivering as they rushed through a strange silence...a steady roaring that sucked away all other sound into a dreamlike hush....

MORGANA

They hurried north up the coastline, fog swirling and drawing around as the wind at their backs shoved them unevenly forward. Morgana led them, enjoying the cooling wild air, the scything, scattered bursts of rain.

They followed a Roman road which ended, suddenly, at a man-high stone wall. They rode beside along it towards the Channel Sea. It abruptly ended in a crumble of bricks and they continued north within sound of the waves, now. The fog had finally blown to shreds in the shifting, slanting, weakening rainfall.

"Ride the wind," she called back to them. "Fear it not!"

She had no ideas, now, no memories, an emptiness gazing out from herself so that the force and power of the wind filled her and she was floating on it. She let herself fly forward. That was the power of her power. She didn't want sex, love, wealth, or worldly pomp. Only, maybe, Merlinus understood her need.

So she flew forward, ahead of herself and her horse the way you might in a dream and looked at her destination: a roughly heart-shaped island surrounded by surf that heaved chunks of ice onto a grim, gritty beach...at the same time she was rocking, gusting forward on the horse....

If you're there, Merlin, she said to herself, *you'll not block me....*

MIMUJIN

There were too many tracks: hoofprints, footprints, as if a small army had passed. The fog was so dense he had no idea of direction. Instead of blundering on, he stopped and watched the diffuse, graying glow that showed where the sun was arcing south and west. He waited for it to move a few degrees, to be sure, then pointed his pony almost dead east. He rode until the two tracks he wanted separated out.

Grunted with satisfaction. He'd calculated well.

Finding you I will, he said to himself. *Finding you soon....*

He was riding, steadily, nodding in semi-doze, imagining a sweet scene: Parsival and Lego nailed side-by-side, upside down, to a tree while Mimujin, with a dull, notched knife stripped off their skin, reveling in the unspeakable pain, urinating in their contorted, swollen faces...roasting the bloody strips of flesh and sucking on the crispy treats....

He dreamt of these and other delights the way a lover might dwell on the sweet sights and scents of passion.

About then the aberrant wind from the south (that was driving the Viking ships madly north and pushing Morgana and her party up the coastline) hit him so hard he nearly went over his mount's shoulder. The gray vapor billowed wildly and seemed semi-solid.

He was instantly driven at right angles to his course and tried to force his pony to tack back except the terrified beast backed and charged along with the gale. Sticks and bits of vegetation flashed by, appearing and disappearing in the fog mass.

"Witch work," he snarled, kicking hard. "Foul betrayer."

PARSIVAL

The longship was finished, caught from behind by a tremendous sea, it pitchpoled, bow going under, the weight of the wave shoving the stern up and over, spilling everything and everyone on board into the freezing, wild water.

As Parsival went in, he was holding both Lego and Gralgrim the Viking by their respective leather collars. In a survival reflex he clutched them as if they were buoyant, and saved both without realizing it because he kicked up the back of a monster wave, just starting to feel the actual artic shock as they sledded down the face like surf-riders...rushing on...then, suddenly, in a welter of ice...suddenly out of the fog, there was a beach of dark, stony sand and they slammed into it as the surf crumbled, rolling, gasping, blinded....

He kept his grip and started dragging them both up the raspy beach, falling, twisting ...going under...ice chopping into them....

They staggered out of the undertow as the waves drained back. Parsival dragged Lego clear and got well up the gritty, dark, ice-flecked sand until they dropped, gasping and shivering....

This could be the place I saw, he thought.

Lego was shaking hard, gagging seawater, cut and bruised from the harsh shore.

"Hah," he gasped. "The damn land is rocking...by Saint Paul's piles...unnn...nothing left to puke up..."

"He has," said Parsival, indicating Gralgrim who was on his hands and knees, shadowy in the billowing mist, coughing and vomiting. They all were shivering violently.

Stay here and we die, the knight thought, getting up.

"Fire and shelter," he said, over the wind and surfsmashing. Kicked Gralgrim lightly on his butt end as they passed him. "Follow along, mighty master of the sea. I think we've come to Viking heaven."

SHINQUA

The second night away they had been camped in a dell under a dulled moon that hung, nearly full, above the fog. The heavy air barely stirred. The fire was dim and smoky a vague glow on the forest floor beside the road.

He shifted himself closer to her.

"Shinqua, I must go back."

"Leave me here?" She'd been waiting for something like this. "What manner of man does that?"

"A man with duties...at the manor....A man with...."

He drank in her face from closer, now, in the subtle, almost sourceless gleaming, those smooth, rounded matchless features. She could feel him react, the catch in his breath. She thought his pale, bony face improved in the gentle blurriness.

She was back against a tree bole. Raised one bare foot and ran it along his cheek and neck. He stayed very still. He might have been breathing.

"Duties?" she wondered, softly. "Really? Duties?"

He didn't move at all, saying:

"I am not some knight free to ride here and there."

Her toes nibbled, a little at his ear.

"You are a responsible fellow," she agreed. "I am a poor, unfortunate woman from a far land."

He cleared his throat, staying very still.

"Well," he began. "I am no brainless knight...I...."

She brushed his cheek, again. He lightly rested his fingers on her instep.

"Come a little way more with me," she suggested.

'Ah...I...."

"Yes?"

Held her ankle and knelt himself forward between her legs in the loose dress that had fallen away from her long, amazing thighs. He seemed giddy, gasped and fumbled with his codpiece, almost trembling with welling need.

"Sweet creature," he almost gasped.

"Sweet dark magic," she amended, not resisting. "So I am told. Duty has you in its grip, seemingly."

"Ah, sweet...sweet...."

"Yet, not tonight," she told him.

"Nay, nay," he said, cried, humping himself up onto her lap. "Ahhhh, my dear black ewe."

"Nay, nay, my white ram, not tonight. We must travel on still, by moon and mist."

"Nay, nay...."

And then he stopped, codpiece popped free and dangling, all his heat instantly chilled because he knew that the cool, flat metal suddenly resting along his testicles was a dagger blade. He recalled what he'd heard about her deadly skill. He nodded and took a long, deep breath.

"Aye," he agreed. "As you say, sweet...Chinqua. Aye...."

"As I say." She was amused by his gaffe. "I, *Shinqua*."

In the diffused moonglow her smile was a clean shock of whiteness.

So on into the massed fog as the moon was a blurry, general roundness overhead; a soft subtle glow which left them just shadows, vague stains floating into muffled vagueness.

While his wife's face set in scorn and fury was clear in his mind, the dagger blade gleamed just as vividly....

GAWAIN

He and the masked lady or witch were now riding side-by-side along the inland road through the same strange fog that seemed to cover a huge section of the coastal country as if the solid earth itself were heatlessly smoldering. The wind had faded quickly as they moved from the coast.

"What about your followers?" Gawain wondered. "Did you leave them the map?" Didn't quite chuckle.

"I left them the priest. He'll lead them to where we meant to go."

"And where are *we* meant to go?" He rubbed his good cheek with his real hand. "A love nest?"

"You really know no fear," she commented, "do you?"

He tapped his helmet where it hung from one side of the saddle (his shield on the other) with his knuckles.

"At this point," he said, peering into the featureless dullness before them, still masses that barely now stirred as they rode with the unseen dawn at their backs. "At this point I live only for fancies so absurd...what could be done to me that might worsen my lot, save, maybe, a too-long life?"

"I can think of things."

"You, who lead into obscurity as if your unseen nose were a lodestone."

"Still on my nose."

"I mean if in truth you have one." Except it wasn't that funny anymore. The mood was all fog which threw him back into himself – not his favorite place. "Though I'm not sure I care, where are we bound?"

"As you don't care. As you hope to be healed."

"Healed."

"You are a great knight." She aimed her mount with her knees like a man. "Who would have expected to find you? There is a great king under the world. Pay him homage and you may be more than healed."

"Healed."

"Believe this, O knight, were you but content even as you are, you would be whole again."

"Were I content."

Moving on, at a walk, the little circle of gray blur moved with them as they went (so far as he could tell) directly into nowhere.

LOHENGRIN AND JANE

"Halll!" he yelled into the dull, stifling mists. His voice fell flat and died. "Youuuu! Hallll!"

Moving inland the wind fell off east and weakened. Jane had her own horse, this time, riding a few feet behind and beside him. The wet mist trailed from her like a fairy robe. Lohengrin had found the beast tethered near the beach.

Cruel to leave an animal like this, he'd said to himself.

"You call to the lost," she said.

"Hal is...well, I brought him hence."

"You might as well call to yourself."

"I know not whence I go?"

"If I'm to be lost," she told him, shrugging, "I'm content to be lost with you."

"You're only lost if you have a destination," he reflected, peering at the featureless screen of billows. "So said my deep-thinking father, once."

"Do you really hate so....?"

"So many reasons," he cut her short. "Like waves on the shore, as one dies another rises behind. Yet...I'm not sure I hate...my father wastes his gifts. Lets everything slip through his hands...so I inherit, his only son, mind you, as if I were the bottom name on an entail." Shook his head. "He's here...he's there...he's nowhere. He...he might have been a great lord...instead he merely kills well."

"Yet they say he is a kindly man."

"Who says? Tale-tellers? Bah. I can find what he failed. I have the map in my mind."

"Maybe better to be lost," said she. "I weary of map-talk."

"When I met you," he commented, grinning, "you were the handmaiden of the map-folk."

"I am a woman. Like the moon, we find beauty and delight in changing."

"I'm Mar's son. He must have topped my mother. I don't look like him, anyway."

"Mars?"

"My father."

"Topped," she said, with a quiet, sighing hum.

"You'll wear me thin," he told her. "I need assistance. Hal! Halll!" he cried again and this time she giggled. "Oh fair and mighty Hal, come lend me thy rough vigor!"

The shouts fell dull and dead.

"Follow the map in your mind," she suggested. "As for me, I am but guided by love."

"And so are lost."

"No. With love I am always where I wish to be."

"Love." He stared at the nothingness. Had he but known it, he was, now, much like his father, long ago, struggling to grasp the obvious.

"You are finer than you think," she said, easing her mount close enough to touch his hand, bare below the steel sleeve, with her pale smooth fingers.

"I'll find my father's footprints and not fail as he did." He gestured with the other fist, glaring at the blankness ahead.

"The Grail is a sacred quest, they say, Lohengrin."

"Sacred?' he snorted. "Like love?"

PARSIVAL

The icy mist seethed in the steady, offshore wind.

"There were more of us," he murmured, remembering the vision or dream when he'd sailed high above what he believed was this place, the heart-shaped island.

"More?" grunted Lego, leaning back into the gusts.

Gralgrim spraddle-legged it along, now, semi-upright and, still spitting drool.

That fate again, that I have come to expect and will one day desert me and leave me in ruins, he thought. *That fate dropped us so close to shore you'd think it meant something...then, maybe, this Berserker and Lego and what all else mean something?*

Because his armor would have dragged him to doom. Water still dribbled out of the joints.

"What now?" Lego wondered.

"If I remember aright," said the knight, "not far ahead there's rock and twisted trees,"

"So you've been to heaven before, my Lord?"

"Nay. But I've seen it, notwithstanding."

"The map, then?"

Leaning back into the hard wind that blew them onshore, they reached the top of the beach in coils of streaming, chill smoke. Light snow and small hail whipped into them, clittering on their metal.

"Heaven, ya say?" growled Gralgrim.

"Mayhap you sinned, unknowing," suggested Lego, "and came wrong. What are Viking sins? Are there such?"

"Hah," snorted the Norseman, "Letting enemies live. Listening to lying foreigners. Foundering a longship."

"This can't be Viking Hell, in any case," Parsival decided, "or you'd be in better spirits."

"I lost me fucked ax," the Berserker pointed out. "There's a true sin."

Parsival and his captain's weapons were still at their belts. Lego tossed a two foot dagger to the Viking.

"Here," he grunted.

Gralgrim missed the catch, then scrabbled it up from the frozen sand.

"Arr," he emitted, "a toy for a woman to scrape her toenails."

"Better a short cock than no cock at all," said Lego.

Now among the black, wet rocks and stunted trees stiff with thorns and bristly leaves, the wind was somewhat broken up.

"Heaven," said Lego. "Full of wonders and ease." He huddled down in the shelter of a ragged wall of rock.

Shivering, Parsival went to the nearest tree, drew his sword and chopped branches.

Here's better use for it, he thought. *The world lost a great woodchopper when I went to head splitting....*

He chipped kindling and set up the fire.

"It'd take Merlinus to light that," he commented. He sensed or felt or just imagined the old wizard was close by. Somehow. "Merlin," he whispered, striking the flint from his leather waist bag, in the wet, clutching, icy draughts.

His fingers felt thick and numb, hands quivering as he struck and struck. Shut his eyes and kept striking....

"Good Christ," said Lego. "There's witchcraft."

"There's fire, anyway," said Gralgrim.

Because the flames caught and held, sucking and wisping left and right and around in the eddying wind.

Suppose all my actions really have meaning, the knight thought. *Tend to some purpose I but dimly grasp....*

"Thank you," he murmured, like a prayer.

Because he was here and it meant something....

LAYLA

The voice had stopped talking or crying or whatever so she paused to listen. Near her a single, twisted tree vaguely seemed to form and un-form as the mist wavered. Seemingly far away, directionless, she heard the muffled drumming of many hooves...or, maybe not....

"Most strange."

Am I dead her mind asked. *This seems no natural world...the land of ghosts...yet seem I solid...why dread death except to meet again, mayhap, the oafs and fools who plagued me while I lived....*

She walked, again, heading towards the scraggly trees, thinking about going to her cousin's in the midlands so if the baby proved real she might have and leave it there...ideas floated like mist....

"What an existence," she murmured.

Unless I'm dead, then, what a death....

She was hungry again. That could be the baby, alone. She didn't want to think. Layla never could help thinking too much about almost everything which (her mother once told her) made her need to drown things out. Which was why she liked honey wine so much, she supposed. She always kept a jug in her chamber and found reason to go there, from time-to-time, during the day. She told herself it was but the sweetness of it. Well, she wished she had some, now. The bitter ale of the Pilgrims of the map had been pretty unsatisfactory.

Now there was a voice, to her right. Stopped again. Maybe the little killers were upon her or survivors of the Map People. She wasn't sure which would be worse.

"Jane?" asked a male voice, closer, familiar. "Hullo? Be it Jane, I...."

"Greasy Jane from the kitchen?" wondered Layla. She knew the accent, close to her on. "Are you greasy Jack?"

Taking shape out of the wet smoke was Hal, wide face unnaturally pale and apprehensive. She recognized him at once except his normal ruddiness seemed faded.

"My lady," he said, amazed.

"I am relieved to meet a ghost I know, young Hal. But it worries me there may be more about."

"Ghosts? Think you I am a ghost, my lady?"

"What else, out here in nothingness?"

So like my life since I were wedded, she thought, automatically.

"I know not. Maybe we had come near each other. In any case, do ghosts hunger?"

"Well reasoned. It is said they suffer divers miseries.

"Do you have aught to eat, my lady?"

"I have ought," she informed him. "Where is my son? Is he among the vaporous souls?"

"Well," Hal allowed, sullenly, "I know not."

"A quarrel?"

"Well," he replied, shrugging heavily.

He seems changed...still dull, yet...a spark of something...time with my son could change anyone, I suppose....

"Is he safe?'

"In the arms of a fair maid," Hal muttered. "If that be safe."

Ah, she thought.

"A maid, say you?"

"Well, not so much a maid as I was raised to suppose."

"My son was raised, yet how he lowers himself."

Play what tune you like, she thought, *the dancer finds his own steps....*

"I'm very hungry," he said. "Which way do we go?"

"First, in my sack, take something to eat." She held it out. "Then we follow the straight road before us."

"I see no road," he pointed out, rooting in the bag.

"No surprise."

"You say things like your son says," he observed, chewing hard bread.

"Then pity one of us," she told him, starting to walk into the curtain of undulant blankness. "Come along, young Hal. We wander in nowhere, as my husband loves to do. You see, as someone said, long ago, you become the thing you dread and dislike, sooner or later."

GAWAIN AND THE LADY IN THE MASK

Gawain just sat there, as the impossibly dense gray flowed past. He reckoned they were heading southwest. He didn't know that the weather had cleared due west where Lohengrin and Jane headed.

"Do I get a reward for my adventure with you?" he suddenly wondered.

"Still you seek to top me?" she asked amused.

"Umh," he shrugged, verbally.

"Follow me and you may find a fair countenance, again.

"Another Grail to heal me." Smiled in his hood. "If I'm made fair why I'll return to darkness and you need never dread my love-longing."

"You came from darkness? Well, the womb is dark enough."

"Nay. I lost my darkness. I loved my darkness. I could not return to her. I'm a tragic fellow. Sometimes I grind my teeth in rage. Teeth that are ever bared. My emblem."

"You amuse yourself, at least."

He was suddenly distant and bored with it all. He didn't want to think about Shinqua.

I need to be drunk, he thought. *Been too long....*

"Have you wine about you?" he wondered. "Share it and I'll show you how I drink through the side of my face."

She took this in.

"I have none," she told him. "Yet be patient. Theirs is a liquor that heals."

"Dull talk enough," he muttered in disgust.

He decided the fog would have to lift, sometime. Back to the manor where she still lived. He was disguised. He would look at her, once more. Just look. Look at her children to see if one in some strange stripe or shade resembled him. He'd watch the way a ghost (which he believed he was) might return for a final moment and incommunicate farewell.

And then he'd make his way back to the coastal town and see if the innkeeper's wife would reopen her door and arms and legs, too. More than wine to get him to sleep at night was unnecessary. He felt less crazed.

Still, he thought, *there's no telling if I won't be mad again tomorrow....*

Just then he felt contained, without heat or self-pity. Rocked easily with the horse's gait, stretching good arm up and out to ease a crick in his shoulder.

Ride into nothingness without even hope to trouble me...beside a female who might have a dagger-blade between her legs where the sweet gate ought to be...stick it in her and I'd likely come out with a split prong to match my halved face....

He didn't quite laugh aloud. Into nothingness, a ghost without dream of future joys and conquests, like someone in the lengthening shadows of old age, no longer staring at far horizons he'd never reach...just eating, sleeping, aches and pains draining away into the inevitable, looming oblivion....

"Small wonder men seek the Grail," he said, feeling very deep and almost spiritual. He felt close to understanding some mystery: things that had troubled him little enough in the past.

Her voice seemed directionless, blurred by the dense atmosphere.

"Small wonder," she agreed. "Soon you may be changed and the world will mean nothing. No false questing. There will be no more world for you."

He grinned with the half of him that could.

"Small wonder," he responded. "So tell the featherless hawk he's done hunting." Shifted his rear around to relieve a pinch. "Who do you truly serve, lady?"

"I'll bring you there, to him," she promised. "This day's ride."

"I'm surprised you serve a mere man."

"More than a man. And you are fit to meet him and pledge thyself."

"I doubt it." Spat neatly out of the good side of his mouth, missing the cowl. "Have you really no jug? I thirst."

She rummaged in her slung bag and handed one over. He unstopped it and eagerly drank. Then nearly spit again.

"I've slain folk for less," he told her.

"We need water on a long ride," she said.

"Water is fit for fish. I'll suck mine from this cloying air."

She liked that. Returned to her point.

"You are well-seasoned," she said. "Sad and bitter enough to pledge to the true king. We go to his fortress. Enter and come out a dark god."

He chuckled, amused again.

"Every direction you take leads to madness," he concluded. "If we went south I ween you show me the trees that blossom into cooked meat." Laughed. "What say these journeys about poor Britain?"

LOHENGRIN – QUO VADIS

"Which way?" Jane asked, alongside him on her spare, bony mount.

Lohengrin watched the mist fold and unfold as they moved on at a walk.

"Some way," he said.

He was sure from the vague sunglow diffused behind them, that they were heading inland again.

"What does your map say?"

"No more maps. I follow what my mind's eye sees."

"Bare ladies and great glory?" she wondered archly.

"Nay," he corrected. "Power."

He smiled. She was looking at his hawk profile, dark and sullen against the ghostly backdrop. Her lips said: *I love you,* silently. She believed there was something hidden in him, locked behind the casual gate of his personality, young cynicism and edge of cool violence. She believed she could touch and warm him and, maybe, dull the edge of his gnawing fury.

He hath curly hair like a Moor, she noted. *Mayhap the dark blood runs in him...*

She imagined strange, blindingly hot tropic places where queer trees (she'd seen pictures in a copy of the gospels showing Adam and Eve in the garden) and amazing beasts where wild, dark peoples loved and hated with terrifying passion....

She wanted to stop again and open her soft places to him, take his keen edge into herself.

"It's foolish," she almost murmured, "to ride now. We needs must wait for this fell smoke to lift."

He smiled, slightly.

"Sweet one," he replied, "I imagine to myself that suppose it never does. That the world has forever changed. Now we are all creatures of the mist and so must learn, like babes, the ways of a new world."

"As in a dreaming," she said, impressed. "You thought this?"

"It's easy to invent with the mind," he told her. "Doing is harder. My father grows forests of nonsense from seeds of idle talk."

"Well, that knight has great fame, my love."

He slit his eyes as if seeing through the obscurity.

"I'll find in fact what he'll find in fancy," he said.

MORGANA ET AL

Now the mists of the land had flowed to meld with the fogs from the breaking, chill sea that, wind-wracked, crashed into the rocky northern coastline where no ship could beach or launch. The setting sun was a vague, rosy staining in the western blur.

At the end of what had to be a spit of land jutting way, way out into the North Atlantic, the party waited, even her restive son silent and still for the moment.

"We wait," Morgana said, "for my poison fang. He hath been well-sharpened."

The faded dark red went blue-black and then the vague, blurred silver where the unseen, nearly full moon rose opposite, hinted its glow into the mist.

"What of the little killers, my queen?" a half-masked woman asked.

"I have set them loose," was the reply. "They are a drop of poison in the tub of milk. "Soon all will curdle." She gestured one delicate, pale hand. "Terror will spread and when we return we will gather all these lands to ourselves." Looked up. "Ah, the fang comes."

Because the mist stirred the masked handmaiden shuddered a little, imagining she-knew-not-what hellish manifestation; except it was the small, lean, furious Mimujin on his shaggy pony trotting dourly out of the wall of faintly luminescent fog.

He reined up, eyes slit. Morgana gestured, all but her hand perfectly still on the motionless, pale horse, black robe seeming to gather the darkness into her so that everything else seemed slightly brighter.

"Your revenge," she told him, "is over this bridge. We will cross together."

"Bridge?" he wondered, fierce, abstractly desperate, tensed for a final (if futile) explosive effort to slash her throat.

"Come," she commanded, turning her mount and starting along the narrow strand of rocky land that went out and disappeared into the wind-ripped shrouding at right angles to the coastline where surf crumbled unseen and massive.

JOHN

Flailing the chill water, near the end of his strength, a shadow loomed over him like a wall. A ship. He shouted, beat the water, found his natural voice though each cry hurt:

"Here! Down here! This is a sign! I am saved! Triumph is at hand!"

Gasping, he forgot to paddle in his excitement and his head ducked under in a welter of sputtering. Resurfaced, sputtering yells, this time.

A long, pale, gap-toothed face (that resembled a chewed joint of beef) peered down.

"Pull me aboard!" John cried up at the face.

"It's himself," said the face. "What yer doin' down there, then?"

"A rope, you dolt!"

Another face, now, round and red.

""Drownin'," it opined, squint- eyed.

"Fools!"

"Eh?" responded joint-face.

"Help me…." Now bubbling and blowing as the ship-side drifted slowly past.

"If we haul him up," said red-round-face, "he'll go to makin' speeches again."

"Ah, that's so," said the other.

Next a woman peered down at the pale, frantic face in the dark water that kept going under as the hands gesticulated, the mouth yelling bubbles as it resurfaced.

"Yuh follered him this far," she pointed out.

"Aye," said, Round-face, "an see where we come."

Silence. John was just splashing, now, trying to keep pace with the drifting ship. Then a rope came looping down; he caught it desperately clutched. The faces withdrew as if enough had now been done.

So he was dragged alone, unable to climb to the high deck of the ponderous, top-heavy craft that resembled a kind of floating castle. Wood creaked and popped and groaned. There was no direction visible, ghostly hints of other aimless ships all around as he trailed near the stern at the end of the rope…soft splashes, voices of pilgrims and lookouts called and shouted, unseen…insubstantial…shades in some aquatic limbo…

PARSIVAL

Pieces of the vision kept flashing as they moved inland at chilly dawn. There was no visible sunrise, but after an hour or so, the mist thinned somewhat and their range of visibility increased. The landscape was bleak, sharp-edged, pale grayish with patches of ice and snow. The cold was deep and damp with a steady wind from the sea hustling them inland.

"Viking heaven," commented Lego.

His lord was pondering one of the remembered images.

"Up ahead," he announced, "there's little killers."

"My Lord?"

Parsival shrugged and gestured, vaguely.

"Visions," he explained. "Better in these situations to trust moonshine than common sense."

MORGANA ET AL

The tide had done something or else (as Mimujin believed) the witch had put a spell on the very sea so that a narrow, serpentine promontory had emerged before them, vanishing ahead as if melted by the sea-mist.

Modred was less ill, now, sitting straighter in the saddle. The mask on the lower half of his face made his voice tinny and dulled.

"Ah, Aunt," he said, "this is like unto the deed of the great magician 'Mose' in scripture."

"All forward," she commanded, in her own mask-voice. "You will claim your father's weapon since he cannot hide from me now. The Red Knight will be drawn to him and this little fang to the Red Knight." Gestured to the little killer.

Which was why she hadn't slain Parsival outside Camelot. She'd set him to attract King Arthur. She'd need Mimujin because (she believed) on the island that some called Avalon, her powers would be ordinary and leave her vulnerable to any of these enemies including the barbarian. She'd never intended to set foot on that soil. She meant to populate it with slaves and vassals under her son while then rest of Britain fell to her. Only Merlinus ever guessed her full ambition.

"And brother's weapon, too," said her eldest crony, amused.

Morgana didn't mind. Nodded, aiming her horse along the narrow, twisting way, massive waves dividing and crashing past on either side. The sea-spray stung.

"We are all brothers and sisters," she declared. "One way or another."

"Witch," Mimujin called out, keeping close to her where two horses could barely stay abreast, "Whatever doom coming, I strike you at the last. Death nothing to me."

Turned her half-masked face to him, voice metallic and wind-wrung.

"Nor are brains," she told him, very amused and a little annoyed. "And with a face like yours why live, in any case? Your nose alone...when you blow it, does snot pop out your misshapen ears?"

"Ha, ha," he responded. "When I cut throat I blow nose in you hair.'

"Witty retort," she said. She was thinking about Arthur, her brother and whatever.

You struck the flat of the great blade on a rock in your pique and it snapped like your failed prick when you heard of Guinevere's horizontal dance with fly-wit Lancelot and needed a new helm cut around your cuckold horns...you look a stag, now, repenting you slew neither whore nor knight you broke thy steel prick and flew to the lost land to have it made whole again...your flesh one would take ten Merlins to recreate....

"We'll have it," she said. "The true power."

"Mean you the Grail, mother, that all men seek in vain?"

"No," she explained. "Not that. We don't want that. That's best left forever lost."

SHINQUA

When she woke up under the tree in the mist-diffused, cool morning glow she was stretched-out on the rich softness of the pine needles. The tall, well-spaced trees blurred into grayish smoke. There was a faint pittering of rain in the great hush...then a birdcall, up high...a lyric trill...somewhere...brief....

The cart stood empty on the road, the mule unhitched, looped loosely to a tree trunk, nuzzling the weeds.

He is gone, she thought, not caring much. *That one was much scared of his woman...with reason....*

She felt relieved. At least he'd left the cart for her. And the foodsack, before padding off, noiseless on the pine-matted ground.

She relieved herself by a tree and rinsed her mouth from the waterskin and washed her face. She untangled her tight-curled hair and retied it in a high knot and thought about Gawain...her child...which way to go....

When I come to a stream I will wash my body, she thought. She hated feeling grubby and took particular care of herself. The hygiene was barbarous compared to her culture: she missed those baths, oils, soaps, perfumes...all of it. *What will he think when he sees me again? Mayhap he's found another spare black woman in this pale country who's stolen his heart....*

She softly laughed. The last other black face she'd seen had been at a tournament in London Town where her lord's son had fought. She'd seen her father, the Moorish Knight called Iron Heart, fight when she was very little. The watchers cheered as the men, with round shields and pointed helmets, dashed their swift, slim horses around each other. Close to where she stood clutching her mother's robe the horsemen came together on the sandy soil and she saw the tip of a spear crease her father's cheek, saw the blood and his wide, bright smile as he struck viciously back. She felt chill fear but didn't turn away. She never forgot that moment: the flash of his teeth, blood running like tears from under his eye, the glitter of brilliant, dry sunlight on the steel....

At the London Town tourney she'd chatted with a dark Saracen warrior and his saffron-skinned woman who were guests of some high-and-mighty. They'd asked her if she missed her people and she'd answered that it was all in what was familiar and, in any case, her memories were scars. The woman asked if she were content with her blocky, pink-skinned husband (who was not even a knight) or was there a true and noble lover somewhere? The woman loved romantic tales, it turned out. Why not? Shinqua had said nothing much but images from her childhood came back in fragments: pitching through blazing heat, white desert, high on a camel's back, the straw-musk reek of its hair, a man's iron-hard, leathery hands holding her virtually in her lap...his smell (still cloying in her memory) pungent and thick, oil and sweat, high-pitched laugh like a shout as he groped under her white robes plucking, stroking, scraping over her tender nine-year-old body...memories like scars...somebody saying "Now you are married, girl." Riding into the blue and white fire of the day in the terrifying embrace and shout-laughter of the man (husband) whose face she'd never dared look straight at, riding her out of the white-walled, blindingly bright town in the land known for exquisite women...riding, tilting along as people danced and called out stylized felicitations....Scars....

Not long after, she was taken by the Christian knights and ended somewhere in the unstable territories west of Turkey and was held in a great castle. She was about twelve. They baptized her at once. She became the prize of a knight with a partly slashed-off nose and squinty, runny eyes. His face was so reddened by bad skin and drink she feared to look at him. He brought her to his home in Brittany where she met a touring troupe of English jugglers and actors: the leader saw profit; she saw escape so went away hidden in a trick coffin with a false bottom they used for miracle plays. It was a great attraction to have a jet-black, beautiful infidel girl, with a long, narrow nose, on stage.

She toured Britain for two years and took only one lover, a young man-at arms who brought her home with him. He was killed in a combat concerning a point of what wasn't yet called heraldry, a matter (incomprehensible not only to her) about a raven on a crest. She saw him carried from the field, thigh shattered; later he died.

Eventually she'd married the armorer because she was already a Christian so none could oppose it. This was her life. It had been bad but might have been worse. She was a black Ruth among the alien corn and that was alright, too.

In fact, she'd been about to leave her girlchild in the hands of her in-laws and go on a holy pilgrimage (it had to be allowed) when the tedium of castle life was broken forever by the coming of Gawain.

This world, she thought, now, among the misty pines, *is either dull or painful....*

"I'll go on, anyway," she murmured. "Find Camelot. Find him."

Even a hopeless dream, she'd concluded, years before, is better than no dream at all.

PARSIVAL

It was true. The mist had thinned and there were grayish-green fields before them. Except the crisscrossing ravines hadn't been in the dream. It was a kind of maze of shallow and some deeper cuts.

As they went on straight they'd scramble down and stump up the other side of each one. This had to be one of those tests (he thought) as he tried to explain to Lego, where his actions cast exaggerated shadows.

"Christ Jesus," said Captain Lego, as they marched through this up-and-down landscape. "What a fine view, now."

They could see about 100 feet, for a change. Parsival had a feeling the intercuts were going to get deeper and closer together as they went along. It stood to unreason.

"Ho," uttered Gralgrim, "where is them as inhabit heaven here?"

"Hoo," responded Lego. "Where, indeed?"

Parsival was carefully scanning the periphery where the mist thickened.

"Don't doubt they're here," he suggested. Loosened his sword unconsciously, as they went down a steeper cut which bent out of sight, right and left, all wet earth and rock croppings. It was deeper than Parsival was tall and as they went up the far side he advised: "Spread apart, somewhat."

"Eh?' grunted Gralgrim.

"So they don't hit us the first time."

"Who?" asked the Viking.

"More dreams, lord?" wondered Lego.

"My nose," said the tall knight, shaking his head.

"I smell nothing much," said the Berserker.

They came up the far side of a steeper, trench-like cut. The next was fairly close ahead, as he'd expected. There was movement in the mist.

"Duck down," said Parsival as several little pointy helmets popped up as one and fired arrows almost point-blank.

As he and Lego fell flat, one zipped through the Viking's bushy hair. The knight realized he knew only one way to fight, being just stupid enough. He sighed and followed the other's mad, instant charge. Heard Lego grunt to his feet behind him.

The three were suddenly too-close as the little, eastern-looking fellows were re-nocking for a second shot so their next volley was weak, half-drawn and ragged. One had stuck about a quarter of an inch in the Berserker's massive forehead, flopping as (hissing in rage) he plunged among them, chopping and flailing viciously, smashing bows, flesh and bone with a gnarled broken tree limb he'd picked up. Scimitars flashed but too late as Parsival and Lego arrived and the survivors fled down the trench-like watercourse. One with a broken leg was trying to crawl away but Gralgrim cracked his head with a terrific downstroke.

The Berserker stood there, seemingly unaware of the arrow sticking in his skull. The knight plucked it out and a bright crease of blood ran down his snub nose and lost itself in the matted beard.

"Hoo," he commented, weighing his improvised club. Rubbed the wound as if it were a bee sting.

"Your good luck you were but struck in the head," said Lego, smiling. "And now you think this is your heaven?'

"Closer to the mark," agreed the Viking. "But where be the wenches?"

"Move on," said the knight and they went on down and up the other side, again and again as the number of intercut creases became more true ravines and they had to use hands and feet both to get up the steepening sides.

They were soon all panting. The mist stayed the same fifty to one hundred feet around them. No more little men popped up. It seemed more of a gesture than a real attempt to stop them.

They paused and stared ahead at the deceptively even ground surface. Parsival's image showed the heart-shaped island with the point straight ahead. But the terrain was becoming impossible. Reminded him of something long ago...a place in his youth where he was forced to twist into the grain of that country despite his best efforts to go on straight.

"We should go straight to the heart," he murmured.

"Heart a what?" wondered the Viking.

Parse peered in the now almost windless fog-curtains and shrugged.

"Heart of the same nothing I've come to know and relish," he said.

GAWAIN AND THE LADY IN THE MASK

It was as if something had been poured (something viscous and chill) that somehow set the fog in the shape of a ragged, many-turreted black fortress carved into the side of a cliff face; the same place Lohengrin apparently stumbled into during that great storm.

The ground cover thinned to the west where the landscape rolled green under bright blue sky. At the horizon spurs of dense forest showed dark, rich and clear. Was as if they'd come to the edge of a breaking sea of light.

The knight shook his head. His fancy suggested the shroud had, somehow, flowed from that forbidding structure, her goal.

Something is going to fix me there, he thought.

"No more amazements," he said. "Let us part where I have but half-known you as I have but half-seen you, being, myself, a half thing."

She shook *her* head.

"Are you half-witted, as well?" she asked. "Maybe half your brain was cut away. You are at freedom's gate."

"My luck is too weak," he replied, moving off, slowly, melting by degrees into the surrounding mists, "else my head entire would have been taken off. I have no ambitions. What point? What could any offer me? Riches? Power? Gross pleasures? I've had all. In the end I will die and have *no* face."

She stopped her mount and watched him as he rode out of the fog she still sat in. She was starting to fade behind the mist as he spoke back to her.

"You don't know what you're giving up, Sir Gawain," she told him.

"Nay, I know well. And I go to try once more to...what? Not live for...I but half-live. I go as a ghost come back to look one last time on what I loved and left. That's better said. Not to be just a simple, bloodstained villain riding, dick first, through all my lingering, dying days like all the bloodstained fools who went before me." The mist was closing, melting his dimensions as he slowly eased away. "Down the path of shadows to the last, wearing my yesterdays like a shroud, without leaving more than half a glory to my half a name. Farewell, witch who believes in something. In the end, all paths meet in darkness. Or in the windy raving of a village fool telling my story with violent emptiness." Blurring away now. "I go to view who I most loved in life. For I am, as I say, a ghost now." He felt remorse, longing, and (strangely) even hope. He didn't understand the hope. There was nothing to attach it to. But it lived in him, still, like a lost seed in bitter, winter soil. "I go to look my last."

The ground-clouds filled in behind him so when he looked back again she was a shape, a shadow...gone behind a dimming wash while he blinked in brightness....

He was a shape, a shadow...gone.

She nodded, strangely moved. *Unusual: a knight whose soul had bled within him.*

"I'll show you what's under my mask," she called into the abstract fog.

"Better to have half-known you, my lady," his muffled voice returned from the blankness.

"Farewell then, ghostly knight," she said. "Thou wilt return to the cold smoke. I doubt thou wilt find the solid world, again."

PARSIVAL

"It's as though we were already dead, in truth, good captain," Parsival said. "If we fail here I think we'll never leave."

"What?" responded Lego. "Are we cursed into death with without dying?"

"We are ever in two worlds, I think. We shut one out from the other."

The ravines were now too narrow, numerous and too deep. They started to move along the parallel path of least resistance. The dried blood had left a crease on Gralgrim's wide forehead. He brought up the rear.

"I've seen no game," he commented.

"Mayhap in heaven no food is needed," said Parsival, half-grinning..

"Tell that tale to me innards," scoffed the Viking.

The knight shrugged.

"This is no natural place," he said. "Or, if so, no natural time."

MORGANA

The unseen sea crashed along both sides of the rocky bar that twisted out into the wind and dense sea fog.

"Aunt?" called Modred over the tempest.

"My boy?"

"Where go we?"

She reached back and took his hand.

"Into a dream without sleep," she explained.

"Dream?" Mimujin, almost beside her on the narrow, wild way, cut by wind and flung water, leaned closer, split nose snorting air. "Think you sleeping in bed, eh, witch?"

"Fear nothing, my boy," she said. "If you die here you live on hereafter."

"Ah-ha," cried the little Mongol-like killer. "That good. Only one serve king live anyway."

"King?" asked the boy.

"Only king!" shouted Mimujin. "And I will bring him hearts to eat. Who know who heart?"

"Fear not him, either," said his mother.

"King Arthur?" The boy was uneasy.

"He no king," laughed Mimujin. "Maybe you see king, then know a thing."

Then a gust nearly spilled the three of them over the low but sheer side into certain, crashing death.

"We'll not end suchwise," she said, as if commanding someone.

SHINQUA

She was just sitting behind the mule, staring at the gray before her. The rutted track (that suggested a road the way a thread suggests a robe) blurred away into formlessness.

Which way woman? she asked herself. *No way, woman,* she answered. *Why do you still feel now what you felt so many years behind? Because you are a fool….*

She imagined faces in the sluggishly undulant shapes: the castle, the wide stream that fed the moat, dark, deep water swimming with gleams…a night when she'd first come to Britain and spoke less English (someone had said) than a magpie. She'd leaned over the bank and looked at her face in the twilit water where her eyes were like moon shimmer and her hue melted her features into the gathering night and she'd wondered if she and the white people were two sides of something that mattered or just one thing like the moon in light and shadow, shifting, changing but the same under the appearance….

She used to sings songs from her childhood…soft chants….she'd invent new ones trying to put sounds to her feelings that were long and sweet and true…the changing moonlight on the moving water….

Which way, you fool? Ah, I made him, my strange, sweet, cruel pale and pink faced knight into a song yet he was not a song no more than the light is the moon….Sing, girl-child, sing your dreams and yourself to sleep….

She stared ahead at the unrelenting whitish-gray, closing her in.

"Here's where you come to," she said.

LOHENGRIN

"Is there any point in just riding to nowhere?" Jane asked.

They were going down a gentle slope. The fog was worse, if anything.

"Why not?" he replied, rubbing his eyes which were losing focus from staring at blankness. "There's nothing here worth staying for." Stroked his tight-curled black hair, wet from condensation – as was everything else.

She sighed. It was unnerving. She supposed he was right but was saddle-weary. Closed her eyes, which didn't help. Glad she wasn't alone. This was like some nightmare; she didn't put it but felt it that way.

"I don't know," she said vaguely. "I suppose...."

"Anyway," he told her, "I come from Castle Nowhere. My father is Lord of Nowhere. As I will be someday, since I have no brothers."

"You say things, but...."

"I say I'm heir to nowhere. All you can see will be mine."

"And I, your lady?" she liked saying that.

"Lady Nothing. It may all be yours too."

He was grinning, not harshly, glad she was there. He glanced aside at her pale, thoughtful, fine-nosed profile and dark hair that had a little red in it.

"What I wish," she began. "Ah, well...I thought I wished to follow the Map...I thought...."

"I'll follow my horse, for now," he said. "Even nowhere may have an end."

PARSIVAL

"Don't assume we're in the world," he suggested to Lego. "Don't assume anything."

"Assume, my Lord?"

Gralgrim lagged behind, peering around, club over his shoulder, looking (all scraggly and muddy) thought Lego, a veritable troll with the dried crease of blood dividing his face in two.

"We could use a map in this foul place," the Viking declared, spitting, thoughtfully into the shadows at the bottom of the ravine which was now too steep and deep to cross.

"Are we on an island for certain?" wondered Lego.

"Don't assume it," replied the knight.

Where the fog drew back on the other side Parse could see the partly fallen wall and the grayish, weathered stones of the monastery (or its twin) where he'd stopped with Lego a blur and a time and a half ago. The huge metal door was standing open and he thought he glimpsed the same little monk with the round yet sharp-featured face who'd given him the strange wine that maybe was just drugged or maybe something magical....

"Look there," he said, pointing.

"Where?" asked Lego.

Parsival called to the monk as the fog closed down again.

"You! Is it you? Where is this place?"

They stopped and stared.

"I know not my Lord," said the captain.

"I asked *him*," Parsival said.

"Who, lord?"

"The monk. I swear it was the monk."

"What monk?" wondered the Viking, spitting down the little canyon, again.

"Where, my Lord?" Lego asked. "I see but damp smoke and twisted trees. Was it a vision?"

"Since all's a dream," he replied, shrugging, "why not?"

"Visions a monks," snorted Gralgrim. "That's a great use. We need visions a food an' drink and maybe a woman, in it."

As they went on, Lego was thinking how all it took was fog and unknown country to make the world as strange as any sleep-pictures. He'd never felt so cut off.

"We may be getting close to something," said Parsival.

"There's news," said Gralgrim. "More monks, then?"

"This country is like a child's maze," Parsival commented.

Yet what isn't? he asked himself.

"Where are the little crabs?" queried the Berserker, meaning the Mongol-like warriors. "I'd like to crack their shells."

Always the same puzzle on a different table, the knight considered. The rest of life flowed past like faces in a fever. *How to find the heart of this place in the fog...eyes full of fog....*

"Onward fellow doomed," he said. "All answers are always around the next turning."

MORGANA

The twisting promontory was so narrow the horses went in single file, jerking and starting nervously. The water crashed close on both sides, breaking over the top, in places. The faintly lit fog whipped and shaped past. The waning moon had followed the sun down.

Modred huddled in the saddle. Mimujin was just behind the famous witch. Three of Morgana's women had stayed with them and brought up the rear.

Mimujin hunched and scowled; stayed primed for mayhem. His sliced-off pinky throbbed less but his rage stayed cold and steady. He'd embraced death. It would all be the same in the end.

There was snow in the air. Big flakes swam and flickered past.

"We are close," Morgana said, shouted back against the wind, voice sucked away.

GAWAIN

He'd crossed a road, worn and wheel-rutted. looked in both directions for maybe twenty feet each way before the smooth, glowing wall closed the circle as if (he'd thought) he were in the center of a huge, silken tent.

The day was now windless and warm. He took a draw of tepid water from his leather flask. He wished he had spirits.

Which way? he asked himself.

He laid back his hood, exposing the scarred ruin of his face.

There were trees close to the road so he knew he was well inland. The faint glow descending meant west. Good. On the road he went west.

I believe in nothing much, he thought. *Yet, something like a wind blew me where it willed...maybe, finally it will blow fair....*

SHINQUA

No point in staying where she was any longer, fog or no. Perhaps there was no point in anything.

An you find Camelot, woman, she thought. *I think you'll get no seat at the Table Round....*smiled. *'Where's my Lord Gawain?' I'd ask. 'Why?' they wonder. 'Our son longs to look upon his father's face and I will bring him there. Of course.'*

She knew it was absurd. They might just laugh at her and ask who the child looked like. If Gawain were there it could lead to bloodshed. She might just say she had a message for him from some lady. But these were idle notions because this trip was just a gesture. So maybe the knight was no more than a target to aim at because her longing was for things that never really were but should have been.

"What the moon dreams," she half-sung under her breath, "melts in the sunrise."

Stared at the blunt nothing that softly stirred and swirled around her.

"Melts," she whispered.

LAYLA

They were now stopped at a deep stream bank. Hal paced along the water's edge hoping to spot fish. He had a notion of stabbing one or two with his sword which was ready in his hand. All he saw was dull, dark water reflecting the suffocating grayness.

Layla laid back and rested staring up at the changing blankness.

Upstream there'll be something sooner or later...some village...something....

Unconsciously she put a hand to her belly. Felt the old mix of tenderness and dread.

The sun's unseen angle suggested shapes in the mist overhead and then, in semi-focus, seemed to form a vague and passing image of something long ago where she was coming out of the dark, cool shadows of the arched corridor that traversed the inner castle wall and opened into the rich gardens that enclosed the middle-sized building on almost three sides, running nearly to the narrow moat. The scents were so intense...perfumes...cool stone...and (as she went out) the sudden rush of hot summer-day's air and astonishing richness of herb and flower and fecund, still air seeming tactile as some wonderful food....

And there he was, helmet laid aside, the massed, dense, compacted green summer foliage setting off his bright, Mars red armor, the long blond hair in the caressing breeze and then, looking at her, eyes that seemed to condense and concentrate the blue sky itself with all its untouchable beauty and remoteness and might have spoken (had she the wisdom of the coming twenty years) the secret joy and warning, too....

Because she'd wanted to touch him. Just touch him.

Was that it? Seeing someone in a shock and hush of green-gold summer light; young, welling longing overflowing because it had never really been him: golden hair, red armor, graceful strength and wide eyes (it seemed) full of dreaming...no...he was (she now believed) like a picture on a shield, the emblem of her wishes so that walking out of dimness the eyes first sees bright, edgeless blurs that then resolve into merely beautiful, yet mundane things....

How she'd wanted to touch him, that long gone day. She'd felt lightheaded, afraid, absorbed, lost...stood there, wanting to run to him, at once....

Ah, she'd thought, *Ah....*

GAWAIN

The road was following the little river upstream. In his little circle of sight he mainly watched the whorls and purlings as the water caught and bent around rocks and sticks and stirred darkly along the greenish black, weedy muck of the banks.

It gave him new ideas. He just looked; sensed no metaphoric meaning in the twists and whirlpooling water or the stagnant places where flickering, surface-walking bugs flourished. The muck, the stones, the unending, ever-shifting current were all one to him.

He kept thinking he just might find the castle town by going this way; thought it really made so little difference except for the stupid, incurable hope....

At this pace, with water and forage, the horse hardly needed rest so he could ride and doze in the saddle when the now moonless night fell and the faint, starshine showed where the trees vanished into the ground fog. He considered how the new moon would be rising before the sun.

I've come back at the dark time, he thought, *good for planting, the serfs say...or ploughing under....*

Semi-dozing, things came back, partly memory, partly dreams so there was a hot humid summer night in a barn hayloft at the edge of the village, the castle maybe a mile away....the moon crossed the opening that was like a window space and he was in her and she under him, soaked with one another's sweat and scent, breathless with rocking and thrashing together, leaning above her on locked arms, sore, aching but ever besotted by her sweet abandon...the dark gleaming face, rich, parted lips, amazing long, strong legs and two-toned, long-toed feet (like dark golden honey, he'd fragmentarily thought) lifted wide and softly kicking as he drove himself down into her as if he could ever actually get deep enough...on...on...and on....

"Ahhhh," he whisper-shouted, now, in this moment's bitter longing.

MIMUJIN

They'd come to a cave or ancient tunnel and were now under the sea. The religious little killer relaxed, slightly. Blew his nose into his hand and the snot spurted from the split nostrils. He wiped his hand on his jerkin. The sea sounds faded behind. His people liked caves.

He now accepted she was bringing him to the satisfaction he desired. He would fulfill his pledge to his people. Drink in the Red Knight's agony and eat his heart.

In the next world he would enjoy the slave-souls he'd slain in this life. Yes. And the sweet delights of whored women and boys. He would revel in his heaven.

"Ha," he snarled, kicking his horse forward into the darkness, shadows from himself thrown by the torches the women now held, angling and bending around the damp walls that seemed partly natural, partly worked by who knew what giant race or evil dwarves.

As if he needed so much light; he could smell his way through any cave to serve his king who hated the bright of day. The feeble surface folk feared the dark while he loved it, a fanged shadow, a whisper of death. Imagined finding Parsival in the caves and burrows of his homeland; imagined how he would toy with the arrogant knight before eating him.

MORGANA

Morgana was close beside the shivering boy, one cool, iron-strong hand gripping his forearm. The torch shadows wavered and wobbled around them.

"Hear me," she said in the sudden quiet below, "I mean for you to rule this place we soon will come to."

"But Aunt -"

"Peace. *But* not. At the end of this passage I will have little power and shall need all your strength."

"But -"

"Peace. The little killer will do what he does and you will meet your father."

I have released the demons in Britain, she was thinking. *Plague, fog and fear will melt them into a clay I may work...with his sword my son can be crowned....*

"How can -" Modred began, again. "Rule where? In a cave, Aunt? I want to -"

"You want silence, boy. You'll do what you must, secure in my love for you."

There where mortals can do magic and wizards lose their fire, she mused and then, for some reason asked herself: *Would I do these things were I alone on the earth? What would one seek, then? Were heaven perfect what would make our dramas? If ecstasy were always at a peak would it be ecstasy or ordinary?*

"The world runs on what we do and what results," she murmured.

Remove pain and death and the world is but entertainment...why strive for gain where all are rich? On earth its contrast moves us....

That would be interesting.

PARSIVAL

A bend...another...then a sun-glazed field, rich with shadow-melted bushes where red berries glowed.

A brownish form moved in the filtered light and, for a few moments, the sun slanted, blindingly bright, and then he knew it was a deer...four legs...heavy antlers of a buck, big body. He remembered and smiled. A vision of his childhood.

Am I still asleep in that monk's chamber having but dreamt I ever left?

At what sure point does any dream begin or end? That was his question.

Lego had armed himself with a short, stout bow he'd taken from one of their opponents. He nocked an arrow and drew on the creature in the dappled gleam and shadow of the brush.

"Fresh meat," he murmured but Parsival stayed his hand.

"Nay," he said. "This was my first guide and will not be slain again."

Because his idea was to reverse everything he could and so reverse his life. Because the old memory had blurred away what he was now looking at; a teenager again, still living with his long dead mother on the summer morning when he'd hurled that spear at the surprising, mysterious beast that seemed wrung from the netted light and shadow in the underbrush. He'd watched it shatter the glowing perfection of green and gold, suddenly belching blood in flailing death throes...and he'd run in fear and sick regret to his mother, shouting how he'd just killed something wonderful....

So he now took the bow from Lego and aimed, just as Gralgrim had come up to them, saying:

"Shoot for Freya's sake!"

The knight did, aimed low and the arrow stuck in the pale mossy earth ten feet short of the animal who backed and withdrew with what humans might have termed dignity or disdain, into the dense, scrubby, wind-twisted ragged trees.

"I'd done better with a thrown ax," muttered the Viking.

"We're lucky to have something to follow," Parsival told him.

"We follow the wild beast?"

"Come or not," the knight said, shrugging, heading into the strange forest and thought he saw (where the mist blurred the undergrowth away) what might have been a gowned woman moving into the shadow as if the creature had transformed. He decided that fit and smiled. "See, Mother," he murmured. "I killed nothing this day."

8SHINQUA

She turned the cart and simply headed back through the ghostly glowing mist, wheels bumping and creaking over the ruts and stones of the reverse slope.

The sense of going on, she thought, *is no sense....*

Down and across the short bridge again and it really wasn't far now. There was the broken windmill, the single blade that, for a moment, startled her, looking like a giant with a wide sword, poised to strike.

Not so far, now, she thought, as the wooden wheels clattered dully across the slatted bridge. *You are still the dreamer, woman...see what the dream is....*

The new waxing moon floated on top of the mist, a bow bent at the east, the sun not far behind. She was near the river that fed the moat and knew there were huts maybe 100 yards ahead. She didn't want to see them and just be back. Now she wished she'd gone the other way.

Reined up, got down and found a dry hummock of mossy grass and sat watching the soft, round reflection on the dark surface...after awhile she stretched out and might have dozed off in the slight murmuring of water and night-bugs and the muffled, soft chanting of frogs....

GAWAIN

So the next day when he came to the same wooden bridge he remembered where he was, as the heavy-shod hooves clunked on the damp boards and he took in the rich smell of wet woods and muddy banks. The sun melted the mist down to the bushes so the trees seemed to poke from a cloudy flood. The bright warmth was good and he lay back on soft grasses among summer violets, stripped to the waist; slept away the afternoon.

Like any ghost, he thought, *I need the night....*

The sun was still high when he woke up went to the stream. Stood looking down at the bright rippling. Knelt to top off his near empty water skin. Saw his coweled reflection among the undulant weeds and smooth stones. Threw back the hood and looked on the open ruin, softened by sun and shadow.

What's the point? He asked himself. *Why not stick my head under and draw breath?*

"No point," he murmured. "Not deep enough."

Broke the reflections as he cupped a palm full to drink, then tilted and held the waterbag under. Watched the bubbles rise and pop.

In a little while he went on. After sunset he watched the slim, crescent moon follow the sun down behind the fog. He was getting close to judge by the low forested hills the road had been winding around and over. He knew the country.

Decided to keep on a little longer before eating and soon passed a set of half-fallen-in huts. He halted at one and sat just inside the doorway; smelled damp and sour but almost pleasant. Sucked at strips of salt, dried and barely chewable beef.

Sat among the faintly starlit, shadowy forms and wondered if plague or the roving killers had emptied this place. He thought about Lohengrin and the girl Jane which turned his mind to Parsival.

He liked to talk about being a boy, the knight thought. *I hated being a boy, ruled by others. In that, I am like his son....*

Continued on the road he knew was the right one. His mount was skittish; kept snorting to clear his nostrils. Gawain had taken to calling him Horse. The knight appreciated how footsore the beast must be. He dozed and jerked awake in the saddle a few times in the thick, earth-scented early morning air....

Nothing drags its feet like a dawn you wait for, he thought. *Or comes so swift when the headsman waits....*

The sun was still an hour or two under the earth, he calculated.

"Not far to go, Horse," he said, stroking the smooth neck. "Then what?"

Then an empty cart took form in the luminous mist and he halted and waited, listened, hand on sword hilt. Who would leave an animal in traces out here, unattended? Who might be out here, attending? He dismounted and hitched the horse loosely to the back of the cart.

LOHENGRIN

In that limited area, even soaked in palpable wet air, it was likely that they'd all come to the same stream as they worked their way roughly inland. So (though Lohengrin didn't know it) his mother and Hal were less than half a mile ahead and had already reached the nearest village where they meant to rest and stay out of the fresh light rain.

Jane huddled in her cowl while he removed his helmet because he hated the pitter-pung of raindrops on the metal. His tight curly "Moor's" hair was water-beaded, almost as good as a cap.

Now it was close to evening; their conversation had dribbled away hours ago. She was tired and cranky and felt what she knew were incipient cramps that came with the dark moon. By tomorrow she expected to be miserable and was about to insist they stop when they heard and a creaking thunk and startling splash.

"What noise?" she shout-whispered.

"Sounds like a mill to me," he grunted, saddle-sore and grouchy.

A little further and he heard Hal before he saw him. Shook his head. Dull, wavering flames showed through a doorway in the humped shadow of a hut. The rain was spattering down harder from a thicker sky so the fire was the only light.

As they dismounted she reeled, slightly, and held the saddle. She felt hot and cold and cramped-up. This was something new, she realized, at once. Before he knew he'd moved he was already supporting her.

"What, my lady Jane?" he asked.

"A dizziness...I...."

Her cowl was back. The hair under his face. She was a damp, sweet-sour scent that gave him pleasure. He kissed her forehead. It was too warm.

"We should have stopped before," she said, resting her cheek on his shoulder, "and crushed the grass again."

"Come," he said, "we've found Hal, I think. There's bound to be food and drink."

"I am very dry," she said. Past the horse she saw a well in the ghostly mist, just touched by the reddish light in the doorway.

He started to help her but she freed herself.

"I am better now," she told him. "You go in. I'll be there."

She felt she was going to vomit. All at once everything was churning and nasty.

For some reason he didn't understand, he kissed her forehead again and felt a sick, dim fear and tenderness.

"Are you certain, Jane?"

"Ah...yes, I need to go to the bushes, my love."

"I'll see to Hal."

Heard a female voice as he headed in. Hal and a woman?

Inside was warm and bright by contrast. He leaned in the doorway, enjoying the feel and worrying about Jane.

Hal saw him and reacted, scrambling for his sword which leaned against the wall by the rough fireplace.

"Your doom is upon you, Henry Loutling," he pronounced, amused, going in, then seeing his mother sitting, doubled-up on the rude bed of logs and sacking, clearly in pain. "Mother!"

"Lohengrin," cried startled Hal.

"My son," she said.

"Are you hurt, Mother?"

"Bad food, I think," Hal offered, coming closer. "We found some dry victuals here that -"

"Not food. How have you come here, son?"

"After many turnings, mother," he said, kneeling beside her. "I think we were all closer than we knew. I -" She winced and clutched herself convulsively. Sighed a groan. "Mother, what?"

Then got up, still doubled-over, and half hunkered outside into the dark damp.

"Follow me not," she insisted.

He was torn. Hal was looking at him.

"Bad meat, I'm sure," he explained. "Let her but void it and all will be well."

PARSIVAL

The wet air kept thinning as they went so now they could see as they came around the next bend. He knew he should have been surprised to see a castle set into a hillside that he instantly recognized.

"When in a dream," he told Lego, "make no resistance."

"What place is this?"

"Camelot."

"My Lord, I -"

"In a dream, captain."

Gralgrim came close.

"Eh," he sounded.

"Shh. Don't wake me. You must serve a deep purpose else you would not be here."

As they reached the gate he wasn't surprised to see two armored knights in black and silver with fang faces.

"Come ahead," he challenged the pair, loosing his blade in its scabbard.

"We're right here, my Lord," said Lego.

"I mean these two devils. Here begins the nightmare."

"My Lord," said the captain, "doubt these will hold us back for long."

"They are fearful fighters."

Gralgrim snorted and gripped the devils in his massive fists. Parsival saw the deadly mutes draw and he leaped to assist the rash Viking except the voiceless knights were shaken and snapped apart in wordless gusts of agony.

"What power you have," Parse said, approving.

His companions looked at one another. Gralgrim held a broken, brown-leaved, stunted and rotten pine sapling in each hand. They'd been growing before the broken columns where Parsival saw a castle gate.

"Keep watch out here," he commanded, "whilst I enter. I fear we are tracked by the little men."

"Enter?" wondered Lego.

His master had already stepped between the broken stones and seemed to wander among scrubby trees and wiry brush into a kind of rough glade where scattered clumps of reddish, spiky little flowers gathered around small, dark, narrow rocks that appeared to be set in a rough circle like worn-away standing stones.

"Maybe when your great knight is done talking to trees and bushes maybe we'll find a town or something of use."

"The old priests did talk to earth and tree. The ones of Merlin's ilk still do."

"It's good to converse without fear of argument."

Indeed, Parsival seemed to be deep in discourse with a mossy, thick, short, knotted, leafless tree bearing dark, stone-like berries on the twisted limbs.

He'd entered the lofty, dim throne room as if the mist that domed around him had condensed into the vaulted chambers of Camelot.

The Round Table was empty. A massive hooded figure slumped on the high seat. The knight went up to him, imagining it was Arthur. He saw the beard and nose recognizing Merlinus.

If all things were the same, he thought, *how do you tell a vision from the rest?*

Glanced back to see that Lego had come in the high door.

"Wait there," he commanded, "whilst I speak with this wizard."

Lego winced. Gralgrim grinned, showing various teeth. The blood crease that divided his face wrinkled.

GAWAIN

The mists stayed thin above the stream so that the stars and slim, rising moon were blurred but visible and now shone in the relatively unruffled watersurface. So, as he went past the cart on the soft wet grass, he saw her outlined against the faint luminescence of the stream and the moment she moved her long, graceful arm to touch her hair and shook back her head he knew it was she and his heart and stomach clenched as if in fear.

He stopped at the end of the subtly shifting, cold smoke and watched from under his hood. The droning night bugs were soothing. The air was damp and rich and sweet. He wanted to leave and stay...call her name...flee...wanted....

"Ahhhh," he apparently voiced in his confusion because she turned, quick and fluid, long-fingered hands each holding a dagger, glinting the muted moonlight.

He was pleased. Smiled, feeling the stiff stretching where his lip edge had been sliced away.

"How beautiful you are," came out of him, "even but half seen."

"Keep your distance, brigand," she suggested.

"Have I not?"

She was a blotted silhouette. Only the twin blades showed.

"I know the ways of weapons, fellow," she told him, crouching slightly.

"Well I know it," he replied. "As I am armored, all you need do is slip into the water and I cannot follow."

"You school me, fellow?

"Again, my lady moor."

The knives went away as she came closer.

"You," she said, not even shocked yet. "How can this be?"

He could now make out hints of her soft features. With only one eye he strained less to see in poor light. Then her scent overlaid with the sweat and grubbiness of her recent exertions, seemed somehow sweeter, catching in his throat and heart so that (by the time she was looking up into his face) his impulse to remount and ride had no more force than a tendril of mist.

He twisted his head, keeping his undamaged side towards her, holding a futile but wonderful moment of normalcy.

"Gawain?" her long supple, strong hands closed on both his mailed arms. "You...never came back." He sort of groaned, as she went on: "I set out to find you when I learned you were not dead." It was hitting her now.

"Well...I came back...I...."

"Now, sir? Now?" She shook his mailed arms, slightly. "Now, sir?"

"Ah. I could not, before."

He didn't look at her, face twisted away.

"Were you held captive? Imprisoned in some dread dungeon?"

"Indeed, indeed. In the terrible cell of my head. And there is no hope of parole."

"Cozening riddles?" She pushed his hood aside. He winced. She touched his face, across his cheek…lips. As her fingers moved he caught her wrist. "Will you not look at me, sir?"

"I came back to see -"

"See?"

"Not be seen."

"Not be seen."

He held her away, a little. It wasn't easy.

"Please, Shinqua…."

"So am I called."

"I love you. More than before. As if I'd never had you at all."

That was better.

"Why speak so brokenly, Gawain? Am I not here? How many nights did I wait and wonder. How many times…."

He almost shook her.

"You know nothing!" he cried. The arm with the wooden hand locked behind her long back. "This moment is more…is more than….Yes, even my speech is broken in halves. I am half a knight in half a world and can but half have you…I have half a love, yet how I burn with it! I, who never needed words now eat and drink them! I live on their empty sound. I, Gawain, who did such…such deeds as…as…."

He was weeping as he clutched her. She felt his agony and shuddered with it.

"Oh sad knight," she whispered into his neck, pressing the ripe fullness of her lips there, above the harsh metal of his armor. She could feel his desperation and her own. "What, my poor love? O, kiss me! I beg it."

"Kiss you," he almost shouted, crushing her into his iron skin until she sighed with pain but made no complaint. Her head was prisoned under his chin. "Kiss you?" he murmured, this time. His breath heaved as if he'd run a mile. "Fare thee most well, my dark jewel…my love, my pain, my heart, my hope…." Holding her harder she gasped with pain and pressure. "Lost forever…kiss you? Were I more than half with more than half a mouth, how I might kiss you, then. My heart the only thing left whole and with all that heart, I love thee, from beyond death's utter night! I love thee...out of all this I cry to thee, from hell and fog and ruined earth. But kiss thee I cannot."

"What words you find."

"That gain me nothing."

And he almost hurled her away so that she staggered back and went down on the loamy riverbank, almost disappearing into the shadows from where she called back, with broken breath:

"We have a son!" She just crouched there. "But what, poor Gawain? What?"

"I cannot kiss thee," he said, cried. "Nor may I show myself to him." He backed away, starting to melt into the fog. "I live in mists and nothingness."

He drew his sword and slashed at the blurred, dimly gleaming, empty almost-shapes around him.

"Oh, Gawain," she said, not loud.

"I cannot kiss thee," he repeated, almost shouted. "I cannot."

LOHENGRIN

"Bad meat?" he asked Hal, who replied:

"Since we ate I've had fire in my belly and sour burpings." He opened and closed his hands, expressively. Obviously, he was letting the past quarrel go, in light of present troubles. "I once was up all night," he went on, warming to his subject, "spewing loose, stinking liquids from both ends. Bad -"

"Enough," said Lohengrin, grinning, despite himself. "Far more than enough." He went near the fire, half-consciously drawn to the warmth and cheer.

"I merely state the facts," concluded the young squire.

Lohengrin stared into the flames. Wanted Jane to come in and warm up. He was almost amazed by how troubled he was.

"My mother...." Shook his head. "Jane...ill." Rubbed one finger down the length of his beaked nose. Turned and went back outside.

He stood with the light at his back in the deep obscurity and cool rain. Saw nothing much.

"Mother! Jane!" he called out. For some reason he felt a sinking, cold within as if belly and heart were chilled.

There was a stifled, gagging sound towards the well.

What a plague caring is, he thought.

Hal was behind him.

"Lohengrin," he said.

"Where is she?"

"Jane?"

"Yes."

He crossed the yard through the wet, misty earth smell.

"Jane?"

He found the well. Saw the bucket she'd obviously raised because it hadn't been there before. Hal shadowed him.

"Is she unwell, too?" he wondered.

"She had the same meat I had," Lohengrin said.

She was alongside the hut on the far side. Crouching. Rain dripped from the eaves.

"My love," said she. "I am all cramp and burning."

Lohengrin lifted her up. She clutched him. She was very hot.

He walked her around towards the doorway, lifted her into his arms, slipping a little on the slick mud from the runoff.

So sudden it comes, he thought. *Like snuffing a candle...she's light to bear....*

"The water," she said, weak and giddy, as they angled through the doorway into the low close room.

"You want water?" asked Hal, moving with them.

"No. Drink not the water in the well...."

Lohengrin laid her on the straw pallet. The firelight hollowed her face with shifting shadows.

"I but sipped," she whispered. She seemed, suddenly, so very small and pale; shivered slightly. "It were foul," she whispered on. "Gagged in my throat."

"Poisoned?" asked Hal.

"Did my mother drink therefrom?"

He was already heading back out, as close to panic as he'd ever come.

"I know not," Hal said after him.

JOHN

Was barely clinging to the wet rope as the ungainly, fog-whipped ships drifted with the strong wind. When he thought he could hold no longer, his feet touched bottom and he heard the dull creaking and cracking as the unseen vessels began to pile up on some reef or the shoreline.

All around h-e heard wind-twisted, muffled shouts and cries. He waded and half swam, desperately, up the shore-slope, over muck, stones and crunchy little shells.

He passed around the bulk of another stranded ship that showed through the general cloudiness. He could see a level mucky stretch of beach where masses of oily-looking seaweed clung to dark stones. The standing pools showed the ebb tide was going out....

PARSIVAL

Gralgrim looked up as if he'd just been offered a very rotten bite of fish, watching the knight in red armor discuss matters with the gnarled tree.

"Merlin," said Parsival, "am I come here to finish or begin?"

The Viking watched him listen and nod thoughtfully, as the branches stirred.

"Ah," he murmured. "Yer master asks a good question."

Lego shifted, uneasily.

"There's something deep in it," he decided, without much conviction.

"Hoo. Deep enough, I ween. Deep as the sea and mad as a Frenchman."

"Why don't you go back to your country of drunkards and pirates?"

"I wish no more. Mayhap I'll ask that tree directions when the great knight's done his discourse."

Merlinus seemed too weary to move. His resonant voice seemed to sound from the earth itself, saying:

"There is always the final chance, for all things must end in both heaven and earth. This may be your final chance to live outside the dull world, again like a ship that the fresh tide lifts from some dreary and somber shore."

"What must I do?"

Gralgrim considered this.

"Pick that scurvy-looking fruit?" he wondered. "Hang yerself from a branch?"

"My master sees things hidden from ordinary eyes," said Lego.

"Hears, too, meseems."

"As before," Merlinus was saying. He shifted his cloak, slightly, revealing the haft of a sword in his belt. "Go knowing nothing. Take this and keep it from the witch."

"Yes, I will go, knowing nothing. What has changed?"

"I think he can," said Gralgrim.

"Enough," said Lego. "Ah, see there."

The branches had shifted in the breeze and they saw the knight reach into a space in the trunk and extract a silver and gold-worked swordhilt with about a foot of broken blade.

"I will keep this, as you say, sir," Parsival told Merlin – or the tree – depending on where you stood.

"Should he no ask a sound stone, too?" chortled the bulky Berserker. "Just to be certain he understood the tree."

'Barbarian shitwit," snarled Lego getting ready to break his pact and break the fellow's big, round head.

"Yet," went on the other, pleased by his effect, pointing, "there's a bush adjacent that hath a sage look."

Lego walked away from him and closer to the knight.

"My Lord," he said, "how did you know to find this here?"

Parsival thrust the blade through his mesh steel belt.

"Saw you not the great wizard give it me?" indicating the tree.

"So we did," said Gralgrim. He turned to the knotted trunk and sank to one knee. "I beseech you, great wizard, transport me by the wights of the air to me homeland where…." But could utter no more for laughing.

"No doubt the joke is good," Parsival allowed, striding back out of the great hall, "but tweak not Merlinus overmuch. Come outside you both and on we go. All will soon be clear, I think."

"As soon as we come outside, a course," gasped Gralgrim. "But, yet, the door seems shut."

Parsival shook his head and turned under the arch. Lego, dourly, marched past him.

"Are you short of sight, Viking?" the knight wanted to clear-up. "The gate stands wide."

"Ignore him, my Lord. We ought to toss him back into the sea like a rot-blighted fish."

"A spell may have been set to blind him."

"The gate stands wide," Gralgrim howled, rolling over on the grass. "Wizard's work."

The other two went on ahead and the convulsed Berserker, unwilling to miss anything to come, found his feet and followed.

"There's a point, my Lord," Lego pondered. "We may be spellbound while thou art free to see."

GAWAIN

His sole eye weeping, burning, voice choked with pain and passion, he turned away.

She heard his mail tink and the horse snuff-cough. She was quick so he hadn't mounted yet, just freeing the reins. Maybe he hadn't actually meant to.

So he just stood there in his wetly gleaming, silvered steel, holding the saddle, facing the horse. The arc of moon showed over the low trees across the pond, first hinting of sunrise faintly silhouetting heavy limbs.

She didn't touch him, this time.

"You became tired of me," she said, "for all your words. Half of heart and half of this and that. Is there another who has your whole heart?"

"No," he said, a catch in his voice. His throat felt thickened with feeling.

"Tell me, knight and man." Because she wanted to be free if he would not be bound, one way or another. "But tell me."

"Another?" He thought about the peasant whore innkeeper where (in a sense) he now longed to be, free of knighthood, feeling and purpose, obligated only to eat, fuck and drink himself to blank sleep. "Another who has my whole heart? Ha, ha." He still didn't turn, wooden hand absently hooked on the saddle girth, eye shut. The night sounds droned on as if suspending time as the mist suspended space....

"I went to find you," she told him again, staring at his metal back formed from soft moonlight and burnished harshness. "More than once. Tell me, man and knight, why so silent now? And why do you only stand like a tranced madman?"

His living hand stroked the horse's warm, damp flank as if he touched her. For all the suffering he'd had, this was a new one because he truly loved and longed (as poets would put it) and had no dream, no dram, no speck nor spot of hope.

"I am like one 80 years old," he finally came out with, voice shaking and choked. "Or a dead man come back to endlessly reach for what he cannot grasp. Gawain's shadow. Cans't love a shadow or the dead love you?" And then he sobbed a kind of scream that terrified her for a moment. "To have no hope. None." He flung himself up into the saddle, violent, furious. "A ghost in love with the living."

He wrenched the horse around and nearly knocked her down.

"Gawain!" she cried.

"Fare thee well!" he yelled. "My hour up, I now return to hell!"

LOHENGRIN

He found his mother next, sitting against a massive tree, almost lost in brush and fog. There was just enough light to show her bare legs opened.

"Stay away," she demanded. "Leave me."

"Mother, I...."

"Go. I'll not die of this. I'm partly glad of it."

"Glad to be sick?"

"A kind of purging. Go. Attend your lady."

He was baffled and rueful.

"This is...I know not what I feel, Mother. So many things have happened...."

Images recurred: the lady in the tent; the weird underground fortress and charnel pit; the mad knight using the naked dead girl...and then Jane. "Some things were like enchantments...which I disbelieve...."

"Go inside, my boy. I bid you, go." Her voice was strained.

Inside Hal was kneeling by the pallet where Jane sighed and softly thrashed. He *did* know what he felt; there was nothing to do.

"Christ's words, what?" he demanded of the air and fire-tossed shadows. He was afraid to go near and afraid to leave. "What?'

"She seems most ill," Hal needlessly said.

She rolled on her back, legs straight and rigid.

"Lohengrin," she whispered.

"Ahh," he whispered, "I am here."

"I was thus sick," said the round-faced Saxon boy said, "after bad fish."

He pointed as she spewed some bubbling vomit from the side of her mouth into the dank straw. Lohengrin felt a convulsion of chill dread. He rushed close and knelt there. Wiped the sticky stuff away with a handkerchief.

"Oh, sweet Jane," he said.

"Even bad salt fish," suggested Hal, blinking and staring. "O Holy Mother Mary."

"She had no fish."

Outside Layla stood up and staggered a little. She wanted to wash the blood from her thighs. Saw her son standing in the doorway, looking in and then out.

"Drink not from the well, mother," he called over. "Jane says it poisoned her."

"There's a bucket of rainwater over there," she responded.

"Clean water. I'll give her a drink."

"Then bring it me, son." She held her partly smeared dress up, a shadow in the misty moonlight. She wide-stepped over to the crackly hut wall and sat just under the sagged eaves.

He went in and came back out.

"She could not drink," he said. He put the bucket down close to his mother who was dimness in the wet, still night. The rain dripped here and there from the roof and tree branches. "I think she is most ill."

"I see you care."

She wet a clean linen cloth and wiped herself. He just stood there, breathing steadily, silent. Then he plunged back inside. She sighed. Took and drink, then wet the cloth again.

JOHN

Slogging, feet like lead in the sucking muck, he worked his gasping, shivering, miserable way to the stony shore of rotted fish smells, crushed shells and slimy seaweed.

He could distinguish the side of one ship tilted into the strand. The pilgrims were clambering down and dropping back onto the reeking beach.

"No reason to give up the cause," he muttered. "A false start. A new trail. Yes."

It seemed to him that to the south the fogs were thinning. He thought he could almost make out the sun's disk in the lower half of the sky. "A new trail and trial, too...."

With a sudden rush of energy he stood up and started plopping his feet along the stinking beach towards the people.

"Hear me!" he called ahead. "The sun returns. All will be clear!" Maybe two dozen watched him coming. They were pale, weary, impassive. He half-hopped to them through the muck with stork-like steps. "All will be clear! Clear!"

PARSIVAL

No surprise, he thought, as they came to a clearing where (in the fog, subtly thinned) he saw a blue and yellow silken tent against a dark green background of dense undergrowth.

The sun, again, softly sprayed soft, uneven coins of light around them and the cool day was spring-like, for a moment....

"Wait," he said, "I'll go in and see her alone."

Because it had to be, his memory insisted.

"You'll go in an see her?" Gralgrim liked that idea. Winked one eye at Lego who ignored him.

The knight went to the tent flap and entered quietly.

His companions watched him walk a few steps into the shadow of a fifteen or so foot high bluish, pointed rock, covered with soft green moss and sprinklings of tough, spiny, yellow cold-country blossoms. He stopped there and spoke, fervently:

"Lady I am grieved by what I did to you in those days. I was a foolish boy and caused you hurt. I have been long troubled by this."

The Viking squinted. There was a bird, a smallish, graying wild goose, maybe, he decided, pecking at the scrubby grass near Parsival. Lego shifted his eyes, squinting, trying to see the tent in case there *was* a spell.

"He's grieved," said Gralgrim. "What? Did he once steal its eggs?" Snorted. "Wish I had a fucked fresh egg or even a hard-cooked one saved in salt."

"I am pleased to see you well," Parsival said to the lady who looked like Jeschute. She seemed to sigh and droop her head.

"He's pleased she be well," the Viking said. "Where's that bow?"

"You left it behind," said Lego.

"Even that skinny fowl would taste sweet, I think."

Meanwhile, Parsival had dropped to one knee, with a slight clink of armor and Gralgrim shook his wide-eyed head. Said no more words.

"My Lord, should we not -"

The knight glanced back out of the tent they couldn't see.

"Wait," he commanded. "I'll come out in a moment."

"He'll be out," assured the Viking.

Parsival stood up and studied her averted face.

"I will try not to fail in my purpose, this time," he declared. She seemed to sigh and went into the back of the tent – which faded into soft mist as he passed through the parted flap and kept walking across the open field.

Gralgrim noted the bird had gone into the spiny brush. Sighed.

"So much fer supper," he muttered. "This is whom you follow, fellow?"

"Be still, he's beyond the comprehension of bumpkin barbarians."

"Yet geese understand him pretty well."

"Had you half a bird's brain you might comprehend more."

"Aye. You understand him too," guffawed Gralgrim. "Thus ya must have half a one." The Berserker enjoyed his little triumph of the last word.

Parsival now hurried at a partial trot, metal pinging softly. The dark, massed and twisted trees, melted together by the fog that had closed down around them again, were unlit by sunlight. There was grayness and a graceful tower of bluish stone.

Lego and the Viking watched him heading towards a mass of broken rock that spilled in a twenty foot heap across the tundric plain.

"There before us!" cried Gralgrim. "The lost treasure of Odin!"

LOHENGRIN

His mother came back into the hut, limping, pale, but not entirely miserable.

It's over, she was thinking, *God's will*

"How fares the maid?" she asked. Coming closer she saw and knew and winced.

"I know not, my lady," said Hal.

It's always the worst, she thought.

Her son looked dismayed; she hadn't noted that since he was three.

Ah... my son...my son....

GAWAIN

He kicked the horse ahead, then reined it to a stiff legged, snorting halt because she held on and now was being dragged.

"Damn you," he cried.

"Damn *you*, you white fool," she cried in exchange. "Am I grown a hag? Am I loathly?"

He twisted in the saddle, gripping her with his right hand, holding the false one up to her face.

"See this!" he told her. Let go and drew his dagger, stabbing it into the palm of the wooden hand and left it sticking out. "See!"

"Sad to lose your limb," she said, just standing there, now, weeping. "Many have before you. What care I for that? Save you kept the best one."

"I have lost all hope of thee," he said, quietly, plucking the blade free. "All hope...I came back because I could not help myself. Of all women it was only you I loved entire." His eye was weeping now, in the dark mist and obscurity of his cowl. "There is nothing I would not have done...I...please, let me go, sweet Shinqua. I am a ghost and you must free me to join the shadowy pack."

The horse rocked his head and snorted but barely shifted in place. She still just stood there.

"I am no child," she said. "I can see thou art solid flesh and blood. What spirit has a hand of wood?"

"I beg you, my love, my wonder, my dear night and magic...I beg you...."

"What words...what words...."

"Free this ghost and ask no more, my only love."

"Are you all words? A ghost of words?"

"Ahhh."

"You seem flesh and blood," she said again, baffled, not moving, staring at nothing. "You may be mad...." Paused. "Yet are you intact below?"

"Lady, you know my meaning."

The soft light made her seem an exhalation of grace from the mysterious, murmurous night and he could bear neither to look at her nor look away. Then she gripped his steel-sheathed leg in both hands.

"I know nothing," she told him. "All I wish is here with me now. Show me what you must."

"Show you...."

"Yes, fool. Or leave me cursed in doubt."

He clutched his hood.

"Look then," he said, sobbed. "Look."

PARSIVAL

"At last," the knight exclaimed. "I'll not err this time."

A second chance, he thought, *even in a dream may free me of questions and regrets...any dream might be a lifetime....*

Because he was crossing the moat on the carven and delicate drawbridge that might have been the same from twenty years before except all those memories swam in blurring denser than the fogs they'd wandered through.

The gate was open and he went inside and was surprised by the rich tapestries and metal mirrors, bright painted carvings of holy beings, a rich, almost stifling mist of incense and strange perfumes that smelt of clean fields and herb-clogged gardens washed by soft rains....

He went straight through the empty entrance passage, through the vaulted archway into the big (and suddenly low-ceilinged) chamber where he remembered (twenty years ago) seeing the wounded king who lay, forever bleeding, on the scented, sinkingly soft couch, awash in silken pillows with maidens and pages bearing strange objects...food, scented drink...stifling heat from masses of candles and roaring fireplaces...the castle of the Grail where he'd failed as a boy and left a shadow, a hole forever in his life that was always there, like a spot in the eye, even when he wasn't actually noticing it....

So he was sideways surprised that the place was empty, this time, except for a figure on a massively soft and silky bed.

Lego had his arms folded. Gralgrim stood, stocky, wide, hands on hips, face halved by the dried blood streak; not quite smiling yet.

Because there was Parsival confronting heaps of rock, saying:

"I know what to ask now." He knelt before a scrubby bush. The king moved his head from the shadow of the pillows and, this time, it was Arthur Pendragon. "My Liege!" exclaimed the knight.

This was too many for the Berserker, who hooted:

"He's vassal to the bush!"

"Go your own way," snarled Lego, baited. "Begone."

"And miss these rare things?"

"Bah."

"Hearken, for he speaks further with the leaves an berries." Sank to one knee, chuckling.

Lego shoved the Viking over with one foot; the fellow lay there, convulsed with guffaws.

"Lout!" snarled Lego.

"Parsival," said the king. "Come nearer."

LOHENGRIN, ET AL

Lohengrin lifted Jane's hand from where it lay beside her. It was cool and seemed unnaturally heavy. He understood. Winced and (his mother noted, sitting in her incrementally fading pain) with unaccustomed tenderness, laid her hand across her body, then turned away with a dark, baffled look and went outside. She could see him standing in the foggy yard, back to the door, softly lit by the softly tossing fireplace flames.

Well, she thought, *now he's learned this....*

She wanted to comfort him but her own pain kept her doubled-up. He was so young, she kept thinking. He'd ridden off almost like his father had.

Never thinking about pain....Life was all theirs for the taking...now he's already learned this...I fear this wound will keep ever raw and open and deform his nature....

Hal was trying to give Jane a palm full of water. It trickled past her lips and down her chin.

"I think she's waking up," he said.

Layla sighed.

Oh, Lohengrin, she thought. *Be not as I, my son, confirm not your bitterness....*

PARSIVAL

He leaned close to the listless king.

"My Lord," he said, "I swore to do no more murder for you. On my oath, no more killing save in defense."

"I ask no more. You denied my knights who came to you. Yet it was not killing they were to ask you for. And I am not the same Arthur you knew as you are not the same boy who came to me for the same red gear you wear still."

"Aye, Lord. We change with time."

"Yes and no. We are not the same because we are here in this place where time is as with a sleeper, where moments can seem days or a lifetime."

"We are asleep? I suspected something since that odd monk...."

"This is no dream to wake from in your bed. This is a place neither of us may stay in. We will go back and I will be the unhappy king, again."

The heat of the low-ceilinged chamber made the knight want to get outside but he stayed on one knee, listening.

"My, ah whatever-she-is-to-me-through-copulation's-conscience-smothering-blindness, she, Morgana, has poisoned the world with needless murder, plague and ill magic. She has opened gates that were well sealed. She has awakened Clinschor's father in his ice-cold hole and wants to bring him forth to darken and chill God's light and sweet green earth."

"So I must fight this fight." He was groggy from the stifling air; yawned. "But it's not what it seems."

"Most true. It is not. You will battle and chop down and slay flesh and blood in a world of pain and loss, effort, hope, despair...."

"Yes, yes, Sire." His eyes kept shutting almost as they had in the strange monastery.

"And in another place they will mean other things. The shadows of our acts in life matter more than the lumps who cast them. So I will give you a map."

Another map, Parsival may have said or just thought, eyes shut, now.

"There is a tunnel back to the world. There is a chamber where the knights and their horses sleep and you will find the rest of Excalibur's blade." The gaunt king held out a scrap of pale parchment.

"Yes, my King...."

The stifling heat was too much and the Red Knight sagged to his side with a dull clunk and snored, slightly. His last waking thoughts may not have been his own:

Excalibur...Grail...words? Just a sword and a cup...or something? Things that stop the mind far short of truth and prove the mind a lie....

Gralgrim hadn't gotten up. He knee-walked over to Parsival and shook him.

"I'm here to homage King Bush," he declared, laughing.

Parsival stirred and got up. Staggering a little in the close air he went quickly down the corridor and back outside, breathing deeply. There he held the map before his face.

A map is a dream, too, he thought. *Or, at least, a wish to believe something is really known about something....*

Behind them, still kneeling, the Viking had pulled a branch to him as if it were a hand and kissed it.

"I pledge to serve you," he cried, "an all yer leafs and berries."

GAWAIN

"Look," he said, softly this time, hand clenched to pull back the hood and show her his face. She held him, half-dragged along as the horse restlessly shifted and snorted.

"What care I?" she insisted. "I had heard your face was hurt. What care I?"

"Yet am I monster and man."

"Many are. You are my love. Even were you become a monkey-man all foul hair and stink."

Then she reached up and tore his concealment away. He wrenched his face aside so that only the fine profile showed in the gentle, fog-diffused moonlight.

What? Her mind asked. *He still looks like some pale god....*

"You are like some angel in the Holy Book," she told him.

"Angel?"

"Then ever keep that single half to me, my love," she whispered. "And I'll put out this eye -" She held the dagger to her face. "- with this hand and see you only from one side, forever." He knew she meant it.

"Ahhh," he groaned.

"Then cover yourself, I care not, fool."

"Ah."

"Better to be half myself with you than live out this dull bitterness alone."

He threw himself from the saddle and crushed her to him, to his mail and plate and she gasped with pain and pleasure.

"Shinqua," he whispered.

"I need but part of thee, my Lord," she told him. "Which still you keep from me."

Easy to say, he thought, *in night and fog...yet....*

"Yet daylight will come," he murmured.

"Give me the part I burn for now," she said into his ear so that he sank within himself and his heart pounded. "Strip off this shell." Her fingers skillfully worked at the armor's lacing. "Or slay me here, if you be not white of heart as well as flesh. I'll not part from you alive this night."

Then they just stood there, silent, breathing hard; the horse still too. Head twisted to the left, his eye stared across the flowing water into softened forms and shadows, into the misty night melting into morning, the high leaves now taking substantial form....

He could go neither forward nor back and she knew that, too. He disarmed and let her help him lay aside his armor. She kissed his good cheek again and again and his good hand. They finished undressing and lay down together on the soft, warmish knoll. Her rich body astonished him as it formed out from the brightening vapors that concealed them both.

"Let me hold you, now," she said.

"I know not what's to come...."

"Mayhap little or much. Let me hold you, my lover. And if you must leave me, then slay me."

MORGANA

"Aunt, See there!" cried Modred, pointing.

There was a high arch cut into the side of the passageway and their torchlight flickered into what must have been a vast room or natural grotto.

Mimujin had gone ahead, not looking back. Morgana and her son climbed a few steps into the opening.

"Look," he whispered, excited, pointing at a welter of bright glintings, a slaughter!" The horses resisted, trying to pull back.

Because (at the outskirts of the wavering flamelight) armored men lay in part of what must have been a large circle extending around the chamber. They were laid out, side-by-side.

"Hush!" she hissed at him. "Leave this place!"

Seized his horse's bridle as she backed them both out.

"Aunt Morgana?"

"We'll come here later. Let them sleep."

They went on through the rock corridor.

"They are not dead?" he wondered'

"Death meets in sleep," she said.

They came out of the passageway into a perfectly flat field that could have been used for a tourney. Mimujin was waiting, sitting his pony.

The mist was fading here and they could see for nearly a hundred yards all around.

"They will have to come this way," she said. The little man glared at her, twisted around in the saddle. Snorted through his split nose. His eyes were slits of fury. "Go my little hunting beast," she said. "Find your quarry. You smell them, I think. Bring back the broken sword that Parsival, your beloved, will have found."

"I find beloved, witch," he said, twisting his pony's neck as he held it side-stepping violently. "Then I bring you something back. Yes."

"Call first your brothers whom I sent before you," she added.

"Brothers here?"

"Call them. I doubt those two will have slain them all. Go!"

He started the shaggy, quick mount across the gray-green field.

Maybe I bring the brothers back to you, here where you are too weak to do your own business....

"Wait here," he called back.

"Good hunting," she said.

One of the women was close to her.

"I feel weak," she said. "Almost as when I bleed of the month."

"It is this land," Morgana told her. "Well let them come who comes. They will pursue and we flee until we've caught them." Smiled.

And the sword we could not have found here ourselves as we are near blind in this place...if the little assassin fails it is no matter as the knight will follow...

She sat there watching across the pale fields into a blurred distance where all edges went to mist, and considered how in days to come when all magic weakened, this island would reverse and the powers gather here and fade elsewhere on the earth...unless she succeeded completely, this time, and woke and freed the sleeper in the fortress....

Wondered when the ships of the pilgrims would arrive here led by the demented priest and her sister sorceress. The idea was to populate this isle with serfs for her son to rule and breed legions so this would be the great place as the world beyond went dull and dark. Part of the Great Plan.

"Do we fight when they come?" he asked.

"The point of war, child," she explained, "is not to seem brave but to win and live."

PARSIVAL

He held up the map before Lego and Gralgrim in his mail-gloved left hand.

"We follow this and soon we'll have both halves of the sword," he told them.

"You need to find both halves of yer wits, mad knight," responded the Viking.

"It seems a blank piece of bark, lord," said Lego, looking closely at the thin, silvery stuff that must have been peeled from a smooth, grayish tree like a birch.

"It's perfectly clear," he said.

Here is this dream so deep I wonder I can ever wake again...here where that king I never really trusted has a majesty and meaning as if he were no man but a fable in seeming flesh....

Gralgrim pinched the edge of the bark and made to study it.

"Ar hoo," he emitted, "what could be plainer."

Parsival was already turning and heading back through the jagged heaps of broken stone. The other two followed at a little distance, Lego trying to keep a pace or two ahead of the Berserker.

Or I'm awake, the knight went on, internally, *and magic and amazement overlap the substantial earth and leave us in two worlds at once so all is now new or all is nothing but vapor....*

MIMUJIN

The pony seemed to know so he let it canter. The mist closed in and drew back as he went. The small hooves thumped softly on the moist ground. The gently rolling field ended at a wall of shattered rock, black, volcanic-looking. He rode parallel, sensing his moment might be close. Loosened his bow.

Soon we see, he said to himself.

PARSIVAL

As they followed a twisting path with the dark rock on both sides making a kind of canyon, a gust of mist (it had, generally pulled back hundreds of feet) spilled over and down the broken slope on one side like an airy waterfall. At the edge of Parsival's sight it seemed to shape itself into the archway of a small chapel where (in blurry stained-gleaming) a couple seemed to taking vows before the vague outline of a priest. When he looked directly there was just mist. It made him think of his marriage to Layla, so many years past....

"I wish I'd bolted," he said, loud enough for Lego to hear.

"My Lord?"

"From that wedding." Pointed, unconsciously, at where the mist was spilling shapelessly onto the ground. "What unhappiness might have been averted."

"Which wedding?"

"Mine."

"You cannot be sure," Lego considered, "what good it may have brought and may yet bring."

Gralgrim came nearer, not wanting to miss any new madness. He thought the entertainment almost as good as a meal.

"Hoo," he voiced. "Be these fairy-folk dancing afore ya, now?"

And Parsival saw a huge knight in black and silver steel with a demonic faceplate, mounted on a massive charger. He resembled one of Clinschor's mutes from twenty years before.

"This monster is for me alone," he told them. "Stay back."

This may wake me up, he thought.

In the middle distance was a placidly grazing moose as far as Lego and the other observers could discern. Gralgrim licked his chapped lips, contemplating fresh meat. He knew these animals wouldn't flee one hunter.

The Black Knight had a spear-tipped lance couched. The Red had shield and sword but no mount. The rider waited as Parsival came closer. Now, in the mists behind, more warriors were visible, waiting.

If this is real it will be worth a tale, he thought.

Suddenly the near one charged. Parsival relaxed, waiting to respond. His opponent thundered at him, lance tip flashing the weak light.

"Here we are," he murmured. Like the first time when he won this armor.

A yard away he ducked across the enemy's path and suddenly the lance was on the wrong side of the horse. No time to recover. The Red Knight tossed aside his shield and dove, point-first, at a space in the part-plate armor exposed under the armpit.

The mute emitted an agonized grunting bellow and went over and down with the impact of Parsival's weight.

The other two watched the famous knight criss-cross and stab the huge animal under the right shoulder after the beast had flipped a furious antler at him. Gralgrim was delighted and moved forward to help in the kill.

Parsival was rolled aside by the impact, leaving the blade jammed in the creature's ribs.

"Good strike," Mimujin muttered.

Parsival stood up, stunned, and gestured to the onlooking herd while his victim thrashed around, dying, pinkish foam at his lips. Some of the moose were moving off into the receding mist.

"Your champion has fallen!" he called to them.

Lego raised a warning fist.

"Speak no word," he warned. "Not one."

Except Gralgrim was looking elsewhere.

"What's this?" he exclaimed.

Because Mimujin, moustaches flopping, oiled hair shining, bow in hand, pony loping, had just come around the bend where the wall of rock ended not far ahead. He was close to Parsival who was still watching the herd withdraw as Lego yelled a warning. Mimujin yelled an ululating warcry which was also a signal in case any of his people really were near.

They are on foot, he thought, *and soon die!*

The knight turned in time to take an arrow through his lifted faceplate. Even his amazing reflexes failed to do better than take the missile on an angle so it creased across his eyebrows and wedged in the helmet, blinding him with blood and the shaft, too, before he snapped it away so the next one (shot at closer range) hit and just pierced his backplate, stopped by the chainmail layer. It hurt.

He couldn't wipe the blood from his eyes through the visor with his steel-gloved fingers and assumed the companions of the Black Knight were upon him.

I die here, mind words flashed.

Except the Berserker, brandishing his tree limb club in instant frenzy, bull-charged, roaring with happy anger, amazing Lego with his stocky speed. He went straight at the mounted man who'd halted his pony with his knees, taking dead aim, point-blank, at the blinded knight.

MORGANA

She halted just outside the entrance to the tunnel they could see almost a quarter of a mile, now, across the slightly brightening plain. She almost made out the shape of the wall-like rock mass.

They heard Mimujin's cry and then an answering bellow.

"That's not Parsival," she observed. "Or his man either."

She didn't like that. Frowned and tapped one finger on her half-mask.

PARSIVAL

"Yaaaaarrr!" cried Gralgrim, flinging his oversized club straight at the undersized rider.

Mimujin ducked backwards, spinning his mount – except the blow hit the animal's head so hard blood flew and one eye popped free. The wiry rider somersaulted and landed on his feet (arrow still nocked) as the pony went down.

The killer fired straight into Gralgrim's throat, the point standing out six inches behind his neck so that the Berserker's fighting shout became a bubbling blood-spew into Mimujin's split-nosed, scarred, contorted face as the dying Viking crashed into his little body and knocked him flat and winded and the big hands clawed into his lean throat in berserk pain and fury.

As Parsival finally got his helm and gauntlets off and cleared his eyes, pressing his forehead to divert the bleeding. Lego came up to him, sword in hand.

"Get me a cloth, Lego."

He could now see Gralgrim's massive body pinning down the dead fighter, arrow shaft (hammered through by his falling forward) sticking up nearly two feet from the back of the thick neck.

"My Lord," wondered Lego, "why did you attack that beast?"

"What?" Parse was distracted. Turned to look for the Black Knight's body and saw his blade protruding from the body of the dying moose. "Well...yes...."

Lego was wrapping a strip of cloth, crusted with salt, around his master's head. Knotted it behind.

The knight winced as the salt bit into the wound, still staring at the animal. He went and pulled his weapon free, with a real effort.

Am I awake? Well, my wound stings and that blocky fellow is dead....

"We bury him under those rocks," he said, indicating the dark, broken stones. There was little mist now. "He saved my life."

"He did. It was his nature. That killer had you to rights. I was too far away. I think he saved mine too, if it comes to that. Him mounted with that bow." Looked around at the pale, brightening landscape. "You seem yourself now, lord."

"For what that's worth, captain." He looked at the blank, bark "map." "What I saw showed an entrance to an underground way across the field. We have nothing better." Tossed the piece aside. "I think he were here just to save me." He indicated Gralgrim.

"He would have as soon slain you, lord."

"He wasn't here for that." Went over and pulled the bodies apart, tugging the shaft through then breaking off a short piece including the tip which he tucked into his belt pouch. "I thank thee, fellow."

On his back, his wide, reddened face looked fierce. Lego had stripped off the little man's shirt.

"He's their leader," he pointed out. "With the map and pictures on his body. The one who ate hearts."

"I'll not eat his," said the knight. "We leave him as he lies."

He stared back at the trail that led out of the ravine. Felt as if he were being watched. No more strange shapes though.

MORGANA

They waited on horseback, her two handmaidens, Modred and herself, at the entrance. She shook her head with disgust.

"He's failed," she said. "Now we trap them."

Turned her mount just as Parsival and Lego were in sight across the field and led them back into the tunnel.

PARSIVAL

The slain killer's horse had run off. Parsival and Lego headed across the field. The image from the map lingered, fading, and he followed the last hints.

They came to the tunnel and saw the hoofprints on the faded, grayish-green turf. Easy to read; five riders came out, one went on (the late Mimujin) and the rest went back.

One pony, the knight thought, *the rest horse...the witch and her crones....*

The tunnel-cave was quickly pitch-black but this had been in the map too, and went on straight and they went on straight....

LAYLA, LOHENGRIN, AND HAL

By dawn they'd dug the grave and buried Jane. The light was dull metal though the wet fog had thinned and rain stopped. Layla was still, resting on the rude bed. The bleeding had stopped.

She watched the fire die away into vaguely glowing ash....

She wasn't thinking. Didn't want to. Another sleepless dawn. She was just starting to believe she might go home, again...across the grayness....

Lohengrin left Hal standing at the muddy grave they'd scraped out with bent and rusted spades they'd found leaning behind a hut.

He went to the well and stared down as if there was some answer there in the impenetrable blackness. Just a hole into the earth. He spat into it.

It will always be like this, he thought.

His throat felt swollen as he choked on abstract grief.

"Feelings are shit," he said.

Spat again. His eyes burned.

GAWAIN

Desperate, now, they both finished unloosing his armor, she already stripped and he kept saying *no* without meaning anything so in the din of night-bugs and the subtle, soft dawn-gleaming he lay athwart her, left side aside, locked into the sweet suction, shuddering with agony and relief, good hand under her, intact cheek pressed to hers, lips at her ear adrift in night and sighs and wordless words...she melted fiercely in the sweet air, closed so close that two was one from mouth to loins as if forever....

Because, finally, for them, there was no future and no past or pain...finally under the horned moon and still mists time held in perfect stillness as sometimes it will for lovers, for all the enraptured...crying out like drowning swimmers...rolling over on the crushed grasses they pressed a memory on the earth itself, a momentary shape of love...

PARSIVAL

The map had faded away about where he was sure they were, now. He passed through the dim arch into a faint, greenish, spectral gleaming that showed the still forms of the knights lying in an open circle. Around the curved walls of the huge, vaulted chamber the horses slept.

"Enchantment?" wondered Lego. "Or be they dead?"

"I think not, captain."

Inside, faint slits daylight fanned down from embrasures high up producing a cathedral-like effect. The armored men formed a great wheel, legs all facing out from the center except for one who lay reversed.

They went around and stopped at the one who faced the open center. All but he had their helmets shut, faces pale blots in those (Parsival vaguely thought) private head-caves.

Where they hide from more than blows, he thought.

Knew him at once. Sighed. White-bearded, now, face tense even in death-like slumber.

"This must entertain angels and gods," he said.

But does little for me....

"My Lord?" asked Lego. "Who is this man?"

"Your king. And I suppose I'm to wake him." Sighed again. "Expect no peace and ease to follow."

"How to wake him?"

Parsival shrugged.

"Awaken, Your Majesty!" he said sternly. Tried it a few times more. Nothing.

"He stirs not," observed Lego. "Maybe shake him." Cocked his head. "He seems not at rest."

"That's his royal nature, captain." Then he got it: "It's still the same day and the same problem."

"Which day, my Lord?"

"Twenty years back." He knelt by Arthur. He knew what to ask this time. "What is the matter, Sire?" Drew the broken sword.

The king's eyes popped open. Worked his jaw side-to-side. Grunted. Lego had a strange impression, for a moment, that a cloudiness suffused the face with other, older features; then the blurring drained back into the head as the King sat up, then stood up very straight.

Lego went to one knee beside Parsival. Looking up, the Captain-at-Arms had an impression that the smoky blurring showed only in the eyes, now, where the King stood staring straight ahead as if into lingering dream-sights.

"Better wake him some more," suggested Lego in a whisper.

The cloudy eyes sharpened and rested on the Red knight.

"On your feet," he automatically commanded.

As Parsival and his man stood all the rest began to stir with a gathering clash and scrape. Horses snorted and softly whinnied. Men began standing. Lego was counting them in groups of ten.

"I count 44 knights," he said, half-unconsciously.

We lost 100," the king said, rubbing his face and shaking his head. "Somewhere...my memories are shredded...."

This is all how I should have been...mayhap long, long shadows are cast into another world of each petty cause and nasty business done by all of us...there our murders may seem necessary glories and rape and theft the high unfolding of history....

"We all become stories," he said, thoughtfully, in the unfocused moment, "made from shredded memories."

"This is a tale you could well leave me out of, my Lord. And yourself too, methinks."

Silver-armored Arthur came alert as his troops gathered around, still silent as shadows, as if, Lego fancied, they were stuck in the same blur the king had seemed to somehow inhale.

Tense as ever, observed Parsival. He thought of the king as a tensed, no, stretched bowstring

"My Liege," said Parsival, stepping forward and holding out the broken sword. He wondered if maybe he was finished; doubted it. "Is my service over, now?"

"Half-done," he said. "A little further, Sir Parsival."

Still not quite taking it all in, Lego automatically dropped again to one knee, inclining his head.

"Who is this knight?" asked the King.

"No knight, Majesty," answered Lego.

"Yet with more heart and chivalry, Mesire, than a dozen who stand dubbed," declared Parsival.

"Well," said the king, "only knights should follow us here." Smiled, sardonic even in magic and mystery, Parsival noted. The king hefted broken Excalibur. "Pray thou for God's Grace," he instructed Lego. "I dub Thee...."

"Majesty," protested the commoner, "I neither wish nor am fitted for such elevation, if such it be. I am a fighting man, simple and unembarrassed."

"You speak well, fellow."

Which, Lego realized, was true. He hardly sounded like himself as if he spoke in some minstrel's tale. Well, he considered, he'd heard noble talk constantly and was ever adaptable. Still, it was to trouble him later, thinking how these events had seemed to bend and twist the rules of his world. Things were still going too fast to contemplate much.

"If such it be," quoted Parsival, liking that.

"Thou speaks nobly," said Arturus, staying in a formal mode. "yet forms do matter here, good man. If only for my sake and those who come after." Stepped closer to the kneeling man-at-arms. "Thy master here was less fit than thee ere I raised him up." Touched the broken blade to Lego's shoulder. "I make Thee half a knight with half a sword, so all are satisfied." He smiled. The others stood silent, still seeming half in sleep, Parsival thought, seeming to wait like spellbound automations.

I resist nothing, he said to himself. *Doubt little since here we came...the world has no fixed nature save as we see it....*

"And thus the curse is halved," he said, meaning the knight's creation.

"Yes, Sir Parsival," agreed the king. "But for times and worlds where forms matter, how do I name Thee?"

"Sir Nobody," said Lego, not knowing why.

"So dubbed Sir Nobody-Who-Shall-Be-Known," concluded Arturus, turning away to his men: "Are we ready?" Seeing they were he called his steed to him.

"Sire,' asked Parsival. "How and why was this sleeping done?"

"How? Deep draughts of poppy-wine...a spell?" the king replied. "Why? For the sake of consequences. No more reasoning. My memory, as I say, is shredded. Accept this as this until we come again into the light." He mounted. Brandished the half-sword. "Our enemies are within reach," he cried. "Forward!"

And in an unbearable clashing of metal and hooves loud as a battle, they crashed through the narrow tunnel, in a darkness that Lego wouldn't let himself directly think about, riding just behind his lord and Arthur, waiting for the next disaster....

"Am I mad or in slumber, my Lord?" he yelled.

"Lego," the Red Knight yelled back, "ask not and it matters not."

MORGANA

"Go on!" she commanded Modred and the others.

Her greenly gleaming wand-tip revealed a fork in the tunnel that had been unnoticed coming the other way.

She searched the tunnel sides and found what she expected: an iron lever. She yanked it, strained violently (she was stronger than any normal man) and a massive, rounded block rolled to fill the passageway.

And then out the far end at a fast canter into fogless dawn. The east was dark blood. The world seemed wet and fresh. As the sky brightened the gently dipping fields were a misty, grayish green.

"I've trapped them," the witch said.

"When do I do battle with him?" her son asked.

"He is under us now," she said, amused. "We will descend to his level and destroy him."

"What, Aunt?"

"All trapped."

"Trapped?"

"All roads end here," she said. "All our fates go no further."

"But when," her son asked, "will I join battle with Arthur?" He now wore the scabbard that held the other half of Excalibur.

Arthur must come for the blade else all his works will be washed away, she thought. *He could not bear that....*

"Soon," she answered, "or in ages to come."

PARSIVAL

The tunnel was wider and steadily descended. Neither of them liked that.

"This wasn't on the map," Parsival said.

"What matter?" asked Arthur, riding abreast of him.

They were moving at a walk, now. The ringing hooves and clashing of armor diminished.

"This may be a trap," suggested Lego.

"It has to be," Parsival said.

They probed on through the dimness, down and down....

"I don't understand what's happened to us," Lego murmured.

"Maybe this tale will be told ages hence," his master returned, obliquely.

"What care I for that?" responded Lego. "I think of home and no more sinking boats and mad killers, plague, witchcraft and poisoning of wells."

"I warned you, at the first, to go straight back and follow me not."

"I grant you did."

It was starting to smell dank and foul as an open sewer, rank decay, sweet and nauseating.

Parsival sensed, by the echoes, that they were in a large, cavern-like space. There were sounds of dripping water.

"Hold," he said.

Because there were rumbling and grinding noises as if massive stone were breaking loose and vastly shifting, as if the mountain above them (that they didn't know they were under) was moving.

He suspected all of this was like an afterglow from the vision where something long past and something in the future enfolded together...where what you might dream or say might have the same force as what you did....

We're like fish, he thought, as the rocks screamed and cracked around them, *seeing the sky of heaven only through the water*....Or, now and then, in a brief leap into a breathless world of brilliant light and freedom where no fish could long live....

So he wasn't quite surprised when the huge, cavern-like space was suddenly glaring green and he saw Modred up on a kind of balcony looking down as a twelve foot tall and massive knight in armor came out through and opening just formed by the crashing stones.

The hundred with Arthur charged at once. The giant (eyes twin pits) flailed a mace and three or four, horses and all, flew aside, shattered in a scream of metal and thunk of burst flesh. One actually slammed against the far wall like a crumpled piece of tin.

The machine of doom was wading through the mounted men whose swords and maces chipped, bounced, scraped and sparked futilely. It was making for the king who was looking up at his half-son.

"Where is your stinking mother, boy?" he yelled.

"Know you not, Father?" jeered Modred.

The stone warrior was no quicker than a man, Parsival noted. So it could be dodged. He, Arthur, and Lego backed their horses away.

"The way back into the tunnel is surely sealed," he said, judging the distance to the ledge where Modred stood. "The thing seeks you, your Majesty."

Two more knights had just been slammed and shattered; a horse decapitated as the grinding, clumping fighting machine crashed closer, body worked in filigreed stone armor. One hand reached for the king.

He and Parsival spurred past and headed for the ledged wall. The thing slammed through more knights and followed. About half were down by the time it reached them again.

"Let it come close," said Parsival over the clash and din, "and give me your half of Excalibur."

Arthur hesitated then obliged and the Red Knight stuck it under his sword belt. Now (as he expected) the giant went for him.

A voice spoke through the stone or in the stone.

"You belong to the king of ice and death." Arthur's remaining men kept crowding in but the thing didn't move.

"Stay back," Arthur shouted. "Avoid combat!"

"Resist not," the hollow, flat voice commanded.

Parsival (nimble as any in a steel suit) lunged up and stood in his saddle as the stone hand clawed to crush him.

Except he ran up the arm to the huge shoulders and put one mailed foot on the head jumped up to the ledge beside Modred.

We each have half, he thought.

Modred struck at once and, at the same time, the stone knight (almost at their level) slammed a blow at Parsival. Most would have fallen to one stroke or the other. When backed to the wall, when there was no hope, he always seemed to move as if he'd rehearsed with his enemy; so in that narrow space he danced forward into the Modred's cut so that the giant's mace just scraped his back armor, twisting so the boy's sword just scraped his left side and then he kicked him between the legs so hard with his mailed foot that the iron codpiece crumpled.

Modred screamed and doubled up. Parsival stooped under the following mace-blow (that actually shattered the rock ledge) and took the second scabbard (which had showed where the piece was) from the fallen boy (now puking and gasping) and moved along the ledge. The mace followed, spraying rock chips so hard they pinged and dented his red armor. He thrust the hilt he had into the scabbard with the other half of Excalibur. He had no idea what might happen. He wasn't thinking, just flowing with the pounding at his heels.

And then he was outside the walls of his castle again, nude, the spear to his throat watching the bird soar above the treetops, catching the first sunbeams and seeming to ride the light and Parsival felt the strange power and beauty and vastness....he felt the strange energy as the blade fused itself in the sheath and he drew a whole sword, Arthur, down below, shouting:

"Give it to me!"

"Nay, Sire," Parsival called back, "*you* must not destroy this thing, I think."

Because he was sure it was like the other time when his own armor attacked him outside Camelot.

Now it's my turn, he said to himself. *What came out of stone can penetrate again....*

As the mace swept down, he simply jumped onto the massive shoulders, feet skidding, as he was tossed off the back he timed and struck a blow with Excalibur. The blade flamed, sparked and took the head cleanly off. It hit with a crash and rolled about thirty feet under the knights' horses where they were keeping their distance. As he suspected the thing was hollow. The head was empty.

He crashed onto his back, then rolled to his feet. As he expected, it raised the mace again.

"Useless," he said. "I will kill you, my lady witch. You have no protection, now."

Because he realized if she'd had her own powers down here why would she bother with this stone giant armor that was obviously mechanical?

He rested the bladetip at the center of the carven breastplate and saw the downblow freeze.

The response seemed a voice in his mind, something deep, dark from the stone foundations of the earth itself. An echo, potent and terrible that was not just Morgana herself;

You cannot escape. The world will close down upon you.

He was about to thrust when Arthur eased his mount beside him, facing the unmoving, headless seeming statue. He clamped his hand over Parsival's.

"This is my steel, sir," he said.

Lego was close.

"Why does it hold its stroke?" he wondered, as Arthur took Excalibur.

"Because she's alone in it, now," the Red Knight answered. "Your sister, My Lord."

I hope none of this is happening, he thought, *except in the dreaming or whatever it is…except believing in the dreaming makes you careless of the waking….*

"I'll not slay her, yet," said the king, striking hard but holding the blow so that the stone sheath fell away like an eggshell and, as if she'd just hatched, Morgana stood there, red-haired, graceful, nude and contemplative.

Really so beautiful, Parsival thought.

"Dogs," she said, "now darkness falls!"

"Stupid sister," said Arthur.

"Dull king," she responded. "Sagging prong. The true ruler of all creatures awaits you. All maps lead to him."

Her son had crawled to the edge of the ledge, face pale and squinty.

"Aunt," he gasped, "help me."

She leaped the twelve feet, caught the ledge and pulled herself effortlessly up. She was far enough from the isle to have some strength again.

The chamber was rumbling as rock shifted. Parsival was aware of a flickering effect which he sensed was the dreaming and waking worlds overlapping, trying to either fuse or pull apart and seeming to spin around him like a whirlwind.

"He is hungry!" she yelled, furious, seething. "Go to dinner in the dark."

The spinning blurred around them and the Red Knight sensed it was another chance for him to act, to change, to understand…as when he saw the Grail, he was supposed to do something with the power revealed here….

What, what? His mind asked. *Help me, sweet heaven…help….*

Maybe that was it, too: he'd never really asked before. Not understanding how small and helpless he actually was like the king who attacked the sea with his sword and was knocked flat and tumbled for his pains....

And the floor opened and the walls and roof crashed down and he perceived the pit was, actually, a vast mouth with a tongue of fire, rimmed with fangs.

He fell without a real sense of motion...floating...down...into Hell's mouth....

GAWAIN

The moon seemed to lift the dawn behind it. Now growing He understood it was now slightly less than full. Every moment it was slightly more then, full, it would almost imperceptibly begin to be less. Because they lay there, legs overlapping, side-by-side, on the crushed grass as the water flowed with low, sopping sounds and faint, faint tinkles....

His good half was to her, arm under her head. He lay there hating time.

"The sun will soon rise," he murmured.

"No," she said.

"Ah, no?"

"Never. It will never rise again for us."

"Never."

"*We* will live only under the stars. I will sleep by day and wake for you all night."

"Yet it must rise."

"No," she declared. "It will not."

LOHENGRIN AND LAYLA

They rode in the coolish, fogless air. The countryside steepened and sharpened as they moved into the northern foothills not so far from home.

At least, Layla thought, *I am not with child...at least there are no guests waiting and my husband has gone off again...these are compensations and it seems my son has learned something about finding and keeping...and what have I learned?*

"Try not to be bitter, son," she advised, out of her reverie.

They were climbing, steadily; had drifted to the rear. He was munching a greenish apple. Tiny bright flowerlets almost glittered along the trail where the sun fanned through the thin trees.

"Bitter," said Lohengrin. "I'll try."

And fail, he thought.

Stared. He wasn't remembering Jane. He was deeply tired the way the young are tired but are just a simple, dreamless sleep away from beginning again as if the world still had no real weight – or they simply hadn't yet noticed....

What have I learned? She asked herself, again.

Because, in the end, there was a memory that had no weight either and was about half true: there was (forever) the young man on the silvery-soft grass in the lost moonlight and tender shadows of more than half her life ago when she'd hesitated a few fearful steps away, thinking how beautiful and pale he was, lying there in the delicate night...and she knew (without knowing she knew) that once she went and touched him it would forever open the door her whole life would go through....

And not knowing she'd moved, was suddenly kneeling over him, fingers light on his bare chest, speaking as if she'd rehearsed the words in some time or place long past as this moment cast a shadow of itself, forever, saying:

"My name, though you have not asked, is Layla."

PARSIVAL

In a way he was still standing on the hill under the wall of his castle, naked, hands bound behind, death at his throat and the flash of the bird lifting above the world......above everything...voices of the bandits around him, the mad priest and Gawain with helm shut as if it mattered...one runtish brigand pointing to Parsival's groin, saying:

'See how it's all shrinked up like an old hag's neck!'

Another laughing.

'Ain't much a one to start off, meseems,'

...still staring there and here too as if nothing had changed or ever would so the pit that was just a mouth opened to nowhere and faded away...and there was the stone room in the monastery and the great carven stone coffin, the round-faced monk with his pointy, razor sharp features. Parsival was there too in his red, discolored, rent armor that the salt-sea had stained with spots of corrosion; alone, sword at his side.

"Did I ever leave this place?" was his question, being now well used to impossibilities. He was treating everything like a troubled sleep.

"Yes."

"Yes?"

"You've been in the world wizards' love," said the monk, looking at the doorway as if expecting guests. "Two things can be true at once. You have not been living in one world at a time."

"Magic? I have been bewitched?"

The monk shrugged.

"Words, Sir Knight," he said. "What is, is. Time to go home. You have gone everywhere and done nothing...or have you gone nowhere and done everything?"

JOHN

There was a seaweed-covered, mussel-clotted rock that sat high above the dark and stinking strand.

There was a big turtle working its slow, glopping way parallel to the water. A handful of former pilgrims of the map were standing and sitting in the general area, watching the fog disperse and the steel-gray sea gradually expanding to the horizon, blurring away into the eternal vagueness....

John stood there on his bare, splayed feet clutching the rock like some giant five-toed bird, ragged black tunic still wet, flapping heavily in the sea breeze. He was saying things, mouth open as if swallowing the wind except his voice was too worn away to be audible.

Two boys were tossing shells and pebbles at the laboring turtle. Now and then they glanced off the shell with a dull click and the creature would pull its head in and wait. The boys were delighted and were working up to killing it, as boys will.

So John's mouth moved, the wind blew, the waves sagged into the beach and crumpled there like all that went before. The turtle crawled and paused and paused and crawled into its fate.

John gestured with one skinny hand. His rags flapped; mouth opened and closed. His eyes were bright, avid, full of the power of his vision....

SIR NOBODY

Lego's mind was still ringing, overwhelmed by the shock, crash, bang, and confusion as the masses of stone fell around him. The earth cracked open and he fell (or seemed to fall) down towards the foundations of the earth – except it was about fifteen feet and he rolled, battered, but not much hurt and saw daylight just above him spraying in around the shattered rocks.

"My Lord," he cried out. "Where are you?"

Everything behind him was sealed-off so there was only one way to go. He crawled (no space to stand) over and around the broken stones that pressed so close he felt he was being bent and softened and twisted, doubling and turning so that by the time he actually wriggled and crept on his belly into the actual daylight he almost believed some random beam of the mad magic back there had converted him into a snake.

"Half in...half out,' he muttered, straining. "Christ...urrrnnn...."

Like being born or passing a hard turd....

At the end his head was out, shoulders stuck. The warmish breeze and sea air was refreshing and seemed strange.

Sweat in his eyes blurred and doubled the shock of brightness as he finally dragged and kicked himself free. The cliff face had crumbled well up from the beach and exposed the tunnel Morgana hadn't known about.

Struggling a few steps higher to softer ground he lay on his back panting, looking up into the greenish-blue, pure late afternoon northern sky. The sun angled warmth into him, almost sparkling on the long, mixed grasses of pale, yellowish greens. The thing, he decided, was to forget as much as possible as fast as he could. He felt as if from the time they met the Vikings and set sail, he might as well have been asleep. He hoped he could get home without meeting his master whom he assumed was alive somewhere. He remembered Layla once saying (maybe more than once) that her husband was under a spell to never die until he took full responsibility for something…anything. So he was, she'd concluded, effectively immortal.

Lego never understood her until now as he reflected back on his recent adventures.

"He talked to trees and found swords and whatnot in bushes," he muttered, thoughtfully. "We went underground with cannibals and plague bodies….Almost everybody died, in the end."

I admit, he thought, *he warned me…..*

"Witches and monks and madmen," he went on, still trying to take it all in. "King Arthur!" Shook his head. "As that Viking would say, 'hoo.'"

Holy Mary. He thought. *What madness…and me a knight or half-knight…Sir Nobody…there's some sense in the name an let me stay so….*

He looked at the sun making sharp waves of light as the tall wild grasses stirred in the shifting, comfortable breeze. He didn't want to stay there and he didn't want to get up; either way he might be found by Parsival and drawn into new and unpleasant adventures that resolved into a kind of nauseating and misty confusion….

I'll stay with my married daughter for awhile…there's a notion…I'll live in a cave…I'll….

MORGANA

It was like walking through heavy rain without getting wet, Modred thought, as they made their way through the crashing rocks that seemed like blurs of softness, his hand in Morgana's soft yet steel strong grip.

And then there was greenish-blue sky, pale grasses and a warmish breeze. They went up a little hill with a view of the crystal-blue sea crashing into the rocky coast. Walked higher on to the cliffs.

Almost directly below they saw the King and Parsival walking side-by-side on the actual beach under the sharply pitched rock wall. The red armor was like a blot of blood.

"Aunt," said the boy, "I want to kill him. I want to…."

"We just didn't," she pointed out. "Be quiet." A tic winked under her left eye.

"But I want to kill him."

"Another day," she said, tense and cold with clenched fury.

"But -"

"Another day you will eat his heart." Shook off his hand. "Now be still, weak boy."

"We eat hearts?"

"Aye. But we roast them first."

PARSIVAL

The King was looking up the cliffs at the back-tilted figures (obscured by the misty haze from the breaking surf) he couldn't tell were Morgana and her unhappy son. The knight was facing out to sea where waves like fractured blue-green light cut, humped and sliced into the rocky shore, shattering into spray.

Parsival wasn't remembering anything. He wasn't planning anything. He didn't want to know anything.

"Did you notice how we got out?" Arthur asked.

Parsival liked looking at the waves and the small, white birds that kept circling and suddenly swooping down, darting their long, sharp beaks into the water until one finally came up with a speared fish, a silver glitter that, as he squinted could have been anything from a coin, a jewel to a trick or defect in the eyes.

As he watched the bird soar up with its prize in its beak, into the haze-softened sunlight creasing over the cliff tops, he knew what it meant and refused to think about that either. It was appetite and illusion or something as simple and empty as a curl of wind or water....

"I'm not sure we were anywhere, my liege," Parsival said, at length. "We didn't get out of anything."

"What sense does that make?"

"None, Lord."

"I sent men to find you," the king said. They still faced opposite ways.

"They found me."

"Did you kill them? I hope you did not."

"I retired from violence." He squinted but had lost the bird in the bright haze. "I've hardly killed anyone since then."

"Will you come back to Camelot?"

"I'll go that far with you, my liege. Then…." Shrugged. "I've made vows…well, we'll see…."

"Yes, Sir Parsival. I have made vows myself. But, I, more than another, must stand by the roll of the cast dice which are still bouncing."

He turned at the clinking and scraping sounds to see the Red Knight stripping off his armor and the under padding clothes until he stood on the pebbly sand, bare-legged in his tunic and leather sock-like shoes.

The king watched him scale the plate and mail into the grinding surf where it was tossed, rolled, stuck, unstuck and turned in the foamy undertow.

"Another gesture, Parsival?" asked the king.

"Yes," said the knight, grunting. "Let the sea eat this stinking metal that I might never put it on again." He stared at the birds watching them circle and dive for the quick, silver flickers, spearing into the heaving roils of water. He considered how, to the fish, these soft, weightless, fragile riders of the lucent, substanceless air were deadly as thunderbolts dropping from the unseen void above to stab them through in their own hushed element. "What invisible creatures hunt, poise and drop on us?" he reflected, aloud.

Arthur got it, following his gaze and train of thought.

"The Grail stained your mind, Knight," he said, "so shadows and dreams joust with you."

"The Grail," said Parsival, staring away into the hazy horizon. His inflection told the king little. "I still say nothing really happened and we went nowhere."

Arthur shrugged, glanced back up at the two figures on the cliffs he imagined were fishermen. He drew Excalibur and let it catch the blurry light.

"And how was this recovered?" he wondered. "Made whole again?"

Parsival shrugged.

"Maybe it wasn't," he said. "Maybe you never lost it or shattered it. The Grail blurs my mind, blurs my life, My Liege. Maybe we're both dreaming, this moment." Shrugged again. "Maybe we're not."

"Time blurs mine," said the king, sheathing the blade. "Walk with me, in any case, until we find horses. Then we'll ride."

Parsival nodded.

"Yes, your Majesty," he said.

"I won't ask you about the Grail."

"Nothing happened," the tall, lean, mainly blond, sometime hero said, inhaling the rich, cool salt air, watching one of the birds (perhaps the same one) dip, drop and come up with a flash of glitter in its beak, circling up away from the others, riding a coil of thermal air until it was lost in the bright haze and glare, again; a detail-less flickering...blot...lost.... "Nothing happened at all."

I'm going home, he said to himself. *One way or another...sooner or later.....*

Arthur was looking up at the two figures on the cliff edge. Squinted, because something was moving, a speck, a blur dropping fast, faster...a stone the size of a head was almost on them by the time he reacted, yelling to Parsival and ducking aside.

It was a pretty good throw. The knight glanced up, not having to move, and tracked it to where it cracked, shattering, where the king had been standing. Rock chips zinged around, two or three clipping Parsival hard enough to sting.

"There it is," he said. "As ever."

The two on top were gone.

"That had to be my sister and her twisted child," Arthur said. "They escaped, too."

"Escaped what?"

Parsival was looking out to sea again as if it meant something. Falling rocks left him unmoved, at this point; he was more concerned with the way the waves rode up on themselves as they broke. Never the same twice but always the same. He understood that, too, without thinking about it.

The king was looking at him.

"You don't have to come with me," he said. "Go where you please. I believe I was enchanted though I don't believe in magic"

"No?"

"I believe when it is far off. As I believe in the miracles of our Lord. But were I not enchanted then I would be mad to think what happened, happened."

"You are politic, my liege."

"I believe in stones being dropped on me by supposed witches." Glanced up.

The waves were more astonishing the more Parsival studied them.

"*Credo*," he said, "in falling rocks." Nodded and stared. "I believe waves are never the same but have everything in common. I begin and end with that."

"You don't have to come with me," the king sighed. "I release you. But we were enchanted, you agree?"

"You are right or you're not. I'm mad or I'm not. What use are opinions?"

The birds had circled away along the rocky shore. Parsival could see pieces of the dull red armor scraping, turning and shifting as the angle of the breaking surf moved slowly and resistlessly south.

There goes my life, he thought. *Farewell....*

He stretched and sighed. Tried to see what hurt the worst. Hard to tell.

"We were enchanted," the king repeated.

"I am going home," the knight said at length. "I'll kill no more men save those who ask about the Grail. I'll watch the serfs till the fields. I'll watch the birds nest. The pigs shit and eat. The grasses grow." He turned from the sea and looked at Arthur. "Let us go, your Majesty. You back to the great work of state and me to my family and respect for manure."

"Great work," said the king, glancing up again to see if, maybe, another rock was dropping at his head. "Great work of greed and mayhem. Of course I don't believe you, Sir Parsival."

"You are mistaken, my King," the knight said, starting to walk with him along the beach, looking for an easy way to climb the cliffs. "I truly love cow manure and all manner of horseshit."

EPILOGUE

The king and the knight walked through the late morning into the soft afternoon together; maybe seven miles. Without knowing it they passed Lego who was resting with his back on a rock overlooking the rutted coast road. He didn't move, watching them pass. Shook his head, no, as if he'd been asked something.

December 22, 2004
NYC

www.ingramcontent.com/pod-product-compliance
Lightning Source LLC
Chambersburg PA
CBHW022148010726
47493CB00002B/392